THE LOST LETTERS OF EVELYN WRIGHT

CLARE SWATMAN

Boldw**oo**d

First published in Great Britain in 2024 by Boldwood Books Ltd.

Cover Design by Leah Jacobs-Gordon

Cover Photography: Shutterstock

This book is a work of fiction and, except in the case of historical fact, any resemblance to actual persons, living or dead, is purely coincidental.

A CIP catalogue record for this book is available from the British Library.

Paperback ISBN 978-1-78513-061-8

Large Print ISBN 978-1-78513-057-1

Hardback ISBN 978-1-78513-056-4

Ebook ISBN 978-1-78513-054-0

Kindle ISBN 978-1-78513-055-7

Audio CD ISBN 978-1-78513-062-5

MP3 CD ISBN 978-1-78513-059-5

Digital audio download ISBN 978-1-78513-053-3

Boldwood Books Ltd
23 Bowerdean Street
London SW6 3TN
www.boldwoodbooks.com

For my boys, who are my world

1
———

BETRAYED AND HEARTBROKEN

My husband has been unfaithful to me in the past, but I forgave him. However he has recently begun to come home late again, claiming he is working nights, although I do not believe him. I feel sure he is cheating on me again but I am too afraid to say anything for fear of losing him altogether. However I am very unhappy. I work long hours too and do my housework in the evenings, but the worry is affecting my health. I'm at the end of my tether, what should I do?

First of all, I am sorry that you are feeling so distraught. The truth is that, although many women can do two jobs perfectly well, others cannot. It seems to me as though you have become so occupied with completing your chores in the evening that your house no longer feels like a home, which could be one reason why your husband has sought comfort elsewhere – first from another woman, then in the companion-ship that extra work brought. Could you consider giving up your day job so that you could complete your chores during the day? Perhaps then your husband will no longer feel the need to stay away from his home and you can be happy again.

When I first arrived at Laburnum Cottage, with its creaking windows and wild front garden, I didn't even want to walk through the front door. Because that would have made the last few months real.

That would mean that this was my new life. My new future.

Alone.

But I had no choice, whether I liked it or not.

So, finally, I took a deep breath and stepped inside. The carpet was spongy beneath my feet, the wallpaper in the hallway ripped, and when I pressed my fingers against the wall, it felt damp. I trailed my fingers along as I crept towards the foot of the stairs, where I lingered for a moment, watching the outdated flower pattern repeat upwards and disappear round the corner. The carpet was faded and scuffed, patches of underlay peeking through, while the paint on the balustrade was chipped and worn. Even with the front door still open the hallway felt gloomy.

Taking a deep breath, I retraced my steps and pushed the front door shut until it clicked, then made my way into the kitchen at the back of the house. When I'd viewed this property the estate agent had tried to up-sell its good points – the location, the large garden, the decent room size – but even he hadn't been able to make the kitchen sound like more than it actually was: a tiny room containing an ancient free-standing cooker, a stained Belfast sink resting on a rotting wooden frame, and a small, round table. It was little more than a hovel and as I stood in the doorway surveying it, my heart sank. It really was as bad as I'd remembered.

I turned away and headed back to the stairs, keen to see

whether the bedrooms were as terrible as I remembered too. There were only three rooms up here – the one immediately to my left was the bathroom with its outdated beige suite that I knew I'd have to scrub clean and make do with for several months before I'd be able to afford to change it. The next door on the left was my bedroom – the smallest, as it was only me – while the right-hand door led to the kids' bedroom. I pushed it open and stepped inside. The curtains had been taken down and I was surprised to see that the room was actually brighter than I remembered despite the grimy glass. The carpet was so thread-bare it was practically dust, but I knew that underneath there were beautiful old floorboards, which I planned to sand down and restore to their original glory. There was a battered fitted wardrobe along one wall, while the rest of the walls were covered in a mixture of sickly orange wallpaper and a shade of blue you'd only expect to see in a children's hospital. It was an eye-watering combination and I couldn't help wondering whether the previous owner had been colour-blind.

It was hard to believe that the house had been lived in as recently as six months ago. It felt long-abandoned, and the décor and the state of the place suggested it had stood empty for years. It made me sad to think of someone living here with the house like this.

But it was mine now, and I had to make the most of it.

My first job would be to get the kids' bedroom looking as good as it could, otherwise neither of them would ever want to spend any time here.

As I stood with my back to the window surveying the room again I wondered what Olivia and Jacob were doing right now. I missed them so ferociously when they were at their dad's that it felt as if I had a golf ball lodged in the pit of my belly whenever I thought about them. I tried hard not to picture them there, in their old bedrooms with everything they could ever want, and *her* trying to ingratiate her way into their affections. *Her* being not only Olivia's old schoolteacher, but the woman Rob had been conducting an affair with for over a year, and who he was now shacked up with in my old home.

The rage bubbled up and I swallowed it down, determined not to cry. This house was meant to be my fresh start. So what if it was all I could afford after Rob had bought me out, and so what if it wasn't as beautiful as the house I'd left behind? It was all mine and it marked the start of a new chapter in my life.

If I said it enough times I might even convince myself, eventually.

I was startled out of my thoughts by a hammering on the front door. I raced down the stairs to let the removal firm in. I didn't have a lot of stuff but I hoped the place might look a bit less depressing once my bits and pieces were here.

It didn't take long, and after the men had left, the van rumbling off down the lane, the house felt even emptier than it had before. Echoes of voices bounced off the walls and faded into the carpet, leaving nothing but silence in their wake.

And as I folded myself up into my tiny sofa – the one thing I'd been so determined Rob was not going to keep – and closed my eyes for a moment, I'd never felt so lonely in my entire life.

* * *

I'm sure most people have imagined how their lives might go if they ever separated from their partners, even if only in an abstract way. I know I had, though I'd never really thought it would happen in reality. In those imaginings I'd assumed I would stay in our home and Rob would move into a flat somewhere nearby; I'd pictured civil conversations as we handed over the children during our fair and mutually agreed days with them; I'd even thought how nice it would be to have so much more time to spend with my friends, assuming we'd have lots of evenings slagging off men and putting the world to rights.

None of those assumptions had proven to be correct.

After Rob had admitted he'd been having an affair with Miss Hutchinson – *Natalie* – for almost a year (not that he'd had much choice given that almost everyone else seemed to know about it before I did), everything seemed to fall apart bit by bit, like dominoes in a row, gathering speed as they went.

First Rob went. Then he told me he wanted to keep the house, and that I had to move out so he could buy it from me. As a science teacher I knew I couldn't afford to stay there on my own, and he also argued it would be good for the children to have some stability in among all the upheaval. I didn't say *they would have had plenty of stability if you'd kept your dick in your pants*, but only because I could see he was right, however misguided and oblivious to his misdemeanours he was.

So I moved out and rented a flat nearby while I looked for somewhere more permanent. But house-hunting on my budget had been soul-destroying – even with the money from Rob, it hardly went anywhere. In the end I'd had to look outside the town I'd lived in for ten years – the town where I worked and had made friends and built a life for myself – and settle for something a twenty-five-minute drive away, in a small village. I was not a country girl. I liked hustle and bustle, people, anonymity. I'd never wanted to be a small-town girl, and yet here I was.

This house – the ramshackle cottage with its tumbledown kitchen and jungle-like garden – was the best of a bad bunch. At least it wasn't a grotty apartment, or a terraced house with sofas and fridges piled high in neighbouring gardens. It might have only two bedrooms, which meant that the kids would have to share until I could afford to pay for an extension – if that day ever came – but at least I could put a roof over our heads. A comfortable one, eventually.

But what hurt me more than any of that was the desertion by people I'd thought of as friends.

The mum-friends I'd spent mornings chatting with since the kids were babies; the couple-friends Rob and I had made over the years, sharing gossip and house-price woes over dinner parties and drinks; the neighbours in our street we'd got to know. They'd all melted away since Rob and I had split up so that, now, even those with the best of intentions had faded into the past.

To make matters worse my best friend, Suzie, had given birth to her first baby a month ago and was struggling to get up in the mornings, so the chances of her being able to leave the house and drive fifteen miles to see me were slim, which meant I couldn't rely on her for support either.

Divorce really was shit in so many more ways than you ever imagined it would be.

For now, the only way to keep myself from drowning in a pit of despair was to keep busy.

This week Olivia and Jacob were staying with their dad. It was the school Easter holidays and, although I didn't relish the idea of being on my own for the entire week, it was at least giving me the chance to get on with some renovations.

Starting with the kids' room.

I lugged the stepladder up the stairs, bouncing it on every step, and dragged it into their bedroom. It was a lovely big room, and once I'd ripped the wardrobe out, the wallpaper off, and slapped some paint on the walls I hoped it would look a whole lot better.

I went back down the stairs and picked up a huge tin of paint, a bag of paintbrushes and a roller from the hallway, and tucked an old sheet under my arm. It took two more trips to gather everything I needed, then I plugged in the radio, pushed the creaky sash window up to let in some fresh air, and chucked the ancient sheet over the floor. The paint was a shade of mid-blue that had felt like a compromise to satisfy both of my children – they both loved football and even though the rest of the time they were walking clichés with Olivia's love of sparkles and Jacob's obsession with cars, at least it meant I had something to work with. Sparkly cushions and a tractor duvet cover would be the nods towards their individual tastes.

But before I could even start on any of that, I needed to get this wallpaper off and clean the years' worth of grime from the walls. I filled a bucket with hot soapy water, dipped the sponge in, and began. As the water dripped down my arm and soaked into the ancient paper, I let my mind drift, thinking about everything that had happened over the last few months to lead me here.

After the initial shock and humiliation of Rob's betrayal had subsided, the children had been the first thing on my mind.

'We can split custody between us, can't we?' Rob had suggested, as though it were the obvious thing to do.

'Over my dead fucking body,' I'd retorted, anger flickering like an inferno through me at the thought of being without my babies for 50 per cent of my life. Not to mention the thought of *Natalie* wheedling her way into their affections in my place.

Luckily, after a bitter battle, the court had ruled in my favour, which meant that Olivia and Jacob lived with me most of the time during the week 'for stability', and we split the weekends between us. But it still felt like a dagger to my heart every time I dropped them off, or each time Rob came to the door to collect them.

This week was the first time they'd spent more than a couple of nights away from me since the split, and although it had been agreed that they would spend half the school holidays with their dad, and although I needed the time to get the house in some sort of liveable state, I still felt like an empty shell without them by my side.

The words Olivia had said as she'd packed her little bag on our last morning in my rented flat still stung. 'It's okay, Mummy, because at Daddy's house we still have our own bedrooms so it's better.' She'd seen I was upset and had been trying, in her little girl way, to cheer me up. But those words taunted me as I pictured their idyllic lives away from me, and I couldn't help the ball of anxiety in my belly tightening at the thought that they might never want to leave the comfort of their dad's house. I felt as though I were dangling over a precipice of emptiness, only just clinging on by my fingernails.

I picked up the scraper and ran it up the wall. The paper had been barely hanging on and it came off in huge swathes, dropping to the floor in long, satisfying strips. The wall beneath was painted a dark green and I wondered whose room this had been before, going back years. Had other children lived here? What sort of lives had they had? Had this been a happy family home?

The song playing on the radio shifted from 'Every Breath You Take' to 'I Will Always Love You' by Whitney Houston, and I couldn't help a small smile at the irony.

Finally, wallpaper off, I perched on an upturned bucket and pulled my phone from my back pocket. I was surprised to see it wasn't even lunchtime yet. There were two missed calls – one from Rob's number, which I hoped was the kids ringing to speak to me rather than some emergency, and one from my mum. My heart sank. As much as my mum meant well, she had an uncanny knack of leaving me feeling worse after speaking to her. She always managed to find something for me to worry about that hadn't even occurred to me.

She could wait.

I pressed redial and hoped Olivia would answer the phone. I didn't have the energy to speak to Rob.

'Hi, Beth.' Rob's deep bass rumbled into my ear. I held the phone away and pressed the speaker button.

'I think Olivia rang me,' I said without preamble.

'Oh, hello, Rob, how are you?' he said, and the back of my neck prickled.

'I don't give a shit how you are,' I snapped, and instantly regretted it. I hated losing my temper with him because I hated him knowing he'd got to me.

He let out a breath of air. 'Fine. I'll put her on.'

A few seconds later Olivia came on the line and I snatched the phone back up and held it to my ear.

'Mummy!'

'Hello, sweetheart,' I said, blinking back the tears. 'How are you?'

'Good,' she said.

'What have you been doing today?'

'We had pancakes for breakfast and in a minute we're going to the zoo,' she said, her voice filled with excitement.

'That sounds lovely.' I wanted to ask whether she was spending time with Natalie, whether Daddy was being nice to her, whether she missed me. But instead I said, 'I'm decorating your bedroom. I can't wait for you to see it.'

'Is it blue like you promised?'

'It is, sweetheart. Or at least it will be.'

'And have I got sparkly cushions? Natalie bought me sparkly cushions.'

Of course she fucking did.

'There will be more sparkly cushions than you could ever imagine,' I said, my voice breaking.

'Mummy, Jacob wants to say hello,' she said, already bored

with our conversation. This was one of the things I hated most about being away from them. FaceTime was better than the phone, but I avoided that as much as I could because I didn't want to risk seeing Natalie in the background in my old home. It was all just too hard.

'Mummy?' Jacob sounded uncertain.

'Jakey? Hello, sweetie, are you okay?' I said.

'Yeah.' I could hear him chewing.

'Are you eating something?'

'Chocklit,' he said. 'Creme egg.'

'Oh yum, they're your favourite.' He didn't reply.

'So, you're going to the zoo later, are you?'

'Yip.'

'What animal do you think you'll go and see first?'

'Effefants!' he cried, as I'd known he would. He'd loved elephants since he was tiny, and we'd spent hours curled up on the sofa re-watching the elephant scene from *The Jungle Book* over and over again. I hoped Rob and Natalie would let him spend as long watching the elephants as I knew he'd want to.

'Say hello to them for me, won't you?'

'Yip.'

'Okay then, darling, I love you so much.'

Silence. Then Olivia's voice was back.

'Mummy, Daddy says he wants to speak to you.'

Well, I don't want to speak to him.

'Okay,' I said, careful to keep the disdain from my voice.

'Here you go, Daddy,' I heard her say, and then Rob was back.

'Beth, hi.'

I didn't reply.

'We – I mean, I – wondered if we could have the kids for a couple more days than we agreed? Until Easter Monday?'

'What? No! Why?'

'We – *I* – wanted to take them away for a few days. Natalie's parents have a house on the coast, down near Brighton, and we thought it would be nice to take them down there, go on the beach, you know. Spend a bit of time together.'

Bile rose up my throat. Natalie's parents and their fucking beach house could fuck off and leave my children alone. Of *course* they couldn't go away with someone I barely knew, with these people who were no part of my life.

'I'd rather they didn't,' I said primly. 'The arrangements are very clear.'

I heard Rob let out a little sigh and was overcome with a surge of rage so wild he was lucky I couldn't reach through the phone and smack my fist into his smug, arrogant face. 'I'm well aware of the arrangements, Beth. I just thought they might enjoy a little break. But if you don't want—'

'I wanted to spend Easter with them.' I hated the desperation in my voice even as I said the words.

'I know. Don't worry, I'll tell them no.'

'Wait, what? You've already mentioned this to them?'

'Well, yes. And they were looking forward to it. But it doesn't matter. You're right. We should stick to the arrangements.'

How could I say no now? And, much as I couldn't stand to admit it, it would give me more time to get their room ready.

'Okay. But do *not* pull a trick like this again. Ever.'

'I won't. Thanks, Beth.' I heard a woman's voice in the background and I shuddered. 'I'd better go.'

I ended the call without saying goodbye, and as I did a wave of despair overwhelmed me, and I sobbed until I thought the tears would never end.

* * *

The curtain-less window taunted me, making me aware of the fact that anyone passing by could see in but I couldn't see out into the blackness of the evening. It wasn't a busy road but that made it worse. I wasn't used to being on my own, and quiet places with few people made me more nervous than a city pulsing with life. There, I felt safe. Here I felt vulnerable, like sitting prey.

I found a sheet and some parcel tape and covered the window with the makeshift curtain. I'd get some proper curtains tomorrow as a matter of priority.

My tiny sofa was the only piece of furniture aside from an old coffee table that I'd propped the TV up on, and I sank into it gratefully. The overhead light leaked out a sickly egg-yolk yellow and it was bone-cold in here, but I just needed five minutes to sit down before I did anything else. I picked the remote control off the floor by my feet and switched the TV on, just for some company, then I stretched out lengthways along the sofa with my feet hanging off the end and closed my eyes.

I'd spent the entire day scraping and scrubbing, filling holes in walls and painting and now my whole body ached. It had been a while since I'd been this physical, and I knew it would feel even worse in the morning.

Laughter on the TV made me jump and I snapped my eyes open. God, this room was depressing.

I pushed myself back up to sitting and then stood, stretching my arms above my head. I needed to get some food and dig out a lamp before I could settle this evening. I checked my watch. It was only seven o'clock. The evening stretched before me like a barren desert. No kids, no friends, nowhere to go. Just me, in a village I didn't know, alone. A vast, bottomless emptiness opened up inside me and I shivered. Would I ever get used to being on my own, or stop craving company?

To distract myself, I picked up my phone again and searched

for a local takeaway service, and added a bottle of wine to the delivery. I took a shower and had just got dressed when the doorbell rang. Running down the stairs, I could make out a silhouette through the bevelled glass. Maybe it was a neighbour coming to introduce themselves, to welcome me to the village with a basket of fruit or a home-cooked crumble. That was just the sort of thing that happened in places like this, wasn't it? Despite myself, I found my spirits lifting, just a little.

'Hi,' I said, tugging the door open with what I hoped was a friendly smile.

But it wasn't a neighbour. The man on the doorstep was holding up a plastic bag filled with metal trays. 'Delivery,' he said, and I took it from him, swallowing down my disappointment as he turned and made his way back to his car. Stupid me. Of *course* it was just the food delivery.

Heart sore, I dug out a box of cutlery, but I didn't have the energy to find a plate. It wasn't as if it mattered anyway, as if anyone would even know if I ate my meal off the floor like a dog. Blinking back tears, I sat back down on the sofa to scoop noodles into my mouth and swig wine from the bottle. What was *wrong* with me?

Half an hour later I was dozing in front of *Casualty* when my phone vibrated.

Mum.

I pushed myself up to sitting. Normally I'd ignore her call, ring her back when I felt mentally prepared. But right now I just needed to hear a friendly voice.

I pressed the green button. 'Hi, Mum.' My voice wobbled.

'You're still alive, then?'

I smiled weakly. She didn't change. 'I am very much alive. Are you and Dad all right?'

'Yes, yes, fine. We were just wondering how the move went.'

'It was okay, thanks.'

'And how are the children coping? Do they like the new house?'

I looked round the room, at the peeling wallpaper and damp carpet, and knew I couldn't tell her the truth.

'They're not here yet, Mum. They're staying with Rob for the week while I get their bedroom ready.'

'Oh, right, I see. Well, that's a shame. I hope they don't want to stay there.'

Aaaaaand this was exactly why I avoided speaking to my mother most of the time. It was as though, with every sentence she spoke, she was deliberately poking at my already open wounds, trying to get them to bleed again. When I'd told Mum and Dad about this house, and about how I was sad that the children would have to share a room while Rob got to keep the family home, hoping for a bit of sympathy, Mum had just said, 'Well, what seven-year-old girl wants to share a bedroom with her baby brother?'

'There isn't much I can do about that,' I'd snapped, hurt but unsurprised by her lack of support.

'You could have stayed with your husband,' she'd said with a sniff, as if Rob hadn't decided to up and leave his family of his own volition. It had taken everything I had to bite my tongue.

Her other suggestion had been that the kids and I moved back there, to Lowestoft where, as Mum frequently reminded me, 'you get a lot more for your money'.

'But I live and work here, Mum,' I'd explained yet again.

'You can be a science teacher anywhere,' she'd added when she'd realised I was determined to stay a three-hour drive away from them.

But given how much Mum and Dad had both spent their lives judging everything I did through their own narrow little outlook, was it any wonder I'd got away as soon as I could – or that I wanted to stay away?

'They'll be home in a few days,' I said now, my voice clipped.

'Right, well, as long as you're okay.' I could tell Mum was upset that I wasn't engaging with her more, bending to her will. But could she really blame me?

'I am. Bye, Mum.'

I hung up with a pang of guilt and sat for a moment, staring into space. Why did I always do this – get my hopes up that, for once, Mum would be on my side? That she would be cheering me on, telling me how well I was doing, getting on with life on my own? She never changed, and hoping she would was only getting me down.

I sighed.

I felt restless now and needed something more than the TV to distract me. I dug out a book from one of the boxes in the corner, but couldn't focus on it. I scrolled through Facebook and Instagram but couldn't bear the smug family photos of amazing Easter holiday adventures everyone was posting.

I checked my watch again. Eight-thirty. I never knew when was a good time to ring Suzie with the baby. I tapped out a text anyway.

Can you talk?

I hoped she could. We used to spend all our time together, me and Rob, Suzie and Dan. Suzie had been my best friend since we'd worked together at a school after graduating. We'd drifted apart a bit after I'd had Olivia and Jacob – she'd still been dating and expected me to be there at the drop of a hat to listen to her dating woes even when the kids were tiny, seeming to have no comprehension of how difficult it was to do anything with young children in tow. But when she'd met and fallen in love with Dan, one of Rob's old university friends, we'd become close again. I'd been there for Suzie when she'd struggled to get pregnant – but by the time she finally did, things with Rob and I had gone spectacularly wrong. Suzie had been very firmly on my side, but even still our friendship had never felt quite the same again. Then Samuel was born a few weeks ago, and I'd hardly heard from her since.

I missed her, and just needed to hear her voice, to remember that someone out there cared.

My phone pinged and I snatched it up, hopeful.

Sorry not tonight. Just putting Sam to bed. Tomorrow? S x

I tried not to cry as I trudged up the stairs to my depressing bedroom, glass of wine in hand. This was my life now, alone. I'd better get used to it.

2

FEELING SO LONELY

I recently started a new job, which meant I moved to a new town. I do not know anybody here and I'm finding it difficult to meet anyone and feel ever so lonely. Do you have any ideas how one can make new friends in a situation such as this?

It is always difficult when you move to a new place. You do not say whether you have moved entirely alone so I can only assume you have. Have you considered a new hobby? Joining a club such as needlecraft or tennis – something you enjoy – can be a good way to make friends with like-minded people. Be aware that it may take some time to establish firm friendships, but it's certainly a very good place to start. You could also consider getting a dog. Dog walkers are very sociable people, and having a dog of your own can be an excellent conversation opener, not to mention the companionship they bring.

The next morning dawned bright, the sun pouring through the curtainless window straight into my face at six o'clock. My mood didn't match the weather though, and I groaned as I rolled over, covering my face with my arm.

I was dying for a cup of tea but, as I knew it would involve finding the kettle and box of teabags first, I couldn't be bothered. I dragged myself to sitting, all my aches and pains revealing themselves one by one as I did. My shoulders hurt from scraping and painting, and I had a crick in my neck that jarred when I turned it.

I picked up my phone and remembered Suzie's text from last night. There was a time when I would have simply rung her no matter what, and told her how lonely I was feeling, how much I craved her company. She would have made me laugh until I forgot my woes, or insisted on coming over to take me out for breakfast. The fact that things had become so stilted between us, and that I couldn't just call her on a whim, only made me feel even more lonely.

Rob's betrayal had taken more from me than just him, and I didn't think I'd ever forgive him for that.

I got up and threw on a dressing gown, then walked through to the kids' bedroom. Even though they'd never actually slept in this house before – they hadn't even been in to see it yet, as I'd been determined to get it looking more inviting first – I still felt their absence like a hole deep inside my heart. I shouldn't be standing in this silent, empty, loveless house by myself on a sunny spring morning. I should be surrounded by chatter and laughter and arguments about who had eaten the last of the Nutella or whose turn it was on the iPad.

I turned and trudged downstairs into the terrible kitchen. I picked up a box from the floor, rummaged around and pulled out my kettle and a couple of mugs. The whereabouts of the teabags, though, was another mystery, and I was also ravenous. I couldn't face going anywhere – it was too early for any shops to be open anyway – so I dug through a couple of other boxes until I found an old jar of instant coffee and a packet of custard creams. That would keep me going for now.

Coffee made, I ran back upstairs, showered and pulled on yesterday's old clothes. That was the other thing about spending all your time alone – you stopped caring about what you wore. Not straight away, of course. But as the days passed and you realised there was literally no one to notice whether you'd even showered, or if your clothes were clean, you stopped caring too. I wasn't back at work for another two weeks, and the kids wouldn't be home for four days. What was the point in wearing anything other than my decorating clothes, my hair tied up in an old bandana?

It was still not quite seven, but I decided I might as well get started. I wanted to pull out the old wardrobe today ready for the delivery of a new one in a couple of days' time. I opened one of the rickety old wooden doors and it felt loose on its hinges. Good, it shouldn't be too difficult to remove.

For the next couple of hours I unscrewed doors, ferrying them downstairs and outside into the overgrown jungle of a garden one at a time. With the last one out I stood outside for a few minutes, letting the sun warm my face. I could hear the gentle hum of a distant lawnmower, and a chatter of voices in a neighbouring garden, and I wondered who these people were that I was living so close to now. Would I ever get to know them? Having lived in a large town for most of my life, I wasn't used to the intimacy of introducing myself and wasn't sure if I could bring myself to do it, no matter how desperate I felt for company.

I trudged back inside, back up to the kids' room, and tried to pull out the base of the wardrobe but it was stuck fast. I tugged harder and slowly, finally, it began to give. Then, all of a sudden, the whole thing came away in my hands and I went flying backwards, landing on my backside.

'Shit!'

I sat for a moment, dazed, then propped the piece of wood against the wall and peered into the gap underneath the raised wardrobe floor. There were a few pieces of rubble and some scraps of damp, slightly smelly carpet. I curled my fingers under the base of the next section and tugged. Slowly, it started to give and I braced myself so I didn't go flying backwards again. This time the piece of wood yielded much more easily, as if it had been unscrewed many times before, and it was off within seconds. I laid it to one side too and leaned forward to pull off the next piece. But as I did, I stopped. There was something buried under here, a black plastic box. I reached for it. It was quite big, and heavier than I'd expected. I held it with both hands and stood, looking round for somewhere to put it. The room was empty so I wiped the dust off and took it through to my room and laid it on my bed. It was, I realised now, a box wrapped in a black plastic bin liner, which was held on with a series of elastic bands. I gave it a shake, pressing my ear to the top. There was a bit of movement, books moving around or something like that, but nothing distinguishable. Should I open it? What if it was private?

But then again, if it was important, why would somebody have left it behind?

Before I could change my mind I peeled the bands off one by one, then unwrapped the plastic and eased it off. I let the bin bag drop to the floor, then placed the box gently on the bed. It was large, and made of thin wood, with metal edges.

The lid didn't look as if it was fastened down, so I carefully inched it off. Inside were what looked like piles of old magazines, and some other loose magazine pages. I picked one off the top. It was called *True Charm*, and the illustrations on the front page were beautiful, a stunning woman with a cinched-in waist and a handsome man with his arms wrapped round her. It was dated April 1952. The paper felt crepey and fragile beneath my fingers so I wiped my hands down my trousers and carefully opened it, letting my eyes wander over the contents page.

I flicked through the rest of the pages, careful not to rip them, taking in the adverts for shampoo, antiperspirants, corsets and nylons, recipes for special meat dishes and plentiful desserts, interviews with long-forgotten heart-throbs and photo stories of girls and boys falling in love. These were a treasure trove. But what on earth were they doing buried away under the wardrobe?

I could have spent all day reading them, trying to picture the women who would have devoured these stories so many years ago, but I had to get on. Reluctantly, I put the magazines back in the box on my bed and left them to have a proper look at later.

* * *

The rest of the day was spent getting rid of the wardrobes, sanding down walls, filling holes in the plaster and painting skirting boards. By the time I'd run out of energy the sun was a deep orange disc hovering above the treetops. I gave my hands a quick wash, picked up the box of magazines that had been tugging at my mind all day, and hurried out into the garden. 'Jungle' might have been a better description for it – from here I couldn't see the fence at the bottom, and what I could make out was a tangle of weeds and overgrown plants. Just like the house, it had obviously been neglected for many years. There was a patch of rickety concrete slabs immediately outside the back door that stretched for about two metres until it hit what must once have

been a lawn. The grass was choked with weeds now, towering
dandelions and nettles clamouring for space, thistles stretching
their heads towards the sun. I knew there was a greenhouse in
there somewhere, several glass panels cracked and broken but
otherwise still intact, but I couldn't see even a corner of it from
here. I assumed there was a laburnum tree buried in there somewhere too – or least there must have been once for the cottage to
be named after it.

I placed the box of magazines on the ground then went back
inside to find a camping chair, which I unfolded on the least
damaged section of paving. I went back one more time for a bottle
of wine, an old mug (the best thing I could find) and a blanket to
protect me from the rapidly cooling evening, then settled into the
chair.

I felt my heart thump with excitement as I removed the lid
from the box again. I'd been looking forward to this all day. I
peeled the first two magazines off the top and moved them to one
side, then chose one dated a couple of months later. The cover
was just as intricate and beautiful and I wondered when magazines had stopped being illustrated like this. This time the magazine fell open on an agony aunt page, and I noticed that the
corner had been turned down as if to mark it. The page was called
Dear Evelyn Wright, and it was filled with half a dozen letters from
readers – women, mainly – asking for advice from the homely-
looking agony aunt. I pulled the page closer and began to read.
There were questions from girls asking if they should let a boy
kiss them, or how they could attract a boy they had their eye on;
there was one from a husband furious that his wife wanted to
work because his house was always a mess and he wanted to
know what he should do about it, as well as letters from older
women whose husbands were having affairs, or who were seeking

advice about whether to ask for a divorce. It was like a snapshot into another era.

I put the magazine down and plucked the next one from the pile. Just like before, the agony aunt page had its corner folded down and it fell open easily.

I started reading again, fascinated by the worries of these women – and the occasional man – from seventy years before who had felt they had no one else to turn to except a stranger who worked for a magazine. What must it have been like, back then, to have been so worried about doing the wrong thing and having no one to confide in, or to have people judge you at every turn?

I must have lost track of time because before I knew it the light had faded so much I was squinting to read the words on the page. I stared out into the darkness of the night and felt suddenly cold, and more than a little vulnerable. I wasn't used to being on my own and it still made me feel nervous. I gathered everything up except the chair, then took it all back inside and locked the back door securely. There was no curtain or blind at the window in here either, so I kept the light off and went through to the front room, where the sheet still hung forlornly at the window, and flicked the lamp on. My stomach rumbled loudly in protest at being starved. I promised myself I'd go shopping tomorrow, but for tonight I rang for another takeaway.

While I waited for the food to arrive I devoured more of the magazines' pages. Evelyn's advice, although dated, seemed in the main part fair and considered, and I wondered who this woman was who had advised so many people over the years. How many of them had taken her advice, and how many people's lives had she changed – for the better or the worse? And, more to the point, how had she *known* how to help people?

In fact I felt more drawn to these pages and letters than I ever imagined I would be. It was almost as though Evelyn Wright were talking to me from the past, trying to tell me something. What it was I was too bone-achingly tired to pin down right now, but as I drifted off to sleep later that night I felt comforted, somehow. Because just maybe hidden somewhere in these pages was the key to helping me find happiness again too.

3

SELFISH FRIEND

I have had the same best friend for more than a decade, and we have always told each other everything. But recently we seem to have less in common, and whenever we spend time together, I find the things she talks about boring. I am beginning to dread her visits, but I am not sure how to let her know, or whether I should just stop contacting her.

I think you have probably answered your own question. Over time people drift apart, and what you once needed in a friend may no longer be the case. Friendships come and go and I would suggest that if you really don't feel you want to be friends with this woman any longer then you simply stop contacting her. She will eventually understand that your friendship has run its course, and it will give you time to find some friends that better suit your new life.

'Mummy!' Olivia launched herself at me, almost pushing me over. I lifted her arms and pulled her to me, breathing in the familiar scent of her apple shampoo. My love, my baby. I glanced down to where Jacob was lurking a little behind Rob, his tiny hand reaching up to clasp his daddy's. His eyes were wide. I put Olivia down gently and crouched down to his level.

'Hello, sweetie, are you going to come in and see your new bedroom?'

He shook his head and looked up at Rob.

'He was a bit teary this morning about leaving home, but he's been a big brave soldier, haven't you, Jacob?' Rob said. I bristled at the word *home* but said nothing.

'It's okay, sweetheart, you're home with Mummy now, and you've got a brand-new bedroom,' I said, reaching my hand out. 'Do you want to come and see it too?'

He nodded and let go of Rob's hand, grabbing mine. The warmth of his skin against my palm filled me with so much love I wanted to squeeze him and never let go, but instead I stood and turned back to my ex-husband. He handed me two rucksacks.

'Anything I need to know?'

'I don't think so.' He ruffled Jacob's hair. 'We had fun, didn't we, little dude?'

Jacob nodded.

'Right, well, thanks for bringing them back.'

'No problem.'

I closed the door before he could say anything else, desperate to cuddle my babies. God, I hated them being away for so long. I felt as though I had a limb missing.

'Come on, Mummy,' Olivia said, impatient to get upstairs.

'Sorry, love, I'm just so pleased to have you home.'

The three of us made our way up the tatty stairs, and my heart thumped with anticipation. Would they like their new room?

Given what a good time they seemed to have had at Rob's for the last week, it felt as if there was a lot at stake.

'Is it blue, like you promised, Mummy? Are there sparkles? And a tractor duvet for Jakey?' Olivia kept up a constant stream of chatter as we made our way upstairs and I was grateful for the distraction.

'You'll see,' I said. We reached their bedroom and I swung the door open and flicked on the light as they stepped inside.

'Ta-da!' I said.

They both stood still for a moment, taking it all in. I felt proud of the way the room looked. It had taken me much longer than I'd hoped, which meant that by the time I'd got the final lick of paint on the walls, the new wardrobe and beds built, and all the rugs and cushions in there to finish it off, it was the only room I'd made any progress on at all. Every other room was still just as grim as it had been the day I moved in. But I hoped my hard work would pay off and they'd love their new bedroom, at least.

I held my breath as I waited for them to say something.

'Is this my bed?' Olivia said, approaching the furthest one cautiously.

'It is. Do you like it?'

She studied it for a moment, then sat and bounced up and down. 'Yes, Mummy, it's nice,' she said.

I turned to Jacob, who was still hovering in the doorway, clutching his toy rabbit to his chest. 'Jakey? This is your bed,' I said, pressing my hand on the bed nearest to the door. 'What do you think?'

He didn't move, but just stood watching me with saucer-eyes. I sat down on the bed, sinking into the soft mattress, and held my hand out to him. But instead of coming towards me he walked across the carpet and jumped onto Olivia's bed and curled up beside her.

'Mummy, this is my bed, isn't it, not Jacob's?' Olivia said indignantly.

'Yes, this is your bed, sweetheart,' I said. He shook his head.

'I want to stay with Livia,' he said.

I looked at Olivia. 'Is that okay, love?' I said. 'Just for tonight?'

She looked at me, then at her brother, then, to my utter relief, her face broke into a smile and she threw her arms around him. 'You can stay here tonight, Jakey,' she said.

Thank you, I mouthed at her above Jacob's head. Sometimes I thought she was wiser than me when it came to her brother. Or, in fact, with most things.

* * *

Over the last few nights, rather than dreading the long, solitary evenings, I'd begun looking forward to the time when darkness fell and I collapsed onto the sofa with exhaustion. It meant I could return to the 1950s, and fall into the problem pages once more. As I read I began to feel a real affinity with these people from so many decades past, with their trials and tribulations, worries and insecurities just like me. People, I began to realise, had always been unhappy. And they'd always needed people like Evelyn Wright to help them.

It certainly helped me to feel less alone in my despair.

I settled on the sofa and peeled half a dozen magazines from the top of the box. I'd only just opened the first page when my phone started buzzing against my leg. It was Suzie.

Reluctantly, I pressed answer.

'I'm so, so, so sorry,' she gushed the instant I pressed the phone to my ear. She sounded frazzled and in the background I could hear the baby begin to cry. 'I've been meaning to call since you moved but it's been hectic here. Samuel just won't sleep and

I —' She stopped abruptly, as if she'd suddenly run out of words.

I knew I should say that it was fine, that I understood what it was like when babies were tiny and you couldn't find a minute to yourself to even have a cup of tea without it going cold. But I couldn't shake the memory of when Olivia had been born and Suzie had carried on as normal and expected me to be on the other end of the phone whenever she'd needed to cry or vent or moan. A wave of bitterness swept through me that she couldn't do the same for me now. She knew I was all alone, and even a text every now and then to check up on me would have been welcome. I swallowed the sour taste down like a particularly unpleasant pill.

'How is everything?' I said, reluctantly putting the magazines to one side.

'Fine, fine. I'm just knackered, you know.'

I knew that feeling all too well. I felt a swell of sympathy.

'So, Samuel's not sleeping?'

Suzie let out a little bark of what I assumed was meant to be laughter. 'He's really not. He's awake all night and cries most of the day and I only get any respite if I go out for endless walks and he drops off in the pram.'

'Sorry to hear that, Suzie. It's tough, isn't it, the lack of sleep?'

'Honestly, it feels like torture.'

A silence fell for a moment as we both ran out of things to say and Samuel stopped sobbing at the same time. It was a far cry from the days when we could spend all day together chatting and then all evening nattering too.

'You'd think you hadn't seen each other for two years rather than a couple of hours,' Rob used to say. But it had always felt as though Suzie and I would never run out of things to say to each other. Now, I longed to ask her whether she and Dan had seen

Rob and Natalie together – even though I suspected the answer would be one I didn't really want to hear.

'So, how was the move?' Suzie said eventually.

'Fine. Easy, considering.'

'And how's the house?' I let my gaze wander round the living room with its tired carpet and faded walls, the sheet sagging at the window and the few sticks of second-hand furniture.

'It's nice,' I lied. 'Cosy.'

'Good.'

'I've been decorating the kids' bedroom,' I added, for want of anything better to say.

'Sounds good.' I could tell she was distracted and I was tempted to say goodbye and get back to the magazines that had consumed me over the past few evenings. But this was the first proper conversation I'd had in days, and I was overwhelmed by a sudden urge to keep her on the line; to not be confronted by the humming silence of my own company.

'I found some magazines,' I blurted.

'Magazines?' She sounded confused by the segue.

I barrelled on regardless. 'Old magazines, from the 1950s. They were in the bottom of the wardrobe in the kids' room.'

'Oh. Right.'

I ignored her obvious lack of enthusiasm. 'I've been reading some of them and they're fascinating,' I explained, desperate for her to understand how much these letters from the past had come to mean to me. 'You'd love them,' I added, weakly.

'Maybe you can show me when I come round,' she said.

'Yeah. Yeah, that would be good.' I didn't ask when that was likely to be.

'Listen, I'm really sorry, Beth, I'm going to have to go.'

I swallowed down the disappointment. I hadn't realised until

Suzie had rung quite how desperate I'd been for someone to talk to. My insides felt hollow.

'Okay. No worries. Thanks for ringing.'

'I'll call you soon, okay?'

But before I could answer, she'd gone, leaving me all alone again with just the fruitless clunking sound of the ancient radiators. I rubbed my eyes and let the room slowly swim back into focus.

The letters I'd been so desperate to get back to, that had been consuming my thoughts these last few nights, sat on the floor in my peripheral vision. But I didn't feel like picking them up any more.

My stilted conversation with my supposed best friend had left me feeling odd. Lost. Almost as though I were having an out-of-body experience, looking down at this strange, solitary creature huddled in the middle of an artfully dismantled living room. I tried to get my thoughts in order, to work out what it was exactly that was bothering me, hovering just out of reach.

Was it that speaking to Suzie had made me realise just how lonely I was? That the person I'd always turned to for advice no longer even listened to me? Or was it something else?

And then, a glimmer. A fleeting thought that I snatched hold of, tried to study from all angles.

All of these letters. All of these people – many of whom would have had no one else to talk to, just like me – who had written to Evelyn, desperate for her help. It didn't matter what the problem was – how trivial, or how serious – she treated them all with the same respect. She tried her best to help them all.

It gave me a strange sense of hope. Was that the right word? I wasn't sure. But all I did know was that, somehow, the fact that these people had found someone to listen to their woes and to help them made me feel less despairing.

After all, hadn't Evelyn helped me too? She might not actually be here to answer my questions, to help navigate me through my loneliness, or my sadness at being without my children. But just the fact that she existed, once, as a beacon of hope to so many people, gave me hope too.

And then, the thing that had been floating just outside my vision finally came into view. And I knew what it was I needed to do.

I needed to become an Evelyn for *today*. I wasn't yet quite sure how I was going to do it, but I needed to help people, the way she had helped others. The way she had helped me. I owed it to her, and I owed it to myself.

4

WORKAHOLIC WIFE

I never seem to be able to find a man, and my friends suggest that it's because I work too hard. I admit I do work long hours and am in the office for most of the day, but I can't see how that would put any fellow off? Are they right? Should I work less and make sure I have enough time to spend with a man?

It's important for a man to know that you will be there to give them the attention they require. No man likes to think that you are more interested in your job than you are in them – and if you do find someone you want to marry, you'll want them to know that you are able to look after them properly once you are married. Perhaps you could simply ensure you make it clear to any fellow you meet that they are the most important thing in your life, and not your job. If that means reducing your hours, then that is a sacrifice worth making.

It was another three weeks before I found a moment to sit down and do anything about resurrecting *Dear Evelyn Wright*. The kids and I were back at school, and adapting to our new routine had been a challenge. I'd also been determined to make the house a little less depressing and had spent most of my evenings getting the living room looking and feeling like a place we wanted to be. So far I'd stripped the faded yellow wallpaper and painted the walls a soothing green. I'd hired a sander and sanded the floorboards that had been hidden beneath the decrepit flowery carpet, bought a rug and finally bought some curtains to replace the tatty sheet hanging at the window. It was far from being finished but at least it was beginning to feel a bit more like home.

Now, though, the kids were with their dad and I had two long weekend evenings stretching out in front of me with nothing to fill them. Since my initial thoughts about doing something to help people and alleviate my loneliness at the same time, I'd been trying to figure out a way to make it work.

I fired up my laptop and typed in 'agony aunts'. Articles detailing the history of agony aunts and links to modern-day agony aunts were top of the list, along with round-ups of the funniest agony aunt responses of all time. Apart from a handful of local newspapers and a few magazines aimed at older women, there didn't seem to be the same sort of love for the traditional advice columns as there had once been. I clicked on another story that caught my eye. According to one report, an agony aunt named Dorothy Dix, who was popular in the first half of the twentieth century, received more than one hundred thousand letters every year at the peak of her popularity. One hundred thousand! My mind raced. All those people who had been so desperate for someone to turn to that a stranger had seemed like the only option.

But where did these people go for advice now? A smattering of magazine columns could only scratch the surface, and with people even less connected than ever, it struck me that there must be thousands, if not hundreds of thousands of people out there who could use more focused, tailored advice. People who had literally no one else to turn to.

I walked into the kitchen to pour a glass of wine. I could feel the earlier idea that had taken seed in my mind beginning to grow, and I needed time to think, to let it settle and reveal itself. I stood at the tatty sink overlooking the back garden. It was almost dark outside now and the towering, overgrown weeds were beginning to deepen into ominous shadows. But for the first time since I'd moved here, I didn't feel scared that someone was out there watching me. My mind was too full for that. Full of thoughts about how I could help other people in need, while at the same time helping myself by doing something meaningful to fill the long, empty days when I was all alone.

I knew there had to be a way to do it, and do it well.

I turned away from the garden and went back to my laptop. I found a news story from a year or so ago about the rise of TikTok agony aunts and problem-page podcasts and, as I read, a fully formed idea of what I should do finally began to take shape.

I needed to start an agony aunt page for the modern age. A place where people my age could get advice without having to resort to TikTok. I'd found the odd online agony aunt column and a couple of paid-for problem-page websites, and there were a number of online forums where people shared opinions and advice, but other than that there didn't seem to be anywhere for the ordinary person to go for personalised guidance these days.

My fingers hovered over the keys for a moment while I got my thoughts in order.

And then it came to me.

I opened a link to register my domain name. Then, slowly and ever so carefully, I typed in the name I'd landed on, and pressed *enter*.

It was done. I had a brand-new project to keep me occupied: an agony aunt page.

I'd called it *Dear Evelyn*.

This was the start of a brand-new chapter.

5

SECRET FEELINGS

I am a happily married woman with a wonderful husband and two young children, but recently I had relations with a colleague. We both regret our actions and agreed never to mention it again. However someone we work with has found out and is threatening to tell our boss. I am terrified my husband will find out and I am certain he wouldn't be able to forgive me. I know I made a mistake, but it feels desperately unfair to be so severely punished when we had both decided it would never be repeated.

You did indeed make a terrible mistake, and no doubt you feel worse about having been discovered than the act itself. You must come clean to your husband about your actions. He may find it difficult to accept, but imagine how much worse it would be to find out from someone else. By keeping it between you, he may find a way to work through this.

You should also consider why you turned to someone else

in the first place. Are you unhappy with your husband, and if
so, how can you improve things within your marriage?

By the following evening I had a rudimentary website up and
running. I might need something more sophisticated later, but for
now my simple design was enough, and I was pleased with the
result.

To get the ball rolling I'd made up a couple of problems by
looking at the original *Dear Evelyn Wright* questions and updating
them. It surprised me that, much of the time, Evelyn Wright's
advice had been good, solid, considered guidance. Some of it,
especially the idea that women should be there to look pretty for
men, was old-fashioned and slightly ridiculous, but a lot of it was
easy to bring up to date.

All I had to do now was let people know the page existed, so I
joined some local Facebook groups as Evelyn, set up an Instagram
account, and sent a couple of introductory posts out into the ether.
I felt a flutter of excitement at what this might bring.

The next few days were busy as exam time was coming up for
my pupils, and Olivia and Jacob were with me. But each night
once they were in bed I couldn't wait to check my emails to see
whether anyone had written in.

At first there was nothing. Maybe I'd misjudged this and it had
been a big fat waste of my time.

But I felt sure there was something in the idea, and while I
waited I continued to read through the problem pages I'd found
in the box.

I also got to wondering about Evelyn Wright herself. Who was
she – and, more to the point, why had her old agony aunt columns
been hidden under a wardrobe in my house? Had she lived here?
Maybe she had sat in this very room, painstakingly typing out
replies to people she'd never met, but who were relying on her

advice to help them make what often amounted to life-changing decisions. For the first time I was beginning to feel a little bit of warmth for my new house, a real connection to its previous owners.

Finally, one evening about two weeks later, an email popped into my inbox. I stared at it for a few minutes as if it were a mirage, scared that if I clicked it open it would disappear into nowhere, like a puff of smoke.

My heart thumped as I clicked on the email. There was no name at the top – I assumed whoever had sent it had been so keen to remain anonymous that they'd set up a brand-new email account for this very purpose – but that was okay. The message was short and to the point.

Dear Evelyn

Recently my marriage has been going through a rocky patch. Then two weeks ago I did something really stupid, and slept with one of my husband's friends when we were both drunk. I regretted it instantly, but I'm now terrified his friend will tell him about it. Should I keep quiet and hope it all goes away, or should I come clean and tell my husband myself? Please help.

I tore my eyes from the screen. This was the moment of truth. This woman, whoever she was, really did need my help. The responsibility suddenly felt overwhelming. What if I got this wrong? Why had I thought I was qualified to help other people make the right decisions when I'd made such a mess of my own life?

Overcome with a wave of self-doubt, I pushed my laptop away and stood. I needed time to think. A glance out of the window revealed it was still light, the sky a deep peach above the treetops.

I picked up the box of magazines, then walked through the house and out into the back garden. I'd bought a couple of cheap wooden chairs in a sale, and I placed the box on one of them, went back inside for my wine glass, then sat in the other chair. The air was still warm and if I closed my eyes I could almost believe I was in the garden of my dreams.

The overgrown jungle didn't bother me now as I began to search through Evelyn Wright's letters to see if I could find something to help me give this woman the best advice I could.

By the time I found the perfect letter to help me craft my own response, night-time had stretched itself across the sky and it was almost impossible to read without giving myself a headache. I gathered everything back up and headed inside to read Evelyn's advice more carefully.

The letter I'd found was titled 'Secret Feelings' and was about almost exactly the same dilemma as this, except the affair had been with a colleague. The tone of the advice might have been outdated, but it would definitely help me work out what I needed to say.

My fingers hovered over the keyboard. It was all very good using Evelyn Wright's advice, but what would I want in this situation? Would I have wanted someone else to tell me about Rob's betrayal if I'd had the choice, or would I have preferred to have heard it from him? Might there even have been a chance that I could have forgiven him if he'd confessed?

I knew what I had to say.

As hard as it might be, the very fact that you have asked me this question tells me that you know you should tell your husband about what happened immediately – before someone else does. Think about how you would feel if the situation were reversed. Would you prefer to hear from him, or his friend?

Explain why it happened, apologise for hurting him and breaking his trust, and don't expect him to forgive you straight away. He may not ever be able to forgive you, but at least by being honest you have given him the chance to get over any mistrust and make an informed decision.

You also need to think about why you had the one-night stand in the first place. Are you unhappy with your husband? Do you crave attention that he is not giving you? Or is there some other reason for your infidelity? You need to address the cause and discuss it before you will be able to move on.

I stopped typing and reread the words. Should I send it now or sleep on it, make sure I was happy with my response? I tried to think what Evelyn Wright would have done. Her answers seemed very black and white, her advice confident. That was what was needed here. That was what this woman was looking for: someone to tell her the right thing to do.

Before I could change my mind, I clicked send, then copied the letter and added it to my website.

My first real letter was up!

I was on my way.

6

A MOTHER'S WORRY

My husband and I are divorced. While he lives with his new wife, I am all alone. Our two children live with me, but I am worried I am losing them. My former husband and his new wife have a more extravagant lifestyle than me thanks to his well-paid job, so are better able to offer my children the lifestyle to which they have become accustomed. While I know money isn't everything, it is difficult for them to understand this when their father takes them on expensive holidays and lets them have anything they ask for, while I am unable to do the same. How can I help them appreciate that money isn't as important as love?

You are of course absolutely correct that money is far less important than love, and the truth is that nothing can replace a mother's love and care. The question, as you say, is how to help your children to understand this.

Spend time doing fun things together. When they are not at

school, can you go for walks, or bake, or play games? Is there something they really want that you can offer them? Maybe they are desperate for a kitten or hamster, or even a dog, if you have room, a pet they can form a loving bond with in your home? I really would try not to worry too much. As the children grow they will come to appreciate all that you have done for them.

I couldn't stop thinking about the woman who I'd tried to help, wondering whether my advice had helped her; if she'd told her husband what had happened. I hoped that, whatever she'd decided to do, she at least felt as though someone was listening to her.

The next letter arrived in my inbox on a Thursday morning. I had a quick glance while the children were munching their toast at the tiny kitchen table and I was waiting for my coffee to brew.

Dear Evelyn

I've never done anything like this before, but I came across your website and I literally have no one else to turn to. I hate the way I look. I've tried to talk to friends about it, but they just tell me I'm beautiful, or think I'm fishing for compliments, but I'm really not. All I see when I look in the mirror is a huge nose, a hideous fat face and a disgusting, lumpy body. I spend hours poring over pictures of perfect women online and it makes me hate myself even more. I've become obsessed. How can I learn to love myself – or make myself look better?

Poor woman. I knew exactly how she felt. We were bombarded by so many supposedly perfect images of beauty these days that it was impossible to escape them, and they could knock your confidence further if you were already feeling down.

I tried to formulate a response in my mind. I wanted to tell her she needed to learn to love herself, and to ignore the heavily filtered images she saw online, but I also wanted to make sure I got the advice just right. My mind was in the middle of that when my thoughts were interrupted by Olivia, who, judging by the pitch of her voice, had been trying to get my attention for some time.

'Mummeeee, stop looking at your phone!'

I looked up. 'Sorry, love.' I clicked the phone off and smiled at her guiltily. 'What's up?'

She swallowed her mouthful and gave a melodramatic sigh. She had jam all round her mouth. 'I *said,* why can't we see Daddy this weekend?'

'What?'

She took a gulp of her apple juice. 'Why do we have to stay here this weekend and not see Daddy and Natalie?'

My stomach twisted at the mention of that name. I forced a smile onto my face.

'Because you're with me this weekend, sweetheart,' I said.

'Yes, but *why*? We were with you last weekend.'

'Well, yes, you were. That's the way Daddy and I arranged it,' I said. 'Don't you want to be here with Mummy?'

She shrugged and I felt as though a knife were being twisted in my back. I turned away from her to pour my coffee so she couldn't see how upset I was.

'It's just...' She stopped, as if trying to work out what to tell me. 'We don't have to share a bedroom at Daddy's, do we, Jakey? We get to stay in our old rooms, just like before.'

My coffee turned bitter in my mouth, and I turned round in time to see Jacob look up from his toast, crumbs spilling down his chin. His eyes were wide as he shook his head.

'See, Mummy,' Olivia said triumphantly.

I pulled out the spare chair and sat down opposite them both, my hands wrapped round my mug. 'I know Daddy has more space than us, and you have your old bedrooms there, but you like your new bedroom, don't you?' I said gently, trying not to show them how hurt I was. None of this was their fault, and how could a seven and a five-year-old be expected to understand how unfair the situation was? I wanted them to spend time with their dad, I knew it was important. But none of that made it any less gut-wrenching to hear them say they wanted to be with him more.

'Yes, Mummy,' Olivia said, rolling her eyes. 'But it's not *my* bedroom, is it?' She turned to her brother, who had Nutella smeared across his face. 'You prefer your room at Daddy's house, don't you?' she said, and he nodded. Olivia turned back to me. 'And Natalie lets us stay up late to watch TV. You never let us stay up late.' She picked her plate up and licked the crumbs off. I snatched it away from her and it fell to the table with a clatter. Both of them stared at me. My whole body shook.

'Staying up late is just a treat for weekends,' I said, trying to keep my voice steady. 'It doesn't mean Natalie's a good parent, or that she loves you more. It just means—' I broke off, not wanting to say something I'd regret later. I took a deep breath. 'Mummy only wants you to get a good night's sleep because she cares,' I said. 'And sharing a bedroom has been cool, hasn't it?'

Jacob nodded, Olivia merely shrugged. Mum's words rang in my ears: *what seven-year-old girl wants to share a bedroom with her baby brother?* I knew she was right and that soon Olivia would start to need her own space – but what could I do about it?

I reached my hands out and pressed them firmly against theirs. 'Your home is here with Mummy now,' I said. 'Daddy loves you, and you will always be able to go and stay with him, but you live here with me.' I swallowed down the lump in my throat.

'But what if Daddy wants to take us somewhere cool?' Olivia

flicked a look at her brother, then back at me. 'Daddy said he'd take us to Disneyland. I want to go there.'

My body tensed as anger rose through me. How dared Rob make extravagant promises he probably wouldn't keep just to make himself look good? 'We can do something cool together this weekend if you like,' I said, forcing a smile.

Olivia's eyes lit up. 'Can we? What?'

My mind scrabbled to come up with something that could compete with what Rob had offered them, but also meant I wouldn't have to remortgage the house to pay for it. 'I don't know,' I said, playing for time. 'Why don't you think about it, and let me know where you'd like to go? Okay?'

'Okay, Mummy,' Olivia said, licking jam off the butter knife with satisfaction. I took it from her and moved it out of the way. 'Okay, little man?' I said, turning to Jacob. He nodded wordlessly, then stood up.

As they left together to go and brush their teeth, I looked round at the makeshift kitchen, and thought about the gleaming modern kitchen-diner I'd left behind. The kitchen that Natalie was now treating as her own, moving around the space I'd spent so many hours creating, poring over colour charts and tile choices, lighting plans and worktops. If I let it, the bitterness could eat me from the inside out, but I wasn't going to give either Rob or Natalie the satisfaction.

I wished I had someone to talk to. But I couldn't face the judgement of Mum, and calling Suzie didn't have the same appeal as it had once held. My colleagues were mostly lovely, but snatched chats in the staffroom and the odd drink after work didn't bring the sorts of friendships where you could talk about personal problems – at least not for me.

I wondered whether Evelyn's letters could help me work out

how to stop the bitterness swallowing me whole – or even give me ideas on how I could beat Rob at his own game.

* * *

The children were in bed by the time I finally got round to poring over Evelyn Wright's letters again, desperately searching for an idea to win the children back on side. I wasn't expecting much, but, to my amazement, I found the perfect thing – someone who had been going through almost exactly the same as me all those years ago.

As I finished reading the letter, I felt dizzy and tipped my head against the back of the sofa. The overhead light was harsh, so I reached up and switched it off and stared blindly at the blankness of the ceiling, letting light shadows dance across my vision and allowing my mind to take in what Evelyn had advised. There was one line in particular that stuck in my mind, getting lodged like a needle on a scratched record.

Maybe they are desperate for a kitten or hamster, or even a dog, if you have room, a pet they can form a loving bond with in your home?

For years the kids had wanted a dog. Ever since they were little, they'd begged me and Rob for a puppy, but, thanks to Rob's allergies, we'd always said no. Secretly, I'd always believed Rob would have refused no matter what, because a dog wouldn't fit in with his lifestyle, so if I said we could get a dog now, I'd be offering them something Rob couldn't.

I couldn't deny the thought was appealing, even if I was simultaneously appalled at myself for playing stupid games with my ex-husband.

But then I remembered something else. One of Evelyn's letters had suggested getting a dog as a way of making new friends, too. Perhaps it could be good for me as well as the children.

I pulled my phone from my pocket and typed 'dog shelters near me' into the search engine. Seconds later a list appeared. There were dozens of them, all offering pets that had been abandoned, or maltreated, staring out longingly from the screen, begging for a loving new home. And I knew, as I scrolled through page after page of photos, that I'd already made up my mind.

I'd tell the kids the good news tomorrow.

* * *

I couldn't hear myself think above the shrieking, but I didn't care – because the children's reaction to my announcement was even better than I'd imagined it would be.

'Can we get a girl dog and put ribbons in its hair?' Olivia begged.

'Can we called it Superman?' Jacob said.

'Can I take it for walks every day?'

'Can I take it to school?'

'Can I tell Miranda?'

'Can it sleep on my bed?'

I held my hands up and waited for the questions to stop. Eventually, they both went quiet, and I crouched down to speak to them. Jacob wrapped his arm round my neck and clung to me as I spoke and I pulled his little body in close.

'We need to go to the rescue centre to choose one,' I said. 'But —' I held my finger up in the air to make my point '—the doggy also has to choose us.'

'What do you mean, Mummy?' Jacob said.

'Well, some pets can only live in houses where there are no children. And we need to make sure the doggy likes us, and that our house is all right for them to live in.'

There was a moment of silence, then Olivia said, 'But our

house isn't very nice. Will you have to make it nice before a dog can come and live there?'

I shook my head. 'No, love. An animal doesn't mind if the decorating isn't very pretty. It's more whether the people at the shelter think our house is big enough.' I didn't tell them that my main concern was the garden. I knew dogs liked space to run around outside, and currently our garden was a no-go area. I hoped I'd be able to get it cleared up in time – although I didn't know where to start.

'Can we go now, to choose one?' Olivia said.

'No, it's too late. Anyway, first we have to look at all the pictures on the website, and then we have to go and meet them.' I stood and took their hands. 'Shall we do that now?'

'Yes!' they chorused.

* * *

We spent the next couple of hours scrolling through photos of dogs looking for a new home. From old, arthritic pets whose owners had died, to puppies whose owners hadn't been able to cope, I wanted to take them all in. I wasn't sure how we were going to choose just one.

'Can we have that one?' Olivia said, pointing at an enormous greyhound staring dolefully at us from the screen.

'No, this one,' Jacob said, pointing out a German shepherd with a ferocious look on its face.

'We might need to get a smaller dog than that,' I explained. 'Dogs that big need too much exercise and lots of space.'

Once the kids got bored with looking at dogs they weren't allowed to have, I spent some time registering with a couple of the local shelters. The forms were extensive, and it took me some time to complete them. When I'd finished I went and found Olivia and Jacob in front of the TV.

'Have we got one, Mummy?' Jacob said, looking up hopefully.

I lowered myself onto the floor beside him. 'No, love, not yet. It might be some time before there's a dog suitable for us. But they'll let us know, I'm sure.'

'How long, Mummy?' Olivia turned towards me. I was beginning to regret mentioning this before I'd set the process in motion. I could foresee weeks, maybe even months, of endless nagging. 'I'm not sure, sweetheart,' I replied. 'Hopefully not too long.'

'Good. Daddy said we can have a guinea pig soon.'

For God's sake.

'Did he? That'll be nice.'

Olivia studied me for a minute, then shrugged. 'Yeah, but not as good as a dog.'

I couldn't ignore the surge of triumph I felt. *Ha, fuck you and your expensive gifts, Rob,* I thought uncharitably as I pulled Jacob into a cuddle. I didn't even care when he shrugged me off.

* * *

To my surprise one of the shelters was bursting at the seams and arranged a home visit within a couple of days, and we were able to visit the centre just two days later.

'You will need to clear this garden and make sure it's safe,' Melanie from the rescue centre explained, and I promised I would.

'And you'll need to arrange for someone to walk him or her on the days when you're at work,' she added.

'Of course,' I said, wondering who on earth I was going to ask in this village where I still knew no one. I pushed the thought away, determined not to get caught up in wallowing any more. I'd cross that bridge when I came to it.

And so to my surprise it was just over a week later – much sooner than I'd ever imagined – that we went to pick up Buster, a four-year-old cocker spaniel. Excitement levels were high, and by the time we bundled ourselves into my rattly old car, Jacob was in danger of wetting himself.

'Will we be able to bring Buster home, Mummy?' he said, his voice high as he clambered into his booster seat and I buckled him in.

'Yes, sweetheart, he'll be coming to live with us today,' I said. He clapped his hands in delight, and my heart soared. I sent up a silent prayer of thanks to Evelyn, whose advice had worked better than either of us could have imagined.

Half an hour later we pulled up outside the rescue centre. As we clambered out of the car the air was filled with barking, and as we walked through the front door we were greeted by Melanie.

'Ah, here we are,' she said, shaking my hand and crouching down to speak to the children. 'Buster is very excited about coming to live with you,' she said.

'We're excited too, aren't we, Jakey?' Olivia said, nudging her brother when he didn't reply. Instead he was staring round at the photos of dogs plastered all over the walls, photos sent by their new owners to thank the centre for giving them their new friend. His eyes were wide with wonder.

Melanie stood and wiped her hands on her jeans. 'Right, shall we go and fetch him, then?'

'Yes!' Olivia cried.

'Let's go,' I said, taking Jacob's hand.

The moment we walked through the door into the kennel, the kids ran straight over to Buster's cage. He wagged his tail wildly, and Melanie unlocked the door. Buster bundled out and barked, bouncing up and down around them as they giggled in glee.

'Mummy, look, he remembers us,' Olivia said.

'He certainly does, and he's pretty pleased to see you,' Melanie said, smiling at me. I smiled back gratefully. The truth was I was feeling quite overwhelmed. I'd never owned a dog before and I knew what a big responsibility it was. I just hoped the kids and I could give Buster the home he so deserved.

'Right, let's get you ready to go home,' Melanie said, and I was relieved she was taking charge as she bent down and clipped Buster onto a lead and led him back into the reception area.

'Can you hold him tightly while Mummy signs a few forms for me?' Melanie said, turning to Jacob as we approached the counter.

He nodded and silently took hold of the lead and led Buster solemnly to the row of chairs along the side wall. He sat down and gripped the lead until his knuckles went white. I loved the fact he was taking his role so seriously.

'Let me hold him,' Olivia said, tugging the lead.

'No, love, let Jacob hold him for now. You can lead him to the car, okay?'

She looked at me challengingly, then finally folded her arms across her chest and sat down with a scowl. 'Okay.'

It only took a few minutes to sign all the forms, and then we were leaving, with Buster sitting in the boot of the car, and the kids turning round to talk to him all the way home.

We pulled up outside, then brought Buster into the house and watched as he sniffed everything, his tail wagging furiously.

'Do you think he likes it here?' Olivia said, following him around as if they were fastened together with Velcro.

'Give him some space,' I said, and she pulled back. 'Yes, I think he will be very happy here with us.' The truth was I was still worried about the state of the garden. Despite my promise to

Melanie, it was still overgrown, and only getting worse as spring well and truly took hold. There was a small patch of patio for Buster to run around, but the rest of the garden felt like an over-whelming task to overcome. I had no idea where to start, or how I was ever going to get it safe for a dog – or for us.

I pushed it to the back of my mind for now. I didn't want to spoil the excitement.

The rest of the day was spent with the kids showing Buster round the house, clearing up dog wee from ancient carpets, and making sure Buster got properly settled in.

'I think he's happy here,' Olivia said as the children munched their way through a plate of spaghetti later that evening.

'I think you're right,' I said, pouring a glass of Merlot and taking a long gulp.

'Where is Buster going to sleep?' she said.

'On my bed!' Jacob's mouth was full of pasta and the words were muffled, but he was desperate to get them out.

'No, he has his own bed,' I said, pointing out the small dog bed in the corner of the kitchen. They both looked at it and frowned.

'But he can't sleep in here,' Olivia said indignantly. 'He'll be lonely.'

'And it's yukky,' Jacob said, tomato sauce smearing his chin.

'But dogs don't sleep with humans,' I explained. 'They have their own beds.'

'My friend Jasmine has a dog and he sleeps on her bed every night, she told me.' Olivia looked at me, a challenge in her eyes. Sometimes she was so like me as a child, questioning everything, that it scared me. I was beginning to understand why my parents had found me such hard work.

'Well, let's just see how it goes tonight, shall we?' I said, non-committally.

'I want him on my bed,' Jacob said, his voice a whine.

'No, my bed,' Olivia said, her face like thunder. She looked at me. 'Mummy, tell him. Buster will be on my bed, won't he?'

'No, he won't be on anyone's bed apart from his own,' I said, determined to end the conversation there. Poor old Jacob was such a walk-over, and Olivia knew it. Even though I was glad to be raising such a strong-willed girl because I knew it would stand her in good stead in later life, sometimes she could be a challenge even at the age of seven.

I stood. 'Now, who wants some ice cream?'

'Me!' they chorused and, thankfully, the battle of where Buster was going to sleep was – temporarily – forgotten.

* * *

I knew dogs were hard work, but Buster had clearly been properly trained, and by the time the kids – eventually – collapsed into bed that night, Buster climbed up onto the sofa beside me and settled against my thigh. I casually tickled behind his ears and flipped open my laptop. I'd finally replied to *Ugly Duckling* a few days before, and posted my reply to my website. To my surprise, she had sent me another message, this time thanking me.

> You made me realise that looks aren't everything, and have given me the confidence to actually believe in myself for the first time ever. Thank you so much, it really does mean the world to have someone to properly listen to me.

I smiled.

This was something I hadn't expected – that people would be so grateful for my help that they would reply, and we'd strike up some sort of connection. I'd used some of Evelyn Wright's advice to shape my reply to *Ugly Duckling*, and I was glad that a combination of seventy-year-old advice and my own judgement had helped this woman to feel better about herself.

Sitting in my living room all by myself, I couldn't help feeling pleased. Knowing there were people out there relying on me made me feel far less alone. I wondered whether Evelyn had felt the same way.

I tapped out a reply, and just after pressing send I noticed another message alert flashing. *Dear Evelyn* had another letter!

I clicked it open. This time the email was from a man, calling himself 'Charlie'. Intrigued to see what the first man to write to me needed help with, I started reading.

Dear Evelyn

I don't know whether you can help a man, but there's no way on earth I could ever talk to my mates about this, so you're my last resort.

In a nutshell, I don't think my wife loves me any more. We've been married for twenty-three years, and for twenty-two of them we've been happy. At least, I think we have. I was. But then a year ago the last of our grown-up children left home to go to university and things changed almost straight away. It felt like it was just the kids holding us together, and when the last one left, the string snapped. She goes out all the time and doesn't tell me where she's going, and when we are together, she doesn't seem to want to be near me. She won't talk to me about it, and if I ask if there's anything wrong, she says there isn't. I honestly don't know what else to do. If she won't tell me what's going on, how can we sort things out?

I stared at the email for a few seconds, taking in his words. This was the first time I'd had a letter from a man, but that didn't mean my advice had to be any different. My heart broke for him though, because I could almost feel his pain, and it took me back to the days shortly after I found out about Rob's betrayal. The helplessness. The all-invasive sadness that ran deep to the core.

But what jumped out the most was Charlie's compassion. He was clearly determined to try and fix whatever was broken in his marriage, but he just didn't know where to start.

I might not know Charlie's wife, but I did know how women thought. If I tried to put myself in her shoes as well as his, I was sure I could formulate some sort of helpful answer.

I started typing a reply. But just a few words in, I put my laptop to one side and reached for the box of magazines, which seemed to have found a permanent home down the side of the sofa, within easy reach. At my movement, Buster lifted his head and looked at me accusingly. Once he realised I wasn't abandoning him, he shifted position, put his head back on my lap, and resumed his gentle snoring. I couldn't believe how quickly he'd learned to trust me after being abandoned once already in his short life. If only I could learn to do the same.

I flicked through a few of the magazines looking for something relevant. It occurred to me that, if I was going to use Evelyn's letters to help me advise other people, I really ought to get some sort of system in place for finding letters about certain subjects. The trouble was, filing was most certainly not my strong point.

Finally, about half an hour later, I found a letter from Evelyn Wright where the advice might work.

Dear Evelyn

I'm at the end of my tether and I hope you can advise me. My wife and I have been married for thirteen years. For the first twelve of those years we were happy and loved each other very much. For the last twelve months, however, things have changed between us and I do not know what to do about it.

Now, whenever I come down in the morning for my breakfast my wife is simply sitting at the table with her hair in rollers, and barely even glances up at me. When we go to bed at night she turns away from me and if I try to speak to her, she often doesn't reply at all. I have suggested going out for dinner or for a weekend away but she always says no. She doesn't seem to want to spend any time with me at all. How can I make her come back to me?

Sad Simon

Dear Sad Simon

You know your wife better than I do so you will be best placed to understand what it is she has on her mind. Is there any reason why she might have changed her affections so suddenly? Has anything happened in the last year that could have made her withdraw from you?

What is obvious to me is that there is something on her mind that she currently does not wish to share with you. Perhaps it is about your relationship, or perhaps it is about something else entirely. Is there someone you can encourage her to speak with? Perhaps a good friend, or a colleague, or even a doctor? Maybe once she has spoken to someone else, she may feel more able to open up to you about her worries.

I read it through one more time, then turned back to my laptop and started typing. Much of it would have to go, but the sentiment remained the same: you need to encourage her to talk.

Dear Charlie

Thank you for your letter. I can indeed try to help.

You say something shifted between you and your wife when the children left home. It seems clear to me that this was the catalyst for your wife's change of heart towards you. It could be that she is struggling to come to terms with not being relied upon so heavily by the children. You do not say whether she was their main carer, but, whether she was or not, a mother still feels it strongly when her children move out and gain independence. Perhaps she finds it hard to speak to you about this because she is afraid you won't feel the same, or perhaps there is something else bothering her. To get her to open up, perhaps you could suggest she speaks to someone else first – does she have a best friend, or perhaps a colleague she is close to? Then perhaps she will open up to you too, and allow you to attempt to fix whatever is broken between you.

I read it through one more time then, satisfied, I pressed send, before adding it to the growing number of letters on my website. I was pleased with my reply, and hoped it would help Charlie in some way.

I pushed my laptop aside and tickled Buster's ears, then turned my attention to the TV. There was some cooking show on and I half tuned in but after half an hour my eyes were drooping and I was having difficulty concentrating.

'We should probably go to bed, shouldn't we, Buster?' I said, and as I spoke I realised this was the first time in weeks that I'd spoken to anyone after the kids' bedtime. Buster looked up at me and let out a long sigh, then dropped his head to my lap again. I didn't have the heart to push him away so I tipped my head back and closed my eyes.

I wasn't sure how long I was like that, but I woke with a start when my computer beeped. I looked round, confused, then peered at the screen.

'One new message' flashed.

I rubbed my eyes blearily, then clicked on it. To my surprise, there was a reply from Charlie. I forced my eyes to focus.

Dear Evelyn

Thank you so much for your reply. Writing to you was the first time I have spoken to anyone about the problems between me and my wife, and it was cathartic just getting the words down. Reading your reply really made me think, and I've realised you're right. Maybe it is about her more than it's about me, or maybe she really has fallen out of love with me, but whatever the problem is I do need to try and get her to talk about it. I will speak to her tomorrow and let you know how it goes – if that's okay? I don't want to overstep the mark.

Thank you

Charlie

I looked away from the screen. I felt for Charlie. But at least now he had someone to talk to about his problems, someone to share them with. A problem shared was a problem halved, as they said. I couldn't help wondering how many other people out there were in the same boat as him. Many, I suspected. I might not be able to help them all – but I could do my bit.

I started typing a reply.

Dear Charlie

I'm so glad I could help you. Of course, please do let me know how it goes with your wife, and if you need any more advice I'm always here.

Evelyn

I closed the laptop and stood, stretching. Buster glared up at me.

'Sorry boy, did I disturb your peace?' I said, reaching down to tickle behind his ear. 'Come on, let's go to bed.' He gave me another quizzical look, then hauled himself up and jumped off the sofa and followed me through to the kitchen. While he ran into the garden for a wee, I glanced at his little dog bed in the corner. Olivia was right, it was depressing in here.

I picked the bed up from the floor in the corner, and when Buster came back inside I walked out of the kitchen and up the stairs. I wasn't sure whether he would follow me but, as I reached the landing, I heard his footsteps skittering up the stairs behind me. He sniffed at the kids' bedroom door, then we went into my bedroom, where I lay his bed on the floor beside me. By the time I came back from cleaning my teeth he was curled up on my side of my bed, and I didn't have the heart to move him. He'd already well and truly settled in.

UNHAPPY SINGLETON

I am nineteen years old and feeling unlovable. I have never had serious relations with a man, and now I am at an age when all my friends and acquaintances are meeting their future husbands and settling down. I am not unattractive but I just seem unable to find someone to love. What is the matter with me?

My dear, I would suggest there is nothing the matter with you. All you need to do is to find a like-minded soul, and in order to do this, why not join a club or a group which matches your interests? I shouldn't worry enormously though, as you are still so young. Enjoy being on your own, and if you follow my advice then I am certain you will have found the man of your dreams within a few months.

'Mummy, Buster was on my bed this morning, that means he loves me the best,' Olivia announced as she marched down the stairs the following morning.

'He loves me too,' Jacob wailed, and I rolled my eyes.

'He loves you both, and I'm sure he'll sleep in a different place every night,' I said.

Neither of them replied but I caught Jacob sticking his tongue out at his big sister and hid a smile. He was finding his feet at last, and it was good to see.

'Right, who wants what for breakfast? Shall I make pancakes?'

'Yes!' Jacob said.

'Only if they're better pancakes than Natalie makes,' Olivia said, a serious look on her face. 'Hers were all squishy and sticky and looked rubbish.'

'I make excellent pancakes,' I said, trying not to sound too pleased.

'Can I have Nutella on them?' Jacob said.

'And syrup?' Olivia added.

'You can have whatever you like on them,' I said, digging out the frying pan.

I felt good this morning, better than I had in ages. I'd been thinking about the letters I'd replied to last night, in particular the one from Charlie. Although I didn't even know whether that was his real name, I'd already formed a picture of him in my head as a slightly sad middle-aged man, thinning on top, who was beginning to go to seed. I felt sorry for him and hoped he'd be okay.

With the kids here, Buster bouncing happily from garden to food bowl and back again, and the promise of a warm day, it felt as though this might just be the beginning of a turnaround in my happiness.

The kids were shovelling their third pancakes into their mouths when my phone rang. A glance at the screen told me it was Rob and my good mood dissipated like a magician's puff of smoke.

'Hello,' I said, my voice making it clear his call wasn't welcome.

'Hi, Beth,' he said. He sounded echoey, as if he were in a cave. I didn't say anything, just waited for him to speak.

'How are the kids?'

'Fine.' I refused to give him any more than the bare minimum. He sighed and I felt my hackles rising as they always did when I sensed his disapproval. 'Do you want to speak to them?'

'In a minute. It was actually you I wanted to speak to.'

My grip tightened on the phone and I stepped into the hallway so the children couldn't hear. From the tone of his voice I didn't expect this conversation to be something good. It rarely was with Rob.

'Go on.' I pulled the door shut behind me.

Rob cleared his throat. He sounded nervous. Good.

'I need to talk to you about the summer.'

My stomach dropped. I'd been avoiding talking about this in the hope that if I didn't mention it, he wouldn't either, because I was dreading the first summer holiday apart from my kids.

'What about it?' I said.

'Do you have any dates in mind when you want them?'

'No.'

I held my breath.

'In that case me and Natalie would like them for the last three weeks. We want to take them to Greece.'

'Three weeks?' My voice was a screech. Even though it was inevitable – this was what happened when couples got divorced – the very thought of my children being in a different country from me for three whole weeks was unbearable. How could I let this happen?

Yet how could I say no?

'You'll have to give me time to think about it.' I walked into the living room and lowered myself shakily onto the sofa before my legs gave way.

'The thing is, Beth, I'm entitled to three weeks with them in the summer, so there isn't really anything to think about.'

I wanted to scream. I wanted to tell him he couldn't take my babies away from me, that I didn't want them to spend three weeks with Natalie pretending to be their best friend and ingratiating herself into their lives; that actually, no, he couldn't have them at all. But I couldn't. My hands were tied by the custody agreement and Rob was right. He was entitled to spend three weeks with them out of the six. I felt sick.

'Well, then, why are you bothering to ask?' I hated the belligerence in my voice but I couldn't stop it.

'I was *trying* to be reasonable.'

'Like you always are, you mean?'

'For fuck's sake, Beth, can't we just have a civilised conversation?' His voice exploded down the phone like a bullet and I jumped.

'Why?'

'Why what?'

'Why should I be civilised?'

'For your children? So they don't hear us arguing all the time, and don't think their mother hates their father?'

But I do hate you, I wanted to say. Except he was right, wasn't he? They didn't need to hear this. We needed to be civil, polite. Nice to each other. And yet every time I tried, the bitterness came flooding back and I turned into an angry, combative woman. I took a deep breath in.

'You're right.' I couldn't run to apologising. 'What exact dates were you thinking?'

As Rob outlined the plans he had with my children – our children – I tried to stay calm. My pulse thumped low in my belly and my shoulders were tight, but I didn't let it show in my voice. When he ended the call, I picked up a cushion and screamed into it until my throat hurt. Then I stood, pulled myself together, and went back into the kitchen.

'I've got good news,' I announced brightly as I opened the door. Olivia and Jacob both looked up expectantly, and Buster barked excitedly. 'Daddy's taking you on holiday!'

'Where?' Olivia said.

'Greece.'

They both looked so happy as I told them what Rob and I had agreed, and slowly my anger began to subside, leaving nothing but sadness at the fact that I wouldn't see them for three whole weeks. That, plus the fact I knew I couldn't afford to give them such an amazing holiday. Camping with the dog in Suffolk didn't have the same ring to it somehow, but I'd just have to think of a way to make it special.

'Oh!' Olivia said, suddenly.

'What, darling?'

'But what will happen to Buster when we go away?'

'I'll be here with him, darling. We'll go on walks together.'

She frowned. 'But he can't come with us?'

'Well, no. Buster is our dog, not Daddy's. And dogs aren't allowed on planes anyway.'

She looked serious for a few moments, her legs swinging back and forth. 'But I don't want to leave him.'

I placed my hand on her head, which felt warm from the sun pouring through the window. 'It will be such an amazing holiday that you'll forget all about me and Buster while you're on the beach with Daddy,' I said.

'I won't!' she cried. She looked at Jacob then back at me. 'What if Buster forgets who we are?'

Jacob looked up at me with wide eyes. 'Will he forget us, Mummy?'

'Of course not, sweetheart.' I ruffled his hair. 'How could he ever forget you?' I sat down to face them at their level. 'Besides, it's only for three weeks. It'll go by in a flash.'

'Okay, Mummy.'

As I cleared their plates up and let them dash off to play I couldn't help feeling pleased that, despite Rob's grand plans and expensive holidays, the kids weren't that excited about being away from me and Buster for so long. Maybe he couldn't buy their affection after all.

And even though I hated myself for feeling pleased about getting one over on Rob and Natalie – since when did I use my kids to score points? – the feeling wouldn't go away. Thank you, Evelyn Wright.

* * *

The next day the kids were back at school and I was back at work. I'd found a dog-sitter a couple of villages away who'd agreed to take Buster out for a walk around midday and I hoped he'd be okay on his own the rest of the time. I was usually home around four-thirty after collecting the kids from their after-school club.

We pulled up on the drive and Buster was at the living room window, standing on the back of the sofa, front legs balanced on the windowsill. He was barking furiously and as we unlocked the front door he almost bowled Jacob over with his enthusiastic greeting.

'Down, Buster,' I said, and he bounced a couple more times, then ran away, sniffed his food bowl and bounced back in again. I reached down to stroke him, and Jacob wrapped his arms round his neck.

'Careful, love, we don't know if he likes that,' I said.

'He does, Mummy, look,' he said, practically hanging off poor old Buster's neck. Buster didn't look too concerned.

'Just be careful,' I said.

I picked up Buster's lead from the hook by the back door and held it in the air.

'Right, who wants to come for a walk?'

'Me!' Jacob said as Buster's ears pricked up.

'Me too!' Olivia said.

'You two go and get changed, and meet me back down here in five minutes. Can you do that?'

They both raced upstairs and I clipped Buster's lead on and found a few dog treats and poo bags. By the time I'd got my shoes on they were both standing in front of me ready to leave the house. That must have been a record. I knew getting a dog had been a good idea. I just hoped their enthusiasm continued.

I hadn't had much chance to explore since we'd moved, but now we had Buster and the evenings were longer and warmer, I felt like venturing a bit further afield. We turned left out of the cottage and followed the pavement to a left-hand turning towards some nearby fields. I wasn't confident enough to let Buster off the lead yet – his recall wasn't brilliant and I needed to make sure he knew who was boss before I'd risk him running off on the scent of something or other – but I had bought him a lovely long extending lead, and the kids chased him around as he ran about sniffing and cocking his leg against every tree we passed.

The sun was still warm, and I took my jacket off and tied it round my waist, enjoying the feel of the sun on my skin. The field beside me had been neatly planted in rows of crops that were beginning to poke their heads out of the soil and reach to the sky.

As we strolled along, I couldn't help thinking about how much life had changed over the last year. It had changed for the kids as well, and I was glad they seemed happy, despite everything. I wished I weren't so lonely though. I just had to hope that getting Buster would be as good for me as it seemed to have been for the children, and help me meet some new people.

We didn't pass anyone for a while, but about fifteen minutes later a couple walking their ancient Labrador stopped to say hello.

'You're a lovely boy, aren't you?' the woman said, bending down to scratch Buster's ears as he tried to sniff their dog's backside.

'Sorry about him,' I said, tugging his lead to pull him away.

'Oh, don't be daft. Monty doesn't mind. Do you, Monty?'

The Lab looked up and gave us a resigned look, as though he was used to irritating puppies giving him too much attention.

The woman looked back at me and smiled. 'We haven't seen you out walking before.'

'No, we've not been here long, and we've only had Buster a couple of days,' I explained. 'We just wanted to make the most of the lovely evening.'

'I don't blame you.' She held her hand out. 'I'm Jackie and this is Tony.'

I shook her hand then her husband's, in turn. 'I'm Beth, and these two are Olivia and Jacob,' I said. 'Oh, and this is Buster.'

'Hello, you two,' Jackie said. Olivia said hello but Jacob just gave a shy smile and looked at the ground.

'You've just moved to the village, have you?' Jackie continued.

'Yes. A few weeks ago. I haven't really got to know anyone yet.'

'Oh well, I'm sure you will – especially now you've got Buster to get the conversation started.'

I smiled. 'Yes, I hope so. That was the idea.'

'Well, it's lovely to meet you. We'd best get poor old Monty home before he collapses, but hopefully we'll see you again.'

As they wandered slowly away I smiled. That was the first conversation I'd had with anyone since we'd moved here, apart from the delivery man. Maybe Buster really would help me to make some new friends.

We strolled on a bit further, but Jacob soon began to slow down. 'Mummy, my legs are tired,' he said, stopping in his tracks.

'Come on, Jakey, there's not far to go now.'

'But we've walked for *miles*,' he whined.

'We've only been out for twenty minutes,' I said. 'Come on, let's keep going.'

'No!' He stamped his foot and gave me a scowl.

'Jakey, we have to walk because Buster needs us to,' Olivia said, her hands on her hips. She looked like a mini schoolmarm and I bit back a smile.

'No!' Then he sat down in the middle of the path.

'Come on, love, you can't just sit there,' I said, not sure what to do. Buster ran up to him and sniffed his face and to my relief Jacob started to giggle.

'There's a bench just up there, why don't we go and have a little rest before we go home?'

Jacob looked to where I was pointing and, obviously deciding that a bench was a better place to sit than the middle of a dusty path, he stood and lolloped towards it. Olivia, Buster and I followed.

The bench overlooked the real country scene that spread out before us. There was the odd building dotted among the neatly laid-out crops, a few sheep sprinkled across a few distant fields, then a darker patch of woods beyond, which stretched away towards the horizon. As much as I wasn't a country girl, even I could appreciate a view like this.

'Mummy, I'm hungry,' Jacob said, his feet swinging below the bench.

I pulled out a couple of slightly melted Penguin bars and handed them one each, then gave Buster a couple of dog biscuits, which he wolfed down hungrily. I was just about to close my eyes when a voice beside me made me jump.

'Mind if I join you?'

I looked up to find a figure silhouetted against the sunlight. I squinted.

'No, course,' I said, shuffling up to make room.

The woman sat down next to me and pulled her tiny dachshund onto her lap.

'Sorry,' she said. 'Freddie's little legs get so tired when we walk too far, and we often sit here for a rest. I didn't mean to disturb your peace.'

I looked over at her. She was a few years older than me, with a thick wave of auburn hair scraped away from her face. Her clothes were practical – laced walking boots, knee-length shorts and a plain white T-shirt – and I liked the look of her immediately.

'Don't be silly, it's fine,' I said. 'Anyway, we're the ones who should be apologising for taking your resting spot.'

She laughed and it rang out across the open fields. 'I don't think I get dibs on the bench.' She held her hand out to me and, just like before, I was amazed at how friendly people were when you had a dog in tow. 'I'm Catherine, and this is Freddie,' she said, and I took her hand and shook it. She had a firm grip and her skin felt soft.

'Beth. This is Olivia and Jacob, and this is Buster,' I said, rubbing his head as he sniffed curiously at Freddie.

'How lovely to meet you all,' she said. She looked out into the distance and I followed her gaze. 'You can just about make out my house from here, if you squint.' She pointed at one of the tiny little dots near the line of trees. 'Do you live around here?'

'We're down in the village,' I said.

'Ecclesforth?'

I nodded.

'Ah, lucky you. I used to live there. Have you just moved?'

'A few weeks ago.'

She nodded. I wasn't usually one to overshare, but there was something about Catherine that made me want to tell her more. Perhaps it was precisely because she didn't pry. 'We used to live in Banthorpe, but me and the kids' father are recently divorced and it was too expensive to stay there on my own.'

She nodded. 'I know that feeling.' She placed Freddie down on the ground and he began sniffing around her feet. Chocolate bars finished, Olivia and Jacob jumped down from the bench and began to follow the dogs around, running in circles and throwing sticks for them to chase.

'You're divorced as well, then, are you?' I said eventually, when the kids were out of earshot.

'Twice.' I could hear the laughter in her voice. 'I'm no Elizabeth Taylor but I'm getting there.'

I glanced at her. 'And now?'

'Now? It's just me and Freddie and we're happier than ever.'

'That's amazing. I wish I could be like that.'

She looked at me, her eyebrows raised. 'It'll come. You don't think I got here overnight, do you?' She laid her hand on my arm. It felt warm. 'I've been on my own for five years now and at first I was bitter as hell. But it's fine now.' She shrugged. 'It's better than fine. Life gets easier, I promise.'

I felt tears prick my eyes and I blinked them back. This was the first time in months that I'd spoken to someone who really understood what I was going through.

'I hope you're right,' I said, my voice a whisper.

She nodded. 'I am. Just don't expect miracles.' She took her hand away and looked back out across the fields. 'I'm sure you've got plenty of people to talk to, but if you're ever feeling lonely and just need to chat, I'm happy to listen.'

'Thank you.' A tear escaped and slid down my cheek. I brushed it away roughly.

'I mean it, you know. I know how hard it is to make friends when you have to start again somewhere new.'

We sat in silence for a few moments watching the kids and dogs scamper around. For the first time since the divorce I could actually imagine myself feeling happy here, and the kids being happy too. Maybe Evelyn was right, maybe it really wasn't that hard to meet new people after all; maybe you just had to know where to look, put yourself out there.

'Right, I'd better get the kids back for dinner,' I said, standing. The sun had dipped behind the hill and it was suddenly a little chilly. Beside me, Catherine stood too.

'Wait, let me give you my number,' she said, waving her phone in front of her. 'That way you can decide whether you ever want to speak to me again.' She grinned. 'And if you don't, well, then, it was nice to meet you.'

I took her number and said goodbye, then watched as she marched back down the hill, Freddie scurrying along behind her, desperately trying to keep up. That, I thought, was a woman I definitely wanted to get to know better.

'Right, come on, you two,' I said, clapping my hands. Olivia and Jacob looked up, and Buster bounded towards me. We strolled back down the hill to the house, and by the time we let ourselves in the front door we were starving.

'Go and watch TV for half an hour and I'll get your tea ready,' I said, and the three of them dutifully trudged through to the living room. As I chopped vegetables I thought about all the encounters I'd had in the last couple of days. There was Charlie online, who'd needed my help, Jackie and Tony, who'd been so friendly on our walk, and then Catherine, who could potentially become a friend. It had only been a few weeks since I'd found Evelyn Wright's letters, but already her advice was touching so many people – including me. I hoped she would have approved.

* * *

Later that evening, once the kids were asleep, I finally got round to opening up my laptop. After a busy day at work, the walk with Buster and an evening feeding and bathing the kids I was almost too tired to check *Dear Evelyn* tonight. But I'd made a promise to anyone who had written in that I'd help them, so I owed it to them to at least see if there were any more letters. I was also keen to see whether Charlie had replied, and whether he'd had any luck speaking to his wife.

I turned the TV volume down low and opened my inbox. There were two new messages, both from unknown people. My heart fluttered with excitement as I clicked on the first one and read it, then read the other one. The first letter was a woman asking me for advice about how to get her husband to fancy her again (I wished I knew!). The second wondered why she was always overlooked for promotion at work.

I remembered seeing Evelyn Wright answering a similar question to the first one, so I delved back into the box of letters, once again regretting my lack of organisation skills. For the next hour or so I diligently typed out responses, replied, then added both letters to my website. It was beginning to fill up nicely with questions, and, although I'd need to categorise them soon, for now I allowed myself a pang of pride at what I'd achieved.

I was about to close my laptop when a ping alerted me to a new email. There was a message from Charlie. I clicked on it excitedly.

Dear Evelyn

Well, you asked me to let you know how it went with my wife. Not as well as I'd hoped, sadly. I told her we needed to talk, and eventually she agreed. I asked her if she still loved me and she said she wasn't sure. Despite what I'd said yesterday I hadn't really been expecting her to say that. I'd thought maybe I was imagining things. Hoped I was. But she told me that since the kids had moved out she felt like we were stuck in a rut, and she didn't know if we'd ever be able to get out of it. I told her she should speak to someone about it, like you suggested, but she said she just needed time to figure it out by herself, so there's not much more I can do. But at least things are out in the open. Whichever way it goes, I have you to thank for that.

Charlie

Oh, Charlie. My heart went out to him. I knew how awful it was when the person you loved told you they didn't love you any more. If only I could help him more.

Should I write back? Or should I give him space to work things out for himself? It wasn't as if he'd asked me for any more advice. But I did want him to know there was someone out there willing to listen.

I typed out a quick reply, telling him to let me know if he needed anything else. There wasn't much else I could do. Then I pushed the laptop to one side and rubbed my eyes. It was still early, not even nine, but I was already considering going to bed, just to pass the time.

I tapped out a text to Suzie, asking if she was free, then hesitated as I remembered the number Catherine had given me on our walk earlier. She'd said to message her if I wanted to chat, so before I could change my mind I sent a message to her as well, telling her how lovely it had been to meet her, and hoping we would run into each other on our walks again soon.

I wondered whether either of them would reply.

It was only a few minutes later when my phone pinged and I picked it up expectantly. It was from Catherine.

How lovely to hear from you, I'm so pleased you decided not to ghost me. Fancy a walk tomorrow afternoon, same sort of time? Catherine x

I smiled and replied.

That would be great. 5p.m.? Meet you at the bench? Beth x

Perfect. Bring biscuits. Catherine. X

It looked as though I had a new friend.

8

TERRIBLE COOK

I love my wife and we have a happy marriage, but I have one complaint, and that is about her terrible cooking. She's a clever girl and did well when she worked in an office so I cannot understand why she seems so unable to cook a decent meal. I've teased her, and I've become cross, and have even offered to pay for her to have cookery lessons, but she point-blank refuses. Do you have any advice?

If your wife is as intelligent as you say she is then there seems only one explanation for her inability to master a simple process such as cooking, and that is that she simply doesn't want to. Do you think your wife may be missing her office life, or could she be feeling resentful about something else? It appears as if she is expressing her dissatisfaction by presenting badly cooked food. I would suggest talking to her to get to the bottom of it.

'Come on, boy, let's go for a walk,' I said, plucking Buster's lead from the hook where it hung by the front door.

He wagged his tail wildly and ran around in ever-decreasing circles until I clipped the lead to his collar and pulled my shoes on. We marched to the front gate, and Buster tugged me to the left before I even got there. After only a few days he was already used to his daily walk, and knew where to go.

I was meeting Catherine again this evening, as had become our habit. Ever since that first meeting on the bench just last week, we'd met up most days – apart from when she worked late – and spent half an hour chatting. We'd struck up a lovely friendship and, for the first time since I'd moved, I finally felt as though I had someone I could call a friend.

Today, the kids were with Rob, so it was just me and Buster, and I wondered whether Catherine and I would talk differently without little flappy ears to overhear us. Although I'd already told her a bit about mine and Rob's divorce, there was only so much I could say in their presence.

Buster ran ahead, sniffing fences, walls and trees, and I let the lead out a little. I hadn't regretted taking Evelyn's advice about getting him for a single moment and I felt lucky that he'd fitted into our little family straight away.

It was a beautiful evening, the sunshine a buttery yellow, and as we turned into the field I smiled a greeting at Jackie and Tony as Monty tolerated Buster's usual over-enthusiastic attentions. Saying goodbye, Buster and I continued up the hill, and I lifted my face towards the sky, enjoying the warmth of the sun on my skin. Although I'd never imagined myself to be much of a country girl before, I increasingly found myself relaxing – my shoulders dropping, chest loosening, brow unfurrowing – as I meandered along the footpaths. I loved the tranquillity; the rustle of the leaves in the breeze, the chirrup of birds in the trees, the scratch of wildlife scampering in the undergrowth. All these sounds were so unique to this time and place, and I felt unexpectedly more settled and content than I had for years.

I reached the bench and sat down. There was no sign of Catherine yet but she was often a few minutes late. I let Buster's lead out to its full length and he ran off, tail wagging, nose to the ground. I was surprised by how much I enjoyed watching the scenery change from day to day. The crops had already grown noticeably taller just in the last week, and the lack of rain had turned the grass a crisp yellow. I closed my eyes.

'Room for a little one?' A voice interrupted my thoughts and I snapped my eyes open to find Catherine settling into the seat beside me. Her hair was loose today and blew across her face in the gentle breeze, making her look younger.

'Hello,' I said, smiling at her.

'Been here long?'

'Just a few minutes.'

We sat and admired the scenery for a few moments, the distant rumble of a tractor and the faraway hum of the A road the only sounds we could hear. Buster barked as Freddie trotted up to him.

'The kids with their dad?' Catherine asked.

'They went last night.'

'Tough.'

'Yeah.'

I felt her move beside me and when I looked round she was watching me with a concerned expression on her face. 'You okay? You must miss them when they're not here.'

I gave a small nod. 'I really do. It's the worst bit about everything that's happened.'

'I get that.'

I sniffed. 'I just—' I stopped. 'I hate the thought of them having a brilliant time without me. And I hate that they're spending time in their old home, with their own things, and that being with me feels more like a holiday.'

'Plus, of course, there's the bitch.'

I couldn't help grinning. I'd told Catherine about Natalie in a whispered conversation while the kids had been distracted a couple of days ago, and she understood instantly why I felt such animosity towards her. 'There's that too. I just—' I ran my fingers through my hair and looked at her. 'I *hate* the fact she's there, doing things with my children that they should be doing with me. I mean, how *dare* she?'

Catherine reached out and touched my arm lightly. 'They'll never think of her as anything more than their stepmother. You do know that, right?'

I nodded sadly. I kept telling myself that. But then the kids would come home full of stories of the things they'd got up to with Rob and Natalie, and the treats they'd bought for them, and I wanted to scream and shout and stamp my feet with fury and frustration. But I also knew that they were young, and that they loved me. Biting my tongue and letting things slide was proving tricker than I could have imagined.

'So, how are the renovations going?' Catherine said, deftly changing the subject. I was grateful for her tact.

'Not bad. I'm making a start on the kitchen soon but it's a big old project. And I've got to do something with the garden. It's a complete state, and I promised the dog rescue place I'd make it safe for Buster.'

'He's okay as long as he's got somewhere to go for a wee.' She gestured to where the dogs were playing. 'Look, I think he's happy enough, don't you?'

'I think so.'

She turned to me again. 'So, what are you up to tonight?'

I shrugged. 'The usual. Sitting on my own, drinking more wine than I mean to and going through some letters—' I stopped, remembering that I hadn't mentioned the agony aunt letters to Catherine yet. It felt like something I wanted to keep to myself, at least for a while. I wasn't sure what she'd think about me trying to help other people, given that I didn't seem to be doing a great job of helping myself. But it was too late now.

'Letters?' Her brow was folded in a question.

I stared down at my battered trainers. 'I – I've started an agony aunt column,' I admitted.

'Have you? That's amazing.'

I looked up sharply. 'Do you think so?'

'Of course. Why wouldn't I?'

I shrugged. 'I'm not sure I'm qualified.'

'Don't be daft. I'm sure you are.' Another frown flitted across her forehead momentarily. 'But what made you start it?'

Should I tell her about Evelyn Wright, and about the letters I'd found that had inspired me? Would she think I was mad, to think I could recreate something that had last been a success seventy years before? I decided I could trust her not to judge.

So I told her all about finding the letters, about how helpful I'd found Evelyn's advice, and how I hadn't been able to stop thinking about all the people the other Evelyn had helped.

'So I decided to give it a go myself. I thought that even if I could help just one person it would be worth it. Plus, it's kept me occupied during some pretty bleak evenings alone.'

Catherine didn't reply for a while, and I began to worry. *Did she think I was mad? Had she changed her mind about striking up a friendship with me?* I waited for her to say something, my heart thumping against my ribcage.

'Does this mean you live in Laburnum Cottage?' she said eventually.

'Yes. Do you know it?'

She paused again, as if sifting through the right words. And then she said, 'I used to live there. Evelyn was my mother.'

9

FEELING FRUSTRATED

I have been seeing a wonderful girl for almost a year now, but we cannot afford to tie the knot for at least two years. The trouble is we are both finding it extremely difficult to control our feelings for each other, and my girl is even more keen than I am for us to give into temptation. If we do so, will it make us love each other more or, as I fear, will we lose respect for one another?

Young man, you have answered your own question. Clearly you would feel ashamed if you gave in to your feelings, and I suspect you know you would lose respect for your girl too. I advise you to seriously consider not seeing each other as often so that you are less likely to give into temptation. Perhaps you should also consider getting married sooner before it is too late.

I stared at her as her words sank in.

'Your *mother*? But – that's amazing,' I said.

'Not really.' She met my gaze and I could see sadness in her eyes. 'She walked out when I was nine years old.'

'Oh I'm—' I stopped, unsure what to say. *Sorry* always felt so meaningless.

'It's all right,' she said. 'Well, it wasn't, but it was a long time ago.' She shrugged. 'I'm over it now.'

'Wow. That's a big thing.'

She stared down at her feet for a moment, and I gave her space to order her thoughts.

'Where were they?' she said, eventually. 'The letters, I mean. I didn't know she'd kept them.'

'Under the raised floor of the wardrobe in the big bedroom.'

She nodded. 'That was Mum's bedroom. She used to sit hunched over her desk by the window for hours, scribbling away. Sometimes she got so preoccupied with them she forgot to make me tea and I'd have to get myself some bread and butter or something and take myself off to bed.' Her eyes shone with tears. 'I often thought she loved writing those letters more than she loved me.'

'I'm sure that wasn't true,' I said.

Catherine raised her eyebrows. 'She walked out and left me though, didn't she?'

There was nothing I could say to that. Catherine's revelation cast a whole new light on the house I'd slowly begun to – if not love, then dislike less. I pictured Catherine as a little girl, going to sleep alone in the room that was now my bedroom, while her mum spent hours writing letter after letter to a never-ending parade of desperate people, but never being able to help herself.

'Did she ever come back?'

Catherine's head whipped round. 'Mum?' She gave a bitter

laugh. 'No. She walked out one day, left some crappy note, and I never saw her again.'

'God, that's awful,' I said.

'It's fine. I had Granny.'

'Did you live in Laburnum Cottage with her, then?'

'No.' She threaded her fingers together on her lap. 'I moved in with Granny on the other side of the village. Mum had only rented the cottage, so when she stopped paying rent the landlord let it out to someone else. But I always had vivid memories of it.' She smiled. 'I don't suppose the wallpaper in the small bedroom was still dark purple, was it?'

'No, it was flowery.'

'Ah, he did redecorate, then,' she said. 'I begged Mum for purple walls and she finally relented a few months before she buggered off.' She shrugged. 'It would have been nice to have seen it again.'

'Why don't you come round?' The words were out of my mouth before I'd had a chance to give them much thought, but I knew I wanted her to come and see the place the instant I'd said it.

'Oh! I wasn't fishing for an invitation.'

'I know you weren't. But you're very welcome.'

'Really?' Her voice had risen an octave or two.

I nodded. 'You must. I can show you the letters as well, if you'd like.'

She studied me for a moment, then gave a perfunctory nod and smiled. 'That would be amazing, if you really don't mind.'

'It would be a pleasure. In fact, why don't you come tonight? I can cook us something to eat.'

I was really warming to the idea now. The thought of having someone else in the house, having some company, was so appealing I didn't know what I'd do if she said no.

'I'd love to. Thank you.'

She stood then and looked down at me. 'I'll get home and get changed. What time shall I come over?'

'Seven?'

'Great. See you then.' She turned. 'Come on, Freddie.' Then she stalked away down the hill, leaving me with my mind whirring full of thoughts of Evelyn, agony aunt letters and abandoned children.

* * *

I was nervous about Catherine coming round. I'd always loved seeing friends, but it had been ages since I'd spent an evening with someone other than the kids, and I was struggling to remember how to act. Plus, I was worried about how being in the house again after so many years might affect Catherine. Who knew what memories it might trigger – happy or sad?

'I come bearing gin,' Catherine announced when I opened the door to her, waving a bottle in the air and stepping inside. Buster jumped around her legs, barking furiously.

'Buster, stop it,' I said, pulling him away. He sulked off towards the kitchen. 'That's so kind. Come in.' I stepped aside. 'I'm in here,' I said, indicating the living room. She followed and it wasn't until we sat down that I noticed she was clutching something else. She handed it over. 'This is for you as well.'

'Thank you,' I said, intrigued. It was a square package wrapped in pretty paper with a ribbon tied round the middle. I tugged it and pulled the paper off carefully. Inside was a stunning painting of my house in a white wooden frame.

'Oh, this is lovely,' I said.

'I hope you don't think it's too much, but I wanted to give you a house-warming present. My mum painted it when I was little, and even after she left Granny had it hanging in her hallway.'

'Oh, but I can't take this.'

She shook her head. 'Honestly, I want you to have it. Granny died a few years ago and I haven't looked at it since,' she said. 'Only if you'd like it, of course. Obviously I don't know your taste at all.' She looked round at the pale green walls and the freshly-varnished floorboards. 'It looks lovely in here, by the way. You've worked hard.'

'Thank you. There's still lots to do but at least it's starting to feel like home now.' I propped the painting up carefully against the edge of the sofa. 'Shall we have a drink?'

'Great idea.'

Catherine followed me into the kitchen where I made gin and tonics. 'Here you go.' I handed her a glass and noticed the faraway look on her face as she surveyed the garden.

'Thanks.' She took a sip. 'I have some wonderful memories of this place,' she said, returning her gaze to the window.

'Tell me a bit more about your mum,' I said. 'If you want to, of course.'

She took another drink then placed the glass down. 'She was a pretty amazing woman, from what I've been able to piece together over the years.'

'Did your granny tell you all about her?'

She shook her head. 'No. From the day Mum left, Granny refused to even mention her name. It was as though a piece of her had died and the only way she knew how to cope was by pretending it had never happened.'

'That must have been hard for you.'

'It was, at first, especially as I'd never known my dad. He and Mum weren't together, and I don't think she ever even told Granny who he was.' She shrugged. 'I was nine when she left, and confused, and I wanted my mum back. But as the months passed and it became clear she wasn't coming back, and Granny wasn't going to tell me anything more about her either, I parcelled my memories of her away in my mind and tried to keep them hidden.' She took another sip of her drink. 'I understood then why Granny had done the same.'

'So do you remember anything about her at all?'

'Bits and bobs.' She sighed. 'You think you'll remember everything about being nine. But your mind seems to erase things, like it's trying to make room for more memories as you get older.' She gazed out of the front window, then turned back to me. 'One thing I do remember is that she lived completely in the moment and didn't give two hoots what anyone thought of her. She was always the parent clapping the loudest at school plays, shouting the loudest at sports day, or doing the most ridiculous laugh in the cinema. And she'd sing along to songs she loved at the top of her voice no matter where she was, and never worry about who was listening. It was mortifying as a child, of course.' She smiled. 'She always wore this perfume, Rive Gauche, and whenever I smell it now it makes me think of me and her, wrapped up in her enormous wafty clothes when she climbed into bed with me and made up wild stories to send me to sleep. They were my favourite times.'

'She sounds amazing.'

'I think she was. Until she wasn't any more.'

'And was she always an agony aunt, as far as you remember?'

'I think so. She wrote for lots of women's magazines. They were a big thing, back in the day, those pages. Mum used to sit in her bedroom writing letters late into the night and post them out to the magazine she wrote for once a week. The trip to the post office was a regular weekly fixture.' She looked at me. 'Oh, and you do know she wasn't actually called Evelyn Wright?'

'Oh, no, I didn't.' I felt thrown.

'She was called Lois. Lois Andrews, same surname as me. I assume she didn't want people in the village to know who she was, so she changed her name for the letters,' Catherine explained.

I nodded in understanding. Evelyn was Lois, in the same way that I was now Evelyn to the people who needed my help. It felt satisfying, somehow, to know that it had come full circle.

Catherine picked up her drink again and took a long gulp, draining the glass dry. 'That was delicious, shall we have another?'

The conversation was clearly over, for now. I made more drinks and switched the oven on. 'I've just made a cheesy pasta thing, I hope that's okay,' I said.

'Anything I haven't had to cook sounds perfect to me.' She grinned. 'Could we go into the garden? It was always my favourite place.'

I glanced out of the window. 'We can if you like, although it's a complete state.'

'That doesn't matter. I just really want to see it, now I'm here. If you don't mind.'

'Course not.' I opened the back door and Buster raced outside, sniffing round the edge of the patio. He seemed reluctant to venture any further into the undergrowth and I didn't blame him. I dragged the chairs into the patch of sunshine that was left.

'Mum always kept this so neat,' she said, taking a seat. 'It's such a shame it hasn't been looked after over the years.'

'What was it like before?' I said, keen to hear more about Catherine's memories of the place.

'Most of this middle bit was lawn, with flower beds running down the edges,' she said. 'Mum had a greenhouse at the bottom where she grew tomatoes and cucumbers every year. God, I loved the smell of that greenhouse.' She smiled. 'Then over that side,' she pointed towards the back left corner, which was currently completely obscured 'was a raised section where I had a blue and red climbing frame that I was lucky not to kill myself on in the days before health and safety.'

'I remember those. It sounds lovely.'

'It was. There was a big tree over there as well, somewhere towards the back,' she said, waving her hand in the general direction. 'I assume it was the laburnum the cottage is named after but all I knew was that it was a big tree that I loved trying to climb. Nearly broke my wrist falling from it one day.'

'I'm hoping to get the garden looking good again soon – although I'm not sure whether it will ever be as good as it was in your mum's day.'

'Ah, I'm sure you'll do a great job – but it's a huge undertaking all by yourself.'

'Yes, I know. I haven't got a clue where to start.'

'Maybe I'll come and give you a hand one day soon,' she said.

'Would you?'

'Of course.' She raised her glass in the air. 'Cheers!'

I clinked my glass against hers. 'Actually, we should be drinking this toast to your mum,' I said.

'Should we?'

I looked down at my glass, not wanting to catch her eye. 'I've got a lot to thank her for. It was her letters that made me start my own website, which has kept me company during the long evenings alone, and her advice that made me get Buster as a great way to combat loneliness – and she was right, wasn't she? Because I've met you.'

Catherine held her glass in the air. 'Let's drink to that,' she said.

I clinked my glass against hers again. 'To Evelyn. Well, Lois.'

'To Mum,' she said at the same time. 'Gosh, it's been a while since I said anything like that.' She frowned. 'In fact I don't think I ever have.'

We sat in silence sipping our drinks. A bird bobbed from branch to branch high up in the oak tree in a neighbouring garden, and a cat stalked along the fence, its eyes on the prize. It felt different being here with someone else. I had the kids most of the time, of course, but I'd never been here with adult company. It was comforting, and somehow more peaceful.

'Let's eat,' I said. We traipsed inside, and as we ate our dinner huddled round the tiny kitchen table Catherine told me all about her two ex-husbands.

'Bill was lovely, but boring,' she said, taking a delicate mouthful of pasta and chewing thoughtfully. 'I don't think we were ever in love, but he was kind.'

'What happened to him?'

'I divorced him five years after we got married.' She gave a wicked grin. 'Met Tony a month after the divorce came through and we got married a couple of months after that.'

'Blimey, you don't hang around.'

She shrugged. 'I always thought life was for the taking. If you make a mistake, well, it's fine. You change things, move on.' I couldn't help admiring her bravery, although it was obvious to me where her seeming inability to commit came from – when your own mother walked out on you at such a young age, no wonder you learned to believe you didn't need anyone else to make you happy.

'So what happened to Tony?'

'Oh, we realised we should never have got married,' she said, waving her hand in the air dismissively. 'He moved out six months later and I stayed in the house.'

'And now?'

'Now? I'm more than happy just me and Freddie. Life is so

much easier and I can please myself.' She put her fork down, suddenly thoughtful. 'It's okay for me, I've lived around here all my life and I know people. For you though, it must be so hard, moving here without knowing anyone.'

I nodded, chewing my way through a mouthful of pasta. 'It has been. But I'm getting there. Getting the house into shape has made me feel much more positive.'

I wanted to tell her that meeting her had made me feel better too, but we hadn't known each other long and it felt a little intense. So I was relieved when she said, 'Well, you've got me now. If you'll have me.'

'Of course!'

Later, plates cleaned, we settled in the living room, and I pulled out the box of Evelyn's letters. 'I don't suppose you'd like to read some of these now, would you?' I said, conscious it might be a bit much all at once – the house and the letters, all such reminders of what she'd lost. I needn't have worried.

'I'd love to, if you don't mind?'

'Well, they belong to you more than they do to me, so knock yourself out.'

She pulled the box towards her and picked a magazine off the top. 'These are amazing,' she said, flicking through the pages. I was thrilled she was as enamoured by these perfectly preserved slices of the past as I had been. While she read some of her own mother's words, I flipped open my laptop to check for more emails. There was a new one from Charlie, which I checked first. We'd been emailing each other a bit more over the last few days and I looked forward to his evening messages. I'd told him I had a friend coming round tonight so might not be around until later.

He'd written:

I hope you have fun with your friend this evening. Or was that a
euphemism for a date?

I typed back now, smiling:

Nope, definitely just a friend. She's called Catherine, and I met
her on a dog walk. Speak tomorrow.

I moved on and was surprised to see my inbox indicating
seven unread messages.

'Wow,' I murmured, and Catherine looked up.

'Everything okay?'

'I think so. I've just got lots more problem-page letters.'

'Can I see?'

I hesitated. These people were writing to me in confidence,
and I wasn't sure about the etiquette of showing them to
someone else. But then again, they would be posted on the
website afterwards, so I supposed there was no harm. I angled
my laptop towards her, taking care to make sure she couldn't
read the email addresses – after all, I assumed most of the
people who wrote in were local as they'd found me through my
Facebook page, and I'd hate to think I was giving away the
secrets they'd trusted me with – and we read the first one
together.

Dear Evelyn

I'm so worried about my fifteen-year-old daughter. She's
turned from a lovely, easy-going girl into someone I don't
recognise almost overnight. I worry she's got caught up with
the wrong crowd. How can I get through to her?

'How do you know what to tell them?' Catherine asked.

'I usually try and find something similar in Evelyn's answers to help me, but it's not always possible. This one might be tricky.'

'Do you want some help? I mean, I don't know much about kids, but I was definitely a fifteen-year-old girl once.'

'That would be amazing, thank you.'

We spent the next twenty minutes putting together a reply. Satisfied, I sent it off then added it to the website.

'Shall we do another one?' Catherine said.

I glanced at the screen. There were still quite a few to get through, and evenings were my only opportunity.

'Go on, then,' I said, gratefully.

'I'm rather enjoying it – not other people's misery, but the helping bit, of course.'

'That's exactly how I feel.' I smiled and clicked on the next one. After we'd answered that I clicked on the next one, and the one after that, and before I'd realised, it was almost midnight.

'Blimey, I'd better go,' Catherine said, standing. She swayed. 'Oops, I think that last gin might have been a mistake.' We both squinted at the bottle on the table. It was more than half empty.

'Whoops.' I stood too. 'How are you getting home?'

'I'm walking. It'll clear my head.'

'Are you sure it's safe? Can't you get a taxi?'

'Round here at this time of night? No chance. Don't worry, honestly. I've done it loads of times. I'll be absolutely fine. The walk's only about twenty minutes.'

She shrugged her jacket on, pulled on her shoes, then leaned in to give me a hug. As her body pressed against me I realised how much I'd missed simple physical contact.

'Thanks for this evening, I've had a lovely time,' she said, pulling away. 'And thank you for letting me see Mum's letters. It's been – well, emotional.'

'You're welcome any time.'

She gave a wicked grin. 'You might live to regret that offer,' she said, then opened the door and disappeared into the darkness. 'See you tomorrow at the bench,' she called and then, when I was sure she'd gone, I closed the door. As I settled into bed half an hour later, Buster snuggled at my feet, I realised that, for the first time since the divorce, I hadn't spent the evening pining for my children. I'd actually had fun.

10

DIRE STRAITS

I am in desperate trouble. I am soon to have a baby, but I am neither married nor engaged to be married. In fact the father of my baby is engaged to a friend of mine and while he knows all about my plight, he refuses to have anything to do with me. He is still determined to marry my friend. Should I tell my friend the identity of my unborn child's father?

This man sounds very unsatisfactory. If you were hoping that by turning his fiancée against him you might win him for yourself then I'm afraid that would be very unwise. It sounds to me as though you are far better off without him, as he has already proven himself to be callous and selfish – neither of which are traits you would want in a husband. Perhaps your parents or friends could help to convince this young man to shoulder some of the financial burden for his child. If you really do not have anyone else to turn to then please write to me privately

and I will put you in touch with an organisation which will be
able to help and support you.

Sometimes, life could surprise you. And I was certainly feeling
surprised by the apparent turnaround in my fortunes over the last
couple of weeks. I'd gone from lonely and friendless to making a
new friend in Catherine – and a new companion in Buster – and it
was in large part thanks to Evelyn.

And now, it seemed I'd made another new friend too. Since
Charlie's first couple of messages thanking me for my help, we'd
emailed back and forth a number of times. At first it had just been
small talk, but, as with the nature of online chats, it quickly devel-
oped into a more meaningful friendship.

Every night once the kids were in bed, I sat down with a glass
of wine to answer Charlie's message from earlier that evening. It
was becoming the highlight of my day.

So far I'd learned that his twenty-two-year-old daughter, Polly,
worked as a childminder, and his nineteen-year-old, Ava, was at
university in Portsmouth studying marine biology.

'She must have got the brains from her mother because they
definitely didn't come from me,' he wrote one night.

'Oh I don't know, you seem pretty brainy to me,' I followed my
reply with a winking emoji.

'Why do you think I became a gardener and not a brain
surgeon?' he replied.

'Yeah but at least you run your own business. I just teach other
people about science. I don't actually do anything with it. You
know what they say: those who can, do. Those who can't, teach.'

Charlie told me he loved sky diving, but hadn't done it for at
least ten years. 'I guess getting older makes you realise you're not
immortal after all,' he wrote.

'I can't think of anything worse than throwing myself out of a plane,' I replied.

I discovered he liked drinking pints of bitter and huge glasses of red wine, enjoyed eating fiery hot curries, and loved making furniture but had run out of places to put new pieces.

In return I told him about Buster and all about the kids —

'I love dogs, but my wife is allergic so we've never been able to have one,' he replied.

I even told him a little bit about what had happened between me and Rob.

'I'm so sorry that happened to you,' he wrote. 'It must feel awful.'

I didn't ask him if he was thinking about his own marriage when he said that.

After our chats – long after Charlie had retired for the night and I should have been in bed – I'd think about how strange it was to feel so close to someone I'd never even met. But maybe that was the point. This way, I could paint an image of Charlie in my mind the way I wanted him to be. Perhaps, if we met in real life, things would be much more awkward between us, and he wouldn't be all he seemed after all.

For now, things were just fine the way they were – friendship from afar.

Which was why the message he'd sent me this evening had thrown me.

I've had an idea.

That was it. Nothing more.

Are you going to share it?

It usually took him a while to reply so I was about to put the laptop to one side. But a reply pinged up immediately. I clicked it open.

Let me come and help you with your garden.

My wine glass hovered in mid-air. I hadn't expected that and I wasn't sure how I felt about it.

How do you know I live anywhere near you?

I saw your advert for Dear Evelyn on a local Facebook group so I assumed you must do. Have I got that wrong?

This time I hesitated before replying. Did I want to meet Charlie? I might feel as though I knew him, but as a teacher to teenagers I was more aware than anyone of the dangers of taking people at their word online.

My instincts told me Charlie was fine. But how much could I trust them?

Before I could formulate a response, another had popped up from him.

Sorry, I hope you don't think that was weird or inappropriate. It's just that I've been thinking about what you said about your garden and I just thought I could help you. You know, as I'm a gardener. But I totally understand if you don't feel comfortable about it.

I felt a pang of guilt. I'd told Charlie that the state of my garden was stressing me out. I'd jokingly described the wonky patio slabs, the towering weeds, the broken greenhouse hidden behind the triffid-like plants and grass.

'It's like looking at a post-apocalyptic landscape where all the humans have died out and nature has taken over the world,' I'd typed. 'I'm scared to let our dog run around too much in case he cuts his paws or goes missing presumed dead among the bloody weeds, but I honestly don't know where to start.'

He hadn't said anything more at the time, and I hadn't given it another thought since.

Aware time was ticking by and Charlie would be worried by my lack of response to his kind offer, I started to type.

> It's not inappropriate at all. I just don't want you to think I was fishing for your help.

I waited while he replied. It took seconds.

> I didn't think that. I'd be happy to help you. Anyway I owe you a favour after you helped me so much.

I thought about it. The garden was a state, and the truth was I had absolutely no idea how I was going to find the time to get it sorted by myself – or even whether I'd be able to. It felt over-whelming. Before I could change my mind, I typed a reply.

> If you really don't mind, some ideas would be amazing. Thank you so much.

Instinct told me this would be fine. But, just in case, I'd let Catherine know when he was coming round. You could never be too careful.

* * *

I could honestly kill him. *Bloody* men.

I hung up, and my whole body shook with fury. I needed an outlet for my rage.

I picked up a pillow and slung it across the room, and it clattered against the lamp, sending it toppling to the ground.

'Arrrgggghh!' I roared, and hoped my neighbours were out. I sat on my bed for a good few minutes trying to let my heart rate settle and my anger subside. Finally, I felt calm again – at least as long as I didn't think about the conversation I'd just had with my selfish bastard of an ex-husband.

It was a Monday morning and the kids were still there from the weekend, but had been due back after school. The arrangements were very clear, and we'd agreed it was important for the children that we stuck to them so that they knew where they were from one day to the next. Kids needed stability, we'd agreed, and we'd tried our best to make the most of a bad situation.

But this morning he'd rung with a request that had made me see red.

'Can the kids stay for the rest of the week?'

'What?' My stomach had tightened.

'They're having such a nice time, and they asked if they could stay a few more nights so I thought you wouldn't mind.'

'What the *fuck*, Rob? Of course they can't stay a few more nights. They live here.'

'Well, and here.'

'This is their home. They're happy here. Settled.'

'Except they're not, are they?'

'What is that supposed to mean?'

Rob at least had the decency to sound as though he regretted starting this conversation. But like a dog with a bone there was no way I was letting it go now.

'Well?'

'Well, it's just easier for them because they're nearer to school here, and they have their old bedrooms...' He trailed off.

'Yes, well, they only have all of those things because you cheated on me, Rob, or have you forgotten that part of the story?' The rage had begun building by then and I didn't think I could control it if I had to speak to him for one more second. 'Let me speak to Olivia.'

'She's watching TV.'

'Put her on!' I hated losing control, and I shook as I waited for my daughter to come to the phone.

'Hello, Mummy. We're watching *CBBC*.'

Normally I would have something to say about them watching TV before school, but today I was in no mood for being the bad guy. 'That's lovely, darling. Daddy says you want to stay there for a few more days before you come home to me and Buster. Is that right?'

She was silent for a moment and I held my breath. 'Well, Mummy, I don't mind but Jacob really wants to come home. To you, I mean. But Daddy says he's told his work he can work from home and so he says it's easier to go to school. And it means I can have a play date at Miranda's on Friday too. So can I?'

There were too many things I could have said right then, so I just replied: 'Let me think about it. Can you put your daddy back on, please?'

There was a rustling, then Rob's voice again.

'She doesn't sound like she's that bothered about staying there, Rob. What's all this shit about working from home?'

'Well, I thought it would be nice to spend a bit more time with them so I arranged to work from home for a few days to be here when they got back from school. I don't see there's anything wrong with that.'

'So you've already planned it all, then? Fuck the arrangements, fuck what's best for them. You want them there so you're having them, have I got that right?'

'Don't get so snotty, Beth. You see them far more than I do, and there's nothing wrong with wanting to spend a bit more time with *our* children.'

'Except we have an arrangement!'

'Yes, well, we might need to talk about that.'

My blood ran cold. 'What do you mean?'

'I've been thinking. Natalie and I would like to have them here more often, with us. After all, it *is* their home.'

'*This* is their home, Rob.'

'Look, I can't talk to you when you're like this. Let's have a chat about it when I drop them off on Sunday night, shall we?'

'I haven't agreed they can stay.'

'There's not much you can do to stop me keeping them. But I'd prefer your blessing.'

The only thing preventing me from hurling the phone against the wall was the fact it would leave me out of contact with the kids. Instead I swallowed down my rage and snapped, 'Fine. I'll ring and speak to them tomorrow,' disconnected the call, and threw the cushion across the room with a roar. Now I felt as if a fire were raging through me. How *dared* he threaten me like that?

Just when I'd thought that battles about the kids were over and we were back on an even keel, he threw this into the mix. Well, screw him. If he wanted a battle, he could bloody well have one.

I checked the time and realised I was late for work. I yanked a dress on, slicked on a bit of mascara, grabbed my keys and ran out of the door. The ancient Ford Focus was temperamental and I prayed it would start this morning otherwise it might just tip me over the edge. Luckily, it did, and I tried to steady my nerves as I navigated the half-hour journey to school.

Ten minutes into the drive my phone buzzed. I glanced at it in the phone holder. Suzie.

Normally I would have ignored it, but I missed my old friend, and I hoped she might be able to calm me before I arrived to teach my year nine students. I pressed the answer button.

'Hello, stranger,' I said, my voice echoing back at me.

'Hi, I haven't got long,' she said, instantly putting me on edge. She sounded out of breath. 'I just wanted to say I'm sorry for being such a shit friend, and wondered if I could come and see you. I haven't even seen your new place yet.'

No, you haven't, I thought, but didn't say. 'That would be lovely. When?'

'How's tonight? Dan's offered to look after Sammy, and I'd love to see you.'

I didn't reply. With my agony aunt letters to answer and my chats with Charlie, my evenings felt precious these days. I didn't like anyone or anything interrupting them, and longed to say no. But I knew that was selfish.

'Tonight works for me.'

'Ah, good. Dan thought it might be too short notice but I knew you'd have nothing else to do.' I bristled at her words but didn't bother to correct her.

'Okay, how about seven-thirty?'

'Oh, can I come earlier? Only I want to get back and see Samuel before bedtime and he'll need feeding.'

I sighed. Between walking Buster and cooking there really wouldn't be any time to chat to Charlie. 'Fine. Six-thirty is the earliest I can do.'

'Great. I'd better go, Samuel is screaming the house down.'

She hung up and I was left with the feeling that it wasn't really that she wanted to see me, but rather that she just needed to get away from the house for a few hours. I was merely a convenient excuse.

* * *

In the end the day passed without event. My nerves had calmed and teaching my classes made me feel as if I'd gained some control back. I had a stack of marking to do, and didn't get out of the school until gone five, which meant that by the time I got home poor old Buster had to make do with a quick run around the block.

'Sorry, little guy, I'll make it up to you,' I promised, tickling the backs of his ears. He wagged his tail faithfully.

I chopped some vegetables and left them on the side before dashing up for a shower. A quick glance at my emails revealed a couple of new letters and a reply from Charlie, but before I had a chance to do anything about them there was a knock on the door. It was only quarter past six and I felt a frisson of irritation that Suzie had imposed on my time even more.

'Hi,' I said, pasting a smile on my face as I opened the door. Buster barked furiously beside me.

'Hello, sorry I'm early, I thought it would take longer to get here,' she said, sweeping in and wrapping me in a hug.

'It's fine, it's lovely to see you,' I said, pulling away and taking in her appearance. Suzie was normally so well put together – perfect hair, immaculate make-up, carefully-curated outfits. She'd even had a full face of make-up on when I'd been to visit her in hospital a day after giving birth. And while today she still had the surface sheen, the same polished look as always, I could see the telltale signs of exhaustion in the dark circles beneath her eyes, which she'd smothered in too much concealer, and the vacant look in her eyes.

'You look amazing,' she said. I glanced down at my old jeans and sweatshirt and shower-damp hair.

'Really?'

She nodded. 'You look – different. Happier than I thought you would.' She glanced round at the scruffy hallway. 'Being in the countryside obviously suits you.'

I simply nodded and said nothing.

She bent down to say hello to Buster, who sniffed her hand then ran off, then she stood and clapped her hands. 'Right, I can't stay long. Shall we have a drink?'

'Aren't you driving?'

'Yes, but one won't harm. Now, where are the glasses?'

I showed her into the kitchen and she sat at the table while I poured us wine. 'Wow, this is rustic.' I held my tongue and smiled.

'Yes, it is. I'm getting there though.'

'Bet you're missing your old kitchen.'

'Well, yes. But there's not much I can do about that.' I felt my shoulders tense, and placed the glass of wine in front of her with a little more force than I'd intended. She picked it up and downed half of it, then stood. 'Can we go outside? It's stifling in here.'

'Sure.' I opened the back door and we stepped outside. Suzie stopped abruptly as she took in the garden. 'Oh.'

'What's wrong?'

She shook her head. 'Nothing. It's just—' She looked at me and I could see pity in her eyes as she placed her hand on my upper arm. 'This must be so awful for you, having to downgrade quite so much,' she said. I imagined she thought she was being kind, but her words cut deep and I couldn't believe she was being quite so insensitive. I wondered whether it was tiredness making her so thoughtless, or whether she had always been this self-centred and I'd just never noticed it before.

I led her further into the garden and we stood on the end of the rickety patio, glasses of wine in hand. I was about to start explaining about the plans I had for the garden when Suzie let out a high giggle. I turned to see her covering her mouth with her hand.

'What's tickled you?'

'Sorry, nothing.'

I felt a prickle across the back of my neck. 'Come on, what's so funny?'

'It's just—' She glanced into the tangle of weeds then back at me. 'I'm just so *sorry* for you,' she said, taking a sip of her wine.

'What about?' I kept my voice steady.

She swept her arm in an arc and giggled again. 'It must make you so mad that Rob's swanning around in your swanky place while you've got to put up with this. I mean, you've really got your work cut out to get this looking half decent, right?'

I felt anger flare in me but swallowed it down. The last thing I needed was to argue with Suzie when I hadn't seen her for so long. 'It'll be fine. Nothing I can't handle,' I said, careful to keep my voice breezy. No way was I going to tell her about Charlie's offer of help. 'So, anyway, enough about me. How is everything? How's Samuel? And Dan?' I didn't really care how Dan was, but it would have been churlish not to have asked.

'Yeah, good.' She sighed. 'I'm not getting much sleep and Sammy seems to take over my entire day. I honestly don't know how you did it.'

Without much help from you, I thought.

'It does get easier,' I said. 'He's only a few months old. Anyway, I need to come and see him for a cuddle, he must be huge now.'

'He is, a right chunky monkey.' She pulled out her phone and swiped through. 'Look, this was him a couple of days ago.' I squinted at the screen and a chubby little face stared back at me. He looked too much like Dan to be cute.

'Ahh, lovely,' I said, handing the phone back. But Suzie hadn't finished, and scrolled through countless more photos of Samuel in a variety of outfits and positions. 'This is his first smile, look,' she said, and I didn't have the heart to tell her it just looked as if he had wind. 'And this is him with my parents, and this is his first trip to baby group.'

She continued to swipe through an interchangeable selection of pictures and I felt my smile growing rigid. But then a picture stopped me in my tracks and made my stomach lurch. Suzie clicked off it quickly, but it was too late. I'd already seen it.

'Was… was that Olivia and Jacob with… with *Natalie*?' I stammered.

Suzie had the grace to look shamefaced. 'Yeah. Sorry, Beth, you weren't meant to see that.'

'Bit late now.' I felt my voice shake. 'So…' I swallowed. I didn't really want to know any more, but at the same time I needed to, to rip the plaster off in one go and get the wound exposed. 'Where were you when that was taken?'

She put her phone in her bag as if it might help. 'A barbecue.'

I nodded. 'Right. Recently, I assume.'

'Last weekend.' She picked at her nail and wouldn't look me in the eye.

'I see.' I felt cold, and suddenly I really didn't want Suzie there any more. She was too much of a reminder of everything I'd lost, and everything I was missing out on.

'Sorry, Beth, I am. But you know Rob and Dan are mates, surely you must have realised we'd see him and Natalie sometimes?'

My whole body bristled at the mention of her name. 'I – I

hadn't really thought about it.' *I'd hoped you'd have a bit more loyalty,* I thought.

'Well, we do, and I can't feel guilty about it.' She touched my arm and I flinched. 'You're still my friend but I can't ignore her. And she's actually really nice.'

Get out get out get out, I wanted to scream. Instead I stood there, still as a statue, and hoped Suzie wouldn't say another word because I didn't know if I could keep quiet much longer. But she hadn't finished.

'Anyway, it will be good for me and Samuel once the baby comes. They'll be able to play together.'

It took a few seconds for the words to sink in, but when they did I felt a chill travel from my feet to my head and wrap itself around my windpipe. 'What?' My voice was barely a whisper. I saw the exact moment Suzie realised her mistake.

'Oh, God, I thought you knew,' she said. 'Rob told me he was going to tell you so I assumed he had by now. I thought...' She trailed off. 'Shit, sorry, Beth, I...'

'Natalie's pregnant?'

Suzie nodded, and I felt as though the bottom had fallen out of my world.

It had been bad enough that my children had a whole other life away from me. But now they were going to have a brother or sister that was nothing to do with me too. A whole other family.

I felt sick. On wobbly legs and walked away from Suzie and back into the house. I ran up the stairs and into my room and threw myself on my bed and felt the tears come, soaking through the pillow within seconds. I didn't care whether Suzie thought I was being rude, I just needed a few moments to take in the news. Rob and Natalie were having a baby, and not only had he not told me, but he'd left me open to hearing the news like this. I was totally on the back foot.

I didn't know how long passed but at some point I heard soft footsteps on the stairs and then my door squeaked open and the bed dipped. I kept my face buried in the pillow and felt Suzie's hand on my back.

'Beth, I really am sorry. I honestly assumed you knew. Stupid of me, I know.' She rubbed my back and I resisted pushing her away. This wasn't her fault, I had to remind myself. This was Rob's fault. All of it.

I lifted my head and turned to look at her. I used to feel so much affection for this woman, thought she'd always be the person I turned to when times were tough. But all I saw now was a half-stranger, someone on the other side of the divorce fence who I didn't really know as well as I'd thought.

'Don't worry. Rob should have told me.' I didn't add that she could have been sympathetic about it, asked me how I felt rather than just blurting it out, even if she had thought I already knew. There was no point. I sat up. I felt beaten, and my head ached.

'Do you want me to go?' she said.

'But you've come all this way.'

She shook her head. 'It's fine. I should probably leave you alone before I put my foot in it again anyway.'

I nodded miserably. 'Just tell me one thing.'

She looked wary. 'Okay.'

'Is she nice to them? Olivia and Jacob?'

She shifted uncomfortably and looked down at her hands in her lap. 'She's really good with them.' She looked me in the eye. 'I know it's not what you want to hear but she's a nice person, Beth.'

'So nice she shagged my husband behind my back.'

'He was the married one though.'

I nodded. She was right. He was the one in the wrong. I knew I needed to come to terms with the fact that Natalie was part of my kids' lives now, and that I should really be trying to get to know her a little bit, for their sakes. But until the anger and the bitterness subsided, I couldn't bring myself to do that.

Suzie stood then. 'Right, I'll be off. Sorry about tonight. See you soon?'

'Sure.'

I didn't move to see her out, and I waited until I'd heard the front door close and her car pull away, the roar of the Mazda engine cutting through the peace, until I sat up.

I'd thought I missed my old life, and all that came with it, Suzie included. But all her visit had done was show me I was better off on my own, making my own new life away from Rob. Making new friends. Starting again.

* * *

After I'd splashed cold water on my blotchy face I went back downstairs. It was still light outside, so I made a quick stir-fry from the vegetables I'd already chopped and took my dinner into the garden. Buster dragged himself out of his bed and padded out with me to cock his leg and have his nightly sniff. I placed my laptop on my knee and scooped noodles into my mouth as I read today's letters. The light was fading and the air was turning chilly but it felt good to be out in the fresh air.

I spent the next half an hour answering questions, then clicked on the email from Charlie.

Are you free tomorrow? I thought I might pop over and take a look at that jungle of yours, see what can be done. C

Ignoring the niggle of doubt I had about how sensible it was to be inviting a man I'd never met before into my home, I typed a reply.

That would be brilliant thank you.

I felt strangely excited. About seeing Charlie, or about getting my garden sorted? I didn't need to examine it too closely. I closed my laptop and stood, staring into the garden and trying to imagine what it might look like with some work. I tried to picture Lois out here, lovingly tending to her flowers and shrubs while a young Catherine played. Even though darkness had thrown the garden into shadow, I stepped off the patio into the wilderness and pushed aside the weeds that blocked the path towards the back fence. I could hear scurrying feet and I turned to find Buster behind me. 'Careful, boy,' I said, bending to scoop him up. The last thing I needed was for him to get glass from the broken greenhouse in his paw, or find a piece of fence with a hole in it.

I kept moving forwards. Some of the plants had grown taller than me and their presence felt benevolent, as though they were watching me. I stomped my feet along, squashing overgrown grass flat, until I reached the end. I turned left, trailing my fingers along the wooden slats of the rickety fence until I reached the corner, and then tried to feel for the old climbing frame that Catherine had mentioned. The weeds were so thick here there was a good chance the metal frame had been entirely engulfed by them, but my hands simply flailed around in mid-air. The climbing frame must have been long gone. I peered down into the darkness and tried to imagine Catherine playing here, under her mother's watchful eye.

I hoped that one day soon my children would be able to create happy memories in this very same place.

The shriek of a fox from the nearby woods brought me back to the present with a start, and my heart thumped as I marched back towards the house, shoving the weeds that had already sprung back, closing the clearing behind me. I hurried inside, locking the back door. The house was so quiet when I was alone, and I was grateful for Buster's presence. I trudged upstairs, and it wasn't until I was in bed half an hour later, with my eyes wide open staring into the darkened room, that I allowed the seed of anger that had planted itself in my belly to germinate and unfurl, to let me examine how I really felt about Natalie's pregnancy.

The tears I'd cried earlier had wrung me out, but as I lay there turning it over in my mind it dawned on me that it wasn't the pregnancy I cared about. It wasn't the fact that Natalie existed, or even that she slept in the same bed as the man I'd once loved. Any jealousy I'd been holding onto had evaporated and been replaced by huge tangle of feelings: envy about her taking my place, melancholy for what Rob and I had once been; anger about Rob's threats, resentment about the fact that my life had changed so much while his simply carried on as before; worry about how far he'd go to stop me having custody of my children. But none of it was about any feelings I might still be harbouring for my ex-husband.

It felt like a revelation.

I rolled over and switched on the light. Buster stirred by my feet but quickly settled again, his head resting on his front legs. He looked so content. I climbed out of bed again and grabbed my phone from its charger and typed a message to Rob.

I want the kids home on Friday instead of Sunday and I'll come to you. We need to talk.

I wasn't giving him the chance to argue. I was taking back control.

11

WORKPLACE ROMANCE

I find myself in rather an awkward predicament. I am very attracted to a married man and while he's told me he is not in a happy marriage, I know I mustn't make any moves while he is still married. The problem is that we work together and cannot avoid each other's company, and it is getting to the point where I become flustered when we are in the same room together. I don't know whether I should let him know my feelings or keep them hidden.

I think you know that revealing your feelings would be the wrong thing to do. Whether his marriage is happy or not is quite frankly none of your business. No good has ever come from trying to split up a man and his wife, and if you should try, I suspect it will only be you who ends up suffering. If you truly cannot bear to be in the same room as him then I would suggest you look for a new job. For your own sake, I would

also suggest that you move on and look elsewhere for a satis-
factory romance.

I felt nervous, jittery, as if I were waiting for a date to arrive. But, I
had to keep reminding myself, this was not a date. Very far from it,
in fact, given that the only reason Charlie and I had got to know
each other at all was because he'd been so desperate to mend his
marriage.

Pull yourself together, Beth.

I checked the time again. Five-thirty. He was due any minute. I
glanced at my reflection in the mirror one last time. I didn't look
too manic.

I knew Charlie had arrived before I even saw him drive up the
road because Buster started yapping at the window. Moments
later, a small van pulled up directly outside and I felt my stomach
flip over in anticipation. He was here – this man I already felt I
knew, but who I'd never actually met. What if we didn't get on in
real life? What if he thought I was dull, stripped of my agony aunt
persona?

I took a deep breath and opened the door as he stepped out of
the van. Buster rushed out to greet him and he bent down to say
hello so I couldn't see him properly at first. But then he stood up
to his full height and walked up the path, and I felt my heart skip
a beat and my face flush.

Christ, he was gorgeous.

I'd imagined a man about ten years older than me – after all,
his kids had moved out of home – maybe starting to thin on top, a
slight paunch. But this man in front of me must have been my age
at most, his dark blond hair was thick and wavy, and beneath his
white T-shirt I could see the contour of well-defined muscles.

This was a complication I didn't need.

'Hi, you must be Charlie,' I said as he approached.

'I am, hi,' he said in a surprisingly low and gentle voice. 'And I guess you're Evelyn?'

Oh crap. How had I not mentioned my name during all those long conversations?

'Er, actually I'm Beth. Sorry.' I felt flustered already.

'Oh, right.' He looked round, confused, as though looking to see if Evelyn was nearby.

'No, sorry. I mean, it is me, but Evelyn isn't my real name. Beth is.' Oh *God*.

'Oh, good, I have got the right place then, phew.' He reached me and shook my hand. His skin felt rough and warm beneath my palm. He studied me for a second. 'Actually, you look more like a Beth than an Evelyn anyway. You're too young to be Evelyn.'

'Yeah, sorry about that. I'd completely forgotten I hadn't told you my real name,' I said as he came inside.

'Ah, don't worry. I probably shouldn't have used my real name in the letters. It never really occurred to me to change it. I'm not that subtle.' He smiled and his eyes crinkled.

'You don't mind, do you? That I've used your name? On the website, I mean.'

'Nah. My wife will never read it. And if she did it's not as if she'd be exactly surprised.' I saw a flash of sadness cross his face and said no more.

'Right, well, come in,' I said, leading him through to the kitchen. 'Would you like a drink?'

'Something cold would be nice. It's pretty hot in here.'

You're telling me.

'Coke? Beer?'

'A beer would be awesome, thanks.'

Drinks poured, I led him out into the garden. 'This is it,' I said, trying not to stare at his face too much. I felt sure he could see how flustered I was and I didn't want to make things awkward.

'Wow, you weren't exaggerating, were you?' he said, gazing round the garden in awe.

'Nope. I don't think it's been touched for years.'

'Decades, I'd say,' he said, stepping out confidently into the undergrowth. He pushed weeds and grasses aside as he worked his way towards the end of the garden. I followed, trying hard not to notice the tightness of his combat trousers by keeping my eyes trained on the ground in front of me. He stopped suddenly and I crashed into his back.

'God, sorry,' I said. Why was I behaving like a teenage girl with a crush?

'This is amazing,' he said, looking round. 'A total blank canvas.' He whirled round to face me, his eyes shining with excitement. 'Have you got any ideas of what you want to do with it?'

'Not really.'

He rubbed his hands together. 'Great, we can come up with some plans together, then.'

He walked back to the patio and I followed.

'So, shall we get started?'

I loved his enthusiasm but I was worried that it was going to turn into a big job that he'd expect to be paid handsomely for – and I didn't have much spare money to spend right now.

'I – just some help clearing the weeds would be great,' I said.

He looked at me. 'Nah, we can do better than that.'

'But – it's such a huge job and I... I can't afford that.'

He sat down on one of the wooden chairs. 'Honestly, Beth. I'm happy to help you.' He shrugged. 'You helped me, I really want to return the favour.'

'I don't think I helped you that much.'

'You really did. At least now Helen knows how I feel and that I can't keep pretending everything is okay. What she does next is up to her.'

'Do you think she'll come round?'

He shrugged. 'I honestly have no idea.' He rubbed the back of his neck. 'I – I think she might be having an affair.'

Oh God. This was what I'd been dreading. It had been my instant reaction after his first letter, but we'd skirted round the subject so far. I hadn't wanted to put ideas into his head that hadn't been there before. But then again of *course* this would be on his mind.

'What makes you think that? Has something changed?'

'No, not really. She won't talk to me. If it was just about me and her and how things have changed since the kids left, then I could understand it. But there's something else. It's like she's already left the marriage, in her mind.' He sighed. 'I guess I'll have to wait until she decides she wants to tell me what the hell is going on. Or she just walks out.'

I looked up sharply. This was the first time he had said anything like this. I guess it was different when you were face to face rather than talking to a stranger on the other end of a computer. This felt more personal.

'Do you mean that?'

He didn't reply immediately and I could see the pain and confusion in his eyes. Helen was an idiot if she was cheating on him.

'I honestly don't know.'

We sat in silence for a moment, watching the garden settle down for the evening; the shadows lengthen and the birds quieten down. I tried not to think about what he'd just said, or how the physical presence of this man I'd been getting to know from a distance had made me feel. Instead I tried to focus on my new garden, a place where the kids could play, and have fun. Somewhere they'd really want to be, and where I could sit and relax too. It felt like a dream.

'Sorry, enough wallowing.' Charlie's voice cut into my thoughts. 'Let's talk about your garden.'

We spent the next half an hour sketching out some simple ideas, and by the time we'd finished I felt excited. But first, we'd need to get the whole place cleared.

'Are you free at the weekend?' he said.

'I have the children, but we'll be here,' I said.

'How about we make a start then?'

'Are you sure? Don't you want to be at home?'

He hesitated, then shook his head. 'No. I'd prefer to be busy.'

He obviously didn't want to talk about it any more, so I didn't push. 'Okay, then, that would be wonderful, thank you,' I said. I checked my watch. It was almost seven o'clock.

'Do you want to stay for dinner? It's getting quite late.' The invitation surprised me, so I was even more surprised when Charlie accepted.

'That would lovely, if you're sure,' he said. 'Helen's out tonight...' He paused, and I wondered whether he was thinking about where she might be or, more specifically, who she might be with. 'Anyway, I don't suppose she'll miss me.'

I stood and we went inside. Charlie sat at the table while I peeled potatoes.

'Can't you give me something to do?' he said.

'You're doing enough, helping me with my garden. The least I can do is make you some food.'

He held his hands up. 'Fair enough. Be warned though, I won't ask again.'

'Good.'

A few moments passed, then he said, 'So tell me a bit more about this agony aunt thing you mentioned the other day. You said you found some old magazines that inspired you to start the website?'

'Yes. I found them in the wardrobe upstairs.'

'Amazing.'

I glanced over at him. He was watching me intently and I felt my face burn. I looked away and tried to focus on what I was doing. 'Some of the advice was really dated – you know, telling women they should definitely wait until they were married before they slept with someone, or telling them to put up and shut up if they suspected their husband was having an affair—' I broke off, aware of what I'd just said. 'Sorry.'

'Don't worry.' He leaned forward. 'So what made you decide to start your own page, then?'

I shrugged. 'I'm not really sure. I was lonely in the evenings and I felt a real connection with all these people who needed someone to turn to. I just thought... I don't know, that I could help them.' I glanced over at him. 'It feels as though people are more disconnected than ever.'

He nodded slowly. 'You're right. I mean, I suppose that's the reason I emailed you.' He shrugged. 'I couldn't talk to my mates, and I don't have that sort of relationship with anyone else.'

'I'm glad you did.'

He held my gaze for a beat too long. 'Me too.'

A warmth flushed through me. He looked away first.

'So have you had many people writing in?'

I turned back to chopping the potatoes, concentrating on cutting them into slices. 'A few. More every day.'

'That's brilliant. You're good at it.'

'I don't know about that. Evelyn – the first one, I mean – is the one with the good advice. I turn to her a lot of the time.'

'Don't do yourself down. You helped me.'

'Well, I'm glad.'

I lined the potatoes in a pan with some onions, garlic and cream, and stuck them in the oven, then wiped my hands on a tea towel and sat down opposite him. The overhead light was harsh and it formed shadows under his eyes. I wished I could do something more to make him feel happy.

'I forgot to tell you,' I said, leaning forward. 'I met someone.'

'Oh? Is this your mystery friend who came over the other night and meant you abandoned me?'

'The very one.' I smiled. 'I'm sure you coped without me.'

'I missed you.' The air fizzed between us.

'Anyway,' I continued, clearing my throat. 'She's called Catherine, and it turns out she is the original Evelyn's daughter.'

'No! That's amazing.' His eyes shone and I found the fact that he liked a gossip endearing. 'Come on, tell me more.'

So I told him about Lois being the agony aunt who had lived in this very cottage, and about her disappearance when Catherine was just nine, leaving Catherine to live with her grandmother.

'So what does Catherine think happened to her?' Charlie said.

'That's just it. She has no idea, and her grandmother was so heartbroken by the whole thing that she never mentioned Lois again until the day she died.'

'Wow, that's tough,' Charlie said, looking thoughtful. 'Wouldn't you want to find out?'

'What do you mean?'

'A woman disappears into thin air and nobody looks for her? That's a mystery waiting to be solved. Surely Catherine has at least tried to find out what happened?'

I shook my head. 'I honestly don't think she has. I get the impression it was forbidden to even mention her mother's name.'

'Maybe we should, then.'

'Should what?'

'Try and find her.' He picked his phone up. 'A quick Google search wouldn't hurt, would it?'

I frowned. Catherine had seemed quite adamant that her

family had never wanted to know anything about what had happened to her mother. But then again, Charlie did have a point. I *was* intrigued. 'I don't know. It feels wrong to go behind Catherine's back. Besides, I doubt we'll find anything after all this time.'

He shrugged. 'But what if we do?'

I thought about it. I'd felt a connection to Evelyn from the moment I'd found those letters. Finding out she'd lived in this house and meeting her daughter had only strengthened that connection. I really did want to know what had happened to her. There was even a chance that she could still be alive – although she'd be well into her nineties by now if she was. I made my mind up.

'Let's do it.'

* * *

We searched for hours that night, getting lost down all kinds of Internet rabbit holes in our quest to track down Catherine's mother. But, unless we wanted to pay for various ancestry searches, which we worried might alert Catherine to the fact that we were doing this before we were ready to tell her, we eventually had to admit defeat.

Lois Andrews had disappeared into thin air, and definitely hadn't wanted to be found.

'What do you reckon actually happened to her?' Charlie said. It was well past midnight and I should have been in bed – I had school tomorrow. But I was enjoying Charlie's company too much and really didn't want him to leave. I wondered whether Helen cared that he wasn't at home.

'Who knows? She never told Catherine or her own mother who Catherine's father was, and, although she seemed to have been a good mum while she was around, it's pretty awful to just leave a nine-year-old without her mother. Maybe she had never really wanted to be a mother, and left to live a different kind of life.'

'Or maybe she was kidnapped and has spent the last several decades living in someone's basement?'

I grimaced. 'Or she went to do some shopping, fell over, bumped her head and couldn't remember where she lived.'

'Or she was abducted by aliens.'

'Now you're just being ridiculous,' I said, laughing.

'Says the woman who suggested she bumped her head while shopping and forgot about her own child.'

'Fair point,' I said, rubbing my eyes.

'Well, it looks like we might have to give up for now,' Charlie said. 'If only because you'll fall asleep on the computer otherwise.'

'You're right.' I closed the laptop with a sigh. 'But it was fun trying.'

'It was.' Charlie had been sitting right beside me at the table so that we could read the screen together. Now we both realised quite how close we were. His thigh was pressed up against me and his forearm was almost touching mine on the table. For a moment we both sat still, not saying anything. Then all of a sudden he moved away and cleared his throat.

'I'm so sorry, I had no idea how late it was,' he said, standing abruptly. 'I should go.'

I stood too. 'Are you okay to drive?'

He nodded as he pulled his sweatshirt from round his waist and tugged it over his head. I tried not to notice the flash of toned stomach. 'I'll be fine. It's been at least three hours since my last beer. Besides, there won't be any taxis round here at this time of night so I don't have much choice.'

'You could always stay here,' I said, before I could think about what I was saying.

'I—' He stopped, looked down at his feet. 'I hope you don't...' he stammered.

Realisation dawned and heat rushed to my face. 'Oh God, I didn't mean—' I stopped too. This was excruciating. 'I just meant you could sleep on the sofa if you wanted,' I said, gesturing towards the living room door weakly.

'Oh, yes. Right.' He looked at a point over my shoulder. 'Thanks, but I really should go home. Helen will wonder where I am.'

'Of course.' I cringed at the mention of her name, suddenly relieved that he would be gone in a couple of minutes to give me time to compose myself. Any comfortable intimacy we'd forged over the course of the evening seemed to have vanished in an instant thanks to a misunderstanding, leaving an intense awkwardness in its place.

'Well, thanks for dinner,' Charlie said, hurrying towards the door. 'I'll see you at the weekend.'

'Great, see you,' I said, but before the last words had even formed on my lips, he'd closed the door and was gone.

12

UGLY AND OLD

I am approaching mid-forties, and when I spend time with people younger than me, I feel old and ugly. To make matters worse, my ex-husband's new wife is several years younger than me, and when I see them together I go home and look in the mirror and can understand why he wouldn't want to be with me any more. How can I find my confidence again?

Men often look for a 'younger model' as their wives age, but that certainly does not mean there is anything wrong with you, rather it says more about him. Try to remember that growing old is a privilege that not everyone has.

Having said that, if you really do need a confidence boost, why not treat yourself to a new hairdo, or buy some new make-up? Do you dress for your age? There is no need to wear frumpy frocks in our mid-forties any longer. Take note of what some of the more stylish women are wearing and try to find something that suits you. It may just give you the confidence boost you need!

Despite my mortification about how the evening with Charlie had ended, I didn't have time to dwell on it. The next couple of days were hectic at school, and I spent evenings stripping wallpaper. Before I knew where the week had gone it was Friday and time to pick the kids up from Rob's.

Although I couldn't wait to see Olivia and Jacob, I was dreading the confrontation, and prepared myself for battle by applying a full face of make-up and curling my hair. What else could you do when your ex-husband's new partner was ten years younger than you?

As I drove the half-hour to my former home, memories of the evening with Charlie drifted through my mind. I hadn't dared email him, and just had to hope that when he arrived tomorrow all awkwardness would be forgotten. So what if he was good-looking and funny? He was married to someone else and he wanted to make that work. Besides, he'd given no indication whatsoever that he was interested in anything other than friendship.

I pulled up outside my old house and sat in the car for a minute, preparing myself for what I suspected was not going to be an easy conversation. I studied the home that Rob and I had bought more than nine years ago, back before the kids were born and when we were still happy. It had been little more than a shell, having stood empty for years. Over the next twelve months we'd been more or less living in a construction site, but by the time the work was finished it was all worthwhile. I'd loved choosing paint colours, and browsing kitchen catalogues, picking out light fittings and shower screens. The best bit was when I'd found out I was pregnant with Olivia, and we'd chosen the colours for her nursery. We'd really felt as if we were building a secure future together, one where we could be a happy family and watch our children grow.

And now, to add insult to injury, Natalie was living there, among all the things I'd chosen, playing with my children, and sleeping in my bed.

I climbed out of the car and walked up the driveway. Natalie's Toyota sat there, and it took all my willpower not to give the tyres an almighty kick as I passed. I rang the doorbell, and waited, praying Rob would answer and not her.

'Hello, Beth,' Rob said, filling the doorway.

'Are you going to move aside so I can actually come in, then?' I said, instantly on the defensive. I stepped forward but he didn't move and I smacked into his chest.

'God's sake, Rob, let me in.'

'In a minute.' His hand rested on the doorframe and there was no way I could pass. I took a step back and crossed my arms over my chest like a belligerent child, and waited.

'Don't create a scene, will you? The kids don't need it.'

Anger exploded in my chest.

'Me?' I said, incredulous. 'You tell me you want to start fighting about how often you have the kids all over again while at the same time accidentally forgetting to tell me about your girlfriend being pregnant, and you think it's okay for you to tell *me* not to make a scene?' I shook my head. 'You're unbelievable, you really are.'

'See, this is what I mean,' he said, looking down at me from the doorway. 'You're incapable of being reasonable.'

'You'd better let me in right this minute or you'll really see me being unreasonable.' I stepped forward again, but he held his hand out and I smacked into it again.

'This isn't Natalie's fault, okay? None of it. Just don't be a bitch.'

I took two deep breaths, trying not to lose it, then shoved Rob aside and walked into the house.

'Mummy!' Jacob bundled into me the moment I walked into the living room, and I scooped him off the ground and snuggled my nose into his neck. He smelt divine, and I could have stayed there cuddling him all day, but before long he began to wriggle to get down. I crouched down with him and planted tiny kisses all over his face until he began to giggle uncontrollably. 'Mummy, get off,' he said, squirming away.

'Gosh, I've missed you, my little man,' I said, standing. 'Where's your sister?'

'I'm here, Mummy,' a voice from behind me said, and I turned to find Olivia standing in the doorway. I was about to wrap her in a hug when I saw Natalie hovering behind her, and I froze.

'Hello, Beth,' she said, stepping forward shyly.

'Natalie,' I said, turning my attention back to my daughter. She had her hair in braids with coloured ribbons threaded throughout them.

'What's happened to your hair?' I said, running my hand over them.

'Natalie did them for me when I got back from Miranda's,' she said, and I felt myself tense.

'They look lovely,' I said, gritting my teeth.

'She saw it on a YouTube video and asked if I knew how to do it. I hope you don't mind,' Natalie said. I studied her for a minute, then turned away.

'It's fine.'

Olivia leapt onto the sofa. 'Can we finish watching this film before we go home?' she said.

I glanced at the screen where a group of American teens was standing around wearing minuscule outfits.

'Are you sure it's appropriate? It looks a bit old for you.'

'It's fine, Mummy, everyone at school watches it. Miranda watched it ages ago with her big sister.'

'What rating is it?' I snapped at Natalie.

She looked panicked. 'I'm not sure,' she said. 'Maybe a twelve?'

'She's only seven,' I said. 'I'm not sure it's suitable.'

'Oh, Mummy, ple-e-e-ease,' Olivia begged.

'Come on, Beth, she's watched most of it anyway. You don't need to make a point.' Rob had appeared behind Natalie and was giving me a stern look. I wanted to punch him.

'Fine,' I said. 'But we'll be going soon.'

I stalked past Natalie and Rob and out to the hall, then marched into the kitchen. When I got there I stopped, surprised.

'You've redecorated.'

'Yes.'

'But the kitchen wasn't very old.'

'It's not really anything to do with you how old it was, is it?' Rob said coolly, sitting on a stool at the breakfast bar. The stools were new too, I noticed, and the cupboard doors were now a dark blue instead of the mid grey I'd picked out. There was a shiny, expensive-looking coffee machine on the side, which Natalie started fiddling with. I knew it was more the fact that Rob could afford to splash out on a brand-new kitchen unnecessarily while I couldn't afford to get my kitchen done at all that was getting me so riled, but it didn't mean I could help it.

'Can we have a bit of privacy?' I said pointedly to Natalie.

'I've asked Natalie to be here as well,' Rob said. He reached out his hand to her and pulled her next to him. I stared at him defiantly.

'Don't you think we need to discuss *our* children alone?'

'It's fine, Rob, I'll go,' Natalie said, pulling away. But Rob tugged her back. 'No, Nats, you stay. This affects you too. You're part of the family now whether Beth likes it or not.'

A ball of fury blocked my throat and I swallowed it down.

'Fine, can we just get on with it, then?'

'Fine with me.'

I took a deep breath. 'So, because you've suddenly decided you're ready to play happy families and take an interest in our children, you think I should just roll over and give you fifty-fifty custody, do you?' I knew being aggressive wasn't the best start but I couldn't help myself. The thought of seeing my children even less was tearing me apart and I was determined not to go down without a fight.

'Take an interest in them? You make it sound as though I've never bothered with them before when we both know that's not true.'

'Maybe, but you seemed more than happy to let me do the lion's share of the childcare when we were together,' I said. 'But I guess that was because you were too busy shagging your fancy woman to spend much time with us?' It was a cheap shot but I didn't care. Natalie flinched.

'For fuck's sake, Beth, give it a rest.' Rob laid his hands flat on the table. 'I'm not being unreasonable. I've set up my office so I can run most of the business from home. Natalie works school hours and the children like being here. I really don't see how you can have anything to object to.'

'They like being with me too.'

'And no one is denying that. I just want my fair share of time with them, that's all.'

I could feel my argument slipping away. 'Well, do they want that? It's pretty disruptive for them to be going from house to house every five minutes just to satisfy your whim.'

He didn't reply immediately and I could see a flare of something in his eyes. I'd got him, I knew it.

'Olivia is excited about spending more time here,' he said.

'And Jacob?'

'He'll come round.'

I nodded. 'I see.'

Nobody knew what to say next. To my surprise it was Natalie who broke the silence.

'Rob, why don't you go and get the kids' bags, and I'll make some coffee?'

'But I—'

She touched his arm, and gave a tiny nod. 'Go on.'

He hesitated a moment longer, then climbed down from his stool and walked towards the stairs. We both listened to his footsteps until they reached the top.

'I'm sorry, Beth,' Natalie said. 'I know how hard this is for you, and for what it's worth I tried to talk Rob out of it.'

'What?'

She switched the coffee machine on and it made a loud whirring noise. We waited for it to finish. When it did, she gave me a rueful smile. 'I know Olivia and Jacob have their own bedrooms here, and it was their home originally, but your house is just as much their home these days, and I agree with you. I think they would be more settled if we kept the arrangement as it is too.'

'Right.' I rubbed my head. This was so unexpected I felt rattled, and needed a moment to gather my thoughts.

'So why is he doing it? Is it just to get back at me? Because I really haven't done anything wrong here. It was all him.'

She nodded her head. 'I know. And I am sorry, I truly am. I have tried to tell him, but he's determined.' The coffee machine beeped and she turned round and pulled mugs from the cupboard above her head. 'Coffee?'

'Please.'

I watched as she filled my cup and handed it over.

'You know about the baby, don't you?'

I gave a tight nod. 'Suzie let it slip.'

'I'm so sorry, Beth. We wanted to tell you ourselves. You deserved to hear it from us.'

'True.'

Natalie looked sheepish.

'But I suspect that the bee Rob has in his bonnet about having Olivia and Jacob here more probably has something to do with this baby.' Her hand fluttered to her belly unconsciously and I didn't look down. 'He has this idea about surrounding himself with a big family, loads of kids. You know, like he always wanted.' She filled a glass with water and took a sip. 'But I think if you agree to meet him halfway, he might give up the idea of fighting you over this again.'

'What does halfway mean though? You already have them here more than we arranged.'

She shrugged. 'I'm not sure. But I promise I'll do my best to help you sort this out without making things any harder for the kids.'

I was blindsided. I'd come here all guns blazing, feeling as if I wanted to knock Natalie off her perch, prepared for a huge battle. But instead she was on my side. I wasn't sure what to do with that.

'Well, thank you,' I said, taking a gulp of my coffee. It was still scalding and I almost choked as it burned my throat.

'God, are you all right?' Natalie said, running round the kitchen island and patting me on the back.

'Well, this isn't what I expected to come back to when I left you two alone,' Rob said as he came back into the room carrying two small cases. He placed them on the floor with a half-smile, and for the first time in months I could see the man I used to like.

'Sorry, I was choking on too-hot coffee,' I said, recovering myself.

Natalie moved away from me and back round the other side of

the counter to pour Rob a coffee. I saw the affection on his face as he took the mug from her.

'We were just talking about the children,' Natalie explained.

'And your new baby,' I added.

Rob had the grace to look ashamed. 'Listen, I really am sorry about how you found out, Beth. Natalie and I had planned to tell you ourselves.'

'I know, she's already explained.'

He looked from me to Natalie and back again, his face a picture of puzzlement. I felt secretly pleased that we'd knocked him off kilter.

'Oh, right. Well. It wasn't fair that you found out from someone else.' He moved towards Natalie, but this time, with the two of them facing me from the opposite side of the counter, it didn't feel quite so much like a battleground.

'I think we should go and speak to our solicitors about drawing up a new agreement,' I said.

'Really?' He stared at me.

'Yes. But that doesn't mean I'm backing down. It just means I'm prepared to open up discussions, okay?'

He nodded mutely. I slid off the stool and stood. 'I'd better be getting the kids back now.'

'Yes, course.'

We went through to the living room together. 'Come on, chop chop, you two,' Rob said, clapping his hands.

'But, Da-a-ad, there's still ten minutes left,' Olivia whined. Jacob jumped straight up and clung to my leg. I ruffled his hair.

'You've watched more than enough of that today, young lady, come on.'

Olivia reluctantly peeled herself off the sofa and stomped towards me, and I gave Rob a grateful smile. 'Thanks for being the bad guy for once,' I whispered.

He nodded and we followed them out to the hallway.

'Bye, you two, be good for Mummy, okay?'

'We're always good,' Olivia said.

'Whatever you say.'

Then we left and, as I drove us back to our ramshackle cottage, I felt lighter than I had for weeks. Sometimes, I decided, people could surprise you. And today, Natalie had certainly done that.

* * *

The kids both fell asleep on the drive home, and when we pulled into my driveway they were bleary-eyed and grouchy.

'I'm hungry,' Jacob whined as I bundled him out of the car.

'I'll make us a snack as soon as we get inside,' I promised.

I let us in and Buster bounced around our feet, barking loudly. I bent down to stroke him. 'Hello, boy,' I said, scooping him into my arms and standing up. The house felt tiny and cramped compared to Rob's, but as I looked round and recognised all the hard work I'd put into it so far I felt a sense of pride. I'd managed to make this place feel homely, and no one could take that away from me.

While the kids ate I asked them about spending more time with Daddy.

'I don't want to,' Jacob said. 'I like it here best.'

'I know, sweetheart, but Daddy likes seeing you.' He stuffed a piece of toast into his mouth and didn't reply. I turned to Olivia, who was just playing with her bagel and smearing jam round her plate.

'What about you, love?' I said. 'How would you feel if you spent a bit more time with Daddy and Natalie?'

She looked up at me, her eyes shining. 'I want to, Mummy.'

'Oh. Right.' Rob had said that Olivia wanted to be there more but I'd just assumed he was trying to make me feel bad. 'Well, that's good.'

'It's boring here, and there's more things to do at Daddy's,' she said. Her words opened up an icy cavern in my heart.

'We can get you more things here, just tell me what you need,' I said, reaching for her hand, but she shook her head and shrugged me off.

'My friends live there too. I never get to see them when I'm here. It's so *boring*.' She pushed her plate away. I felt tears prick at the corners of my eyes.

'We can invite your friends here—'

'No!' Olivia pushed her chair away from the table and stood, her eyes flashing.

'Sweetheart—' I reached for her again but she darted away.

'I don't want them to come here,' she said, her voice a sob. 'I hate it here. I hate sharing a room with Jacob and I hate you!' Then she turned and ran up the stairs and I listened until I heard her bedroom door slam. I took a long, shuddery breath, then turned back to Jacob, who was watching me with concern.

'Sorry, Jakey,' I said. 'She didn't mean it.'

He shrugged. 'I don't care. She can go to Daddy's and I can stay here in my own bedroom.'

'Oh, love,' I said, pulling him into a hug. With his warm body pressed against mine I felt as though I never wanted to let him go.

* * *

After much coaxing, Olivia eventually let me into their room, and I managed to convince her to go to sleep.

'Sorry, Mummy,' she said as she settled into bed, Buster curled up at her feet. Jacob was already snoring away in the other bed so both our voices were whispers. I leaned over and kissed her gently on the forehead.

'It's okay, sweetheart,' I said. I pushed her hair away from her face and held my palm against her cheek. Her eyes shone in the glow from the bedside lamp and she looked so young it broke my heart. 'I'm sorry you can't live with me and Daddy together.' She looked up at me and I could see from the look on her face that I'd hit the nail on the head.

'But why can't I? Why did we have to move here and leave Daddy and our house behind?'

'You know why, don't you, darling? Mummy and Daddy stopped loving each other, but it doesn't mean we stopped loving you.' I reached for her hand and threaded my fingers through hers and she didn't resist. 'But I'm sorry you hate it here.'

'I don't hate it here, Mummy,' she said. 'I didn't mean it.'

'It's okay, I understand. Of course you prefer your old house. You've got your own bedroom, all your old toys, and your friends live nearby. But living here is a new adventure, somewhere we can make new friends and get new toys. And this is where you live with Mummy now. Not many people can say they have two homes, can they?'

'Madeleine in my class has two houses,' she said. 'But they're both big houses.'

I nodded. 'I know. And I know this house isn't perfect but I'm trying to make it nice for you. For us. You, me and Jakey.'

'And Buster.'

'And Buster,' I agreed.

She didn't reply for a few minutes, then, in a small voice, she said, 'I do like my bedroom really, Mummy.'

'I know.'

'And I love Buster too.'

'Good.' I let go of her hand and pulled her duvet up to her

chin. 'Now try and go to sleep,' I said. I stood and switched off the lamp, then left her cuddling Buster, drifting off to a dream world where parents didn't get divorced, and everyone was happy. At least, that was where I hoped she was.

* * *

'I just feel so guilty all the time,' I said.

'Only good mothers feel guilty. It's the crap ones who couldn't care less about their kids you need to worry about.'

'Sorry, Catherine, that was insensitive,' I said.

'Don't be daft. I came to terms with the fact that I was the least important person in my mother's life a long time ago. It's you I'm worried about now.'

I'd rung Catherine as soon as the kids were asleep the previous night, and although I'd hoped she might have time for a quick chat, she'd insisted on coming over first thing this morning and bringing breakfast with her. I dabbed at croissant crumbs with my finger and stuck them in my mouth.

'Honestly, there's no need to worry. I was furious when I got to Rob's yesterday, but by the time I left I felt much calmer. Actually I think I was in a state of shock.'

'About Natalie?'

I nodded. 'I just never expected her to be on my side. Not in a million years.'

'People can be surprising sometimes.'

I nodded in agreement and peered through the open back door into the garden. Olivia and Jacob were playing catch on the tiny patch of patio, while Buster ran in circles, barking madly and trying to catch the ball in his mouth. Shrieks of laughter floated through the air and I smiled.

'They seem all right, don't they?'

Catherine followed my gaze. 'Are you kidding? They're two of the most well-adjusted children I've ever met.' She looked at me. 'You do know you're doing a great job, don't you?'

I shrugged. 'Sometimes.'

I looked out of the door again. The truth was there was more on my mind than just what had happened yesterday. I needed to talk to Catherine about her mother. I wanted to tell her that I'd tried to look for her, and to ask her whether she'd ever looked for her herself. But I didn't know how to bring it up.

'Charlie's coming round to help me with the garden today,' I said instead. I'd told her about Charlie's email suggesting he could help me a few days ago, but I hadn't mentioned he'd already been round. I wasn't sure why. But she was here now and he was due any minute so I didn't really have much choice.

She swivelled her head to look at me. 'Well, this is a turn-up for the books. Does this mean you've met him at last?'

I nodded. 'He came round a few days ago.'

'I see.' She smiled. 'And it's strictly business, is it?'

'Well, yes. Except – well, it's not for him because he's helping me as a favour.'

'Because you're friends.'

'That's right.'

She studied me for a moment. 'I know you're still getting over the divorce and are most definitely not interested in anyone else, but humour me. Is he handsome?'

I felt the redness creeping up my neck and bowed my head to hide it beneath my hair. Too late.

'He is, isn't he?' she said gleefully.

I looked up defiantly. 'All right, yes, he is handsome. But we're just friends. He's still married!'

'Ah yes, I forgot about that. The uninterested wife.'

'Charlie thinks she's having an affair.'

'Does he? And do you think he's right?'

I shrugged. 'I have no idea. I've never met her.' I shook my head. 'Anyway, this is all irrelevant. Charlie is married, I'm trying to help him sort out his marriage, and he's coming round to help me get my garden in order. End of story.'

'If you say so.' Catherine reached for another croissant, tore a corner off and stuck it in her mouth. She swallowed. 'So what time is he arriving?'

I checked the clock on the cooker. 'In about an hour.'

'Ooh, perfect. I'll get to meet him.'

'I...' I didn't know what to say. There was no reason for Catherine and Charlie – my two newest friends – not to meet. I just didn't want Charlie to put his foot in his mouth and say something about Lois before I'd had a chance to. The last thing I wanted was for Catherine to think we'd been discussing her past behind her back. I took a deep breath.

'The thing is, when Charlie was here the other day, we got talking. About Lois.'

'Ri-i-i-ight?' Catherine held her croissant in mid-air. A frown creased her forehead.

There was no point in beating about the bush. 'We were talking about the agony aunt column, and I told him about your mother leaving when you were nine and that you'd never seen her again.' The frown deepened. I hoped the words I uttered next wouldn't damage our fledgling friendship. 'We had a look for her.'

Catherine didn't speak for a moment, didn't move a muscle. I could still hear the kids' laughter outside, and Buster barking furiously, but inside the kitchen the air was silent and still. My pulse beat in my temple and I held my breath.

Finally, she looked me in the eye. 'And did you find her?'

I let the air out. 'No.' I cast my eyes down, not wanting to meet hers in case they showed me she was furious.

'Of course you didn't. My mother left forty-five years ago, and she didn't *want* to be found.' I'd never heard her voice sound quite like that before and I couldn't work out what it meant.

I lifted my eyes to look at her. 'I'm so sorry. We had no right.'

She studied her croissant, then she shook her head and gave a small smile. 'It's fine. Really.'

'It was none of our business though.'

'Well, no, it wasn't.' My heart sank. She *was* angry. But then a smile spread across her face. 'But it is fine.' She must have caught the look on my face then because she added, 'Truly.'

Relief flooded through me. Thank goodness for that. I didn't think I could bear to lose my friend almost as soon as I'd found her.

* * *

The day was gearing up to be a hot one, and Catherine and I were sitting in the garden drinking ice-cold freshly squeezed orange juice while the kids dug in the soil when Charlie arrived.

'Hello?' His voice made me jump and I turned to find him poking his head round the garden gate. I leapt up.

'Oh, hi,' I said as he stepped through the gate. I tried not to look at his torso in his snug T-shirt.

'Sorry, I knocked on the door but no one answered. Now I see why,' he said, smiling.

I shook his hand and turned to Catherine, who was watching us with interest.

'This is my friend Catherine,' I said as she stood to shake his hand. 'And this is Charlie.'

'Hello, Charlie,' Catherine said. 'It's lovely to meet you, I've heard so much about you.'

'Oh, have you?' he said as I flushed bright red.

'Yes, Beth was telling me all about your kind offer to help her with her garden. That's very generous of you.'

'Oh, right, yeah.' I realised as I saw the relief in his face that he'd thought Catherine had meant I'd told her all about the problems I'd been helping him with via *Dear Evelyn*. 'Well, it's a huge job. There's no way Beth could have done it all on her own in time to make use of the garden this summer.' Buster was sniffing round his feet and he bent down to pick him up. 'And we can't have this one with nowhere to run around for another year, can we?' He rubbed noses with him and Buster wagged his tail excitedly.

He put the dog back down. 'Right, I'll get started.'

'Give me a sec, I'll get changed and come and help out.'

'You don't have to if you've got other things to do.'

'No way, I'm not leaving you to work all on your own.' I turned to Catherine. 'Sorry, Catherine, do you mind if I abandon you?'

'Abandon me? I'm helping!'

'Are you sure? You didn't exactly sign up for this when you came over this morning.'

'Absolutely positive. I've got bugger-all else to do, and it'll be fun. Although actually...'

'What's up?'

'Would you mind if I brought Freddie over so he's not on his own all day? He gets ever so grumpy if I leave him for hours on end.'

'Freddie's her dachshund,' I explained to Charlie. 'Course not. He can keep Buster company.'

While I got changed and Catherine popped home, Charlie unloaded tools from his van. I watched him from my bedroom window as he heaved spades and shears and huge empty sacks into the garden. Sweat was already beginning to gather along his spine and soak through his T-shirt, and his legs were tanned in his shorts. I felt a flutter of attraction in my belly. I needed to stop this.

Half an hour later, Freddie and Buster were napping in the kitchen, the kids were watching TV in the living room, having been introduced to Charlie and Catherine, and Charlie and I were cutting back the plants at the outermost edge of the garden nearest the house.

'If we start here and work our way towards the back fence then we'll start to get an idea of the space,' Charlie explained. The discarded hacked-off branches were beginning to pile up, and after a while Charlie disappeared to get something else from his van. He returned with a huge contraption.

'What on earth is that?' I said, wiping the sweat off my brow. I was sure I must look a right state in my oldest T-shirt and too-short shorts with my hair frizzing up round my head in the heat.

'It's a chipper,' he said. 'Do you want me to show you how to use it?'

Behind Charlie I saw Catherine waggle her eyebrows but I ignored her. 'Sure.'

He moved behind me and I didn't dare look at Catherine as he gripped my hands and showed me how to feed a branch into the top of the chipper. The press of his chest against my back was quite distracting.

'And look, there it is,' he said triumphantly, pointing to a pile of sawdust underneath the machine. 'Now we just have to do all this lot as well.'

I glanced at the pile of branches. 'Shall I do this while you carry on cutting them back?' I asked.

'Why not? You seem to have mastered it already.'

Behind Charlie, Catherine's eyebrows rose so far up her forehead they almost disappeared into her hairline and I smothered a laugh that bubbled up in my throat. I'd have words with her later.

The next couple of hours were spent happily shredding branches and shoving piles of weeds into green sacks as the children ducked in and out of the house, restless. The gloves Charlie had given me to protect my arms were barely up to the job and my forearms were covered in scratches, but I didn't care. For the first time since I'd moved in, I was beginning to see the size of the garden. The space that was opening up was vast, bigger than I'd pictured, and it made the entire back of the house feel different. Less oppressive.

I stood with my hands on my hips and tried to imagine what it would be like when we'd finished. I closed my eyes and pictured a young Catherine on a climbing frame at the end, or Lois on her knees, tending to her flowers.

'Penny for your thoughts.' A voice behind me made me jump and I opened my eyes to find Catherine standing beside me.

'I was just thinking about you playing out here with Lois – your mum, I mean,' I said.

'Are you sure you weren't thinking about a handsome young gardener?'

I nudged her in the side. 'You've got to stop that,' I hissed as Charlie walked by a few feet in front of us with an armful of leaves.

'What?' she said, mock innocently.

I gave her what I hoped was a stern look. 'You know what. You know he's married and he's actually asked me for help to sort it out – which, by the way, you shouldn't know about so please don't mention anything.'

She nodded in agreement.

'But seriously. Please don't make him think I have a thing for him, or that I'm hoping for something more.'

'Because you don't, or because...?' She grinned and I rolled my eyes.

'Because it doesn't matter either way and I don't want to scare him off. I could do without losing any other friends.'

Catherine threaded her arm through mine and pulled me close. 'I'm sorry, Beth. I was only teasing, but I promise I'll stop, okay?'

'Okay. Thank you.'

She leaned in so her mouth was right by my ear and I felt her breath on my skin. 'But I wouldn't blame you if you did fancy him.'

'Catherine!' I laughed as I pushed her away. Charlie turned towards us. His skin glistened and he wiped the sweat from his head with his forearm. 'Any chance of a drink?'

''Course!' I said. 'Let's all take a break.'

He put down his clippers and walked towards us, squinting into the sun. 'You two look like you've been taking a break for a while,' he said, flopping down into a chair and stretching his legs out in front of him. A bead of sweat ran down the side of his face and his hair stuck to his skin.

'I'll have you know I've been working very hard indeed,' Catherine said. Charlie raised one eyebrow and she burst out laughing. 'Okay, okay, maybe I'm not cut out for this hard graft,' she said. 'But I do make a mean margarita. Fancy one?'

'How about we stick to soft drinks for now?' I said.

'It's a bit early for me too,' Charlie said, grinning.

'Oh, you're such spoilsports,' Catherine said. She turned and walked to the kitchen. 'Diet Cokes all round, then, for the light-weights,' she called over her shoulder, and flounced inside, letting the back door slam behind her.

I sat down next to Charlie. The sun felt hot on my head and I felt dizzy. Dehydration, no doubt. Plus Charlie's proximity, although we definitely weren't thinking about that. My shoulders burned from the physical work, and I could feel my skin prickling in the heat. Buster was slumped at my feet, tired out from all the running around he'd done earlier.

'Catherine seems lovely,' Charlie said, shielding his eyes from the sun.

'She is.'

'And you haven't known her long?'

I shook my head. 'A couple of weeks at most.' Was it really only such a short space of time?

'Wow, you seem really close.'

'I feel like we are,' I said. It was true, too. I felt as though Catherine had become an important part of my life quickly, far more than Suzie or any of my old life friends had been. Was it because I'd met her on my own terms, rather than through the kids, or through Rob?

'I told her about our search.'

His head whipped round. 'But we didn't find anything.'

'I know. But I thought she should know that I'd mentioned it to you.'

'And did she mind?'

Had she minded? I didn't know her well enough to be certain. 'I'm not sure,' I said. 'I don't think so.'

'What don't you think?' Catherine's voice was a sing-song behind me and I turned round to find her walking towards us with a tray full of drinks – plastic beakers filled to the brim with ice cubes and translucent brown liquid.

'Oh, nothing,' Charlie said guiltily.

I risked a glance at him, but Catherine must have noticed. She put the drinks down carefully and handed us one each. 'Were you talking about me, by any chance?'

I looked up at her to see whether she was cross, but I could only make out her silhouette outlined against the sun.

'Sort of,' I admitted.

'Yes, sorry,' Charlie said at the same time.

Catherine stood there for a few seconds and time seemed suspended in the moment. I held my breath. And then she pulled an upturned box towards her, put her drink on it then sat down and studied us both. A smile danced on her lips.

'Come on, then, tell me what you were saying about me. Was it that I'm getting in the way and won't leave Beth alone?' Her grin told me she was kidding.

'We were talking about Lois,' I said, holding her gaze.

She gave a small nod. 'I assumed so.' She looked at Charlie. 'So, what do you think about my terrible mother? Do you think she's worth looking for, forty-five years after she abandoned me?'

Charlie looked panicked, his eyes wide, his mouth hanging open. 'I—' He looked from me to Catherine and back again.

Catherine burst out laughing. 'I'm sorry, I'm only teasing you,' she said, picking up a glass. The ice clinked as she sipped from it. 'I'm mean, I apologise. It's just that Beth told me about the little search you two did and I've been thinking about it ever since.'

'Have you?' This was as much news to me as it was to Charlie, and I leaned forwards, elbows on my knees.

'Yep.' She took another sip and wiped her mouth with the back of her hand, leaving a trail of dirt across her cheek. 'I've spent years pretending I don't care what happened to her or why she left. I've built my whole life, my whole persona, around it, if I'm honest.' She swallowed. 'But do you know what? I'm in my mid-fifties now, I only have Freddie for company, and I have a brand-new friend – *two* brand-new friends, perhaps,' she corrected herself, raising her glass at Charlie, 'who seem determined to find out where my mother disappeared to and it feels like...' She trailed off. 'I don't know. I suppose what with you finding those letters that I hadn't even known existed, and resurrecting *Dear Evelyn Wright*, it feels as though the universe, fate, whatever, is trying to tell me something. And maybe I do want to know what happened to her, after all.'

Neither Charlie nor I said anything for a moment or two, me because I wasn't sure what to say. What right did we have to make her think about the past, something she had spent most of her life burying? She seemed happy enough. Why spoil it now?

'I'm sorry,' I said, and my voice sounded weak. 'It was wrong of us to poke our noses in.'

She looked at me, and tipped her head to one side. 'Didn't you hear what I just said?'

'Well, yes. But—'

She reached her hand out and placed it on my knee. Her palm felt warm against my skin. 'I'm *glad* you've poked your noses in, if that's what you want to call it. I want to find out what happened to my mum, and I want you to help me – if you will?'

'Of course,' I said. I looked over at Charlie in surprise; he was nodding.

'I can help too if you want me to?' he said, uncertainly.

Catherine held her hands out, palms up. 'I reckon I'm going to need all the help I can get.'

She stood and drained her glass. 'Right, I'm going to pull some more weeds out. Unless there's something else you want me to be getting on with, boss?'

Charlie shook his head and stood too. 'Nope, weed-pulling is perfect,' he said. 'We've made good progress this morning, and if we can get most of this gone by the end of the day, we'll be able to make a start on the rest of it.'

I dragged myself out of my chair too, and retied my hair in its ponytail. My hands were grimy but it was too late to worry about that now.

'Let's do it.'

* * *

It wasn't until later that evening, when the kids were in bed and the sun was going down, that the three of us got round to talking about Catherine's mother again – but it had been on my mind all day.

Catherine was making the promised margaritas in the kitchen after a quick dash home to shower and get supplies, and I could hear the clink of bottles and glass, the clatter of ice as she shook the cocktail shaker. I'd strung some solar fairy lights along the fence and they twinkled in the twilight.

'I can't tell you how grateful I am for your help today,' I said to Charlie as he stretched out his legs. His thigh grazed my knee and I shivered at the contact.

'Honestly, I've really enjoyed it,' he said. He wiped his hands on his shorts. He hadn't been home yet, and, although he insisted he had to go soon because Helen was expecting him, he showed no signs of actually moving. 'I love watching a garden transform from a wilderness to a stunning but functional space.' He shrugged. 'It's why I do this job, I guess.'

'Well, I appreciate it. But I don't expect you to do any more for me. You've given up half of your weekend and I'm sure I can take it from here.'

He gave a slow smile and I watched his eyes crinkle at the corners. 'To be honest, the way things are right now I'd rather be here with you than at home trying to avoid a slanging match.'

My heart fluttered. I'd assumed things were getting better between him and Helen – he hadn't really mentioned it in the last couple of emails, and I didn't like to pry.

'Oh, right,' I said, hoping he'd say more. I stared into the deepening blackness of the garden. Where just a few hours ago there had been towering weeds, the space was now bare and forlorn, like a teenager with an accidental buzzcut. The cracked green-house in the far right corner was just visible now, and the back fence peeked shyly through the remaining plants when they shifted in the breeze. I waited for Charlie to say something else. But before he had a chance, Catherine came clattering through the back door, preceded by the tinkle of ice against glass.

'Ta-da!' she said, placing the tray carefully on the upturned box we were using as a makeshift table. We'd dragged another dining chair out and she perched on that and handed us our glasses.

'These look amazing,' I said, holding mine up to the light.

'They're pretty potent,' she said, grinning. 'In for a penny, though, eh?'

She held her glass up. 'Here's to new friendship,' she said.

Charlie and I held our glasses up and clinked them against Catherine's. 'To new friends.'

'And detective work,' Catherine added, smiling as she took a sip. She grimaced. 'Christ, that is strong. Sorry, guys.'

I took a cautious sip and the rum warmed me from the inside out, the fiery taste leaving its mark on my windpipe. I tried not to cough. Charlie did the same – but he almost spluttered his all over his legs.

'Good grief, woman, how much alcohol is in that?'

Catherine shrugged. 'Enough to get us all disgustingly drunk.' She grinned. 'Cheers.'

We sat in peace and quiet for a few minutes, listening to the sounds of the neighbourhood fade into the evening.

Then Catherine said, 'So, have either of you got any ideas about where we should start looking for my mother?'

'I have, actually.'

I looked at Charlie, surprised. 'Have you?'

'Yep.' He leaned forward and cradled his drink in both hands, which looked huge round the delicate glass. I tore my gaze away.

'Are you going to tell us or do we have to guess?' Catherine said, but I could hear the smile in her voice.

'There are, what, a few hundred people in this village, right?' he said, looking at Catherine questioningly.

'Must be at least three or four hundred,' she agreed. 'Probably more.'

He took another sip of drink and I tried not to laugh at the grimace on his face. 'Right. And there are quite a few old people too. Over eighty.'

Again, Catherine nodded. I had no idea who lived here, and it made me realise how little I'd done to integrate into my new community.

'Well, someone must have known your mum, and there has to be someone out there who has an idea of where she went.'

Catherine fell silent for a moment, thinking.

'But surely someone would have told her, if they knew?' I said.

'Not necessarily,' Catherine replied. She stared down at the ground in front of her. 'I think lots of people round here were wary of my mum. She – she didn't really fit in. She had different ideas about right and wrong from most people, let's just say.'

'In what way?' I said. Ever since I'd found the letters Evelyn – Lois – had written, I'd been curious about what kind of woman she had been. I wondered how much Catherine could really remember about the mother who'd left her when she was just nine years old.

'It's hard to say. I was so young. But my grandmother made it perfectly clear that she disapproved of the way my mum lived her life.' She rubbed her hand across her face. 'I always wondered what she'd done that had been so terrible, but assumed it was just that she'd left. But now I wonder whether there might have been more to it after all.'

'Can you think of anyone who might have been friends with her back then, who might still live in the area?' Charlie said.

Catherine shook her head. 'No. But I suppose there's no harm in asking around, is there?' She turned to me. 'I'm not sure about knocking on people's doors out of the blue though. I was only young when Mum left, and I doubt anyone would want to talk to me even if they did know something. I don't suppose you've met anyone who might be able to help, have you?'

I was about to shake my head when something occurred to me. 'I have actually,' I said, telling her about Jackie and Tony, who I'd met a number of times since that first dog walk with Buster. 'They aren't old enough to have known Lois well, but they might know someone who had.'

'Got to be worth a go,' Catherine said. 'If you don't mind asking them, that is?'

'I'll speak to them next time I see them. I bump into them most days.'

'Thank you.' Catherine took another sip of her drink with a flinch. She seemed deep in thought.

'Actually, I've just thought of someone else,' she said eventually. Her glass was already half empty. I glanced down at mine and wondered how I was going to drink it all when every mouthful felt as if it were burning my insides.

'Who?' Charlie said.

'There's this woman, Annie Hargreaves. She lives across the other side of the village in one of those big old town houses towards the main road.' She smiled. 'We used to called her Old Park Woman when we were kids because she always sat on the bench next to the park, watching us playing after school. Some of the kids were scared of her, said she was a ghost who haunted the area, or that she was deciding which one of us to kidnap to take back to her house. I never corrected them, but I knew her a bit and knew she was perfectly harmless. She used to visit Mum and they'd natter for ages, and sometimes I'd hear them talking about her daughter, who'd died a few years before.' She swallowed. 'I got the impression Annie only watched us playing because she missed her little girl so much.' She shook her head. 'Anyway. She wasn't really old, about the same age as my mum, more or less, and last I heard she was still around. Still in the same house too as far as I know.'

I looked down at my feet, stretched out in front of me. The nail polish was chipped in my flip-flops, and they looked tiny next to Charlie's huge work boots.

'Do you think she'd be up for a visit, if she's still here?'

Catherine shrugged. 'I mean, Mum would be – what? Ninety-one now?' She drained her glass and put it back on the tray carefully. 'So even if Annie is still alive she might not have the greatest memory. But it's worth a go.'

'Are you absolutely sure about this?' I said. 'You've managed to survive for the last forty-five years not knowing where your mum is. I don't want you to feel I've pressured you into anything.'

She shook her head. 'I don't. Like I said before, I feel like it was a sign, you finding those magazines and me meeting you when I did.' She pursed her lips and looked at me and Charlie in turn. 'Let's try and find out what happened to my mum.'

13

MISSING MOTHER

I am forty years old and was brought up by my father. I've always believed that my mother died when I was a baby, but I recently discovered that she abandoned me. I have always blamed myself for her death, but now I blame myself for her leaving instead. It has made it hard for me to commit to anyone, and I have never had children of my own. Nobody in my family will talk about this but I can't stop thinking about whether she is still out there.

I hope it is clear to you that the way your mother behaved has absolutely nothing to do with anything you may or may not have done. However I do understand that discovering something like this can be traumatic. Have you tried speaking to your father about it? As for looking for your mother, please know that it is notoriously difficult to find someone, especially as your mother may well have changed her name. Since you are now forty years old, perhaps it is best to try and put your mother out of your mind and move on with your life. If you really do feel you would like to try and find her then please write to me privately and I will put you in touch with an organisation which may be able to help.

Catherine stopped a few yards short of the house, her hand resting on the crumbling brick wall. She'd gone pale.

'Are you sure this is a good idea?' I'd never heard her voice sound so uncertain before and I took a step back to join her.

'We don't have to do this if you don't want to.'

She didn't reply for a while, just stood staring at the house. 'She might not even be in. She probably isn't actually.' She took a deep breath and rubbed her hand across her face. 'Oh God, what am I doing?'

'Shall we go? We can always come back another day and—'

'No.' She pulled herself up, smoothed down her T-shirt. 'No, let's do this right now, before I change my mind again.'

Catherine and I had come to see whether Lois's friend Annie was still here and, if she was, whether she would talk to us about Catherine's mother. Charlie had offered to come too but in the end he'd agreed it was best for him to stay and carry on with my garden, and keep an eye on Olivia, Jacob and the dogs.

'It's perfectly normal to have a wobble, you know,' I said as we pushed the rickety old gate open. It squeaked on its hinges like something out of a horror movie. I could understand why Catherine and her friends had thought Annie was some sort of ghost when they were younger, especially if her house had looked like this back then.

'For most people maybe,' Catherine said.

I looked at her, eyebrows raised. 'But not for you?'

Catherine shook her head. 'Nope.' She smiled. 'I know it probably sounds daft, but with most things in my life I'm pretty black and white. I don't want to be with my husband any more, so I tell him to leave. I don't want to find out about my mother, so I don't. I want to be your friend so I make sure it happens.' She shrugged. 'It's the way I've always been.'

I reached over and touched her shoulder. 'Nerves are not a sign of weakness, you know.'

She gave a small nod but didn't reply, and after a couple of seconds we both took the last few steps up to the front door. I held my hand up to pull up the knocker. 'Ready?'

She raised her eyebrows at me again. 'Of course I am.'

I laughed, lifted the metal knocker and rapped it gently a couple of times.

At first there was nothing.

'How long should we wait?' I hissed under my breath.

'I don't know.' Catherine moved away and I turned to find her peering through the front bay window.

'Can you see anything?'

She shook her head. 'It's hard to tell through the net curtains, but I can't see any movement.'

'Shall I knock again?'

'Yes. Try a bit louder, in case she's deaf.'

I banged the knocker louder this time, but just as I let it drop for the second time, the door inched inwards and I almost fell into the space left behind.

'Oh!' I said, righting myself.

'You don't have to hammer quite so loudly,' said a small, wispy voice. I looked down to find possibly the smallest woman I had ever seen in my life standing in front of me. Her hair was a shock of white round her head, like feathers, and she was dressed neatly in a primrose-yellow cardigan buttoned all the way to the top, and cream trousers, with navy-blue slippers on her feet. She might have been tiny but her eyes were wide and bright, and they were staring at me, waiting for me to introduce myself.

'Hello,' I said. I found myself almost crouching down to speak to her, as I did with the kids. 'My name is Beth and I live on the other side of the village.'

'In Laburnum Cottage.' It wasn't a question but I nodded anyway. How did this woman know where I lived?

'Village grapevine,' Catherine whispered behind me. I turned to let her step forward, but before I could introduce her Annie's face broke into a smile, revealing a line of incongruously straight white teeth behind her pale lips.

'As I live and breathe, it's little Kitty!' she said. She clasped her hands together under her chin and her eyes glistened.

'It is, hello, Mrs Hargreaves,' Catherine said, stepping forward and holding her hand out. But rather than shaking it, Annie clasped her own birdlike hands round it and held it to her as if it were a precious gift.

'Oh shush, enough of the Mrs Hargreaves, it's Annie now,' she said, still clutching Catherine's hand. 'Gosh, it's been a long time since I saw you. I thought you moved away years ago.'

'Ah yes, well, I did. But I came back. I live in Bourwell now.'

'Well, well, well,' Annie said. Then, seeming to notice where we were, she let go of Catherine's hand. 'Come in, come in,' she said, ushering us into the hallway. 'You can't be standing on ceremony on the doorstep all day.'

We bustled indoors and slipped off our shoes as Annie waited in the doorway of the adjoining room. Through the open door I could see a dim room, the light muffled from being filtered through the heavy net curtains.

We followed Annie along the hallway into a back room next to the kitchen. This room was light and airy, and a breeze slipped through the open window, making the chrysanthemums on the table dance.

'I was just having a cup of tea in here,' Annie said, turning to face us. 'Please won't you sit down and I'll make you one too.'

Catherine clearly felt as uncomfortable as I did about a ninety-odd-year-old woman waiting on her, because she remained standing. 'Won't you let me make it?' she said.

Annie eyed her for a moment, as if trying to work out if she was being patronising or kind. 'I may be ancient, but I'm more than capable of making a cup of tea for guests,' she said. Then, before we could argue, she disappeared into the kitchen.

Catherine and I sat down. I could hear the clatter of cups from the other room and had to resist the temptation to rush through and help. Instead I gazed out of the window at the garden. It was blooming, roses swaying in the breeze, honeysuckle climbing the neighbouring fence, and I wondered how Annie kept it looking so neat and tidy on her own.

'I've never been in here before,' Catherine whispered. 'It's not what I expected.'

'What did you expect?'

She shrugged. 'I always pictured it dark and dingy and covered in cobwebs.' She smiled. 'Although I haven't given it much more thought than that since I was about twelve years old.'

'It's nice.' I glanced towards the door. 'I can't believe she lives here all alone. She looks so...'

'Frail.'

I nodded. 'Like she's about to snap in two.'

Annie came back into the room, clutching a teapot in one hand. She steadied herself on the door handle and the pot shook in her hand. 'Would you mind ever so much fetching the cups and milk for me please?' she said. 'They're just on the side there.'

Catherine leapt up before I had the chance and returned with a tray containing a jug of milk, a plate with slices of fruit cake, and three cups with saucers. I recognised the pattern from my parents' house, where the tea set was always locked away in a cabinet 'for best', as if they were waiting for the Queen to come for tea. Catherine placed the tray carefully on the coffee table and took the pot from Annie. We all sat.

Annie looked from me to Catherine and back again. Her hands lay neatly in her lap. 'So, what can I do for you?' She blinked slowly. 'I assume you haven't just come here to check up on me after all this time.'

Catherine flushed pink and rubbed her arm, a habit I noticed she had when she was nervous.

'It is really lovely to see you, Mrs – Annie,' she said, flashing her a smile. 'But you're absolutely right of course. We do have something we want to ask you.'

Annie waited patiently. Catherine continued, shuffling forward slightly on the sofa.

'I—' She stopped, swallowed, and glanced at me. I gave her what I hoped was an encouraging nod. 'The thing is, I wondered whether you ever heard from my mum, after she left.'

If Annie was surprised by the question she didn't show it. We waited while she reached forward, lifted the lid from the teapot, gave the contents a stir, then tapped the spoon on the edge of the pot and replaced the lid.

'Has something happened?' she asked, unexpectedly. 'Has she died?'

'Oh, I...' Catherine faltered. 'I... I don't know.' She looked at me in bewilderment. Annie look unperturbed.

'Everyone seems to have died,' Annie continued. She fixed us both with a watery stare. 'I think I'm the only one left.'

'I'm sorry,' I said, although I wasn't quite sure what I was apologising for.

Annie gestured at the tray. 'Please pour yourself some tea and help yourself to a slice of cake. It's not often I get visitors and it is nice to make an occasion of it.'

Catherine half stood and poured three cups of tea, adding milk to each and handing them round. Annie's shook so much in her grip that she placed it on the little side table next to her. I reached for a slice of cake and took a bite. Which was why I couldn't reply to Annie's next question.

'Well, if she hasn't died, then what has happened?' she said.

'We don't know whether anything has actually happened,' Catherine said. 'It's more that – well, Beth found some things in the house that belonged to Mum, and it's got me thinking. Wondering about what happened to her.'

Annie's gaze felt stern as she processed what Catherine had told her. 'What was it you found of Lois's?' she asked, turning to me.

'Some letters. And magazines,' I said.

'Ah, she kept them, did she?' She smiled. 'I assume you mean the agony aunt letters she spent so many years replying to?'

I nodded.

'I wondered whether there was ever any record of them. She did so enjoy writing those.' She laced her fingers beneath her chin. 'She loved helping people, you know. She was ever so kind.'

'Not to her daughter,' Catherine muttered beside me. Annie didn't appear to hear her or, if she did, she chose to ignore it. 'The thing is,' Catherine said, louder this time, 'finding the letters and seeing how she helped other people, it's got me thinking about her, and wondering...' Her voice wobbled slightly and she took a deep breath. 'The thing is, Granny never talked about Mum after she left. If I asked about her she refused to answer me, so in the end I stopped asking. And I thought that was all right. I really did.' She stopped.

'Only now you've found these letters and you're thinking about her all over again?' Annie said.

'More or less,' Catherine admitted.

Annie reached for a piece of cake and placed the plate on her lap. Her hands fluttered above it but she didn't eat any. She was so delicate I couldn't imagine her eating anything that substantial; she looked as if she might blow away if the breeze through the window picked up. Catherine and I were both waiting for her to say something.

'I can't tell you for sure what happened to her,' she said. 'When she walked out that day she must have been determined not to have been found because she didn't leave a forwarding address, or tell anyone where she was going. But I've always had my suspicions.'

We waited, both of us watching as Annie broke off a tiny corner of cake, popped it in her mouth and chewed it slowly. If the suspense was almost killing me, I dreaded to think what it was doing to Catherine. Annie swallowed, took a sip of tea, then turned back to face us.

'For months before she left I had my worries about Lois's state of mind.' She licked her lips. 'She told me she'd met someone, but that they didn't live in the village. She seemed—' She stopped, seemingly trying to pluck the right word from her head. 'Giddy,' she said, satisfied.

'Giddy?'

Annie nodded. 'Of course, it was a long time ago now and I haven't thought about it for years, but when I think about Lois back then, I remember her as giddy, and over-excitable.' She coughed, a rattly sound. 'I'd never seen her like that before. She'd always been so... sensible. Had her head screwed on.'

'So what else did she say, about this man she'd met? Did she tell you anything more about him? Where he lived, or... or... I don't know. Anything?'

Annie screwed her face up. 'I don't think she told me anything else. If she had I feel sure I would have remembered.'

'And you never heard from her again?'

'Not for a long time.'

Beside me, Catherine sat up, suddenly alert. 'But then you did?'

Annie nodded slowly, as though the memory was just coming back to her. 'Now I come to think of it I think she might have written to me, once.' She shook her head. 'But it would have been years later. Maybe even ten years later, when it was all so far in the past I'd almost stopped worrying about her.'

Catherine was rubbing her arm again, her nails scratching across her skin. I could sense the excitement coming off her in waves.

'Did – was there an address on this letter?' She sounded breathless.

'An address?' Annie frowned again. 'Gosh, I don't think there was. I—' She stopped, and for a minute I thought she'd forgotten we were there. Then she stood and shuffled across the room to the dark wood dresser and pulled open a drawer. After a few seconds of rummaging she closed it and walked carefully back to her seat, empty-handed, and lowered herself back to sitting.

'I'm sorry, I had an idea that it might have been stuck some-where at the bottom of that drawer, but it doesn't appear to be.'

'Oh.' Catherine sounded dejected, her voice subdued.

'I'm sure I must have it somewhere though. I don't get many letters so I do tend to keep them.' She gave a small smile. 'My family think I'm mad, tell me my memories are all in here—' she tapped the side of her head '—but there's something nice about holding a memory in your hand, having something concrete to look at. It stirs up all sorts of other recollections that would other-wise be long gone.' She looked from me to Catherine. 'Don't you agree?'

I nodded. 'That's probably why Lois kept the agony aunt letters, so she didn't forget.'

'Except she walked out and left them all behind with every-thing else in her life and didn't give them another thought,' Catherine said. Her voice was bitter.

Annie leaned forward then, her hands clasped. 'She never forgot you, dear,' she said.

'She walked out and never contacted me again,' Catherine said.

Annie shook her head, keen for us to understand. 'No, no. She didn't forget you. She loved you. She—' She looked down at her hands. She seemed to be shaking. 'You were her world. But she never thought she was good enough to be your mum.'

Catherine frowned. 'Not good enough? What on earth does that mean?'

Annie shrugged. 'She could never quite articulate it. But what was never in any doubt was that she loved you and wanted you to have the best life.'

Catherine didn't speak for a moment. Her eyes were glazed, locked on a memory, an image, far in the past. Then as quickly as it had clouded, her face cleared.

'Well, thank you,' she said, standing abruptly. I stood too. Annie watched her from her position in the chair. 'I won't keep you any longer. Thank you for the tea and cake.'

'I'm sorry I couldn't be of any more use,' Annie said, her voice unsteady. 'But when my grandson comes over in a few days' time I'll ask him to have a look in the loft. If I kept Lois's letter, that's where it will be.'

'Really, it doesn't matter.'

Annie stood and looked up at Catherine. She was only half her height but her voice was strong this time. Determined. 'It does matter and I will do my best to find it. And when I do maybe it will help you find out what happened to your mother.' She held out her hand and laid it on Catherine's arm. 'It seems as though it's long overdue.'

Catherine didn't reply for a moment and the room held its breath. Then she gave a small nod. 'Thank you, Annie.'

We moved towards the door together. As Catherine and I stepped out into the bright sunshine Annie spoke again.

'Don't forget to leave me your telephone number.'

Catherine swivelled round, confused. 'Number?'

'So I can let you know if I find your mother's letter.'

'Oh yes. Right.' Catherine rummaged in her bag. 'Have you got a piece of paper?'

'Just a minute.' Annie disappeared back inside the house and we waited so long I was beginning to think something had happened to her. But just as I was considering going inside to look, she emerged from the shadows of the living room.

'Here, why don't you put both your numbers on here for me?' she said, handing a piece of paper and a ballpoint pen to Catherine, who wrote her number neatly then handed me the pen to do the same.

'I promise I'll call you the minute I have any news,' Annie said, her eyes shining brightly. 'And you'll come around for tea again, won't you? Both of you.'

I smiled. 'Thank you, Annie. That would be lovely.'

* * *

Catherine didn't speak for a good two minutes after leaving Annie's house, and I let her stew as we walked along in the warm early summer sunshine. The village was busier than usual, tourists arriving to make the most of the local walks and nearby stately home blocking the roads. When we reached the end of the high street, Catherine stopped.

'Well, that was a waste of time.'

'Really?'

'Of course it was. There's no way Annie is going to have Mum's letter still. Who keeps things that long even if they mean something to you? Which this clearly didn't as she didn't say whether she'd even replied.' She puffed out her cheeks. 'I don't know why I got my hopes up.'

'I disagree. I think Annie might just come up trumps.' Catherine didn't say anything else so I ploughed on. 'But we don't have to wait for that if you don't want.'

'What do you mean?' Catherine started walking again and I hurried to keep up with her long strides.

'Well, I'm sure with a bit more digging we can find out where your mother lived – or still lives. It's pretty hard for people to just disappear off the face of the earth.'

Catherine shook her head. 'Not back then. There wasn't the same digital trail. If Mum hadn't wanted to be found, she could easily have changed her name and lived anonymously.'

'But why would she have done that?'

She stopped so abruptly I almost tripped over her. 'God, I don't know, Beth. I didn't know her at all, not really. I've got no chance of second-guessing why she'd have done anything, especially if one of her closest friends didn't even have a clue that she was about to vanish.' She rubbed her hands over her face. 'I'm sorry. I just—'

'I know. It's brought back memories.' I sighed. 'I'm really sorry, this is all my fault.'

'How on earth is it your fault?'

'I was the one who found those letters and told you about them.' I flung my hands up. 'I was the one who stirred up the hornet's nest by restarting *Dear Evelyn* in the first place. I should have just minded my own business.'

'Don't be daft. It was my decision to speak to Annie. And if it hadn't been for those letters then we might never have become such firm friends.' She laid her hand on my arm. 'I'm so grateful I've met you.'

I felt tears prick my eyes. 'I am too.' We stood there, letting the moment pass between us, until it was rudely broken by a woman bashing her carrier bags into the backs of my legs as she bustled past.

'No, don't worry, it's fine,' I said sarcastically as she hurried off without a backward glance. Catherine grinned and hooked her arm through mine.

'Come on, let's go and buy something nice to take home for lunch. I'm starving.'

* * *

It was lunchtime by the time we arrived back at the cottage, and Buster and Freddie were excited to see us. The kids were nowhere to be seen.

'Hello, boy,' I said, scooping Buster up and kissing him on the nose. He settled into my chest and sniffed my ear.

'Good timing, I was about to stop for a bite to eat,' Charlie said, popping his head out from behind a hedge on the far side of the garden. I felt a flush of pleasure to find him still here. 'The children are watching TV, sorry.'

'Don't be daft, it's fine. Oh, you've worked wonders!' I said as I made it further into the garden. With the jungle cleared the sky felt enormous, stretching over our heads like a canvas painted with streaks of yellow, blue and hazy white. There were only a couple of stubborn hedges left at the edges of the garden, which Charlie was working on now, and a mini digger stood in the middle of what had once been a lawn.

'I was about to start digging, but I'm ravenous,' he said. As he approached I noticed he'd caught the sun, the skin on his neck pink, his forearms tanned.

'We bought some supplies,' I said, holding up the carrier bag of sourdough bread, tomatoes and a selection of cheeses we'd picked up at the delicatessen.

'Perfect, let me just clean up.'

He tugged the grubby T-shirt he was wearing over his head, exposing his toned stomach and chest, and my face flushed. I averted my eyes to find Catherine grinning at me.

Flustered, I scurried into the kitchen and tried not to stare out of the window where I could see Charlie pulling on a fresh T-shirt that he'd pulled out of his rucksack. *For goodness' sake, Beth, stop ogling him!*

I busied myself with slicing bread and arranging the cheeses and salad onto plates and tried to ignore the fact that my mind kept picturing Charlie's toned torso. I was just digging out some knives from the drawer when Catherine came into the room.

'Well, that's cheered me right up,' she said, grinning.

'What has?' My voice came out higher than intended and I cleared my throat as I laid the cutlery carefully on the table.

'Oh, come on, Beth, you're not blind – and neither am I. I saw the way you blushed when Charlie took his top off just now. And no wonder.'

'Shhhh,' I said, glancing into the garden through the open door.

'Oh, don't worry, he can't hear me. But don't deny it. You think he's hot.'

'I do not!'

She folded her arms across her chest and gave me a look. I tried to ignore her but it was impossible. 'Oh, all right, then, I noticed. How could I not?'

'I know, right?' She opened the cupboard and pulled out glasses and placed them by each setting. 'You know it's not a crime to look, don't you?'

'He's married, Catherine,' I hissed.

'So?'

'So – I'm meant to be helping him sort things out with his wife, not develop a crush on him—'

'Ah, so you *have* got a crush on him?'

'I—' I started, but thankfully was interrupted by Buster racing into the kitchen barking his head off, followed swiftly by Freddie and, seconds later, Charlie. I hoped he hadn't heard any of our conversation.

'Oh, wow, this looks great, thanks,' he said. 'Where shall I sit?'

'Anywhere,' I said, placing a carton of orange juice on the table. 'And it's the least I can do when you've been slaving away in my garden all morning.'

'I've enjoyed it.' He tipped juice into the three glasses. I took a sandwich through to Olivia and Jacob, glad to get away from the kitchen to compose myself for a minute. When I got back both of them had already sat down and the only spare seat was next to Charlie. I lowered myself into it, trying to avoid Catherine's eye.

'I was hoping to get the lawn area dug over today, and then hopefully I can pop over and lay the turf during the week,' Charlie said, taking a sip of juice. 'Would it be okay to come over again? You haven't got plans, have you?'

'Oh, no, I haven't got any plans...' I said, trailing off. God, did I want to sound like more of a loser?

'That's very kind, isn't it, Beth?' Catherine said. Her eyes sparkled with mischief. I tried to kick her underneath the table but missed and smacked my toe against the chair leg. I winced. Catherine looked as though she were about to burst.

'Very kind, thank you,' I said. 'But I don't want you to feel you have to. Surely you'll be exhausted, working all day and then coming to do this?'

Charlie had a mouthful of food and I waited while he swallowed. 'Honestly. It's a pleasure. I...' He hesitated, and looked down at his plate. 'I'd rather be here than at home right now, to be honest.'

'Oh...' I didn't know what to say. I wasn't sure whether he'd want to talk about it in front of Catherine – although he was the one who'd brought it up. 'Has something happened?'

His chunk of bread and butter hovered in mid-air, then he dropped it back to his plate with an enormous sigh.

'Sorry, I probably shouldn't have said anything.' He hesitated, casting a glance at Catherine.

'Don't mind me, I'm a disaster around relationships so no judgement here,' she said, taking a huge bite of cheese. She swallowed. 'Although I'm happy to disappear for a bit if you two want to...' She indicated between us with a pointed finger.

'No, it's fine. We don't need to talk about anything, it's my fault. Sorry,' Charlie added, and my heart sank. I'd been hoping he'd open up to me, that talking about his problems would help him and me.

'Seriously, she gives great advice,' Catherine said.

Charlie gave me a look I couldn't read, then smiled sadly. 'She does. But now isn't the time to bore you all with it. I'll shut up.'

We sat in silence, chewing on our lunch for a few minutes. Then Charlie piped up, 'Oh, how stupid of me, how did it go today, with – Annie, wasn't it, your mum's friend?'

'Yes, it was.' Catherine wiped crumbs from her mouth and

stared down at her plate, her shoulders dropped. 'It was okay. It was – it was good to see her but...' She shrugged. 'I don't think she'll be able to help.'

I turned to Charlie. 'Annie told us she always thought Lois had disappeared because she'd met someone, but that she never said who,' I explained. 'And she remembered she'd had a letter from her once, years later, that we, Catherine and I, hoped might have had an address on it. But she couldn't find it.'

'Well, that doesn't sound like nothing,' Charlie said.

'That's what I told her,' I said, turning to Catherine in triumph. But she merely shrugged.

'Maybe. But what are the chances of her actually finding the letter?'

'You never know. And anyway, didn't we say we could make a start looking for your mum without that? I bet we can find something.'

'But you've already tried.'

'Hardly. We only did a very quick search. I'm sure there's loads more we could find if we put our minds to it.' I glanced at Charlie, who nodded in agreement.

Catherine pushed crumbs around her plate with her finger as Freddie sniffed round her feet, searching for morsels to eat. I leant down and fed him a tiny piece of cheese, which made Buster come racing over to see what he was missing out on.

'I don't know.' She ran her fingers through her hair, leaving it sticking up wildly in places, then looked up at me. 'I think I've changed my mind.'

I didn't reply. I didn't want to talk her into doing something she didn't want to do. After all, as she'd said, she'd got through the last forty-five years without knowing where her mother had disappeared to. What had changed now?

Except I had a feeling this was something she needed to do.

Something in the way she talked about her mother's disappearance told me she'd never really dealt with it, and that she blamed herself for her mother upping and leaving. I felt it would do her good to at least find out what had happened, if only to prove to her once and for all that it wasn't her fault. That sometimes, people were simply selfish.

But I had no idea how to convince her. I wish I knew what Evelyn Wright would have suggested.

* * *

'Mummy, can I help?' Olivia was bouncing round on a giant orange space hopper, her hair flying out around her.

'This isn't really children's work, love,' I said, pushing my hair back from my sweaty face. My neck burned beneath the afternoon sun.

'But I'm bo-o-o-ored.' She bounced precariously close to where Charlie was digging the earth and my stomach dropped. The engine cut suddenly and Charlie clambered down from the seat.

'Tell you what, why don't you do a bit of this for me?' he said, pointing to the mini digger that had arrived while we were at Annie's.

Olivia gasped and looked at me, her eyes wide. 'Can I, Mummy?' she said, breathless.

I looked at Charlie. 'Do you think it's safe?'

'Perfectly,' he said, smiling. 'I'll be up there with her.'

I looked over at where the digger sat idle in the middle of the garden. 'Go on, then, what's the harm?'

'I want to try too!' Jacob tugged at my leg.

'I think you're a bit small, sweetheart,' I said, bending down and hoisting him into my arms.

'It's not fair.' He squirmed away from me, but I held onto him.

'I know, darling, but sometimes you have to wait until you're a big boy to do things.'

I glanced towards the digger, where Olivia was balanced on Charlie's knee. He was showing her how to move the machine, and how to lift the arm up and down.

'Tell you what, why don't we do our own digging, with this?' I pointed at a spade that was lying on the ground, but Jacob shook his head.

'No, I want to do that.' He jabbed his finger at the digger. Charlie noticed, cut the engine, and beckoned us over.

'Right, little man, why don't you be in charge and tell us where to dig?'

Jacob looked at me, his face shining with excitement.

'Can I?'

'Course you can, love,' I said, setting him down on the ground. 'But be careful and stay away from this scoop thing, okay?'

'Okay, Mummy,' he said.

Thank you, I mouthed to Charlie as Jacob shouted, 'Dig here!' Charlie fired the engine back up and winked at me. Why did my knees feel weak?

* * *

'God, I'm knackered.' Catherine lay flat on her back on the living room floor, arms stretched out like a starfish. 'There are muscles aching in my body that I didn't even know existed.'

'Me too.' I rolled my shoulders and listened to the satisfying crunch.

Catherine sat up and crossed her legs. 'Honestly, I don't know how Charlie does it all day every day.'

'Me neither.' I squinted at the screen and clicked on my inbox. There were thirty-three new messages! I opened the first one and started skim-reading it. It was from a man called Alan, who was worried his wife had stopped fancying him and was looking for some ideas to spice things up a bit. I closed it and clicked on the next one.

'Beth! Are you even listening to me?'

'What?' I looked up in confusion to find Catherine frowning at me. 'Oh no, sorry, I was reading this.'

'What, so you didn't even hear me teasing you?'

'About what?'

'About fancying Charlie!'

'No!'

'Gah, what a waste,' she said, throwing herself back down onto the rug.

I shook my head. 'Honestly, what are we, twelve?'

She peered at me through one half-open eye. 'So are you saying you don't fancy the delectable Charlie, even after he's spent the entire day parading round with his washboard stomach and bulging biceps on display, and being a hero by helping out with your children earlier?'

I tried not to smile at the thought of any of that, and put on a stern face. 'No, I do not fancy Charlie.' I crossed my arms. 'I'm not sure why you're so obsessed with the idea.'

She grinned wickedly. 'Well, as you know, I've been around the block a few times, and I've seen the way you two look at each other. And quite frankly if Charlie really still believes he wants to make it up with Helen, or whatever she's called, then I'd say he's kidding himself.'

I shook my head. 'You've got it wrong. We don't look at each other like anything.'

'Uh huh.'

'Catherine! We don't!' I could feel myself getting irritated, and I didn't want to lose my temper.

'Okay, okay, if you say so.' She held up her hands in surrender. 'But just one more thing. There are not many men who would give up their entire weekend to help someone out the way Charlie is, if they weren't interested in them – or spend so much time being kind to their children. Believe me.'

I rolled my eyes.

'Right. I'll leave it now. Promise.'

'Good.'

'For now.'

I picked a cushion up from beside me and threw it across the room at her. It landed on her face and she sat up with a shout.

'You little shit!' she cried, chucking it back in my direction. I caught it before it did any damage.

'That'll teach you.'

'I doubt it.' She scooted over to where I was sitting, leaning her back against the sofa and peering at my screen. 'Anyway, what's got you all distracted over here?'

I pointed at the screen. 'I've got thirty-three new emails!'

'Wait, what?' She pulled herself up to sit beside me so she could see the screen better. 'Are they all *Dear Evelyn* letters, or have you already got dozens of junk emails demanding you transfer thousands of pounds into a Chinese bank account?'

I ran my eyes down the list. 'At first glance they all seem to be genuine,' I said.

She craned her neck to have a look. 'Ooh, I wonder why they're all finding you all of a sudden?'

I shrugged. 'I put a few more posts up on Facebook the other day, just locally, and have done a few Instagram posts too. I wasn't sure it would do much but it must be that.'

'That's brilliant.'

'I dunno. It's a bit overwhelming, to be honest.'

She twisted round to look at me. 'What do you mean?'

'I just—' I sighed. 'I'm starting to wonder whether this was such a good idea after all. I mean, look...' I waved my hand at my laptop. 'There are all these people out there looking for my help and I don't know anything. And even if I was qualified to help them, how on earth can I keep up with everyone at this rate? It seems to be taking on a life of its own and I'm worried I'm going to just let people down.' I slumped back into the sofa and closed my eyes. I felt Catherine take the laptop from my knee. She went quiet for a few seconds and I opened my eyes again to see what she was doing. The light from the screen lit up her face.

'I'll help you,' she said, eventually.

I snapped my eyes open. 'What?'

'I'll help you answer the questions. If you like.'

'But—'

'It's fine if you don't want me to.' She smiled.

'No, I do! I just—' I rubbed my eyes, which felt scratchy after being outside all day. 'I'd love that.'

'Honestly?'

'Honestly. I mean, it *was* your mum's problem page that started all of this in the first place.' I reached down the side of the sofa and dragged out Evelyn Wright's box of letters. 'Speaking of which, do you still want her help with it?'

She looked at the next question on the list, and grinned. 'Hell, yes, we're going to need it!'

* * *

In the end, we agreed to divide and conquer – we split the questions between us and answered them one by one, before swapping and checking the other's answers. From time to time we referred to Evelyn Wright's responses for inspiration, but, otherwise, we worked methodically through them until there were just five left.

'These are the only ones from men, aren't they?' Catherine said, peering at the screen.

'Yep. I always leave them until last because I'm never quite sure if I'm answering them right and want to give myself time to think it through. Lois usually has something up her sleeve though.' I reached for the pile again but she stopped me.

'Hang on. There might be a better way.'

'What do you mean?'

A slow smile spread across Catherine's face and I began to feel suspicious. 'Catherine?' I asked, a warning.

'Why don't we ask Charlie to help us?'

'Charlie?'

'Yes!'

'We can't ask him to do that!'

'Why ever not? I think he'd love it. Especially if it meant helping you out.' She shot me a cheeky grin.

'Oi, you promised!'

'Sorry, sorry.' She took a sip of the beer beside her, which must have been warm by now. 'But I'm serious. Think about it. He already knows about the problem page because it's helped him, and he seems like he's got his head screwed on. He'd know better than us how men think, right?'

'I guess so. But – I was meant to be helping him. It feels wrong to ask him to help other people.'

'You can still help him if you want. But I reckon he'd be up for it, don't you?'

'I don't know.' Although Charlie and Catherine were the people I spent most of my time with – apart from the kids – and Charlie had opened his heart up to me before we'd even met, the fact was we still hardly knew each other and I wasn't sure whether I could second-guess what either of them were thinking.

'Do you want me to ask him?'

I nodded. 'Okay, then. But make sure he knows it's your idea and not mine, all right?'

Catherine grinned and held her beer bottle up. 'Deal.'

14

JUST GOOD FRIENDS

I fear I am falling in love with a friend. I am single, but he is still married, although I know his marriage is unhappy. Should I end the friendship? How can I learn to be happy just being friends with him?

You clearly know that you must remain nothing more than friends with this man. Whether he is happy or not in his marriage is nothing to do with you. Learning to see this man as just a friend will be tricky, so I would suggest spending some time away from him to see whether you can rid yourself of your infatuation. If it is merely infatuation that you have mistaken for love then a short break will soon see to that.

I didn't sleep much, and when I woke my eyes felt gritty. I'd spent the night tossing and turning, my mind whirring with thoughts about Catherine, the kids, Rob, and all the people who'd written to me asking for advice.

When I'd had the idea to start the problem-page website it had been as a distraction; something to get me through the long, lonely evenings in a house I hated in a village where I knew no one. It had been the perfect tonic, back then, to spend my evenings reading through problems from the past, and replying to the occasional cry for help from the present. Since then, though, the website had morphed into something else. It had gone from being a small local project where I knew that most of the people asking for my help lived within a small radius of my house, to becoming a bigger beast, spreading its wings far and wide across the county and even the UK, if my website analytics were accurate. *Dear Evelyn* had become about other people now, far more than it was about me, and I owed it to them to help them as best I could. I knew what it was like to feel cut adrift with no one to turn to.

The page had done something else for me too, of course. It had helped me make new friends. Evelyn Wright's advice had led to me getting Buster, which was how I'd met Catherine, who'd quickly become an important part of my life. And, I couldn't help thinking, a far better friend than Suzie had ever been. We'd just clicked, and I never felt as though I had to pretend to be something I wasn't.

Plus, of course, the problem page had brought Charlie into my life.

And he was the other thing that had kept me awake last night.

Something Catherine had said about Charlie earlier that evening had stuck in my mind: *I've seen the way you two look at each other. And quite frankly if Charlie really still believes he wants to make it up with Helen, or whatever she's called, then I'd say he's kidding himself.*

I'd turned it over and over in the early hours, trying to examine it from every angle.

Did I have feelings for Charlie? Forget the fact that I found him attractive. That didn't matter. But what *did* matter was if I was developing feelings for him that were more than just friendship. And if I was, was it time to take a step back?

My mind flashed back to the image of him taking his T-shirt off in the garden, and my skin tingled, and my face flushed.

Oh *God*. Maybe I should stop spending so much time with him before things got out of control.

I glanced at the clock. When Charlie had found out it was an inset day for the kids and me today he'd insisted he wanted to help out again. It was already eight o'clock now, and he was due at ten. It would be far too rude to tell him he couldn't come at such short notice, even if I really wanted to.

Which I didn't.

Besides, he probably had no inkling of my feelings, and I wasn't about to tell him, so what did it matter?

I dragged myself out of bed, checked on the kids – still sound asleep, a gentle snore emanating from Jacob's bed. I watched them for a few seconds, my heart full. They seemed happy enough, didn't they? I was still waiting for the explosion, for the reaction to being dragged away from their formerly happy life with Mum and Dad, but so far, apart from the little flounce by Olivia the other evening, it hadn't materialised. Maybe I really was doing better than I gave myself credit for.

I showered and by the time I was dressed Jacob was in my room, scrolling through photos on my phone.

'Hello, love,' I said, perching beside him. His hair stuck on end and he was sleep-rumpled. I pulled him into me for a cuddle.

'Heeey!' he said, squirming away.

'What you looking at, mister?'

'Photos.'

I craned my neck to see and my heart contracted when I saw that he'd been scrolling through photos of us all together, before Rob had torn the family apart.

'Do you remember that day?' I said gently.

He nodded.

I pressed my lips against his warm little head. 'Do you miss Daddy?'

His shoulders lifted. 'I still see Daddy. At home, with Natalie.'

The word 'home' sliced through me like a hot knife and I took a long, slow breath in. 'This is your home too now, isn't it?'

He didn't say anything, but eventually gave a small nod. 'Yes, but Daddy's house is my real home. It just doesn't have Mummy in it any more.'

I knew I should let it slide, but I couldn't help myself. '*This* is your home just as much as Daddy's is, sweetheart. This house, with Mummy and Olivia, is where you live now, and then sometimes you stay with Daddy in your other home too.'

He looked up at me then, confusion showing on his little face.

'So will Daddy's new baby get to live there all the time, or will it come and live here with me, you and 'Livia too?'

My legs felt jelly-like, and the words caught in my throat. Poor kid, no wonder he was so confused. I couldn't believe I hadn't sat down and explained this to him properly. I doubted whether Rob had bothered. I climbed under the duvet and snuggled up beside him. This time he didn't pull away.

'This baby will be your brother or sister, but only a half-brother or -sister. So he or she will have the same daddy, but a different mummy. Do you understand?'

'So it won't come and stay here with you?'

'No, love, it won't.'

'Oh.'

'But you will see it when you stay with Daddy and Natalie.'

He was silent for a moment, thoughtful. 'Do babies cry a lot?'

I laughed. 'Yes, they do, sometimes.'

'So when I'm there will the baby cry a lot and stop me from sleeping?'

'Hopefully not.'

He looked up at me again and I wanted to cover his little face with kisses, keep him wrapped in cotton wool for the rest of his life. 'But when I'm here there won't be a baby crying?'

'No, just a silly doggy barking sometimes.'

'Good,' he said. 'I prefer a doggy barking.'

We sat for a few more minutes, looking through some of the older photos on my phone, family day trips, birthdays and parties, before Olivia burst in and jumped onto the end of my bed.

'I'm hungry, can we have pancakes?' she said, bouncing up and down so that the bed felt like a ship on a stormy sea.

'Only if you stop making me feel seasick,' I said, laughing as I rolled off the bed and stood.

'Sorry, Mummy,' Olivia said.

'Yay!' Jacob clapped his hands together.

'Pancakes and chocolate spread coming up,' I said.

* * *

By the time we'd finished eating, Charlie's van had pulled up outside. I opened the back gate to find him hauling a potted bay tree down the side of the house.

'Are you okay with that?' I said, laughing as he stopped and wiped his brow.

'Christ, it's heavier than I thought,' he said.

'Where on earth did you get it?'

'My neighbour was getting rid of it, so I rescued it before he threw it in the skip.'

'He was just going to chuck it out?' I said, incredulous. 'But it's gorgeous.'

'I know, mad, isn't it?'

I bent down and tried to lift the base of the pot but Charlie was right, it weighed a ton. 'Come on, let's drag it together,' I said. As we hauled the tree along the path, the pot making a terrible screeching sound along the paving slabs, I tried not to notice how good Charlie smelt, or how handsome he looked with his curls bouncing around, or how his biceps bulged as he worked. Nope, I absolutely wasn't going to notice any of that.

We got the tree into the garden and stood. I was breathless with the effort.

'It's going to be a hot one again,' Charlie said, wiping his hands on his shorts.

'I'll get some drinks.' I turned. 'Have you eaten?'

'A bit.'

'There are a couple of pancakes left if you want them. The kids bullied me into making them.'

'I shouldn't. I'll get fat if you keep feeding me like this.' He patted his washboard stomach and I averted my gaze. 'But go on, then, if they're going spare, thanks.'

I scurried into the kitchen, suddenly desperate to get away. This was ridiculous. Charlie was a married man. I needed to sort myself out.

'Cooee!' A voice interrupted my thoughts and I almost dropped the glass in my hand. I whipped my head round to see Catherine just inside the back door.

'What are you doing here?'

'I haven't got much work on so I thought I'd come and help too. But maybe I should just go home again?'

I put the glass down and let out a breath.

'No, sorry, it's me,' I said.

She stepped into the kitchen and put her bag down. 'You look exhausted. What's the matter?'

'I didn't sleep well.' I fixed my gaze on her. 'Too much on my mind.'

'You shouldn't let other people's worries keep you awake,' she said, picking up the glass from the side and filling it with water. 'You're doing as much as you can to help them.'

'It's not just other people's problems that were bothering me,' I said pointedly. She didn't get the hint so I spelled it out for her. 'I'm worried my friendship with Charlie might be ruined,' I whispered, checking the garden to make sure he was still out of earshot. He was hovering by the back fence studying something at knee level.

'Ruined?' she said. 'Why?'

'Well, partly you putting thoughts into my head about having feelings for him,' I said. 'Making me think about him as more than a friend.'

She folded her arms. 'I didn't put the thoughts there, Beth. I just spotted them.'

I let her words linger for a minute. Was she right? Had I made it obvious that I found Charlie attractive? And if Catherine had noticed, had he?

'Don't worry, he will be oblivious to it,' she said, as if reading my mind. I buried my face in my hands.

'Oh God, this is mortifying,' I said. Because of course she was right. Charlie and I had connected right from the word go, when we were only emailing each other and had no idea what each other looked like. Back then I'd only thought of him as a middle-aged married man who, although I liked as a person, I'd assumed I'd never have any interest in.

Then we'd met. And ever since, things had felt different. For me at least.

I suspected that for him nothing had changed.

'Don't be daft. Men aren't observant enough. You don't need to worry about it. Although I do think he likes you too.'

'How many times do I have to repeat myself? He's married!'

She shot me a look. 'Yeah, and that's going well.'

I shook my head. 'No, we're not talking about this any more. Charlie is off limits. He's just a friend who needs my help to sort out his marriage, and who is helping me sort out my garden. Nothing more.' I took a long drink of water. Catherine was watching me. Eventually, she spoke.

'Okay. If that's the way you're determined to play it, that's fine. I promise not to mention it ever again.'

'Thank you.'

'Now let me go and ask him about helping with the last of those questions.' And before I could object, she'd gone, leaving me feeling more confused than ever.

* * *

I'd pulled myself together by the time I went back out to the garden. The kids were happily installed in the living room with Lego and all-day CBeebies. 'I promise you can use the garden as soon as it's safe,' I assured them, popping down a couple of plastic cups of squash and trying to ignore the pang of motherly guilt at them having to stay indoors yet again on a beautiful sunny day. Neither of them replied.

I went back outside to crack on.

'Charlie says he's happy to help with the letters, aren't you, Charlie?' Catherine announced as I walked into the garden. The tray of drinks and pancakes wobbled precariously as I placed it on the small table, and Catherine swiped a pancake from the plate.

'Hey, that was for Charlie!' I protested.

She looked shamefaced. 'Sorry.'

Charlie shook his head. 'It's fine. I don't need that many anyway.' He reached for the plate. 'Thank you though.'

I sat down. 'So Catherine told you about all the emails that came through yesterday, did she?' I said, picking up a glass of icy water and taking a sip.

'She did.' He took a mouthful of pancake and swallowed. His eyes were wide. 'I can't believe the page has taken off so quickly.'

'I know.'

'Beth's worried she's letting people down if she doesn't answer every single one though,' Catherine said.

'But surely agony aunts get hundreds of letters they don't have time to reply to?' Charlie said through another mouthful of pancake. Syrup dripped down his chin and he licked it. I looked away.

'Maybe. But this feels personal, like they're writing to me.'

'But they're not, they're writing to Evelyn,' Catherine pointed out, wiping her mouth with the back of her hand.

'I know. But I set this up to help me as much as to help other people. I could have done with someone to write to when Rob cheated on me, and when I was on my own the letters gave me something to think about in the evenings.' I blushed as I saw Charlie watching me intently. I'd told him all about this, of course, when we emailed. But somehow it felt more personal now we actually knew each other. 'If I don't reply I might be making things worse rather than better because they'll really think they have no one.'

'Well, don't worry, between us I'm sure we can reply to everyone,' Catherine said. 'Can't we, Charlie?'

He nodded sadly. 'I'll help if I can, but I'm not sure how much use I'll be with other people's problems. I can't even sort out my own mess.'

He looked down at his feet and I tried not to catch Catherine's eye. This was the first time Charlie had mentioned his own problems properly in front of Catherine, and I didn't want her to let on that she already knew about it.

A few seconds passed, then Charlie stood, pulled on an old cap, and said, 'Right then, let's get started.' To my relief, the moment had gone.

* * *

By three o'clock we were all exhausted, grubby and starving, having decided not to stop for lunch – except a quick sandwich for the kids of course.

'I'm always here, will you both let me cook you dinner tonight at my house?' Catherine said as we flopped back onto the garden chairs.

'I've got the kids,' I said, gesturing to where Olivia and Jacob were playing in the dug-up lawn. I resisted the urge to tell them to stop. That was what baths were for.

'I meant them as well,' Catherine said, rolling her eyes. 'How about you, Charlie? You up for it?'

'That would be lovely but I really should get home.' He didn't look thrilled at the prospect but if I was to do my job as agony aunt properly I should encourage him to do just that.

'That's okay, you've spent enough time with us, I'm sure you need to spend a bit of time at home with Helen,' I said. My voice sounded shrill even to my ears, and Catherine shot me a look.

'Of course, but I have a lovely piece of cooked ham that will only go to waste,' Catherine said, fluttering her eyelashes.

Charlie looked from me to Catherine, then gazed off into a spot in the middle of the garden. Finally, he said, 'Go on, then. I'll just let Helen know. As if she'll care.'

As he got up and pulled his phone out, disappearing to the end of the garden to speak to his wife, I gave Catherine a gentle smack on the thigh. She looked at me innocently.

'What was that for?'

'You know full well,' I whispered.

'I have no idea what you're talking about,' she said, turning her face away. Too late though, I'd seen her grin.

'You promised you'd stop,' I said.

She turned back to face me. 'I promised I'd stop teasing you about it. I didn't promise to stop trying to throw the pair of you together.'

I shook my head, infuriated. 'Come on, Catherine. He's speaking to his *wife*, for goodness' sake.'

'His wife who he doesn't appear to want to spend any time with, do you mean?' she said, indicating Charlie on his phone a few metres away.

'That's—' I started, but then stopped as Charlie ended the call and began to walk towards us.

'Everything okay?' Catherine said innocently.

Charlie nodded. 'Yeah,' he said dismissively.

'So are you staying or going?'

'It looks like I'm staying.' He nodded at his phone. 'Helen's gone out with "friends" again anyway.'

None of us said anything for a moment, letting his words hang in the baking afternoon heat. Then Catherine leapt up. 'Right, you lot get cleaned up – I think those two might need a dunk in the bath,' she said, grinning at Olivia and Jacob, who were smeared in mud from neck to knee. 'I'll head home and meet you there in – what? Half an hour?'

And before either of us could object to being left alone together, she'd flitted out of the garden gate and gone.

'Right, that's us told,' Charlie said. He shuffled his feet. 'Do you want a hand with the kids' bath while you jump in the shower?'

'Um – the shower is in the same room as the bath,' I said. My face flushed at the thought of him being in there with me.

'God, course it is.' He slapped his forehead. 'Well, I'll clean up down here and then – is it okay to take a quick shower before we head over? It's not worth me driving all the way home only to come back again.'

'Course,' I said. 'Have you got anything clean to wear?'

He nodded. 'I always carry a spare T-shirt.' He picked up his rucksack from the floor and pulled out a crumpled heap of fabric. 'Oh.'

'You shower first, I'll run an iron over this, then me and the kids can sort ourselves out.' I clapped my hands together. 'Come on, you two, let's go,' I said. As they stripped off their muddy clothes by the washing machine I tried not to think about Charlie upstairs in the shower, naked.

No, I definitely must not think about that…

* * *

'People are starting to talk about *Dear Evelyn*, you know,' Catherine said, handing us a glass of wine each as we walked into her kitchen. The kids were in their element with a cup of chocolate milk and a plate of chocolate biscuits while we waited for the potatoes to cook.

'What people?' Charlie said, as we walked out into the garden. It was almost dark now and the solar lights strung around Catherine's fence made his eyes shine.

'Folk round here.' Catherine waved her hand round vaguely. 'I heard a couple of women talking about it in the post office the other day, and someone else at work said their friend had written in.'

'Seriously?' I said.

'Seriously. They seemed to like it too.'

'Wow.' I took a sip of wine. It was rich, a dark, throaty red. I savoured it for a moment, holding it in my mouth before swallowing. 'Probably just as well I didn't use my real name, then. People are much more likely to be open about things if they're talking to a faceless person rather than their next-door neighbour.'

'That's true,' Charlie said. 'I don't think I would ever have written in for help if I'd known there was a chance I was going to bump into you at the chemist's buying pile cream.' He grinned. 'Not that I buy that, of course.'

Catherine cackled. 'Well, Beth's glad you did, aren't you, Beth?'

'Yes,' I said, my voice small.

'We both are,' Catherine added, slightly too late. I shot her a warning look. Luckily Charlie seemed oblivious.

'Anyway, Beth, tell Catherine what happened just before we left to come over here,' Charlie said excitedly. He was fidgeting in his seat like a little kid.

'What?' Catherine said. She sat forward in her seat, watching us intently, and it struck me that she was probably expecting us to tell her that we'd kissed or something. I smiled to myself at how wrong she was.

'The phone rang just as we were about to walk out of the door,' I said. 'It's why we were a bit late.' I glanced at Charlie, who gave me a nod. 'It was Annie.'

It took a second for the name to register, then Catherine's eyes opened wide. 'Oh, Annie Hargreaves,' she said. 'What did she have to say?'

'Well, she said she'd tried to ring you but there'd been no answer, so she'd tried my number instead. Anyway, she's found that letter.'

'Oh!' Catherine's face turned pale.

I ploughed on, pulling the piece of paper from my bag that I'd made some notes on as Annie had spoken. 'She said Lois – your mum – didn't tell her much, just that she missed their chats over elevenses, and that she hadn't made many new friends. She said people were—' I squinted to read my scrawled notes in the semi-darkness '—judgemental and not very friendly.' I looked up. 'I suppose that was because she'd run off with someone she wasn't married to. It was still very frowned upon, even then.'

Catherine didn't reply so I carried on. 'But she said she was happy despite everything and not to worry about her because she'd found love at last and – yes, then she asked her to pass on her love to her daughter.' I lowered the piece of paper and waited.

Finally Catherine spoke. 'Is that it?'

'Well, yes.'

'Huh.' I wasn't sure what that meant so I stayed quiet and looked round Catherine's garden, which was a complete contrast to mine. It was only small, two or three metres wide and not much longer, but it was neat; the tiny patch of lawn was mown short, a couple of beech trees dominated the other end of the garden, where birds fluttered from branch to branch and one pecked forlornly at the empty bird-feeder. The decking we were sitting on was freshly treated, and the fairy lights, outdoor sofa and rugs made it feel like an extension of the house. Jacob and Olivia were playing a game of Swingball that Catherine had found buried at the back of the garage and, once the dust had flown off it, they were having great fun trying to smack the ball round the pole to each other.

Finally, Catherine spoke.

'I guess that's that, then.'

I looked at her. 'What's that?'

'The end of that little adventure.' She looked half relieved, half disappointed.

I glanced at Charlie. 'I—' I stopped. I didn't want her to think we'd been talking about her, but Charlie and I had had an idea. 'The thing is, Annie also had the name of the village where your mum was living.'

Catherine looked up in surprise. I continued. 'There was no actual address, but I had a quick search as Charlie drove over here and it's not a very big village and I don't think it would be difficult to find her. Or at least to find someone who did know her.'

Catherine nodded slowly. I knew it was a lot to take in.

'One more thing though. She told me that Lois had changed her name. Her surname, that is, so I guess she married whoever this guy was that she ran off with, eventually.'

Catherine stared into the deepening twilight for a minute, before turning to look at us. Her face was hard to read.

'Where is this place?'

'Lincolnshire. About a two-hour drive from here.'

She nodded again.

'And you think I should go, do you?'

I saw Charlie glance at me from the corner of my eye. I let him reply. 'It's entirely up to you. But we'd be happy to come with you, for moral support... if you want, of course.'

'But we totally understand if you'd prefer to just leave it. I mean...' I trailed off, aware I was babbling.

'I have to do it, don't I?' She fixed us both with a steely look.

I shrugged, held my hands up in the air. 'Only if you want to. I don't want you to feel bullied into it.'

She shook her head. 'Don't worry, I'm far too old to be bullied into anything I don't want to do.' She smiled. 'But you're right, we've come this far, we might as well finish it now. And you never know, either Mum or her husband might even still be alive. Now wouldn't that be a thing?'

15

DESPERATELY UNHAPPY

My children are the most important thing in the world, but sometimes I worry that they might be better off without me. It is always just me and them alone during the day and there have been occasions when I have had some dark thoughts, and imagined walking out or, worse, leaving them for good. I do not want to talk to my husband about this as I know he will not understand, but I am not sure what else to do.

My dear you are suffering from your nerves, which is common following the birth of a child. You do not say how old your children are but I assume they are quite young if you are with them all day. I would suggest speaking to your husband if you feel able – his response may surprise you. But if you really feel as though you have nowhere else to turn then please do make an appointment to see your family doctor as a matter of urgency, and it is imperative, of course, that you do not act on your urges. In the meantime, do try to find some like-minded

friends. Could you perhaps take the children to the park and
meet some other mothers there with whom you could spend
your days?

The following weekend the kids were due to be with Rob so we
agreed it was the perfect opportunity to make the trip to
Lincolnshire. But first, we had work to do.

'We should at least try and find an address before we trek all
the way there,' Catherine said as we ate dinner that evening. 'It
might be a small place but we don't want to go randomly
hammering on doors.'

'It's worth a go,' I agreed.

'So what was her married surname?' Catherine shovelled a
huge forkful of ham and lettuce into her mouth.

I peered at my notes. 'Morrison,' I said.

She nodded, chewing slowly. 'Hang on.'

She stood and left the room, then came back a minute later
with her laptop. 'Let's see if she comes up in a search.'

We waited while Catherine tapped something into her laptop,
and seconds later she looked up. 'Bingo!' she said, turning the
screen round to show us. 'It might not be her, but there's someone
called Morrison in that village, so there's a good chance they
might at least know her.'

'That's amazing,' I said. I hadn't expected it to be that easy, and
I hoped Catherine wasn't finding it too overwhelming that things
were moving so quickly. 'So what do you want to do?'

'I'm going to ring them.'

I almost choked on my piece of potato. 'Now?'

Catherine looked up at me, the light from the monitor shining
in her eyes. For the first time since we'd started this search, she
looked excited. 'There's a number here. What have I got to lose?'

She grabbed her mobile from the worktop and carefully typed

in a number. Then she looked up at us, uncertain. 'God, I'm scared now,' she said.

'Do you want me to do it?'

She hesitated a moment, then straightened her shoulders and shook her head. 'No. I'll do it.'

We sat in silence as we listened to the phone ringing. I could see Catherine's hand shaking, and I held my breath. Charlie sat, his hand hovering in mid-air, fork loaded with food.

And then the ringing stopped, there was a click, and an answerphone cut in.

Hello, I'm not currently in. Please leave a message after the tone and somebody will get back to you. Thank you.

'Hello, my name is Catherine Andrews, and I'm... I'm looking for Lois. Lois Andrews. Or Morrison. I – I don't know whether I have the right number but please could someone call me back?' She then left her number and ended the call.

For a moment she didn't speak, and when she did, it came out as a whisper.

'What if they ring me back?'

I reached over and grabbed her hands. They were still shaking. 'Let's deal with that if they do. And if they know your mother, well – then you can decide what you want to do. But I'll help, whatever you choose.'

She gave a small smile, took her hands away and picked up her fork. 'Thank you, Beth, and you, Charlie. I don't think I would ever have done this without you.' She held her glass up. 'To new friends. Worth their weight in bloody gold. Cheers.'

'Cheers!'

* * *

By the time I bundled the kids into the car to get them home, nobody had called Catherine back.

'Sorry I can't stay, I've got to get these two to bed, they've got school in the morning,' I said.

'Don't be daft, course you've got to go,' she said, shooing us out of the door. 'I don't expect you to hold my hand.'

'You'll let me know if someone rings back though, won't you?'

'You'll be the first person I ring,' she promised, hugging me.

'Thanks for dinner,' Charlie said, shrugging on his sweatshirt.

'You're very welcome. Now go, both of you,' she said. 'I'm perfectly fine on my own.'

As she closed the front door she gave me a wink and I rolled my eyes, then turned to Charlie, suddenly shy. It was getting dark now, and the air had turned chillier.

'Right, well, I'd better get back,' Charlie said, shuffling from foot to foot. I tried not to think about Helen at home waiting for him.

'Of course,' I said, smiling. 'Thank you so much for all your work on my garden this weekend. I don't know where I would have started without you.'

'I've really enjoyed it,' he said. He unlocked his van and opened the door. 'I'll let you know when the turf arrives, okay, and try and come over later this week and lay it for you. Gives it a chance to settle in before next weekend.'

'Honestly, Charlie, you've done so much already. Please don't feel obliged to do any more.'

'I'm not going to leave you with a half-finished garden, that would be worse than not having helped at all.' He peered down at his dirty boots. 'Anyway, I've enjoyed spending time with you.'

'Oh!' I said. 'Yes, er, I have too. Enjoyed spending time with you, I mean. I—' *God, Beth, stop babbling.* I cleared my throat. 'It's been fun to hang out with you, and Catherine.'

He watched me for a second before replying. 'Yes, exactly.' He dipped his head in acknowledgement. 'Anyway, I'd better get going.'

'Yes, me too. These two are exhausted.'

'I'm not tired, Mummy!' Olivia yelled from the back of the car, and Charlie grinned.

'Good luck getting her to sleep tonight.'

'Thanks. So. Night, then.'

'Night.'

And then Charlie got in his van and left.

* * *

The next night the kids were in bed and I was contemplating the same when my mobile beeped. I'd spent the evening replying to a couple more *Dear Evelyn* letters that had arrived while I'd been out and my eyes were tired and heavy. I squinted at the phone. It was Catherine.

Can you talk? I've got news. C x

I sat up, suddenly wide awake, and rang her straight back.

'Beth, thank goodness,' she said breathlessly. In the short time I'd known her she'd always been so together, this undone woman sounded like a different person.

'What's happened?' I said.

'Someone rang me back!'

'And?'

'I—' She stopped. 'It was a woman called Andrea, and she said she knew my mum well and she's happy for me to go and speak to her.' The words came out in a rush.

'Oh my God,' I said. I couldn't believe how quickly things had escalated. If I was struggling to take it in, how on earth must Catherine be feeling? 'What else did she say? Is Lois still alive? How does she know her?'

'Well, that's the thing. She didn't want to tell me anything else on the phone. She said she thought it would be best if I went to see her.'

'But she wouldn't tell you any more than that?'

'No. Frustrating, isn't it? But will you come with me?'

'When?'

'Saturday afternoon.'

That was four agonising days away but at least the kids would be with Rob and Natalie so I wouldn't have to worry about them. 'I'll be there. Do you want me to ask Charlie too, for a bit of extra support?'

'Would you like Charlie there?'

'It's not up to me.'

A silence. Then: 'Yes, go on, ask him. He's as involved in all of this as we are.'

'Okay.'

'I don't know how I'm going to get through this week. I think I might burst,' she said. Her voice wobbled.

'Are you okay?'

I heard her swallow. 'I'm fine. It's just overwhelming. I didn't expect to actually find someone who knew her. I mean she – this woman – could be her stepdaughter or something. She's got the surname Mum changed her name to.'

'How would you feel if she was?'

'I'm not sure. It would be pretty nice, I suppose, to have a long-lost sister I knew nothing about.' She sighed. 'I know my brain's going to go wild this week dreaming up different scenarios. I just wish she could have told me on the phone.'

'I guess she thinks it's too important not to do face to face.'

'I guess so. And I've waited all these years, what's a few more days?'

She didn't speak for a while, then she said, 'Anyway, night, Beth. And thanks for everything.' Before I could say anything else, she'd ended the call.

16

HIDDEN SECRET

I have discovered a secret about a close friend that could be potentially life-changing. However I am unsure whether I should tell her the secret or not. I do believe she ought to know it, but it may also upset her and I do not want to be the one to do that. What should I do?

You have told me the details of the secret in your letter but I have chosen not to print them for the reason I am sure you will appreciate. On most occasions, I would always recommend honesty as the best course of action. However in this instance I would say that the subject is not your business, and as such you will merely be causing unnecessary harm by divulging what you know.

'Here you go,' Charlie said, clicking open the back of his truck. There was a huge pile of rolled turf, and several plants in pots.

'Wow, this is going to take you ages,' I said, rolling up my sleeves.

'It's not as bad as it looks,' Charlie said, tugging his jumper over his head. His T-shirt rose to reveal his toned stomach and I looked away, my face flaming.

'Well, what can I do to help?'

'Tell you what, while I get this lot off the van, why don't you put the kettle on, then you can come and give me a hand putting it in place if you like? If you feel strong enough?' He grinned at me.

'Course I'm strong enough,' I said, holding my arms up like Popeye. He squeezed my pathetic biceps and I yelped, my skin warm beneath his touch.

I headed to the kitchen and watched from the window as Charlie ferried the turf into the garden on a wheelbarrow. It was hard not to admire him – you'd know he worked outside just from his physique.

'Mummy!' I jumped as a little hand tugged my T-shirt.

'Oh, hello, little man,' I said, bending to lift Jacob onto the worktop. He kicked his legs against the cupboard. 'What's up?'

'Can I have a snack?'

'Dinner won't be long.'

'But I'm *hungry*' he said.

I glanced at the clock. It was already five o'clock and it was likely to be a while until I could get round to making dinner. 'Go on, have a packet of crisps or something,' I said, helping him down before his wriggling made him fall to the floor.

He took some crisps from the drawer and ran back to the living room. I counted to five, six, seven... and then, right on cue, Olivia marched into the room. 'Jacob's got crisps, can I have some too?'

I grabbed a packet and handed them to her, and she turned and marched back into the living room. I smiled to myself.

The kettle boiled and I poured tea into mugs. I opened the fridge to find the milk and pulled out a packet of fresh pasta that needed eating. That would do for the kids' tea anyway. Just as I was about to take the tea out to Charlie, my mobile rang. A glance at the screen made my heart sink.

'Hi, Rob,' I said, trying not to sound annoyed.

'Hello, Beth.' His voice sounded clipped and I assumed he was still in the office. I pictured his desk, which we'd once had sex on when I'd visited him after hours, and I blushed as Charlie came to my mind instead of Rob.

My attention was pulled back to the conversation by Rob's voice. He sounded insistent about something.

'Sorry, what?'

'I said, Olivia tells me you've got a boyfriend.'

'What? When did she tell you that?'

'When we spoke earlier. So it's true, then?'

'No!'

'So who's this Charlie, then?'

'He's a – he's a friend.'

'Is he now?'

I bristled at his tone. 'What do you mean, *is he now*? I've told you he is, and he is. Although I don't know what it's got to do with you.'

'It's got everything to do with me when another man is spending time with my children.'

It was so absurd that he had the audacity to say this to me that I let out a bark of laughter.

'What's so funny?' he said.

'Are you serious?'

'If you're referring to me and Natalie then you know full well that's entirely different.'

'How?'

'Of course it is! I've known Natalie for years, and she was Olivia's *teacher*, for fuck's sake!'

'And you think the fact she slept with someone she knew was married makes her more suitable to spend time with our children than someone I might meet, then, do you?'

'Ha, so you *are* seeing him, then?'

Rage flared through me. 'Oh, fuck you, Rob,' I yelled, and ended the call, throwing myself into the nearest chair. I was still shaking with fury when Charlie popped his head round the back door.

'Have you forgotten the tea?' he said, but then stopped dead when he saw my face. 'God, what's happened?' he said, sitting down beside me. He took my hands in his and I felt a jolt of electricity surge through me. A tear plopped onto the table and I shook my head.

'It's fine,' I said, my voice thick. 'It's nothing.'

'It clearly isn't nothing. You were fine a few minutes ago, and now look at you. You look like you've seen a ghost.'

I swallowed. I couldn't tell him what Rob had said, it was too mortifying. But how could I explain it otherwise? I took a couple of deep breaths and felt my pulse slowing. I looked Charlie in the eye. His hands were still wrapped around mine and I met his gaze.

'Olivia told Rob you were my boyfriend and he just rang to ask me about you.'

'Oh.' Charlie snatched his hands away and looked down at where they lay on the table. 'I... sorry.' He shrugged.

'Don't be daft. Olivia's got the wrong end of the stick and I put him right, of course. I'm just so furious that he had the *gall* to tell me it was his business after what he did to me.' I banged my fist on the table, making us both jump. 'Sorry.'

He shook his head. 'Don't apologise. I'd feel the same.'

'I didn't mean to drag you into my problems. I mean, I was meant to be helping you!'

'We're friends now though, aren't we? And that's what friends do, help each other.'

I nodded sadly. Of course friends was all we could ever be, but it didn't stop me feeling sad that he was so matter-of-fact about it. 'Thank you.'

'Nothing to thank me for.' He stood. 'Now, can I drink this tea before it gets totally cold?'

'Ha, of course,' I said. 'Oh, I've just remembered something.'

'Go on.' He took a sip of his tea and winced. 'No sugar.'

I handed him the sugar bowl and watched as he heaped two teaspoons in. Rob had always been so scathing of people who took sugar in their tea, claiming they were philistines for ruining the flavour, that it made me like Charlie even more because he cared so little about what people thought of him.

I told him about Catherine's phone call, and that she was going to pay a visit to Lincolnshire at the weekend.

'And she'd like you to come as well. If you've got time, of course. Although I'm sure you've got better things to do. With Helen.'

He held my gaze as he took another gulp of tea. 'Of course I'll come. I'm as invested in this as you are now. But are you sure she wants me there?'

'Positive. I think she's feeling more wobbly about it than she's letting on.'

'Then I'll be there.'

* * *

'Mummy, why's there a big grey patch on the ceiling?' Olivia called from the bathroom where she was splashing in the bath.

'I don't know,' I said, holding Jacob's pyjamas out for him to step into. He clung to my neck as he slipped his feet inside one by one. He smelt of baby shampoo and I inhaled deeply. My boy.

I stood and made my way into the bathroom, Jacob following close behind.

'Now, what's this big patch you're talking about?' I said, handing Jacob his toothbrush distractedly. I felt guilty because Charlie was still outside finishing the garden before it got dark, but I'd had to come indoors to get the children ready for bed so my mind wasn't fully in the moment.

'Look, there,' she said, pointing a soapy hand at the ceiling directly above her head.

To my horror, there was a huge damp patch stretching from the corner above the shower head, to almost halfway across the bath. It hadn't been there that morning, I was sure of it, which meant it had happened quickly.

'Bugger,' I said.

'Mummy!' Olivia admonished me.

'Sorry.' I ran my hand through my hair.

'Why's it there?' Olivia insisted as I squirted toothpaste onto Jacob's brush and handed it to him.

'I'm not sure, love,' I said, glancing up nervously as though the whole ceiling was about to cave in. 'But maybe you should come out of the bath just in case.'

'But I've only just got in!' she said, sulkily.

I stared at the ceiling for a few seconds longer. 'Okay, but just five minutes, all right? Then I need you out.'

'*Okay.*'

I thought of myself as fairly capable. I'd always been happy to put up shelves, change plugs, paint walls. But when it came to plumbing, I was stumped, and I needed someone to help me out. But I couldn't risk leaving it any longer.

I went into my bedroom and opened the window and yelled to Charlie, who was on his hands and knees rolling out one of the last pieces of turf. He glanced up, confused.

'Can I borrow you a minute, please?' I said.

'Upstairs?'

'Please.'

He stood, wiped his hands on his shorts, and disappeared into the house. Seconds later I heard his footsteps on the stairs and I went out to greet him on the landing.

'I think I've got a leak,' I said as Olivia emerged from the bathroom wrapped in a towel, water dripping from her hair all over the carpet. I thought about what she'd told Rob about Charlie being my boyfriend and made a note to myself to set her straight later. She disappeared into her and Jacob's room and I showed Charlie the problem.

'Looks like you've got water coming from your pipes,' he said. 'How long has it been there?'

'Not long, I don't think. I'm worried it could bring the ceiling down.'

'I doubt it.' He reached up and pressed his fingers against it. 'Plumbing isn't my strong point but I could go up and have a look for you, if you like, see if there's anything obvious going on?'

'If you don't mind?'

'Course not. Got a toolbox?'

'Er...'

'Don't worry, I'll grab mine.'

While he fetched it, I dug a torch from the drawer in the kitchen and stood at the bottom of the loft hatch while Charlie heaved himself up from a chair I'd pulled from my bedroom. The sound of bumps and scrapes and shuffles floated down as I waited, and then I heard a loud tapping sound, like metal being clunked against pipes.

Charlie's head popped out in the gap in the ceiling. 'I've found something. Can I pass it down?'

'Of course.'

'Hang on.' There was some more shuffling, then an ancient-looking carrier bag was passed down through the hatch. I grabbed it with outstretched arms and clouds of dust billowed in my face, making me sneeze. Charlie followed me down swiftly, brushing dust from himself too.

'I think it's been a while since anyone went up there, there were huge cobwebs,' he said, swiping at his face.

'Sorry,' I said.

'Don't be daft, it's no big deal. Anyway, there was a leaky pipe on the water tank. I've tightened it a bit for you, but you should probably get someone to come over and have a proper look before it gets any worse.' He reached up and put the loft hatch cover back in place and turned to me. 'Any idea what might be in this?' he said, indicating the dusty carrier bag. 'I was afraid it was getting damp. It was pressed right up against the pipes.'

'None at all.' It was heavier than it looked. A spider crawled out of one of the creases in the plastic and I squealed.

'Why don't you have a look at what's inside while I go and lay the last couple of bits of grass and I'll be right back?'

'I'll get the kids to bed and we'll look together, all right?'

'Deal.'

He headed back downstairs and I left the bag outside my bedroom door and went to find the kids. Jacob was already tucked up in bed, but Olivia was still brushing her hair. She turned when I came in.

'Is it fixed, Mummy?' she said.

'Not yet.' I sat down on Jacob's bed and planted a gentle kiss on his forehead. 'Night night, sweetheart. Want me to read to you or are you too tired?'

'Too tired,' he said, rolling over onto his side and sticking his thumb in his mouth. I knew Rob wasn't keen on him sucking his thumb but if it helped him get to sleep I was all for it. Besides, he was only five years old, for goodness' sake.

'Come on, love, get to bed now,' I said, moving to Olivia's bed.

'But I'm not tired, Mummy,' she said.

'Why don't you read for a bit? You've still got the rest of the spy story to finish.'

She stood and walked over to her bed and sat down on top of the duvet, her legs crossed. 'Okay. But I'm not going to sleep straight away. I should go to bed later than Jacob. He's only five and I'm nearly eight.'

I sighed. 'I know, sweetheart, but it's hard when you share a room.'

She looked at me a moment, a look of defiance on her face. 'Daddy lets me.'

I felt a flare of anger but tamped it down. 'I'm sure he does and that's lovely. But you're usually at Daddy's at the weekend and you've got school tomorrow. It won't do you any harm to get a good night's sleep. Think of how much better you'll be able to concentrate if you sleep a lot.'

'Hmmm.' She rolled over and pulled her duvet across her legs and reached for her book. 'Still not fair.'

'I know.' I leaned over and kissed her forehead too but she pulled away.

'Mummy?'

'Yes, darling?'

'Is Charlie going to be my new dad, like Natalie is my new mum?'

Her words felt like a blow to my stomach. 'No, love!' I said, a bit too sharply. 'He is not – and Natalie isn't your new mum. I'm your mum, and nothing will change that. Not ever.'

She nodded. 'Yes, but when we're at Daddy's we need a mummy to look after us, and when we're here, we need a daddy too. So it makes sense, doesn't it?'

Ah, the logic of a seven-year-old. 'It doesn't really work like that, Liv,' I said, taking her hands.

'Why not?'

'Well, not everyone has both a mummy and a daddy. All families are different, and it just so happens that your mum and dad don't live together any more. But it doesn't mean you need anyone to replace us.'

'But Daddy said Natalie is my stepmum. Doesn't that make her another mum?'

Bloody Rob. 'Sort of. But not really. A stepmum isn't really a mum – not when you've still got your real mummy.'

'And so she won't be my mum when she marries Daddy, then?'

'She's *marrying* him?'

'That's what Daddy said.'

'When?'

She looked worried, and a flash of guilt ripped through me. I shouldn't be quizzing my seven-year-old daughter on her father's plans. 'Sorry, love. It doesn't matter. But no, even if Daddy and Natalie get married—'

'*When* they get married,' she corrected.

'Yes. Okay, *when* they get married, I'll still be your only mummy. Okay?'

'Yes, okay.' She scratched her head. 'So Charlie isn't my step-dad, then?'

'No, love. Charlie is just Mummy's friend. He's not my boyfriend, so it's different.'

'But why?'

'Why what?'

'Why isn't he your boyfriend? He's very nice and he likes you lots. You like him too, don't you?'

My stomach flipped over. If only everything were as simple as kids made it seem. I swallowed. 'Charlie is married to someone else,' I said.

'Oh.' She sounded disappointed. 'That's a shame. I would have liked him to be my new stepdad.' She frowned. 'So why is he always here and not at home with his wife?'

'He—' How could I explain it so she would understand? 'He's a gardener and he's just been helping me with the garden. Once he's finished that he'll be back home with his wife and we won't see him as much.'

'Oh. I wish he could come round all the time.'

'Me too.'

I didn't know what else to say so I leaned over, gave her another kiss and stood. 'Come on, little miss procrastinator. It's time to sleep now.'

'Five minutes reading, please?'

'Five minutes. Night, sweetheart.'

'Night, Mummy.'

I closed the door and stood on the landing for a moment, letting my heart settle. Our conversation had left me feeling even more confused about my feelings towards Charlie, and I wasn't sure how I was going to untangle them if I didn't find some space to be by myself soon. But I could hardly chuck Charlie out when he'd been so kind this evening. I took a few deep breaths, picked up the carrier bag Charlie had found in the loft, and went downstairs.

* * *

Half an hour later and Charlie and I were huddled over the kitchen table, in shock. We'd made a discovery that neither of us had been expecting.

We'd eaten a plate of pasta – I'd expected Charlie to rush off home, so when he'd accepted my offer of dinner I'd been pleased, but surprised – and had finally got round to looking in the carrier bag I'd found in the loft. It had contained two bundles of paper, one held together with paperclips, the other with ribbon.

The first pile was more agony aunt columns, but this time trimmed neatly from their pages so that there were just a few small clippings held together. We huddled over these first, trying to work out what their significance might have been.

'They're all from the same person, look,' Charlie said, pointing at the name signed at the bottom of the letters.

'Dot.' I frowned. 'I wonder who Dot was?'

'Who knows? But whoever she was, she wrote to Evelyn quite a few times, and Evelyn replied every time.'

We read a bit more. It soon became clear why Dot, whoever she was, had been so worried.

'Look at this,' Charlie said, running his finger along a line about halfway down the second clipping.

I leaned closer, trying to ignore his proximity, and read the words he was pointing out.

I don't love my husband. But I don't think I could love any man. I don't think it's men I feel attracted to at all. Is it always so wrong for a woman to love a woman?

I looked up, my eyes wide. 'Dot was gay?'

Charlie nodded. 'It looks like it.' He rubbed his hand over his face. 'God, what a time to be gay. I mean, it wasn't exactly the most accepting time, I'm guessing?'

I shook my head.

'No. Even sex before marriage between members of the opposite sex was seen as wicked back then according to the advice Evelyn dished out.'

I read some more.

'It looks as though Evelyn really wanted to help her. Poor woman, I hope she found some happiness.'

I put the clippings to one side for a moment and pulled the second bundle of letters towards me and loosened the ribbon. The paper remained curled over, and I smoothed it out with my palm.

'These are handwritten letters,' I said, scrutinising the top page. It was addressed to Evelyn, in loopy, curling handwriting. I skimmed my eyes down the words and turned the page over. It was signed 'love Dot'. I turned it back over and read it more carefully. When I got to the end I glanced over at Charlie, whose eyes were still running back and forth along the lines. When he finished he looked at me, a frown creasing his forehead.

'Is this...?'

'I'm not sure.'

I pushed the letter to one side and read the next one. Once again, it was addressed to Evelyn, and signed from Dot. I ran my eyes down the page again. This time, a few lines stood out.

I know you say it doesn't matter, but you said yourself you would advise anyone else against giving in to their feelings if they were to ask the same, and I'm scared. I'm scared that if I do give in to my true feelings, I will lose everything.

Then later:

What are we going to do? Will we ever be together?

I stopped reading, my heart caught in my throat, and looked at Charlie. His lips were curled into the wisp of a smile.

'What's so funny?' I said.

'I don't know. I'm just – surprised,' he said, then looked at me. 'We're thinking the same thing, aren't we?'

'I think so.' I looked back at the letter, just to confirm. There was no doubting it. Dot had written these letters to Evelyn – Lois – because she had fallen in love with her. I turned back to Charlie. 'Lois was in love with a woman, wasn't she?'

'I think so.'

'Do you think that's why she ran away? I mean, they would never have been accepted, would they? And it sounds like they really wanted to be together.'

'Probably.' He frowned again. 'But why do you think she left the letters here?'

'Perhaps she forgot about them?'

'Or more likely left in a hurry.'

'Yeah.' I sighed. 'Poor Lois.'

'Never mind poor Lois. How do you think Catherine is going to take this? And who's going to tell her?'

17

My darling D

I am certain we should be together. In fact after all these months of writing to each other, I am absolutely positive about it. The only problem is the shame I know it will bring on my family. I am not sure how to overcome this, so I am going to give it some thought. I won't be in touch until I have worked out a solution, so please do not be alarmed if you do not hear from me for a little while. But please never forget that I love you, and we will be together, no matter what.

L x

It felt like forever since Charlie and I had made our discovery. After much discussion we'd both agreed not to say anything to Catherine about what we'd found, because there was still a chance we'd got it wrong. But keeping it from her felt awful, no matter the reasons for doing so.

Now we were on our way to Lincolnshire to meet the woman who said she'd known Lois well, and who, hopefully, was about to reveal the reason why Catherine's mother had walked out on her daughter all those years ago. I wondered how much of our conjecture would turn out to be true.

Catherine had insisted on driving, even though both Charlie and I had offered, convinced she was too wound up to drive safely.

'I'm fine,' she'd said. 'It'll keep my mind off things.' I'd never seen her looking quite so terrified though, and her pale face and set expression gave away her nerves. I sat beside her in the front, while Charlie had taken the back.

'How long left?' Charlie piped up.

I turned round and grinned. 'It's like having the kids in the car.'

He pulled a sulky face and stuck his tongue out.

'We're fifteen minutes away,' Catherine said.

She was staring straight ahead at the road, and her knuckles were white on the steering wheel. Tension radiated from her, pulsing like an electricity pylon.

'Hey,' I said, laying my hand on her arm. 'Are you okay?'

Her shoulders slumped but she didn't take her eyes off the road. 'Yeah. I just need to get this over and done with.' She glanced over at me. 'I keep imagining all kinds of things and it's the not knowing that's worse.'

I didn't dare look at Charlie. I hoped we'd made the right decision, not telling Catherine what we'd found. Would she have been less terrified if she'd had some sort of inkling about what she was about to discover?

'Not long now,' I said, weakly.

She gave a wisp of a smile.

The rest of the journey passed in silence, and I stared out of the window at the scorched fields, scrappy hedges and clusters of cottages as they zipped past the window. Finally, we were pulling into a village not dissimilar to the one where we lived. Catherine pulled over outside a tiny Spar, shut off the engine and closed her eyes. Her hands still gripped the steering wheel, and she took a couple of deep breaths.

'I'm not sure I can do this,' Catherine said. Her voice sounded small. 'I don't know why I've come.' She smacked the steering wheel with the palm of her hand and it bounced off the plastic.

I glanced at Charlie in the rear-view mirror and he looked as worried as I felt. He placed his hand on Catherine's shoulder. 'You don't have to, you know,' he said. 'It's not too late to change your mind.'

She opened her eyes and shook her head. 'I know.' She looked down at her lap. 'For forty-five years I've told myself I don't care about my mother. I convinced myself I didn't care why she left, and I didn't want to know anything about her or her life. But now... I don't know. Seeing the letters she wrote, thinking about her again, it's...' she sighed and looked up. 'I can't stop thinking, what if she's still alive? What if she's right here, in this village, and I get the chance to speak to her? What will I say?' Her voice broke and she let out a drawn-out, wobbly sigh. 'What if I can't forgive her?'

'We're both with you. You don't have to do this alone, okay?'

She nodded. 'Thank you.' She turned back to face the front of the car and took a deep breath. 'Right, where are we going, then?'

It took us another few minutes to navigate the narrow lanes of the village, and before we knew it we were pulling onto a small street made up of half a dozen houses set back from the road. Catherine killed the engine at the end of the road.

'Which one is it?'

I squinted at the numbers and pointed towards a house on the opposite side of the road. It was a small semi-detached, with a neat garden and roses climbing up the outside wall. A wind chime hung above the front door, and the window frames looked freshly painted.

'It looks like they're house proud,' Catherine said, peering through the windscreen.

'Like you.'

She smiled and nodded.

'Right, let's go, before I change my mind again.'

We climbed out of the car and made our way through the gate and up to the pale blue front door. There was no doorbell, but a polished silver knocker, and Catherine hammered it twice. My heart thumped in my temple, and I could see Catherine's torso was rigid, her hands shaking. I reached out and grabbed one of them and gave it a squeeze before releasing it again.

Then the door swung open, and a woman, who I presumed to be Andrea, was smiling at us. She was younger than I'd expected, a few years younger than Catherine, and her hair was styled in a perfect grey bob. It was her smile I noticed first though, as it seemed to take over her entire face. I felt myself instantly relax, and Catherine's shoulders seemed to lower a couple of inches too.

'You made it!' she said, gesturing for us to come inside. 'Please, come in. I've made some scones, I thought we could eat them outside on the patio.' We traipsed inside one by one and followed her through to the kitchen, a huge room with wide windows that let the sunshine flood in. It was warm, and the sliding doors were flung wide open, letting a cool breeze dance across the worktop. Something smelt divine.

She turned as she reached the counter where the scones were piled on a plate, and smiled warmly at us. 'So, obviously I'm Andrea,' she said, laying her hand on her chest. 'You must be Catherine?'

'Um, yes. I am,' Catherine said. She looked bewildered and I hoped it wouldn't be too long before we found out exactly what was going on, and how Andrea knew – or had known – Lois.

'Wonderful. It's so good to meet you after all these years.'

Andrea turned to me and Charlie. I stuck my hand out and she shook it firmly.

'I'm Beth. Catherine's friend,' I said. 'And this is Charlie.'

He shook Andrea's hand too and smiled. 'Lovely to meet you.'

Andrea clapped her hands together, making us all jump, scooped up the plate of scones and indicated the small tray laden with jam, cream and plates on the side. 'Would someone mind grabbing that for me, please? It's such a lovely day we might as well sit in the garden.'

Charlie picked up the tray and we made our way outside. Andrea's garden was lush and green. The lawn was immaculate, the flower beds either side were weed-free, and huge, blowsy roses danced along the fence. It was so long it was hard to make out where the garden ended and the woodland behind it began.

'This is stunning,' Charlie said, setting the tray carefully on the table.

'Ah, it's a bit of an obsession of mine, gardening,' Andrea said, putting the scones down too. 'Since I took early retirement I spend most of my time out here no matter the weather. Please, sit wherever you like.' She turned to Charlie. 'Do you like to garden?'

'Actually, it's my job,' he said.

'Ah, how wonderful to be able to spend all of your days being outdoors,' she said. 'I always wished I'd done something like that, but at least I could do it in my spare time.' Her smile was infectious and I felt myself relaxing even more as I took a seat at the huge wooden table. 'Now, give me one minute while I make some tea – oh, I presume you all drink tea and wouldn't prefer something else?' We all nodded. 'Good. I'll be back in a jiffy and I'll tell you everything I know.'

She disappeared inside the house again. Catherine leaned towards me.

'God, I can't stand the suspense,' she hissed through her teeth. 'Who *is* she?'

I risked a glance at Charlie, and wondered whether I should say anything about our discovery before Andrea came back out. It felt unfair that Catherine was at such a disadvantage. But then again, what if we were wrong? After all, even if our theory about Lois leaving home to be with a woman was right, Andrea was clearly far too young to have been her girlfriend so we didn't know much more than Catherine did.

Before I could make a decision, Andrea re-emerged with another tray, this time with a huge teapot, a glass bottle of milk and three large mugs. Charlie leaped up and took it from her and laid it on the table.

'Ah, thank you, what a gentleman,' she said, and Charlie blushed.

Finally, Andrea sat down. 'We'll leave it to steep for a few minutes,' she said. 'Please help yourself to scones, we don't stand on ceremony here.' She clapped her hands again, something I'd noticed she seemed to do to indicate the start of a new subject. 'Now, I don't know how much you know about Lois – your mother, I mean?' she said at last, turning to Catherine.

'Not much.' Catherine's voice was wobbly. 'She left home when I was nine so I was brought up by my granny and I only received a birthday card once a year. Granny wouldn't talk about her, so I only have memories from being very young.' She looked at Andrea expectantly.

Andrea nodded serenely, clasped her hands beneath her chin, and leaned her elbows on the table. She closed her eyes, then started to speak.

'I expect this will come as a bit of a shock to you, I'm afraid,' she said. Charlie looked at me and my eyes widened. This was it. 'Your mum passed away five years ago. She'd been ill for a few years and it was very peaceful. I don't know whether you knew, but if not then I'm so sorry to be the bearer of such sad news.' Catherine gave a tiny shake of her head, but the colour had drained from her face. I felt my own breath caught in my throat. Andrea continued. 'Your mum came to live with us when I was five years old, and she became like a mother to me.' She opened her eyes and they were filled with sorrow. 'I'm sorry, that probably sounds awful, when she left you to be here. But there's more.'

Catherine gave a tight nod but didn't speak.

'Lois and my mother were in love.'

I watched Catherine's face for a reaction. A flush rose up her neck and her eyes widened, darting round the table as though searching for answers to all the questions that were buzzing round her mind.

'She—' She stopped, swallowed, and took a deep breath. 'You're saying my mother was having an affair with a woman?'

Andrea dipped her head in acknowledgement. 'That's exactly what I'm saying. Except – well, it was more than an affair. Lois and my mother were one of the first same-sex couples to get married when it became legal in 2014.'

Catherine was so still it looked as though she had frozen. Of all the things she had expected, I wasn't sure this was high on her list. I hoped it was better than most of her imaginings, particularly as it proved her mother's disappearance had been nothing to do with any failings she'd always wondered about.

'But—' Catherine started, and stopped again. Andrea didn't try and fill in any gaps and I admired her for that. It showed real kindness to allow Catherine space to think, and to let the news settle. Catherine looked down at her hands, which were clasped in her lap, then up to the tree top and finally her gaze settled on Andrea. 'But I had no idea.'

Andrea smiled kindly. 'No, I don't suppose you would have

done.' She leaned forward. 'The thing is, back then, even though it had stopped being illegal to be gay in 1967, it was still a taboo subject in the seventies. Very much frowned upon. People just weren't *allowed* to be gay, not in polite society.' She smiled. 'I'm sure you know all this. But I'm trying to put it into context for you, because I know how much Lois struggled with it.'

Catherine gave a small nod but didn't speak. Andrea continued. 'My mum told me the story of how they met lots of times. She started writing to your mum – as Evelyn – back when she was still writing her agony aunt column. Mum was only a teenager then, and she already knew she wasn't the same as everyone else. She told Evelyn – Lois – that she didn't feel anything for boys and found herself thinking about her best friend much more than she should.

'Anyway, Evelyn started writing back to her privately, telling her she shouldn't worry, that these feelings would pass, but that if she ever felt she needed someone to talk to, she should write to her again.' Andrea coughed and took a sip of tea.

'Years later Mum remembered that, and when she was married to Dad and I was only a few months old, she took her up on that offer. She wrote to Evelyn, even though she had no idea whether she'd even still be at the same address, and she told her that nothing had changed, that, even though she was married now and had a little girl, she didn't feel anything for her husband and she thought she might like women.' She sighed. 'Poor Mum. Her parents were so old-fashioned they would never have got their heads round it, and she truly felt as though she had no one else to turn to.'

Catherine nodded slowly. 'So, what happened? How did they actually meet?'

'Well, that's just it. They didn't for a while. Lois wrote back and told Mum she understood, and that there was nothing wrong with her feelings. Mum said to me one day, many years later, that if she hadn't heard back from Lois she didn't know what she might have done. I suppose she was suffering from post-natal depression, and, combined with the fact that she was trying so hard to hide her true feelings, she was struggling.' She shrugged. 'So your mum saved my mum's life.'

Andrea fell silent for a moment and we all sat quietly. I watched a bird hop across the branches of a cherry tree, and the leaves rustle in the gentle breeze, and tipped my head back into the sun. I wondered how Catherine was feeling about this story. I hoped it was giving her some sort of insight into her mother's frame of mind when she'd finally walked out and left her behind.

Eventually, Andrea spoke again. 'Are you all right? Do you want me to carry on?'

'I'm fine,' Catherine said. Her voice was clipped but I knew it was because she was trying not to cry rather than through anger. 'Please, tell me the rest.'

Andrea nodded. 'Okay. Well, after a year or so of writing back and forth, your mum came to visit. And from the moment they met, I think that was that. They'd already fallen in love with each other via letter, but the spark was instant, and they both knew there was no going back. So Lois came to live with us.'

Catherine stared up into the silky sky, her brow furrowed. 'But that doesn't explain why she abandoned me,' she said. 'It doesn't explain why she didn't take me with her.'

'I know,' Andrea said. Her voice was gentle. 'I did ask her that, years later. And all I can tell you is that she loved you very much, but she didn't want you to be – what was the word she used? Tainted. That's what she said. She didn't want you to be tainted by what she had done, and so she made the hardest decision of her life and left you to be brought up by her mother.'

'But that was hardly a conventional upbringing either, was it?'

Catherine said, her knuckles turning white on the arm of the chair. 'I mean, what part of that scenario did she imagine was going to be preferable to being brought up by a gay woman?' Her voice wavered. 'Granny point-blank refused to talk about Mum from the moment she left. Just before she died she told me she was sorry for erasing Mum's existence, for pretending she had never existed, but that she was ashamed of what she'd done.' She shook her head. 'I always assumed it was because she'd walked out and left me, but now I understand. Granny was ashamed of Mum for being gay.'

A silence fell again. I picked up my mug and took a deep gulp. The tea was tepid now but I needed something to do. I glanced at Charlie and he shrugged his shoulders helplessly.

Catherine stood abruptly, her chair almost toppling over. 'Sorry, excuse me a minute,' she said, and disappeared into the house before anyone could speak.

'I'm sorry—' I started.

'I hope I haven't—' Andrea began at the same time. I smiled. 'Go on.'

She shuffled in her seat. 'I hope I haven't upset her too much. I always wanted to make contact with her, let her know the truth about her mum but – well, you can't, can you, with something like this? I had no idea whether she even knew I existed, so I had to let her come to me.' She looked towards the house. 'I always hoped she would.'

'She'll be okay,' I said, not sure whether the words were true even as I said them. 'I think it will just take a little bit of time for the news to sink in.'

Andrea looked up at me. 'I hope she isn't too disappointed.'

I shook my head. 'I haven't known Catherine that long, but one thing I am absolutely certain of is that she won't be disappointed about her mother being gay. She just wants to understand why she left her. She's always blamed herself for not being good enough.'

'Oh gosh, how awful,' Andrea said, clasping her hands together. 'Lois adored her. She missed her terribly and—' She stopped. 'But I suppose it's going to be hard for Catherine to see that, isn't it?'

I nodded. 'Especially given that she lived with you. Obviously your mother didn't have the same qualms.' I shrugged. 'It's hard for any of us to understand what went through Lois's mind. I can understand the shame, at the time. But I think it will be much harder for Catherine to get her head round why she thought bringing one girl up with two mothers was acceptable, but not two.'

Andrea held her hands out helplessly. 'I really wish I could explain it myself. I've always assumed it was to do with her own parents' attitudes.' She shook her head. 'That's not to say I've ever agreed with it though.'

We fell silent again. When it became clear that Catherine wasn't hurrying back, Andrea stood. 'I'll go and find her, make sure she's all right, shall I?'

I nodded. 'I think you probably should.'

Charlie and I watched as Andrea disappeared through the patio doors into the kitchen. As soon as I was sure she was gone, I turned to Charlie.

'Poor Catherine,' I said.

He puffed his cheeks out. 'I know. I mean, I know that it must have been hard to live as a gay couple in those days. But to choose that over your own daughter? I don't get it. I couldn't imagine ever leaving my girls.'

I thought about how hard I found it when the kids were with Rob – how much I pined for them, felt as though a part of me were missing – and I just couldn't fathom it either. 'I guess we're looking at it from a modern perspective though,' I said. 'I mean, now it wouldn't make any sense to do that. But then? Well...' I tailed off.

'But to leave your kid?'

'I know. But you saw some of those letters Evelyn received. It's hard to remember how judgemental people used to be. And I don't just mean that people would have been disapproving, making comments about them.' I leaned forward, keen to get my point across. 'I think about the kids at school now, and how open-minded they are. They don't give a toss whether someone is gay, straight, bi... male, female, non-binary...' I sighed. 'Honestly, it's amazing how far things have come even in the last decade or so.' I jabbed my finger at the air. 'But remember what it was like when we were at school? People didn't get it, even then, and we thought we were so progressive compared to our parents. So I understand it. I do. I can see how it would have seemed so shameful that Lois might even have believed Catherine's life could have been in danger thanks to the lifestyle she'd chosen. And what mother would want that?'

Charlie pursed his lips. 'I know what you're saying. Really, I do. But it still doesn't explain why it was considered acceptable for Andrea to be brought up that way.'

I rubbed my hand over my face. 'No, you're right. I suppose it might just have been her own mother's choice.' I looked at Charlie. 'We'll probably never know now though.'

We both looked round at a noise by the house. Andrea and Catherine were emerging, arm in arm.

'Sorry about that,' Catherine said, lowering herself back into her seat.

'Don't apologise,' Charlie said.

Catherine shook her head. 'No, I am sorry though. I just

needed a minute to sort my head out.' She looked at Andrea. 'And sorry for barging into your bathroom without asking.'

Andrea grinned. 'It's fine. I'm just relieved I had the foresight to clean it this morning.'

Catherine smiled back at her and I waited for them to explain what they'd been talking about. I wondered if they'd had a similar conversation to the one Charlie and I had just had.

'Andrea was telling me about my mum,' Catherine said, still smiling. 'Tell them what you said, Andrea.'

'I was trying to show her how much Lois loved her.' She held her hand out to reveal a thick wad of loosely bundled papers. 'These are letters Lois wrote to Catherine through the years.'

Catherine took over, excitement shining in her eyes. 'Andrea found them in her mum's things when she died a couple of years ago,' she said, her words tripping over themselves to get out. 'She showed me a couple of them.' She looked back to Andrea for confirmation. 'She always missed me. She never stopped thinking about me.'

Andrea nodded. 'It's true. She talked about you all the time. She used to tell me stories of when you were a little girl.' She smiled, remembering. 'She told me about a red umbrella that you loved so much you took it everywhere with you for a year. Even when the sun was shining and you were trying to play, you'd march around with your red umbrella up, only putting it down to climb on a bike or scramble up a tree.'

'I remember that,' Catherine said.

'And do you remember how you used to have your own secret language for things that you refused to explain to anyone else so they had to try and work it out themselves?'

Catherine nodded, but her smile had faltered, like a crown that had slipped slightly, just off centre. I put my hand on her arm. 'Are you okay?'

She glanced at me as if she'd forgotten I was there – as if she'd momentarily lost track of where she was, even – and nodded. 'Yes, sorry. I just – I'd forgotten about those things. I've forgotten so much.' She closed her eyes briefly. 'These memories are all well and good, and these...' she flicked her hand over the letters that Andrea was still clutching, making a sharp cracking sound '... these are great, but they're just words.' She gave a bitter laugh, and I was glad I hadn't told her about the letters Charlie and I had found yet. 'Words my mother never even let me see. And words can't make up for the fact that she never gave me the chance to make any new memories with her.' A tear traced a path down her face and landed on her lap where it spread out, staining the fabric of her trousers with sadness. My heart broke for her.

'I know it's a lot to take in,' I said, gently. Catherine looked up at me, the pain of all the years she'd believed her mother hadn't cared about her etched onto her face like markings on rock. If only there were something I could do to make this easier for her.

'I wish Mum hadn't been so scared to live the way she wanted,' Catherine said suddenly. She turned to Andrea. 'What was it like?'

'What was what like?'

'Living with gay parents, back then?' She rubbed her hand over her face as though trying to wipe away the exhaustion. 'Was it really as terrible as my mother assumed it would be?'

Andrea studied her for a moment as though trying to work out how honest to be with her. Eventually, she spoke, choosing her words carefully.

'I can't pretend it was easy,' she said. 'Some children were cruel and tried to make me feel bad about not having a dad.' She swallowed. 'But it was the other parents who were the worst. Some of them, they...' she stopped. 'They didn't understand it. They treated Mum and Lois like dirt, as if they were no better than dog shit they'd scraped off the bottom of their shoes. There they'd be, these women, at the school gates, watching us with their pursed lips and disapproving eyebrows, tutting as we walked past.' She sighed. 'At first I hated arriving at school, knowing everyone there thought we were scum. But as I got older I stopped caring. Then when I was about thirteen another family moved into the village, young parents, from London, and they were so different from these people we spent our days surrounded by, and for the first time I saw us through their eyes. They didn't think we were evil, or perverted. They just accepted us.

'But their attitude made me realise what our parents were up against. Bigotry, hatred, threats, they were all there, barely concealed beneath the surface of these do-gooders.' She shrugged. 'Learning not to care was the best coping mechanism, and I expect that's what happened to your mum, in the end. She'd made her choice, and she had to live with the consequences, even if that meant losing you. I'm sure she thought she was protecting you.'

A silence fell, filled with the sounds of nature and other people's domesticity.

'Did she ever talk about me when she was older?' Catherine's voice punctuated the peace.

Andrea nodded. 'All the time. In fact as she got older she talked about you more and more.' She smiled. 'She even considered coming to see you at one point, but in the end she talked herself out of it. If I pushed it, she stopped talking about you altogether, as if she'd erected some kind of barrier to protect herself against the pain.'

'I wish she had.'

'Me too. But she was a stubborn old bugger – just like my mum, they were well suited – and I suppose she decided it was simply her punishment for leaving you in the first place. That she didn't deserve you, after walking out on you. And then she fell ill very suddenly and it was all too late.' She sighed. 'I only wish I'd known about these letters when she was still alive. I might have been able to convince her to send some of them to you, at the very least.'

Poor Lois. I thought about all the help and encouragement she'd given other people over the years as Evelyn Wright; all the times she'd been more tolerant and understanding than the era generally permitted, and I wondered how she'd really felt about other people treating her as less than human simply because she'd fallen in love with someone they didn't believe she should have done. What must it have been like, growing up in a time when something as simple as loving the 'wrong' gender was considered evil?

Although I'd never understand how someone could walk out on their own child, I was at least beginning to understand the circumstances that must have led to Lois doing just that, given the scrutiny and the judgement she would have been subjected to.

'Poor Mum,' Catherine said. Her voice was so quiet I wondered whether I'd heard her right, but one look at her face told me I had. She'd understood it too. Whether she could learn to forgive Lois was something only time would tell. But she was, at least, on her way to understanding her.

18

My darling Kitty

No doubt this letter will join the growing pile of unposted letters I have written to you since I last saw you, but I can only hope that, one day, I will summon the courage to post them to you or, better yet, bring them to you in person.

I miss you every day. I've considered endless times what it would be like to come and find you, and I almost did once. But in the end I couldn't bring myself to do it. I know your grandmother has washed her hands of me, and I don't think I could bear to see the look on your face if she refused to let me in the house. I'm a coward.

But I hope you know how much I love you. Not a day goes by when I don't think about you. I walk past a children's play park and I picture you, ribbons flying, feet outstretched, as you swung higher and higher, screaming with glee. I only have to hear the shouts and cries of children in a nearby school for my heart to clench and for a memory of you running out of school, one white sock pushed down, desperate to hug me at the end of the day, to hit me.

I know I've hurt you. I hope you're happy with Granny. One day, I can only pray that you will understand why I had to leave, and that you will forgive me. Until that day, know that I have always loved you, and I always will.

All my love forever

Mum

'I wish I'd asked her more about what Mum was like,' Catherine said as we drove home. It was cooler now, the heat of the day fading into early evening, the sun hovering on the horizon.

'You haven't lost your chance.'

She sighed heavily as the car wound round the country lanes. Andrea had made Catherine promise to stay in touch, and they'd already agreed she would come for dinner soon. I could see the idea of getting to know someone who had been like a daughter to Lois was having a strange effect on Catherine. On the one hand, she was jealous that her mother had brought up someone else's daughter but hadn't wanted to do the same for her own. But on the other hand, Catherine seemed thrilled about the idea of getting to know Andrea better and, through her, getting to know more about her mother.

'I know. I just hope Andrea doesn't think I only want her friendship to find out more about my mum.'

'We all need to know where we come from,' I said gently. 'There's no shame in wanting to get to know her because she knew your mum. None at all. Andrea understands that, and probably expects it. But it doesn't have to be the only reason for spending more time with her. She seems really nice, too.'

'She does, doesn't she?' she replied, a smile flitting across her face. 'Not as nice as you though, obviously.'

'Obviously.'

I settled back into my seat and watched the world speed by

through my window. The lush hedges had thinned now, and the occasional farm building had morphed into short parades of shops, rows of housing and schools. My eyes flicked back and forth and I let my mind drift to what Andrea had told Catherine this afternoon.

We hadn't intended staying as long as we did, but when Andrea had invited us for a late lunch, we'd all agreed. As we'd chatted around the wooden table in the warm sunlight, we'd learned much more about Andrea, her mother Dorothy – or Dot, as she was almost always known – and Lois.

Catherine already knew that her mother had never been married – in fact her father had never even been on the scene. But she'd obviously had no inkling whatsoever that her mum was attracted to women. Andrea, though, had never known anything different, so had never questioned it.

'I barely knew my dad,' Andrea had explained. 'When my mum left him, my memory of him in my young mind was not much more than a shadow, rather than a fully formed person. He visited from time to time, but when Lois came to live with us, he stopped coming at all. The only thing I remember feeling about that is that it was sad I wouldn't get the bar of chocolate he always used to bring with him, rather than any real feelings about missing him. I realised much later that he'd been ashamed he'd been dumped for a woman and disgusted by the whole thing. But back then I'd had no idea.'

Lois and Dot had been happy from the word go, as if they'd finally realised what had been missing in their lives before they'd found each other.

'Lois used to talk about you all the time, and it was obvious how much she always missed you. Mum thought she should have brought you to live with us, but, for whatever reason, Lois said it wasn't possible. It became the only fly in the ointment between

them that I'd ever been aware of, and it was still there on the day
Lois died.'

The family had been through a lot, it seemed. As well as the
inevitable gossip and disapproval, some people had tried to take it
a step further. They'd had eggs thrown at the front door and
through windows, graffiti spray-painted on their walls and, one
time, a woman in the butcher's had screamed when Lois had
walked in and demanded that she was removed from the shop, as
though she'd had some sort of contagious disease. But they had
never given up on each other, until Lois had died after a short
fight with lung cancer five years ago.

'I just wish she'd been brave enough to have gone and found
you,' Andrea said. 'I would have loved a sister, and I feel as if it
would have rid Lois of the sadness that always pervaded her, like a
dark cloud that followed her round throughout her life.'

Catherine didn't say anything, but I could see her taking slow,
deep breaths, as though she was trying not to cry.

'She obviously thought about you all the time,' I said. 'All
those letters.'

She nodded and gave a weak smile.

'You know she also carried on writing agony aunt letters
though, don't you?' Andrea added.

Catherine looked up sharply. 'No, I had no idea.'

Andrea speared a piece of asparagus, nodded. 'Yep. I think it
was probably some sort of attempt at redemption – she thought if
she could solve other people's problems, give them some hope, it
would somehow cancel out what she'd done.'

I glanced at Charlie, eyebrows raised in a question. Should I
tell her about the letters we'd found? He was clearly having the
same thought, and gave a tiny nod.

'We found some of them,' I said, touching Catherine's arm.
She looked at me, confused.

'What do you mean?'

I took a deep breath. 'Charlie and I found a few of her later ones, in the loft.'

Catherine's face creased into a frown. 'What are you talking about?'

I told her about the letters we'd found that Dot had written to Evelyn asking for advice and, later, the more personal ones the two women had written to each other.

'And you found these when?'

'A – a few days ago.'

Her eyes widened. 'And you didn't think to tell me?'

'It was my fault,' Charlie said, diving in. 'I said it would be best to see what Andrea had to say first.' He looked at me. 'I'm sorry if that was the wrong thing to do. We didn't want to jump to any conclusions and then have it completely wrong.'

Catherine watched us both for a second. I prayed she wouldn't be angry. Finally, after what seemed like forever, she let out a long breath. 'Wow.' She rubbed her eyes, leaving a smudge of mascara on her cheek. 'I wonder how long she carried on answering agony aunt letters. Maybe it was longer than we thought.'

'She stopped years ago,' Andrea said, and I was glad the attention was off us – for now at least. 'Maybe the eighties.' She smiled. 'I think the problems youngsters were having then became too much for her to cope with. She might have been forward-thinking for her time, but time marched on quicker than she did in the end.'

'It comes to us all,' I agreed.

Now, in the car on the way home, I couldn't help thinking about Lois's decision to never contact her own daughter again. How ashamed must she have been of that decision despite clearly adoring her? All those people she helped, and nobody was there to help her work through her sadness, to tell her everything would be all right.

And seeing Catherine's pain at the way her mother had behaved had made me realise one thing. No matter how wronged you felt or how bad you felt about decisions you'd made in your life, you must never, ever let your children be the ones to suffer as a consequence.

I needed to sort things out with Rob once and for all.

* * *

That was easier said than done, of course. The moment I stepped in the door, my mobile rang and Rob's number flashed up. I was so exhausted I almost didn't answer it, but then I remembered my promise to myself on the way home from Andrea's, and I clicked 'answer' at the last minute.

I knew I should have trusted my instincts.

'Beth, your daughter wants to speak to you.'

I bit my tongue, determined not to make a sarcastic comment about his lack of manners, and waited for Olivia's voice to come on the line.

'Mummy?'

'Hey, sweetheart,' I said, kicking off my shoes and smiling at the sound of my little girl's voice. 'How's your day been?'

'Good, thank you.'

'Good.' I made my way into the lounge. 'What did you want to talk to me about, darling?'

'Can I stay at Daddy's this week?'

'What?' The backs of my legs felt weak and I dropped onto the sofa before they crumpled beneath me. 'All week?'

'Yes.'

'Any—' I stopped. I didn't want her to hear how upset I was. I cleared my throat. 'Is there a particular reason?' They'd both been due home tomorrow and the thought of not seeing them for another week made my stomach hurt.

'No, Mummy. I just like it better here.'

Ouch, the honesty of an almost-eight-year-old. I swallowed down the ball of hurt that had lodged in my throat. 'I—' I stopped. I'd been about to ask her what was so much better about being there, but the self-preservation part of me stopped me. I so desperately didn't want her to stay there, and yet I knew if I tried to stop her, she'd resent me. I tried another tack.

'Buster is really missing you. Don't you want to give him cuddles and take him for walks?'

'Walks are a bit boring. We always go to the same field. And Buster won't mind if I stay a few more days. We can have cuddles when I get home.'

I couldn't argue with that. I wanted to feel angry, to blame Rob and Natalie for taking my little girl away from me. But he was still her father, and of *course* she'd want to spend time with him – and in her old bedroom, too. The anger melted away, leaving a trail of self-pity behind.

'Okay, you can stay this week, but just as a one-off.'

'Yay, thank you, Mummy!' I tried not to mind too much that she was quite that excited. 'But, Olivia—' I stopped, aware suddenly that she was no longer on the other end of the line. I was about to end the call when I heard my name.

'Beth?'

'Rob.'

'Thank you for this.'

'It doesn't seem like I had much choice.'

'You did. You could have made it difficult, and I appreciate it that you didn't.'

I didn't reply. I didn't want him to know how much this was hurting me. He spoke again.

'I wanted to tell you something as well, and I wanted you to hear it from me.'

I waited, the line humming.

'Natalie and I are getting married. In Crete.'

'In August?'

'Yes.'

'Wow, so soon.' It took a mammoth effort to keep my voice steady.

'Yes, well, with the baby and everything we just thought…' He trailed off and cleared his throat.

'Well, then, congratulations,' I said, and ended the call, cutting off Rob's next words in their tracks. I knew I was being rude but I needed time to recalibrate.

Weddings and holidays without me, my daughter not wanting to come home… it was beginning to feel as though my children were slipping away from me, piece by tiny piece, like sand falling through an hourglass. I thought of Lois and what an impossible situation she must have felt she was in, and how incredibly painful it must have been for her to leave her daughter behind, and I knew one thing for sure: I couldn't lose my children, the way Lois had. I had to fight for them, no matter what it took.

19

FRIENDSHIP AT STAKE

I am great friends with a man who I have known for some time. He is married to someone else and there has never been anything between us, although he means a great deal to me. One night recently we kissed and now I fear I have lost him forever. I am beside myself. How can I save our friendship?

If you are absolutely honest with yourself you will know that you did the wrong thing by kissing this man. But nobody is perfect, and sometimes love and desire can overcome us. I suspect you have mistaken your feelings of friendship for this fellow with feelings of love, in which case I suggest you talk to him and agree to forget about it and continue as before. If, however, you feel unable to do this, then I fear you may have no choice but to end the friendship for good.

'I want to live with Daddy and Natalie.'

The words pierced my heart as cleanly as if they had been tiny little needles. I felt my breath leave me and if I hadn't already been sitting down I would have fallen.

'Wha—?' I couldn't even get any words out. The sight of my daughter's defiant face on the other end of the Zoom call was sucking all the air from my lungs.

'Olivia, who are you talking to?' Rob's voice in the background got closer, then his face filled the screen.

'Oh, sorry, I didn't know she'd rung you already,' he said. He had the grace to looked shamefaced.

'I—' I coughed and tried to recover my voice. 'She said...' No, I couldn't say it out loud. It was too painful.

A look of something flitted across Rob's face, then cleared. He rubbed his cheek and the scratching sound made me shudder. 'Look, Beth, sorry, she was meant to wait for me to speak to you first, but I—'

'What's going on, Rob?' My voice shook.

'She's asked if she can come and live here.'

'Permanently?'

He shrugged. 'For a while, yeah.'

'But—' I stopped. What could I say? Why had she chosen her father and his girlfriend over living here with me and her baby brother? I could only imagine the fun things they'd bought her to keep her happy. Her own bedroom, new clothes, all the toys she could ever ask for. He'd even bought her an iPhone recently, for fuck's sake, even though we'd agreed a few weeks before that she was far too young.

'She says everyone's got them,' he'd said, trying to justify himself. But we both knew what it was really. Bribery.

And now this.

'I hope you're happy,' I said. My voice sounded like dozens of shards of glass shattering. My throat felt ripped to shreds.

'Don't be ridiculous, Beth, of course my daughter feeling

miserable doesn't make me happy. But if it's going to help her, then I'm going to support her.'

Rob was lucky he was fifteen miles away because I wanted to scratch his eyes out, pummel my fists against his chest, kick him where it really hurt. Instead all I could do was feel this pathetic, pointless rage simmering inside me, with absolutely nowhere for it to go.

I took a deep breath and said, 'Why?'

'Honestly, I don't know.' He glanced over his shoulder. 'She just said she preferred it here. I don't think it's personal.'

'Not personal?' The words spluttered out of me like scalding tea. 'Are you *fucking* kidding me? How can my own daughter not wanting to come home be anything but personal?' I swallowed, trying to gather my thoughts. The phone shook in my hand and I propped it against a glass and put my head in my hands. 'I don't know what to say to you,' I said, my voice quiet. 'If Olivia feels she gets more from you and your girlfriend than she does here then I guess there's nothing I can do to compete with that.'

'It's not a competition, Beth.'

'Isn't it?'

I almost ended the call then too. But I needed to know something else.

'I assume you're letting me have Jacob back?'

'Don't be like that. Of course Jacob's coming back.'

You mean you haven't managed to bribe him, I thought, but didn't say. I needed to be the bigger person here.

'Can I speak to her, please?'

'I don't think that's a good idea, she's—'

'Put her on, Rob.'

A sigh, then I watched him walk out of the room to find her. Seconds later she appeared in the screen and my heart clenched with love. Her face peered at me, a tiny little crease in her forehead.

'Hello, Mummy.'

'Hello, darling. So you want to stay there a bit longer?'

'Uh huh.'

'I see. Don't you want to come back home to Mummy with Jacob tomorrow?'

She shook her head mutely. She was looking somewhere off camera.

'Olivia, can you look at me, please?' She tore her gaze away from whatever had caught her attention and stuck her thumb in her mouth. She'd started sucking her thumb when Rob and I had split up and had only stopped when we'd moved out here. It rang an immediate alarm bell. I moved closer to the screen so that all she could see was my face.

'What's going on, sweetheart? Has something happened?'

She shook her head.

'Jacob, Buster and I will miss you.' I kept my voice low, unsure whether Rob was still listening.

She still wasn't quite looking at the screen. I wished I could reach in and pull her towards me, feel her little body press against mine, keep her safe. Instead all the screen did was increase the distance between us.

'Can I see Buster?' she said.

'Of course.' I reached down and scooped him up. He wriggled in my arms.

'Buster!' Olivia called his name and he looked at the screen with his head cocked to one side. 'He's looking at me, Mummy, he knows I'm talking to him.'

'He is. He misses you.'

'I miss him too, Mummy.' Her voice sounded sad, faraway. The screen was angled half on her face, the rest showing the living

My world stilled.

'What?'

He tried a smile but gave up. 'She said she wants all her old friends to come and we've promised her a pony party and...' He trailed off. 'You're welcome to come though.'

Rage bubbled in my belly, rising up and burning a path through my throat. 'A *pony* party?' I said, my voice a screech. 'A fucking pony party?' My breath came in gasps and I swallowed down a ball of anger. 'Is this what we're doing now, Rob? Bribing our children so they choose us, using them like pawns in some warped game of control?' I shook my head in disbelief. 'This is the lowest thing you've ever done, and you've done some pretty fucking despicable things in the last couple of years.'

'I can't talk to you when you're like this, Beth,' he said. His arm moved and rage exploded in my head.

'Don't you *dare* end the call!' I screamed. He stopped.

'Are you going to calm down?'

I looked at his face in the screen and for the first time since we'd met and fallen in love, twelve years before, I felt repulsed by him. His skin was tanned but had a strange, yellowy gleam to it, and he'd tried to style his hair to conceal what I could now see was a rapidly receding hairline. I wasn't proud of the spark of triumph that flickered through me as I wondered what I'd ever seen in this man.

'I'll be calm when you stop trying to buy our daughter's love,' I said. Then, even though I wanted to speak to Jacob, and even though I had so many more things I wanted to say to my ex-husband, I closed my laptop and cut him off.

* * *

room behind her. My old living room, the one I'd spent so ma
hours choosing the furniture for, agonising over wallpaper.
looked different now, a new coat of paint on the walls and
brand-new corner sofa where my beautiful velvet ones had bee
but I still felt a pang for my old life.

I knew pushing Olivia too much would only make her dig he
heels in further – we were too similar like that – but I had to give i
one last shot before I gave in.

'We can plan your birthday party if you come back tomorrow,'
I said. 'You can choose who you want to invite, and you can do
whatever you like.'

I'd hoped it might just do the trick, but, instead of squealing
with excitement the way she usually would when I mentioned her
birthday, she was deathly quiet. I checked the volume was still on.
It was.

'Livvy? What's the matter?'

'Nothing.' She looked down at her lap.

'Olivia, darling, you can tell me.'

She shook her head again and I wanted to scream in frustration. What the hell was going on? Before I could ask her again she
stood up and ran out of the room. I watched the empty room for a
few seconds in shock, wondering whether to hang up and ring
Rob back, or whether she was coming back. Just as I was about to
give up, Rob's body reappeared in the doorway and his face filled
my vision again.

'What's going on? What's wrong with Olivia? Have you
poisoned her mind against me?'

'Don't be so ridiculous. You know me better than that.'

'I used to.'

He rolled his eyes and I clenched my fists, jabbing my nails
into my palms until it hurt. 'Listen, Beth, Olivia has said she wants
to have her birthday party here instead of at your house too.'

'Give her time, she'll be back before you know it.' Charlie poured two large glasses of wine and passed me one. I took a huge gulp and whacked the glass back on the table with such force it almost shattered.

After my conversation with Rob I'd been boiling with rage and desperate for someone to rant to. Even though Rob had tried to ring me back several times, I'd ignored him. Instead I'd tried to call Catherine to ask if she was free.

'He's an utter bastard and I'd love to come and slag him off with you all evening, but I've got a friend here,' she'd said.

'Oh.' Catherine and I had only known each other a few weeks and it was completely unreasonable of me to expect her not to have any other friends, or to want to spend time with them. And yet I'd still felt put out.

'Sorry, Beth. You know I'd be there in a flash usually.'

'It's okay.' I'd felt like a sulky child. 'Honestly,' I'd added.

After ending the call I'd felt even more frustrated, and before I'd even thought about what I was doing I'd rung Charlie.

'Are you free?' I'd said when he answered.

'Oh, Beth. Hi. Are you okay?'

'No.' My voice had come out as a squeak, and to my horror I'd burst into tears. It had taken me a good few minutes before I could speak again, by which time I'd been a snotty mess. 'Sorry. It's fine. I'm fine.'

'Clearly.'

I'd sniffed.

'Do you need me to come over?'

'Aren't you busy?'

A hesitation. Then: 'No. I can come over if you need me.'

'Yes, please.'

I'd regretted being so needy the moment I'd ended the call, but Charlie had already been on his way. Besides, I always enjoyed seeing him. In fact, more than enjoyed it. I'd realised, as I'd been on the call with Rob, that me not finding Rob attractive any more was not only about him, but about Charlie too. Because whether I meant to or not, there was no doubt I was comparing them in my mind – and Rob was definitely not coming out favourably.

Despite what I'd told Catherine – and what I'd tried to convince myself – I did have feelings for Charlie. And the more time I spent with him, the more those feelings were growing, unfurling like the plants he'd planted in my garden.

So it probably hadn't been a good idea to ask him to come round tonight. But he was here now, and I was so grateful to have someone to talk to I could have cried (again).

'It feels like I can never compete with anything Rob can offer her,' I said, swirling the wine round the glass. We were sitting at the small kitchen table, the bottle between us. Condensation ran down the outside of the bottle and gathered round the base. I ran my finger through it and smeared it across the wood.

'When Polly was about ten years old, she packed a suitcase, left the house and was halfway to Helen's parents' house before we even realised she was missing,' Charlie said suddenly. I looked up at him. 'We were terrified, and it wasn't until Helen's parents rang half an hour later after Polly had arrived at their house, soaked to the skin from the rain and dragging her little case behind her, that we knew where she'd gone.' He ran his finger round the top of his glass. 'It was the longest half an hour of my life, and in that time I couldn't stop thinking about how I might never see her again.

'But actually, that wasn't the worst bit. Because Polly had decided she couldn't possibly live with us any more, that we were the worst parents in the world, and she'd made her grandparents promise she could stay there with them.' He looked up at me and shrugged. 'They were a total pushover, the pair of them, but there wasn't anything we could do. If we dragged her back kicking and screaming she'd never have forgiven us. So we let her stay.'

'And?'

He met my gaze and I shivered. 'She stayed for six weeks in the end.'

'Six *weeks*?' The thought of being without Olivia for six weeks was almost more than I could bear.

'Yes. But it was the best thing we did. Helen's parents spoiled her, at first. She got all the food she loved, she had more space to herself in their spare bedroom, she didn't have her little sister there to annoy her. They even put a TV in her room. She was living the life of Riley. But it didn't take long for her to realise that, actually, Nanny and Grandad were stricter than us. They didn't let her have her friends over, after the first couple of days they made her eat whatever they served for dinner whether she liked it or not. And they definitely didn't put up with any of what they called her 'nonsense' – they were firm believers in children being seen and not heard, and Polly couldn't stand that. So finally, one day, Helen's mum rang us and said Polly wanted to talk to us – and she admitted she'd made a mistake and wanted to come home. And that was that.'

He shrugged and placed his hands flat on the table. I studied the back of them. 'But the point is, only she could make the decision to come back. We had to wait for her to realise how good we were to her by experiencing something else, and then she never wanted to leave again. In fact we had to almost throw her out of the house a couple of years ago when she kept moving back.' He grinned.

He was right. I knew he was right. Olivia might think she was better off with Rob and Natalie – after all, she had her old bedroom back, a room to herself, and both of them all to herself, at least until the baby came. Plus it appeared she only had to ask for something and Rob bought it for her. But living with them full-time? I was fairly sure they'd both run out of patience eventually. I just wasn't sure how long I was prepared to wait.

'You're right,' I said.

'I often am.' He smiled to show he was joking. Our hands were almost touching on the table and I wondered what would happen if I moved my fingers and interlaced them with his. I tried to imagine how his skin would feel. His hands would probably be quite rough thanks to the nature of his job.

Heart thumping, I snatched my hands away and wrapped them round my glass. 'Thank you, Charlie. That's just what I needed to hear.'

'Honestly, I think she'll be home before you know it. And she'll love you even more.'

'I hope so.'

Charlie took a sip of his wine and I did the same. The warm glow from the alcohol was helping my body to relax, and the tension slipped from me limb by limb. I tipped the last of the wine down my throat and topped up my glass, then moved to refill Charlie's. He placed his hand over it.

'I'd better not have too much,' he said. 'I shouldn't be too late back.'

He hadn't said Helen's name but it hung in the air between us anyway, like a fly buzzing round a light bulb. The bottle hovered over his hand, unmoving, as though waiting for something. It felt as though everything was suspended, as though whatever happened next could change everything as easily as the flip of a coin.

And then Charlie moved his hand away and gave me a goofy grin. 'On second thoughts, who gives a fuck? It's not like I've got anything to get home for. Let's get pissed.'

I filled his glass almost to the brim, and we chinked, before taking huge gulps. I wiped my mouth on the back of my sleeve. 'Cheers to not giving a fuck,' I said, not wanting to ask any more details.

'Amen to that.'

I wished I could ask him more about Helen, about how things were between them. Before, I would have done – whether they were getting on, if he could see any improvement between them – after all, wasn't that how we'd met in the first place, through me helping him? But somehow, over the course of the last few weeks, something had shifted between us and now it felt wrong to pry. I wondered whether he felt it too, or whether it was all on me.

Buster's manic barking by the front door jolted me out of my daze and I leapt up, almost spilling my wine.

'Hang on,' I said. I doubted there was actually anything going on outside but I was glad of the excuse to get away before I said anything I'd regret. I stood tickling the backs of Buster's ears as he woofed half-heartedly at absolutely nothing in the quiet street, and took a few deep breaths to compose myself. Charlie was just a friend. He was here to help. It didn't mean anything more.

If I said it enough times, perhaps I'd begin to believe it.

When I got back to the kitchen, Charlie was rummaging in the cupboard and turned to face me guiltily, like a naughty boy who'd been caught doing something he shouldn't.

'Sorry,' he said, closing the door, a packet of crisps in his hand. 'I was getting peckish. D'you mind if I...?' He held the packet up forlornly.

'We can do better than that,' I said. 'Let's go out for something to eat.'

'Out?'

'Yes, you know. A restaurant, where someone else cooks your food and they serve it to you at the table. That sort of out.'

'Oh. Yeah, we could do...' He looked at his feet and it took me a moment to realise what had caused his change of heart. My face flamed and I smacked my forehead.

'God, stupid me. Of course you can't go out for dinner with me, that would look totally wrong,' I said, pulling open a cupboard and pretending to look for something in an attempt to hide my embarrassment. 'I keep forgetting this is a small village where everyone knows everyone else's business.'

'No, it's not that, it's—' He stopped and I whipped my head round to look at him. He wouldn't look me in the eye.

'Charlie? What's wrong?'

He shrugged and finally looked up. His eyes were full of pain. 'I think Helen might be out with someone else tonight,' he said, his voice soft. 'Another man.'

I stared at him for a moment. I took in his long nose, his chiselled chin and his soft blue eyes. What sort of idiot would cheat on this man?

I stepped towards him and put my hand on his arm. He didn't move away. 'I'm so sorry, Charlie,' I said. 'I thought you were sorting things out.'

He gave a small nod. 'Me too. And I don't have any proof but... She said she was going for a drink with a friend, but sometimes you just know, don't you?'

I thought back to when I'd found out about Rob's affair. Although the discovery had been like a blow to the head, I'd realised afterwards that I'd suspected it for a while, but had been trying to deny it to myself. All the nights he'd 'worked late'. All the times he'd said he was going for a quick drink, or had popped out for some unexplained errand at the weekend. Sometimes our brains were good at telling ourselves what we wanted to believe.

'Do you want to talk about it? You know I've been through it myself.'

He stared down at where my hand was still resting on his arm and put his other hand over it, enveloping my fingers in his long, lean, work-worn ones. His touch felt like a lightning bolt to my skin, and a low pulse started in my belly, like a slow, rhythmic drumbeat. I moved imperceptibly closer to him, and the air between us hummed with expectation. The line between his eyebrows deepened, and finally, slowly, he raised his eyes to meet mine.

'Do you know what, let's not bother even thinking about Helen tonight. I've done enough worrying about her. Let's just get drunk and have a bit of fun.'

Then he moved his hand away, leaving my fingers floating momentarily in mid-air. They felt cold and I dropped them down by my side. The moment was gone. But we both knew there had been a moment.

I snatched up the wine bottle, refilled our glasses as full as they would go, then pulled another one from the fridge.

'Takeaway and a night on the sofa?' I said.

'Sounds perfect.'

* * *

Takeaway cartons littered the coffee table, and two empty wine bottles stood beside them, reminding us how much we'd sunk between us. Charlie and I were pressed together on the sofa, huddled round my laptop, giggling like schoolchildren. I hadn't been this happy for a long time, and I was desperate for him not to notice the time, or our state of drunkenness, and leave me here alone again.

I didn't dare think about the hangover I'd have for work in the morning.

'I feel this one is for me to answer,' Charlie said, tugging the laptop slightly closer to him. The screen was angled away so I couldn't see it, so I tugged it back, and he pulled it again and slapped my wrist gently.

'Oi!' I said, smacking him back.

'Hey, that's abuse in the workplace,' he said.

'You don't work for me!'

'What do you call this, then?' he said, gesturing at the screen where we were reading some of the hundred-odd new *Dear Evelyn* letters.

'This isn't work. This is a friend helping a friend out of a sticky corner,' I said, grinning.

He thought for a moment, then grinned back. 'Fair enough. But you do need to let me type if you want me to answer this properly, otherwise I'll be sending some poor sod a right load of gobbledegook.'

I sighed and moved away slightly. After we'd eaten, I'd told Charlie about the *Dear Evelyn* column getting out of control, and how I wondered whether I should stop doing it because I didn't want to let so many people down by not having time to reply to them all.

'You absolutely must *not* stop it,' he'd said. 'What you're giving people is vital.'

I'd giggled at his seriousness, but he hadn't joined in. 'I mean it, Beth. When I wrote to you I really, really needed someone to talk to. Ideally someone who didn't know me or Helen so they could give me objective advice. And then there you were, like a beacon of light among all the shite on the Internet. It felt like a sign.'

'But I didn't even really help you.'

He'd pulled away and given me a stern look. 'Are you kidding?'

'No! You and Helen still haven't sorted things out.' I'd shrugged. 'It seems to me I didn't really do much at all.'

He'd shaken his head. 'You absolutely did. Just writing to you helped me to get things straight in my mind. It helped me decide whether my marriage was worth fighting for, or whether to throw in the towel.' He'd smiled. 'And I know this can't be the same for everyone, but it also meant I made a new friend who has, by some miracle, become really important in my life.'

I'd watched his face as he'd said this, and tried not to feel disappointed at the use of the word friend.

'You're right, I am pretty special,' I'd said, joking to cover up my awkwardness.

'And?'

'And what?'

'You're supposed to say how important I am to you as well.'

'And you're not meant to fish for compliments.' I'd grinned.

'Fair enough.'

But his words had made me realise he was right. *Dear Evelyn was* important. And Catherine and Charlie had both agreed to help me with it, so I really had no excuse. 'No time like the present,' Charlie had said. Despite my protestations about not replying while we were drunk, he'd written some great responses so far. I had, however, made him agree not to actually send them today, so I could double-check they weren't drunken gibberish before emailing them back and adding them to the website in the morning.

'Fine, fine,' he'd agreed. 'Although I think drunken replies would add a bit of spice to the site.'

'I'm not sure spice is what the people writing to me are looking for.'

'Good point.'

So far we'd answered around twenty of the letters that had arrived recently, and Charlie was starting to formulate a response to a man who was worried his new girlfriend was only with him because of his gym-honed body.

'Obviously I know a lot about being a trophy boyfriend,' Charlie had said, 'being such a fine specimen myself.'

I had tried not to look at his toned arms and firm thighs in his jeans beside me.

'What are you telling him?' I said now, trying to peer over his shoulder, but he turned the screen away from me.

'Hang on, let me finish.' He leaned down for his glass of wine on the floor and his T-shirt rode up, exposing his tanned back. I looked away quickly as he sat back up again.

'I don't think I should answer any more, I think I'm too drunk now,' I said, draining the last of the wine from my glass and plonking it down with a bang on the table.

'Yeah, I should probably make this my last one too.' He glanced at his watch and I wanted to kick myself for alerting him to the time. *Don't go, don't go, don't go,* I chanted in my mind.

But he didn't say anything about how late it was and I settled back into the sofa and waited for him to stop typing.

'There, done,' he said, then closed the laptop with a click and placed it carefully on the table beside the detritus of the evening. He swivelled round to face me. 'I think we've had a successful night,' he said.

'Me too.'

I was about to look away when I noticed his eyes searching my face. I met his gaze, my heart thudding.

'What?' My voice cracked.

'Nothing,' he said, but he didn't look away. My pulse thumped in my belly again and I held my breath. I knew I should say something – ask him about Helen or offer him a coffee – anything to break the intensity of this moment and stop whatever was happening here from happening. It was what I *should* do. But it wasn't what I *wanted* to do. So I stayed where I was, caught like a butterfly in a net, unable to move.

The seconds ticked by. I became aware of his arm resting along the back of the sofa, his hand just inches from my shoulder. I felt the press of his leg and his warm breath on my cheek. And still I didn't move.

Then his fingers were in my hair, entwining themselves slowly through it, and his leg moved a tiny bit closer, and his eyes bored into me, and I felt myself sinking into the moment as if it was the most natural thing in the world, as if it was inevitable. Then he closed the gap between us and his lips grazed mine, and something in my brain exploded. The kiss deepened frantically, urgently, as if it were something we'd both been waiting our whole lives for, as if everything had been building up to this moment, and I didn't ever want it to end. We tore at each other's clothes, only pulling apart to get his T-shirt over his head before our lips smashed back together again. My hands ran over his chest, round his back, and I gasped as he pushed the straps of my top down and slipped his hand inside my bra. I didn't think I could take much more and it was almost a relief when he pulled away.

'Shall we go upstairs?' he said. His voice was low and it seeped into my bones.

I nodded, mute, and followed him upstairs where we fell onto my bed the instant we walked through the door. I wanted to fill myself up with him and as we moved together I couldn't think of anything else but Charlie, his body, and me...

* * *

It was early when I woke, and it took me a second to realise that the lemon-yellow light was sunlight pouring through my open curtains. Confused, I tried to lift my head to look at the clock, but as I moved a pain shot through it and I groaned. I lay staring at the ceiling for a moment, trying to work out why the curtains were open, and what had happened last night.

And then, like being struck by a bolt of lightning, I remembered.

Charlie.

I realised then that I could hear slow, steady breathing beside me, a gentle snore. It had been so long since there had been anyone sharing my bed apart from Jacob or Buster that it had taken me a while to notice. I turned my head, slowly, slowly... and there he was.

Charlie.

Charlie was in my bed.

Oh my *God*, Charlie was in my bed!

I rolled over and pulled myself upright, swallowing down the nausea as I stood. I needed to think, but before that I needed water so I didn't kill off any more of my brain cells. I wobbled across the floor, stark naked, and plucked my dressing gown from the back of the door, wrapped it round me and crept downstairs. I didn't want to wake him, not yet, not before I'd worked out how I felt about what had happened between us last night.

Despite myself, I shivered at the image of Charlie in my bed.

Stop it, Beth, he shouldn't be here. This is wrong!

But it didn't feel wrong.

I made coffee on autopilot, and fed Buster, who was fussing round my feet. As he wolfed down his food I opened the back door and let the cool air flood in and wash over my tired eyes, my sore head... my guilty conscience.

I stepped outside and lowered myself into a chair. It was still only six-thirty in the morning but the sun was already warm, and I tipped my head up and closed my eyes and let myself drink it in.

Aside from the nausea, my main feeling was one of excitement – although it was tinged by the guilt of what Charlie and I had done. I didn't want to think about what this might mean, or what it might have done to our friendship if Charlie regretted it instantly. Meeting Charlie and Catherine had changed my life, and I wasn't ready to lose him already, so quickly on the heels of losing my daughter. I opened my eyes and took a sip of coffee. It was still too hot and I felt the burn as it slid down my throat.

'Ahem.' I almost jumped out of my skin at the sound, and I whipped my head round to find Charlie hovering behind me. He was fully dressed and had his hands stuck awkwardly in his pockets, and any thought I might have had that he wouldn't be regretting what happened last night disappeared into the gentle morning breeze like a wisp of smoke. Of *course* he was going to regret it. *He's* married, *for God's sake, Beth, what else were you expecting, a declaration of love?*

'Hi,' I said, suddenly shy in front of this man I'd been so intimate with only a few hours before.

'Morning,' he said, but didn't move.

'You're allowed to come closer, you know, I won't bite,' I said, forcing a smile onto my face.

He nodded. 'Can I just—' he jabbed his thumb behind him '— get a coffee?'

'Oh yes, of course.' I stood and almost spilt my own coffee over myself. It splashed onto the paving stone.

'It's fine, I'll get it. If you don't mind?'

'No. No, of course not. Help yourself.'

I sat back down as he disappeared into the kitchen and allowed myself to emit a low groan. The fact that he was asking permission to make himself a coffee told me all I needed to know about how last night had affected our friendship.

It had ruined everything.

I stared into the garden where the freshly laid turf was beginning to flourish, although you could still make out the edges where the pieces had been joined together. It was so fresh it wouldn't take much to ruin the young blades of grass, to trample them into oblivion. All it would take was some reckless behaviour, a moment of stupidity, and it would all be spoilt forever.

Yes, yes, Beth, lovely metaphor – I would have laughed at myself for being so ridiculous, except it didn't feel very funny.

Footsteps behind me brought my attention back and I waited for Charlie to sit down in the chair beside me. We both sat in silence for a few minutes, watching the still peaceful garden slowly come to life. A plane drifted high above, leaving a lazy trail in its wake. It felt as if the whole world were just waking up.

I needed to say something, but nothing I tried out in my head sounded right.

'I've never done anything like this before.' Charlie spoke first and I turned to look at him. He was staring into his coffee cup.

'Me neither.'

He gave a small nod and I looked away.

'So what happens now, then?'

I shrugged, then realised he couldn't see that. 'I don't know,' I said. *I want to be your girlfriend, I want to get to know you better, spend the rest of the day in bed – anything!* I wanted to say. But none of those words came out.

'We probably shouldn't have let that happen.'

My heart dropped to the base of my stomach. Of course.

'No.'

From the corner of my eye I saw him turn his head towards me but I couldn't look at him. To do so would be to see how stupid I'd been, thinking a drunken mistake could have meant anything more to him than that.

'I was going to say I wish it hadn't happened but – well. I don't mean that. Not exactly.'

I didn't reply.

'I'm glad it happened,' he said. 'I just—'

'It shouldn't have done,' I finished for him.

He paused a moment, then said, 'No.'

A bird tweeted, Buster snuffled in the soil, and a neighbour opened a window with a squeak. I wondered what they'd make of me sitting out here so early in the morning in my dressing gown with somebody else's husband.

'I'm sorry,' I said, although I wasn't.

'Please don't say that. I don't want either of us to feel sorry about what happened.' He puffed out his cheeks. 'I wanted it to happen, Beth. I've wanted it to for ages but...'

'You're married.'

He nodded. 'I've never cheated on anyone,' he said.

'I'm not judging you.'

'No, but I am.'

I felt a flash of anger surge through me. 'You've got nothing to feel guilty about, Charlie. Didn't—?' I hesitated. I didn't want to make Helen seem like the enemy, it wasn't the cool thing to do. But it felt justified. 'Helen hasn't exactly treated you well and... well, didn't you say you thought she was out with someone last night? A man, I mean.'

He looked up sharply. 'Didn't anyone ever tell you two wrongs don't make a right?'

I met his gaze and tried to work out what was going on behind his eyes. 'They did,' I said quietly. Something occurred to me then. 'Are you going to tell her? Helen?'

He shook his head. 'I don't know.' He paused. 'I doubt it. I don't know what good it would do.'

I didn't reply. I hated the thought of being the other woman, especially after going through it myself with Rob. But the truth was I couldn't bring myself to feel much sympathy for Helen, and not just because I was the other woman in this case – but because she'd treated Charlie like dirt and he deserved so, so much better. But I also understood that this wasn't the time to tell him this – and I wasn't the person to tell him. He needed to come to that conclusion himself.

Charlie stood and drained the last of his coffee. 'I'd better get going.'

'Okay.'

'Thanks for the coffee and – well... everything.' His face flamed and he looked away, somewhere over my shoulder.

'No worries.'

I sat mutely and watched him as he went back into the house. I wondered briefly where he was going to tell Helen he'd stayed last night, but it was none of my business. Seconds later he emerged with his jacket and phone. He hovered, and for a minute I thought he was going to change his mind and stay. But then he gave a small nod, turned on his heel, and let himself out of the side gate.

'Bye Charlie,' I whispered. Then I went inside to get ready for work.

20

LETTER FROM THE HEART

I am eighteen and have a good friend who I have known for some time. We go to dances together, and often go to the pictures. But for the last few weeks I haven't seen her and I am worried I might have done something to upset her. She appears to be ignoring my telephone calls, and whenever I have gone to visit her at her parents' house they have told me she is not in. How can I get my friend to talk to me again?

Could it simply be that she is busy and has not realised how much time has passed since you last spoke? If you honestly believe you have done something to upset her then only you can know what that was, or how serious it was. I suggest writing her a letter. That way you can tell her exactly what is on your mind without becoming flustered. I am sure there is nothing to worry about and that your friendship can resume, but in the meantime, perhaps you could try to find someone else to go out with in case your friend doesn't wish to rekindle your friendship.

The house felt quiet with just me and Jacob in it and I felt myself longing for the noise and incessant questions my daughter asked when she was here. But at least having Jacob home with me helped to take my mind off Charlie.

'Shall we go out for dinner tonight?' I said, once Rob had left and I'd finished unpacking his little suitcase.

'Daddy took us out for dinner last night.'

Course he did.

'So don't you want to go out?'

'Can we have McDonald's?'

The nearest McDonald's was about a twenty-five-minute drive away and my first instinct was to say no. But then I thought of Rob and all the things he bought for the kids and, as much as I detested feeling as though I were in some sort of popularity contest, I knew I wasn't going to refuse.

'Come on, then. Let's have burgers *and* a milkshake,' I said, grabbing my keys.

'Really?' he said, eyes wide.

'Really, little man,' I said, scooping him up and covering his face with kisses. He tried to wriggle free. 'Get off, Mummy!' he said, giggling. I wanted to hold onto him forever and never ever let him go, but Buster had other ideas and started barking at me.

'Mummy, can Buster come?' Jacob said as I set him back on his feet.

'Come on, then, let's all go,' I said, and he cheered.

As we drove along I played Jacob's favourite songs, and we sang along at the top of our voices. Buster barked at random occasions, which made us both laugh. But no matter how much we laughed, or sang, nothing covered the conspicuous absence of

Olivia. And as much as I was desperate to quiz Jacob about his sister – *Has she said anything to you? Do you think she'll change her mind and come home soon?* – I knew it was neither right nor fair to put that on him.

I also knew he might have answers I didn't want to hear.

* * *

Work was always a good distraction from my worries, and the day I had on Tuesday would have been testing even at the best of times. I didn't know whether it was the hot weather sending the kids wild, or the approaching end of term, but it was a disastrous mix for a science teacher trying to keep the attention of a classroom full of fifteen-year-olds. I was grateful when the end of the day finally arrived.

As I collected my bag from the staffroom and gathered up the books for marking that night, a voice made me jump.

'Tough day, eh?' I turned to find my colleague Jason behind me.

'Yeah, I can't wait to get home and relax in the sunshine,' I said with a sigh.

'Is that all you're up to this evening?'

Jason taught PE and a few of the female teachers thought he was hot. He was, I supposed, but he was a bit young for me. More than that, though, I'd always felt a little awkward round him because it was common knowledge he'd had a thing for me since he'd started at the school last September. I hoped he wasn't going to ask me out now. I couldn't cope with being the one to make his cheery smile disappear.

'Yes. I'm exhausted.' I smiled at him. 'I think I've got end-of-term-itis, like the kids.'

'I know what you mean.' He smiled back. I thought I'd got

away with it, but then he said, 'Seems a shame to just go home on your own in this weather. Do you fancy going for a quick drink?'

'I—' I stammered. 'Sorry, I really need to go and pick Jacob up.'

'Ah yes, course. Sorry.' He shifted awkwardly. 'So are they... are you...?' He ran his fingers through his hair. 'Sorry,' he said. 'I'm rubbish at this sort of thing. I just wondered if you were child-free at all over the holidays and might fancy doing something? With me,' he added, in case it wasn't clear enough.

'Oh, I—' I stopped. It would be the easiest thing in the world to say yes. I'd been burying my head in the sand about the summer holidays, and the long days and weeks I was going to be completely on my own when Rob and Natalie took the kids to Greece for their wedding. I suppose I'd assumed I'd spend some of it with Catherine, or even Charlie, but after the other night Charlie was looking a lot less likely as a companion, and I couldn't rely on Catherine all the time. Jason was kind, funny and sweet, and spending some time with him might actually be quite nice.

But something was holding me back.

'I'm not really sure yet, can I let you know?' I said, taking a step towards the door, away from him.

'Right. Yeah. Course.' He looked so dejected I wanted to change my mind right there and then but I knew it wouldn't be for the right reasons, so I stuck to my guns.

'Sorry, I'd better go, got marking to do,' I said, holding up my bags of exercise books. And before he could say anything else I turned and almost ran out of the staffroom to my car. It wasn't until I'd closed the door and started driving that I let myself think about what had just happened. Under normal circumstances, there would have been no reason to have turned Jason down. He was handsome, plus having someone to hang out with would have been nice. But my mind was still in turmoil about

Charlie, and until I'd untangled all of that, it felt completely unfair to spend time with someone else, even as friends – especially as I was fairly certain Jason was hoping for more than that.

My phone buzzed on the seat beside me, and when I pulled up at some traffic lights I glanced at the screen.

I hope you don't mind me asking you out. Sorry if I made you feel uncomfortable. Have a lovely evening. Jason.

Poor Jason. I tapped out a quick text to let him know it was fine, and vowed to speak to him properly tomorrow.

For now, though, all of my attention had to be on an entirely different man, and the only one in my life who didn't give me any hassle. Jacob.

* * *

I didn't hear from Charlie after he'd left on Monday morning and I was damned if I was going to be the first one to message. By the time Thursday rolled round and there was still nothing from him, I decided it was time to confess to Catherine what had happened. I hadn't even spoken to her to tell her about Olivia either, I realised.

So on Thursday night I bought a bottle of wine and drove Jacob and I over to Catherine's house to see her. I felt this needed more than a text message.

It was only just after six when I pulled into her road and it occurred to me that she might not be home from work yet. But I was relieved to find her car on the drive. I hadn't realised quite how much I'd missed her these last few days.

'Come on, love,' I said, holding the door open for Jacob as he undid his buckle. Buster jumped out behind him and I clipped his lead on.

'Buster and Freddie can play,' Jacob said as we opened the gate and made our way to the front door.

'They'll love that,' I agreed. I rapped lightly on the door and waited for Catherine to answer. Inside, Freddie started to bark, but a few seconds passed and there was no sign of Catherine.

'Maybe she's in the garden and can't hear me,' I said, and I grabbed Jacob's hand and walked round the side of the house.

'Catherine!' I called. 'It's only me!'

I pushed the gate gently but it was locked. I grabbed an empty flower pot, turned it upside down and stepped on it so I could peer over the gate. There was no sign of her in the garden either. Odd.

'Where is she, Mummy?'

'I don't know, sweetheart.' I knocked at the door one more time, Jacob clutching my hand, but still there was no sign of Catherine.

'She's not in,' Jacob said.

'It looks like you might be right, little man,' I said.

'Are we going home now?'

'Yes, I suppose we should.'

We walked back to the car. I felt dejected. Freddie was in the house so she wasn't walking him, and her car was on the drive. I hadn't heard from her for almost a week, and it dawned on me that perhaps she was avoiding me. A knot of worry twisted in my belly.

I turned suddenly at the sound of a window being opened, and a voice shouting my name. Catherine was hanging out of what I presumed to be her bedroom window – I'd never actually been upstairs in her house. She had a towel wrapped round her head and her dressing gown on.

'Sorry, I was in the shower,' she said. I stopped and smiled up at her.

'I didn't mean to disturb you,' I said. 'I just wondered if you had time for a quick natter. I haven't seen you for a while and...' I trailed off.

Catherine glanced up the road behind me and tugged the belt of her dressing gown tighter. 'I er...' She stopped.

'It's okay if you're busy,' I said.

'Sorry, Beth, it's not the best time, I was just – I was about to pop out. Can we do it another time?'

'Oh, right. Yes. Of course.'

'Sorry. I'll give you a ring, okay?'

'Okay,' I said, and before I could say anything else she'd closed the window and given me a wave. I got the feeling I'd been dismissed and as I drove home I tried to work out what I might have done to upset my friend. I hoped it wasn't because she felt I'd bullied her into looking for her mum. Andrea had seemed lovely and when we'd left her house I'd had the distinct impression that Catherine was glad to have found some connection with Lois. But maybe I'd misread the situation.

It was still early when Jacob and I arrived back home, so I let him play with Buster in the garden while I opened the bottle of wine I'd taken to Catherine's. As I watched my little boy I felt a heavy weight settle on me. After the excitement of making new friends and starting to finally find my feet in my brand-new life, over the last few days it felt as though everything was beginning to unravel again. First there was Olivia wanting to live with her dad and, even though I was still hopeful she might change her mind the way Charlie's daughter had when she'd realised the grass wasn't always greener, there was still a chance this arrangement might be more permanent. I wasn't sure my heart could cope with that. Then there was Charlie, who, it was beginning to seem, was ghosting me after sleeping together, which meant I faced losing his friendship. Suzie hadn't been in touch since her visit almost three weeks before, so I assumed that ship had sailed for good. And now Catherine was acting strangely.

I picked up my phone and opened a new message. The situation with Charlie was a bit more complicated, but surely it would be okay just to check in with Catherine? I tapped out a message asking if she was okay and whether I could see her in the week, and waited. The message was delivered, but there was no indication it had been read. After about ten minutes of checking I was driving myself mad so I went inside and made myself some toast. I wasn't in the mood for cooking, and Jacob had already had his tea. I didn't check my phone while I bathed Jacob, or while I got him tucked into bed, or while I read him his favourite story. When I kissed his flushed little cheek and flicked out the light, I felt the knot of worry in my belly tighten. I hurried downstairs and picked my phone off the kitchen table. There was a reply from Catherine from about twenty minutes ago.

I'm fine, just out with a friend. Am quite busy this week but will let you know if I have an evening free. Take care, C.

I reread the message three times, trying to work out why it was bothering me. There was no kiss at the end, which was unusual, although she could have been in a hurry. But it was more than that.

I felt as if I'd been dismissed, as though she was trying to find a polite way to let me down. And I realised, as I pocketed my phone and made my way up to bed with a glass of wine, Buster trailing behind me, that I was back to square one again. Only this time I didn't see a way out.

21

UNHAPPY DAUGHTER

My daughter is eleven years old and I am ever so worried about her. Ever since she started at senior school she has been extremely unhappy and it has got to the point where neither I nor my husband can raise a smile from her. I so want to understand what the matter is but she refuses to talk to us. How can we get to the bottom of her worries?

Children can be such a concern and it can be difficult to know what is going through their minds. Perhaps you could take her out for the day or persuade her to accompany you on a walk. Children often find it easier to open up about their feelings when they are not feeling confronted. Failing that, I suggest speaking to her teacher, who may be able to put your mind at rest. But try to remember that children go through all sorts of phases, and this is likely to pass as quickly as it came on.

A couple of days later and I still hadn't heard from Charlie or Catherine, apart from a brief text message from Catherine where she assured me she wasn't upset with me, and that she'd see me later. With only two weeks to go until the end of term, work was busy, I was also getting on with some more work on the house in the evenings, and trying to keep my spirits up and not worry too much.

It was easier said than done.

Something else was hanging over me too. Olivia's eighth birthday. For all her birthdays since she was born, I'd been the one to organise everything, to book the hall, the entertainer, send invitations to her friends. I'd buy her presents, wrap them carefully, and put decorations out the night before so that when she came down in the morning there were balloons and streamers all over the ceiling, and a themed birthday cake waiting for her – it had changed over the years from Peppa Pig to princesses, but the ideas were always mine.

This year, though, Olivia was still refusing to come home, so her birthday party was taking place at Rob's house. I had been invited to my own daughter's birthday party.

Talk about a kick in the teeth.

On the morning of her party, I gathered up the presents I'd bought her – a dance outfit that she'd asked for and a book about ponies – and drove on autopilot to my former home, to attend my own daughter's party as a guest. I felt as though I'd swallowed a pill of acid that was leaking into my bloodstream and spreading around my whole body, until my entire body was filled with bitterness. I felt needy and angry and, worst of all, tearful.

It wasn't my finest hour.

I pulled up outside Rob's house – *my* old house – and took a few deep breaths. The weather had been warm all week but now some ominous-looking clouds were approaching above the rooftops. I hoped they'd planned for rain, I thought, not-exactly generously.

I checked myself in the pull-down mirror, wiped away some smudged mascara, and climbed out of the car. I started walking towards the front door, planning how I was going to act when I got inside. Would I wrap Olivia in the hug I was longing to give her, or should I play it cool and let her come to me? But before I even reached the door it was flung open and Jacob barrelled along the path towards me, almost knocking me over.

'Hello, sweetheart,' I said, bending down to lift him up. He wrapped his arms tightly round my neck and his legs round my waist and buried his face in my neck. 'Hey, what's wrong?'

He shook his head but refused to move it away from me, so I stood holding him, trying to ignore the pain in my back and the ache in my arms from holding my not-so-little boy. Rob appeared at the door, a quizzical look on his face.

'Jakey?' he said.

'He's fine, we'll be there in a sec,' I said. He hovered a moment, but then turned and walked away, half closing the door behind him. I sat down carefully on the garden wall and peeled Jacob's face away from my neck. 'Now, I love a cuddle as much as any mummy, but is everything all right at Daddy's?' I said, keeping my voice soft.

He looked up at me then, his eyes huge, his lower lip wobbling. 'It's not the same,' he said, his voice catching on a sob.

'What's not the same, love?'

'Daddy's house. He doesn't know how to do birfdays properly and it's all rubbish.' A tear shimmered in the corner of his eye and I wiped it away before it could escape.

'Oh, Jakey, I'm sure it's not rubbish,' I said. 'It's just different, that's all.'

But Jacob was having none of it. He shook his head vehemently. 'There's no balloons, and no cake and no happy birthday song when we got up this morning so it can't be 'Livia's birthday because we haven't even had cake for breakfast...' He ran out of steam and rested his cheek on my shoulder. I smoothed his hair off his face and tried not to smile at the realisation that Rob had messed this up.

I stood, and gently lowered Jacob to the ground and took his hand.

'Don't worry, Mummy's here now so Olivia's birthday can begin properly,' I said.

'Have you got cake?'

'I've got a small one. But I'm sure Daddy and Natalie have bought one really. They're probably just keeping it as a surprise.'

'But cake's in the *morning*,' he said, with the insistence of someone who had never known anything different in his five years of existence.

'I know, but it's still not quite afternoon, so let's go and have some now, shall we?'

'Yeah!' he said, his face clearing.

We made our way into the house. I pushed the front door open and heard the sound of voices coming from the kitchen at the back. I closed the door and walked towards them – then stopped dead. From the tone of the voices it sounded as if Rob and Natalie were having an argument. I hovered, unsure what to do with myself.

'I *told* you to keep it the same,' Natalie hissed.

'Just because Beth gives them cake for breakfast on their birthdays does *not* mean I have to,' Rob said, his voice a little louder.

'Come on, Rob, don't make this about you.'

'What's that supposed to mean?'

'I mean this is not a competition between you and Beth.' I flinched at the mention of my name. 'This is about your daughter, who is upset and needs to know things haven't changed as much as she's worried they have.'

A huge sigh, then footsteps. My heart stopped. I needed to let them know I was coming before they found me out here, listening to every word they were saying. I quietly opened the front door again and slammed it shut behind me.

'Hello?' I called. 'It's only me!' My voice was falsely bright. I poked my head into the living room, hoping to find Olivia there, but it was empty.

'Beth, I'm so glad you're here,' Natalie said, emerging from the kitchen. She was very clearly pregnant now and I tried not to look at her swollen belly. She smiled and gave me a brief hug and I was so taken by surprise I didn't reciprocate. Besides, my hands were full with Jacob on one side and a bag on the other.

'I wouldn't miss my daughter's birthday,' I said, more harshly than I intended.

'Well, no.' Natalie looked dejected and I felt a pang of guilt. After what I'd just overheard it was clear that none of this was Natalie's fault. I tried again.

'I'm looking forward to it. Do you know where Olivia is?'

'She's in her room, sulking.' Rob came out of the kitchen. He looked tired.

'Go up if you like,' Natalie said, and although I would usually have made some snotty remark about how generous it was of her to allow me upstairs in my own house, the truth was it wasn't my house any more – and Natalie didn't deserve to be spoken to like that either.

'Thanks,' I said, slipping my shoes off.

'Wouldn't it be best if I just called her down?' Rob said.

'I think Beth's okay to go and find her,' Natalie said.

He stood for a moment, clearly torn. Then his shoulders slumped and he waved his hand dismissively, the way he always did when he knew he was wrong. 'Fine, do what you like.' He turned and disappeared back into the kitchen.

'Sorry about him,' Natalie said. 'He's just upset because Olivia wanted cake for breakfast, but he told her she had to wait until her friends were here because he'd spent so much on the pony cake she'd asked for, people might as well see it before they cut it.' She gave a lopsided shrug.

I smiled sympathetically. I could only imagine how well that would have gone down with Olivia.

'I've got a small cake,' I said, holding up one of the paper bags in my hand. 'Maybe she could have a bit of that now?'

Natalie glanced behind at the kitchen door, then back at me. 'Great idea. Just don't let Rob find out, eh?'

I bent down to Jacob. 'Let's go and eat secret cake, shall we, Jakey?'

'Yeah!' he said, in a loud whisper.

We scurried up the stairs and stopped outside Olivia's bedroom. I tapped lightly on it and pushed the door open. Olivia was sitting on her bed, arms wrapped round her knees. When she saw me her eyes widened and a smile flashed across her face before she remembered she was supposed to be cross with me too.

'Happy birthday, darling,' I said, heading towards her bed and perching on the end.

'It's not,' she said.

'Mummy's got cake!' Jacob blurted, and Olivia looked at him suspiciously.

'No, she hasn't, Jakey. Daddy said we weren't allowed it, *remember*?'

'She has, haven't you, Mummy?'

'Actually, darling, I do have some. You, Jakey and I can have some, but you both have to promise not to tell Daddy.' I should have felt guilty about undermining Rob, but this felt like a minor infringement.

Olivia watched in amazement as I pulled the small glittery cake out of the box and slipped it onto her bed. 'Are we eating it in *here*?' she said, her eyes shining.

'Yes, yes!' Jacob said, clapping his hands.

'Ssshhh, Jakey!' Olivia admonished, and he sat back down again.

'Jakey, could you go and get Mummy a towel and some toilet roll from the bathroom, please?'

He ran off and, while he was gone, Olivia watched me divide the cake into quarters with my credit card. Crumbs spilt all over the bed but I didn't care.

'We're not allowed to eat in our bedrooms,' Olivia said.

'I know. But if Daddy doesn't know, he can't tell us off, can he?'

Olivia's whole face lit up and I realised it was the first time I'd seen her properly smile in weeks. Jacob returned with a small towel and a loo roll, and I tore pieces off then handed the cake round on toilet-roll napkins. I brushed the crumbs into the towel and shook it out of the window.

'Happy birthday, darling,' I said, but she couldn't reply because her mouth was already stuffed full of chocolate cake.

It felt like a small victory.

* * *

Even I had to admit the party was fun, but, having seen Rob's attempts at organising things in the past, I could only assume Natalie had sorted out most of it. Ten of Olivia's classmates had traipsed into the garden, and I'd had to field the parents' looks of surprise at seeing me there when they'd dropped their children off, as well as bat away questions from a couple of them. The pony the entertainer had brought for the children to groom had been brilliant and the party bags at the end were ridiculously extravagant. But Olivia had seemed to have fun, and when everyone had left she was in a much better mood than when I'd arrived.

'Thank you for that,' I said, scooping up a few forgotten scraps of wrapping paper and stuffing them into the overflowing bin. 'It was a roaring success.'

It took every bit of self-restraint I had not to mention the times Rob had been outraged at the price of a party entertainer, adamant that the kids didn't need anything like that. It seemed as though, now that he was trying to win them over, those worries had gone out of the window.

'Don't go, Mummy,' Jacob said, tugging at my sleeve.

'Sorry, darling, Mummy's got to go home, but you'll be coming back tomorrow ready for school.'

'I want to come now!' he said, fat tears falling down his cheeks and plopping on the floor by his feet.

I glanced over at Rob, but he appeared to be pretending not to notice his son's distress, so I crouched down to Jacob's level.

'Hey, sweetie, it's all right. You're staying here with Daddy and Natalie for tonight and then you can come home and see Mummy and Buster tomorrow, how does that sound?'

He shook his head. 'No. Home now.'

'Oh, love.' I wrapped my arms around him and held him. My baby. There was nothing I wanted more than to take him home with me right now, Olivia too. But I knew if I tried to suggest it, Rob would be cross. The way things were between us, it wasn't worth rocking the boat. Not until Natalie had convinced him to stop his custody battle.

Thankfully, Natalie came to my rescue.

'I think it would be okay if Jacob went home tonight, wouldn't it?' she said. I glanced up to see her laying her hand on Rob's arm, a placating gesture. 'I mean, it makes more sense if...' She trailed off.

'If Olivia's still refusing to come too, then it does save you a journey tomorrow,' I said, realising what Natalie had been about to say.

'But we were going out for lunch for Olivia's birthday tomorrow,' Rob said, his voice tight. He was terrible at backing down, always had been, but I had a feeling he was already considering Natalie's suggestion.

'I can take him for lunch. And Olivia's had such a lovely day today I'm sure she won't mind.'

He stood for a moment, looking from me to Natalie and back again, his lips tight. I could almost see his mind working out how to agree to the plan without losing face. Finally, he gave a small nod.

'Okay, I suppose it does make more sense than everyone driving backwards and forwards again tomorrow, given you're already here,' he agreed.

I gave Natalie a conspiratorial smile, and she smiled back.

'Thank you, Rob,' I said as Jacob cheered. 'Go and grab your stuff Jakey while I just say goodbye to Olivia, then we'll get going.' I made my way through to the living room where Olivia was sitting surrounded by presents, thumb stuck in her mouth, watching a show called *Sam & Cat*. She barely glanced up as I sat down beside her.

'Hey, lovely girl,' I said.

'Hmm,' she replied. Her eyelids were heavy.

'Mummy's going now,' I said.

'Okay.'

I didn't want to leave without addressing the elephant in the room – her thumb-sucking. I decided a roundabout approach was probably wisest. 'Is everything okay at school?' I said, brushing her hair back from her face. She flicked her eyes up to me and gave a barely perceptible nod. I studied her for a few seconds – her eyes just like her dad's, her blonde curls just like mine – and let out a breath. Her thumb-sucking was definitely a sign of something, but I knew pushing her wouldn't get me any answers.

I leaned down and planted a kiss on top of her head. 'Happy birthday, beautiful girl,' I said, standing up.

'Bye, Mummy.'

Then Jacob and I left.

'Just you and me against the world now, kiddo,' I whispered to myself as I pulled away from Rob's house. He was already fast asleep.

22

A CHANGE OF HEART

My husband and I have been married for two years but sadly
we have already begun to drift apart. However I am still very
fond of him and would like to try and save our marriage. We
live with his parents and agreed we would not have children
until we could afford a home of our own. But I thought that
having a baby might help bring us closer together again. My
husband has said it is not the right time but I think he might
change his mind once the baby is here. Do you think this is a
good idea?

It is never a good idea to have a baby for any other reason than
that you want one. Bringing a poor little child into the world as
a way of trying to mend your marriage would be unfair to the
child and yourselves. The best way to sort things out is to talk
to your husband, try to work out where things went wrong, and
discuss how you can mend things between you. Only if a child
is part of that solution should you consider it.

The last days of term always zoomed by in a flash, and before I knew it there was just over a week to go. The kids at school were like zoo animals, desperate to spread their wings, ready to come back a whole lot older and smarter the following term. I knew how they felt. Olivia was still at her dad's, Catherine had only rung me for a quick chat once since Jacob and I had turned up at her house, and Charlie seemed to have disappeared off the face of the earth. I wanted a fresh start as much as anyone.

I was trying not to think about how lonely the holidays would be.

As I cleared up at the end of the day I felt a presence behind me. I turned, expecting to find one of my students waiting to ask me something. But it was Jason.

'Hi,' I said.

'Hey,' he said, moving towards me from where he'd been standing in the doorway.

'The kids are as desperate to get out of here as I am,' I said, grinning.

'I don't blame them.' He smiled falteringly. He was usually so confident, and I realised before he said anything else what he'd come here for. He cleared his throat and his face reddened. 'I – I was wondering whether you might be up for that drink some time soon?' He looked just over my shoulder at the whiteboard behind me where the words 'anaerobic respiration' were scrawled.

'I—' I started. I wanted to say yes. What would be the harm in going for a drink with a sweet, funny, attractive man? But then I thought of Charlie and, even though he appeared to be ghosting me, I knew it would be unfair on Jason if I went out with him when I was still working through my feelings for another man. 'I'm sorry, Jason, I'm not sure it's a good idea at the moment.'

'Ah. I thought you might say that.' He caught my eye. 'You're probably right. It would be a bit awkward, right?'

'Exactly,' I said, grateful to him for giving me an easy way to let him down.

'Never mind. I guess I'll just go to the gym instead.' He turned and walked towards the door. He stopped before he got there. 'But if you ever change your mind, you know where I am,' he said, then flashed a grin and left.

* * *

To my surprise I couldn't stop thinking about Jason as I drove home, wondering whether I should just have gone for that drink after all. The kids were with Rob and the house was empty tonight. The house, in fact, was going to be pretty empty all through the summer holidays, especially when they went to Greece with Rob and Natalie. I was dreading it. Some company would have been nice.

But it was more than that too, I realised. I really liked Jason, more than I'd expected to. He was kind and much more self-deprecating than I'd imagined and in any other circumstances I would definitely have wanted to get to know him better.

But I'd rejected him twice already. It was too late now.

I let myself in the front door and Buster jumped round my feet excitedly. I scooped him up, snuffling my face into his fur. 'At least someone's pleased to see me, eh?' I said.

I sighed as I kicked my shoes off and made my way into the kitchen. I was exhausted, physically and emotionally. All I wanted to do right now was to have a shower and an early night, but first I needed to take Buster for a walk. I downed a glass of water, ran upstairs to throw on some old walking clothes, then came back down to find the lead. At the sight of it, Buster went wild.

'Come on, then, boy, let's get you out,' I said, clipping his lead to his collar. We made our way out of the front door and along the path towards our usual fields. As we walked I was reminded of the day I'd met Catherine all those weeks ago and I felt a pang of sadness. I'd felt so lonely back then, and had been so thrilled to have met a new friend, someone I really liked, who wasn't linked to my old life with Rob. Catherine was refreshing – different, funny, honest. I'd loved our new friendship and was thankful to Lois for helping us find each other. But I hadn't seen her for two weeks and so now here I was, back to square one.

I felt a tear slip down my cheek and I brushed it away.

Stop feeling so sorry for yourself, Beth.

I needed to give myself a shake. What would Catherine do if she stopped hearing from me? What would I advise someone to do in the same situation as me?

Ring your friend. She's probably wondering where you've got to and will be glad to hear from you.

That was exactly what I would tell someone else to do.

We reached the bench where I'd first got chatting to Catherine. I let Buster off the lead and he raced away through the long grass, chasing some imaginary prey, so that all I could see of him was the swish of the blades of grass accompanied by the occasional bark of joy.

I pulled my phone out, ready to call Catherine and ask if she was okay. I'd tell her where I was sitting, and that I missed her. I was sure everything would be fine.

But when I looked at the screen I stopped. I had a missed call. From Charlie.

It had been almost two weeks since we'd slept together, and I'd assumed he regretted that night so much that he just found it easier never to speak to me again. So why was he ringing me now?

I felt a strange feeling creep across me, like a small flame trying to ignite. Was this hope? Or anger? I wasn't sure.

My thumb hovered over the green call-back button. Should I

call him, find out what he wanted? Or should I give my poor, bruised heart a break, and leave it, try to carry on getting over him?

I didn't know why I was dithering. I already knew what I was going to do.

I pressed the button.

* * *

You know those children's books where you can choose your own adventure – pick what happens next in the story and see where it takes you? The good thing about those was always the possibility of changing your mind. Don't like the decision you made? Don't worry, you can go back to where you were before and make a different choice, and see whether that option was any better.

Sometimes, I wish life were like that. This was one of those times.

After ending the call with Charlie I sat staring out across the field, blindly. It felt as though there were a heavy stone sitting on my heart, and it was difficult to swallow. But I absolutely wasn't going to cry.

I could see someone approaching in the distance, so I tried to think about something else and wait for them to pass. The man walking his dog got bigger and bigger, then gave me a nod as he passed, and a mumbled 'evening', then I watched as he retreated, shrinking until he disappeared round the corner.

I watched as Buster sniffed a bush, and cocked his leg up, then trotted away, off on another adventure. I wondered whether he was missing Freddie as much as I was missing Olivia. I wished my life could be as simple as his.

Charlie was going to try and make things work with Helen. That was what he'd rung to tell me.

'I didn't want you to find out from someone else,' he'd said, after he'd apologised for his silence, and broken the news to me.

'Okay,' I'd said, not sure whether I could trust myself to say anything else.

'I'm... I'm sorry if you were hoping for something else.'

'I wasn't. It's fine. I always knew you were married.' My voice had been clipped but it had been the only way I could get the words out.

'I wanted to say thank you, Beth. For everything.'

I'd stayed silent for a moment. Then, before either of us could say anything we might regret, I'd ended the call. My hands had been shaking and I'd felt a pressure on my chest.

I *had* always known he was married. It was how we'd met, for goodness' sake. He'd wanted advice on how to make things right with his wife, and now he'd done just that.

I had absolutely no right to feel this way.

I just wish I could have told my heart that.

23

REBOUND LOVE

I have just started stepping out with a fellow I really like. We enjoy going to dances and have been out together a number of times. He is eager to take our relationship to the next stage but I am not sure whether I am keen enough on him as I cannot stop thinking about my last boyfriend, who is now engaged to be married to someone else. How do you know when someone is the right person for you? Should I agree to settle down and to simply be content?

If you are still having thoughts about your former boyfriend then I would suggest that this fellow, as nice as he may well be, is not the right one for you. Although you shouldn't be too fussy when looking for a husband as you risk being left on the shelf indefinitely, I do think that you need to be rather more keen on someone if you are going to agree to spend the rest of your life with them!

I wondered whether the offer of a drink was still on the table?
I've found myself unexpectedly free this evening. No worries if
not! Beth x

It had taken several attempts to get the tone of the text to Jason
right – one kiss or none, more explanation of why I'd changed my
mind or not? – but once it was done I sent it before I could change
my mind. It didn't take him long to reply.

Of course! I'll pick you up at 7.30 if that works? J x

After the day I'd had, I was looking forward to seeing Jason
more than I'd expected. Everything that had happened with
Charlie had left me feeling bruised, and it was about time I gave
myself a chance to be happy with someone less complicated. Or at
least have a bit of fun.

He was due in half an hour so I had a quick shower, put some
make-up on and some fresh clothes. I was just feeding Buster
when the doorbell went and I felt my stomach flip over. This was
the first date I'd been on – assuming it was even a date – since
before I'd married Rob. I felt unexpectedly nervous. I breathed in
deeply, walked to the front door and pulled it open.

'Jason, hi!' I said, my voice bright. He looked so handsome in
the evening sunshine, all chiselled jaw and bulging biceps, and
any doubts I'd felt about texting him evaporated like a puff of
smoke in the wind.

'You look great,' he said, smiling appreciatively.

'Thank you.' I felt like a shy schoolgirl all of a sudden.

I was about to step out of the house when Buster came
bounding along the hallway. Jason crouched down and ruffled the
top of his head. 'Hello, little man.' He looked up at me. 'Who's
this?'

'This is Buster,' I said, and smiled as Jason tickled him behind the ears, making Buster roll over on his back and wag his tail furiously.

'I think he likes that,' I said.

'I'm pretty good with my hands,' Jason said, standing and giving me a look that made my insides swirl. I let my hair fall across my face to hide my blushes, then turned and locked the door behind me.

As he drove into town we chatted easily, although we mainly stuck to anecdotes about school – the kids, the other teachers. Even though Jason had worked at the school for the last ten months I hadn't had much opportunity to get to know him, and I was looking forward to seeing what was hidden behind the handsome face.

We went to a pub a little way out of the town where we both taught. 'I hope you don't mind, I'd just rather not bump into anyone from work. You know what a gossip-pit that place is,' he said as we pulled into the car park.

'This is perfect,' I said, grateful he'd been so considerate.

The evening was still warm, and we chose a table outside. While he went to the bar I watched the people around me. There were couples, families with older children, groups of friends, all together on this warm summer evening, leaving whatever troubles they might have behind them as they enjoyed each other's company for a few hours.

And as Jason made his way back across the lawn, I felt grateful to be here with him.

* * *

The evening was even better than I'd hoped for. Jason was great company, and as the night wore on I found myself wanting to spend more time with him. He told me about his divorce three years before – 'It just didn't work out,' he said, and I didn't push for more; he told me he didn't have children and from the way he said it I wondered whether that had been part of the reason his marriage had fallen apart; he told me how much he loved planning sports day, about his love of American sitcoms, and how he played a mean game of Scrabble. 'I'm slightly dyslexic so I think it helps find the words from the jumble of letters,' he explained. In return I told him a bit about Rob's betrayal and how tough the last few months had been, and about the *Dear Evelyn* letters, but not much about the kids, or Catherine. And I definitely didn't tell him about Charlie.

'We'd better get you home,' he said eventually, downing his alcohol-free beer and checking his watch. It was dark and there was only a sprinkling of people left at the tables outside. The air had taken a turn towards chilly and I shivered.

'I won't turn into a pumpkin,' I said, laughing.

'No, but I might.' He stood and held his hand out and I took it and let myself be led to the car. His palm felt warm and I enjoyed the feeling of skin against skin. As we pulled out of the car park I found myself hoping he might kiss me later. I deserved to have a bit of fun after the last few years, surely?

Ten minutes later we pulled up outside my house and he killed the engine and turned in his seat towards me. I felt like a teenager in an American movie being dropped off by her date.

His face was serious in the glow from the streetlight, and I found my heart thumping frantically against my ribcage. My palms were sweaty.

'Thanks for a lovely evening,' he said. His voice was low.

'I really enjoyed myself,' I said, truthfully.

He went quiet for a moment. Then, 'You know I've wanted to take you out for a while now, don't you?'

I nodded, unable to speak.

He reached his hand across the gearstick and threaded his fingers between mine. And then slowly, ever so slowly, he leaned forwards, holding my gaze. He stopped just before he reached me. 'Is it okay if I kiss you?'

I nodded, and then his lips brushed mine. They felt warm and soft, and I let myself sink into it, trying to banish all thoughts of Charlie or anyone else from my mind. It was easier than I'd expected, and when he pulled away, his eyes flickering, my heart thumped.

'You're so beautiful,' he said. He tucked a lock of hair behind my ear and my breath caught in my throat.

'Thank you.' I was glad he couldn't see my face flame. Neither of us spoke for a moment, the heat between us palpable. Then, before anything else could happen, I twisted round and unclipped my seat belt. 'I'd better get in,' I said, aware of his eyes on me with every movement. Then I leaned over, gave him a peck on the lips and said, 'Night, Jason. Thank you for a lovely evening. See you at school.'

* * *

I couldn't sleep. My mind was in turmoil, with Jason, Charlie, Catherine, Andrea, Helen, Rob, Olivia, Jacob, Natalie, churning round and round my head like socks in a washing machine.

I leaned over and switched on the lamp. Buster lifted his head wearily at the end of the bed, then went back to sleep, snoring gently.

I climbed out of bed, shrugged on a cardigan that hung on the back of the chair, and padded down the stairs. The house felt stifling, the residual heat from the day seeping from the bricks and keeping the rooms hot and stuffy. I slung open the back door and let the cooler air flood across my skin and took some deep gulps. The night was still, just the occasional yelp of a fox from the nearby woods or an owl hooting in the distance to break the otherwise smothering silence.

I peered into the blackness and cast my mind back over the last few hours. I replayed the kiss with Jason; the press of his lips, the feel of his hand in mine, and I smiled to myself. It had felt good. Better than good. I was sure something more would have happened if I hadn't left when I did, but I'd known even in the moment that I needed to work out my feelings for Charlie before I took things any further with Jason. It wouldn't be fair to him to lead him on, he deserved better than that.

There was something else on my mind too, though. A flicker of something like guilt. Guilt that I was cheating on Charlie? Perhaps, although I knew how ridiculous that was. He was out of the picture now. So why was I finding it so hard to get the image of him in my bed out of my mind?

I crossed my arms over my chest and pulled my cardigan tighter, then stepped out into the garden. I walked until I reached the newly laid lawn, then I stopped. The garden was so vastly improved, but it still wasn't finished, and I wondered how long it would take me to get the finishing touches done by myself now that Charlie wouldn't be around to help me with it. The grass felt cool and damp between my toes and I wiggled them, letting the night-time envelop me. A sudden movement by the fence made me jump, and I let out a gasp. As I squinted into the darkness, shadows and shapes that hadn't been there before loomed out at me. I shivered, suddenly vulnerable standing there on my own in the middle of the night. I hurried back inside and closed the back door, locking it behind me. My heart thumped in my throat and my legs felt shaky. I pulled out a chair and sat down and put my head in my hands.

When my heart rate had returned to normal, I got up and flicked the kettle on and rummaged around the cupboard for a herbal tea. There was a rogue box of peppermint teabags that didn't look too ancient so I plopped one in my mug, poured boiling water on it and took it through to the living room. The house was deathly quiet when the kids weren't here, and I wondered whether I should have invited Jason to stay over after all. It would have been so easy to have led him inside and up to my bedroom and—

But no. He wasn't there just to stop me getting lonely. I had to be certain I wanted something to develop with him before taking it any further. Assuming he wanted that, of course. I'd done the right thing.

I had.

My mind turned to Catherine next. I was desperate to talk things through with her. I still hadn't had the chance to tell her what had happened between me and Charlie, or about Charlie then going back to Helen, or about my date with Jason. She didn't even know that Olivia was refusing to come home, and I felt an overwhelming urge to hear her warm, reassuring voice. It occurred to me that I hadn't rung her earlier as I'd intended – the conversation with Charlie had distracted me.

Before I could change my mind, I tapped out a text and sent it to her, hoping she had it on silent and would read it in the morning.

I miss you. Are you around tomorrow? Beth x

I was still wide awake and I knew if I went back to bed, sleep would elude me. So with nothing better to do I pulled out my laptop and opened up my emails. The *Dear Evelyn* letters had piled up so much that the sheer volume had become over-whelming.

I scrolled down through the unopened, unread messages. Among the subject headings that told me they were from people looking for advice, I spotted a few different ones, more busi-nesslike messages, and out of curiosity I clicked one open. I read it with incredulity. It was from a local business, asking how much it would cost to advertise on my website.

I closed it down and opened another. It was the same, asking for price details for advertising. I considered deleting it, but then thought twice. Perhaps I should think about it, at least?

I scrolled to the bottom of the unopened emails and started replying to some of the letters that had arrived a good few days ago that had been ignored.

But as I typed out the replies, trying to imagine what Lois would have said, as well as imagining what Catherine would say, I felt like a complete fraud. A messy divorce, a child who didn't want to live with me; a new friend who wouldn't return my messages, a married man I'd stupidly fallen for, and now an added complication of another possible man on the horizon. Why on earth did I think I could advise other people when my own life was such a mess?

But then again, if I didn't do it, who would? Some of these people probably didn't have anyone else to turn to, and if I ignored them, turned them away, they'd have nowhere else to go.

I owed it to them to at least try and answer their questions as honestly as I could. It was what Lois would have done, and it was what I was going to do.

I began typing.

24

DIFFICULT DAUGHTER

My daughter is sixteen and driving me up the wall. Friends and teachers tell me she is ever so polite and charming when she is at their houses or in school, but when she is at home she is rude, untidy, selfish and lazy. She absolutely refuses to help in any way and if I ask her she says I am nagging. I just want her to grow up in the proper way.

I think you will find that this is very common. Most of us, even adults, behave very differently at home from how we behave elsewhere. Teenagers are known for being maddening, but they can also be enormous fun. It is very hard growing up in this modern age so perhaps you should try to refrain from 'nagging' your daughter and tell her that you expect a little more self-discipline from her. Teenagers, I find, respond well to being given trust. Try to laugh with her more and enjoy her company – she won't be around for much longer before she flies the nest!

Agreeing to another date with Jason was, it turned out, the best thing I could have done. Despite my initial reservations, I'd loved spending time with him, and had even started to find some of my missing confidence again. Since that first night, we'd been out for dinner and to the cinema, where we'd held hands like two love-struck teenagers, and tonight, with Jacob back at Rob's for the night, Jason was coming round to mine.

I found my belly doing somersaults in anticipation of his arrival as I chopped vegetables, showered and blow-dried my hair, then got dressed in a carefully chosen outfit that made me look reasonably attractive without trying too hard. We hadn't discussed it, but the implication was that tonight Jason was going to stay over. I tried not to think about how things had been with Charlie just a few weeks before, and concentrate on me and Jason, right here and now. Charlie was in the past, and that was where he had to stay.

The doorbell chimed bang on seven o'clock. Trying to ignore my nerves, I checked my hair in the reflection of the oven, then hurried to the front door. Jason looked as gorgeous as ever and I stepped back to let him in. He leaned into me as he passed and planted a gentle kiss on my cheek, and I breathed him in, his warm, manly scent, lime and black pepper, and something else, an undertone of earthiness. I wondered how many of the teachers – and students – at school would be envious if they could see us now.

'Hey, you,' he said, displaying his perfect white teeth as he smiled at me. I led him into the kitchen where the table was set for two. I'd had a carpenter in to fit some new kitchen cupboards over the last few days and, although it was far from finished, I was glad the room looked less hovel-like than it had previously. He took in the scene and grinned again. 'This looks lovely,' he said.

'I just thought...' I trailed off. I thought what? I'd be seductive?

Romantic? I felt suddenly silly, self-conscious. What if he'd changed his mind about me? What if he'd realised that I was too old for him, or too boring, or, God forbid, had too much baggage? I prayed I hadn't totally misjudged this. But then he took the few steps across the kitchen and closed the gap between us and pressed me against the worktop, his hands in my hair, his lips against mine, and I let myself kiss him back with an urgency I hadn't expected. It was different from kissing Charlie; a more physical sensation, free of doubts and worries.

He pulled away and looked at me, his face so close I couldn't make out his features properly. I felt his breath on my lips and his chest rise and fall against me.

'I've been thinking about kissing you all day,' he said.

'Me too,' I said, then twisted away. 'But you'll have to wait a bit longer otherwise dinner's going to be burnt.'

'Ugh, you're torturing me,' he groaned, laughing.

'Help yourself to a drink,' I said, gesturing at the fridge. 'There's beer and wine in there.'

'How about we open this?' he said, holding up the carrier bag he'd left by the kitchen door when he came in. He pulled out a bottle of champagne.

'What are we celebrating?'

'Us?'

I wasn't sure what to say. It hadn't been long since I'd been desperate to hear another man say those words to me. Was I throwing myself into this for the right reasons? Would I be doing Jason a disservice if I toasted 'us'?

But then I looked over at him, so sweet and expectant – so *sexy* – and I knew I wanted to give 'us' – whatever us might turn out to be – a chance.

'Sounds good to me,' I said, smiling at him. 'Let's get that bottle open.'

As we chatted and ate and drank the champagne, I felt myself relax. This was good. This was what I needed. We hadn't told anyone at work there was anything going on between us – we'd agreed it was probably wise, for now – but the truth was I felt that telling other people about us would make it more real, and that would mean that anything I'd hoped for with Charlie would definitely be over and done with for good.

I shook the thought from my mind. I had to stop thinking about Charlie. It was unfair to Jason and to me. That was the past. This man could just be my future, if I let him.

We moved through to the living room and I put some music on and sank into the sofa. Jason lowered himself beside me, his thigh pressed against me, his arm along the back of the sofa. He tucked my hair behind my ear and ran his finger down my cheek. I shivered. His finger moved down my neck and along my shoulder, then he leaned forward and kissed my neck, so gently it felt like feathers on my skin. I turned my head to seek out his lips and then we were locked together. One of his hands moved around the back of my head, the other up my thigh and my breath caught in my throat. I pulled him closer, and he groaned, his tongue seeking mine hungrily. He moved towards me and lowered me slowly backwards, then moved gently on top of me. I kept my eyes open, determined to concentrate on Jason and not let my mind drift off somewhere else, to another time, another man. He pulled my bra strap down and lowered his head until I could feel his warm breath on my skin then...

And then my phone rang and we both froze.

'Do you need to get that?' he whispered, his voice heavy with desire.

'I probably should. It could be one of the kids.' I pushed myself up to sitting, my heart thumping. Jason moved away, and tugged his T-shirt down while I scrabbled around on the floor for my phone. By the time I found it, it had stopped ringing but the display revealed Rob's number.

'Sorry, it's my ex,' I said, pulling my bra strap up. 'It'll be about the kids. I won't be a sec.'

The phone had hardly started ringing when Rob answered. 'I'm glad you rang me back,' he said. My stomach rolled over.

'Has something happened?'

'No, no, everything's fine. Except—' He stopped.

'Rob! What's going on?' I glanced at Jason, who was at the other end of the sofa scrolling through his phone. Sorry, I mouthed. He smiled and looked back at his phone.

'Olivia got into trouble at school today.'

'Oh.' I hadn't been expecting that. 'But it's eight-thirty in the evening, why have you left it till now to ring me?'

'She begged me not to. Not until we'd had a chance to talk about it.'

I felt a stone lodge in my throat and swallowed it down. I wouldn't cry, not now.

'So, what happened?'

'She got caught hitting another girl and when she was asked why she did it she said it was because she'd said something mean about you.'

'About me? But what?'

There was a pause, and then I heard a whispering. 'I'll let Olivia tell you.'

Seconds later my daughter's voice came on the line. 'Mummy,' she said. She sounded as if she'd been crying and I wanted to throw my arms around her. God, I hated this.

'Sweetheart, are you okay?' I said.

'Yes.' She sniffed.

'Can you tell Mummy what happened today?'

A silence, then: 'Sophie said you didn't love me and that's why I didn't live with you any more.'

'Oh, darling, of course I love you,' I said. My words came out in a sob. 'I love you and Jacob more than anything else in the whole wide world.'

'I told her that but she kept saying it.'

'So you hit her?'

'Yes.' A sob. 'Sorry, Mummy. I didn't know how else to make her stop.'

There was a rustling sound, then Rob's voice came back on the line. 'Are you busy right now?'

I glanced at Jason. 'No.'

'Will you come over? I think we need to talk. All of us.'

'I've had a couple of glasses of wine.'

'Can I pay for a taxi?'

'You really think we need to sort this out tonight?'

'I think we should, yes.'

'Then I'll come.'

'I'll order you a taxi. See you soon.'

He hung up and I turned to Jason. 'I'm so sorry,' I said.

'You've got to go, right?'

'Yes.'

'Shame. I was looking forward to spending the night with you.' His voice was low and a shiver ran through me.

'Me too. But it's my daughter. She—' I stopped. 'She's having a few difficulties.'

He shook his head and reached his hand out to cover mine. 'It's fine, I get it. Of course you have to go.'

'Thanks, Jason.'

He stood, patted his pocket, and smiled. 'See you at school?'

'Bye, Jason. And thank you.'

I waited until I heard the front door close, then I ran upstairs and changed into jeans and a jumper. A text arrived from Rob telling me the taxi was coming, and ten minutes later I was on my way, my mind full of worry about what I was going to discover when I got there.

It didn't take long in the late evening traffic and soon I was running up the familiar path and stepping into the hallway of the house I knew so well. Except, I realised, it finally didn't feel like coming home any more, but simply like visiting a place that was once so familiar to me.

'Thanks for coming over,' Rob said. 'I would have come to you but Olivia was worried about it, given that she's refused to be there for the last few weeks.'

'It's fine. Where is she?'

'She's in her room. I'll call her down.'

I waited in the hallway while he ran upstairs. I shuffled my feet and studied the pictures on the wall. I hadn't seen any of them before and I wondered what had happened to the pictures I'd left behind.

I was distracted by a noise on the stairs, and then Olivia was there, standing in her High School Musical pyjamas looking so terrifyingly young, her blonde hair neatly styled into two plaits. Natalie's doing, no doubt, unless Rob had miraculously learned to style hair after all these years. I felt a pang of gratitude that she was looking after her so well, combined with jealousy that she got to do that for my daughter while I couldn't.

'Hello, love,' I said, walking towards the bottom of the stairs. She stayed where she was, hovering like a ghost, thumb stuck firmly in her mouth.

'Come down and see Mummy,' Rob said. She tentatively walked the last few steps towards me and I wrapped my arms around her and held her little body. She was rigid, unyielding, but

I tried not to feel upset. We just needed to get to the bottom of what was bothering her.

I pulled away and held out my hand. 'Shall we go and talk in the living room?' I said.

She nodded and took my hand and let me lead her in there, Rob following. I wondered where Natalie was.

'Natalie's upstairs, she thought she'd leave us to it,' Rob said, as if he'd read my mind.

I nodded in acknowledgement. I lowered myself onto the sofa, Olivia settled next to me, and Rob sat the other side.

'Why don't you tell Mummy what you told me?' he said, gently. I hadn't seen him on his own with the kids since we'd separated – Natalie was always there too – apart from when we were dropping them off or picking them up, and I was pleased and more than a little surprised at how good he was with Olivia. She took her thumb from her mouth and looked at me with big eyes.

'Sophie said you didn't love me any more because I don't live with you, and when she wouldn't stop saying it, I punched her.' I had to smother a smile at the thought of my tiny ball of fury hitting another child. It wasn't funny, but I couldn't help feeling proud of her for sticking up for herself – and for me.

'And then what happened?'

'And then Mrs Taylor told me I had to spend the rest of the day on my own and she was going to ring you but I told her I was staying with my daddy so she rang him instead, and then he rang you and now you're here and I'm sorry.' The words came out in a torrent, and I reached out for her hand, wrapping my fingers round hers.

'You know it's wrong to hit other children, don't you, love?' I said.

She nodded. 'But she said you don't love me any more.' She

shrugged. 'I told her she was wrong but she kept on saying it, so I got angry.'

I squeezed her hand and she looked back up at me and then at Rob.

'Tell Mummy what you said to me afterwards,' he said.

'I said I hated not living with you and I wanted to but I was too scared you wouldn't want me any more, and *that's* why I got so cross.'

Rob took Olivia's other hand. 'I told her of course you'd want her to live with you again, and that we had to tell you straight away.'

Gratitude washed over me as Rob's words sank in. After everything we'd been through, all the harsh words we'd said to each other over the last year or so, he'd put Olivia's needs over what he wanted.

'Thank you,' I whispered. I leaned down to Olivia. 'I will always want you to be with me, and I will always love you. You do understand that, don't you?'

She nodded. 'That's what Daddy and Natalie said,' she said, and realisation dawned. This wasn't just Rob's altruism. This was Natalie's doing too.

'Well, they're right.'

'Does this mean I can come home with you tonight?' She looked up at me with wide eyes.

'Not tonight, sweetheart,' I said, even though every fibre of my being was screaming at me to say yes, to scoop her up and leave there with her and never come back. 'Jacob's asleep, and he'll be ever so confused if he wakes up and you've gone, won't he?'

She nodded sadly. 'But I can come tomorrow?'

I looked at Rob. Jacob wasn't due to come to mine for another few days, but he nodded. 'Why don't we say Tuesday, once Mummy has finished at school?' he said.

'Is that the day after tomorrow?' Olivia said, wide-eyed.

'Yes, love. Is that okay?'

'Okay, Mummy,' she said, curling into my side.

As I held my daughter, I studied my ex-husband. He looked the same as he always had, but there was a softness about him that hadn't been there for a long time. He looked content, as if he was finally beginning to understand that not everything had to be a battle.

'Thank you, Rob,' I said.

He looked at me. 'What else could I do?'

We sat in a silence for a few minutes, then I stood to leave. 'I'd better order a taxi.'

'Don't worry, I'll take you home.'

I studied Rob a moment, before giving a small nod. 'Thank you.' I turned to my daughter. 'I'll make sure your room is all ready for you when you get home, all right, sweetheart?' I said.

Olivia nodded sleepily. 'Will you tuck me in before you go, Mummy?'

'If it's okay with Daddy.'

'Be my guest.'

I held my hand out and Olivia took it and we made our way upstairs together. At the top of the stairs I stopped as a face poked out from behind a bedroom door.

'Sorry, I thought it was Rob,' Natalie said.

'Olivia just asked me to put her to bed.'

'Great, I'm glad everything's sorted.' She was about to duck back behind the door again.

'Hang on,' I said, and she stopped. I looked at this woman who had taken up so much of my mind over the last few months – who had made me so angry, so jealous – and I realised she wasn't the enemy. She might have been the catalyst that had taken Rob from me, but she wasn't the cause, and I think I'd always known that

Rob and I would have split up, Natalie or no Natalie. Her coming onto the scene had just made it happen more quickly. Besides, it wasn't her that had been the married one. And as I looked at her now, standing in the dim light of the landing, looking small and worried and tired, I felt a surge of understanding for her.

'Thank you for talking to him,' I said.

She studied me for a moment as though trying to work out whether I was being sarcastic. Then she smiled. 'I didn't do anything.'

I smiled back. 'I think we both know that's not true. I just want you to know there's no hard feelings. Thank you for looking after my children so well.'

'They're lovely,' she said, simply.

I nodded, then Olivia tugged my hand. 'Come on, Mummy,' she said, and I gave Natalie one last smile and followed my daughter into her room to say goodnight.

25

FORBIDDEN LOVE

I am in love with someone but am so afraid that if I tell anyone, I will be ostracised, and spend the rest of my life alone. I am a woman of twenty-five and have been in love with my female best friend for the last ten years. Is this kind of love always forbidden, or should I risk telling her?

Although none of us can help who we fall in love with, I am certain that you already know that love between two women, while not forbidden by law in the same way as it is between men, is regarded as highly unusual and deviant. Do you think she feels the same way? If not then you risk ruining your friendship forever. Even if she does return your feelings then your love will be difficult, at best. Might you be confusing the love of a friend with romantic love? I would think long and hard before making any rash decisions, and perhaps try and find a suitable man with whom to spend your life.

I needed to collar Jason in the staffroom when there was no one else about, and to apologise for abandoning him. But every time I saw him there were other people around and, apart from the odd sneaky glance in each other's direction, we didn't get a chance to see each other all day. Finally, at the end of the day when most other people had gone home, I found him outside the changing rooms clearing up.

'Hey,' I said, walking up behind him. He whipped round and gave me a wide, open grin, and held his arms out for a hug. I stopped where I was and he dropped his arms and his smile.

'There's no one around,' he said.

'I know. Sorry. I'm just paranoid.'

We stood looking at each other for a second, suddenly awkward. The memory of his body against mine last night, and the thought of what might have happened if Rob hadn't rung, hovered in the stuffy school air. I spoke first.

'I'm so sorry about last night.'

He shook his head. 'Don't be silly, it's your kid.'

I nodded and looked at the floor. 'Everything okay now?' he prompted. I looked up.

'Yes. Yes, I think so. She's coming home tomorrow.'

'That's great.'

He twiddled the small blue plastic cone he was holding. 'So.'

'So.'

'Do you want to go for a drink over the holidays?' He blurted the words as if they'd been blocked. I looked at my feet and then up at him.

'That would be lovely.'

'Great.' We hovered for a few more seconds, neither knowing what to say. Finally, I broke the silence.

'Shall I ring you, then? Maybe you can come round one evening when the children are there?'

'That sounds like a plan.'

'Great.' I stood for a minute longer, unsure what to say. 'Right, well, I'd better get going. I'll see you soon.'

'Bye, Beth.' Then before I realised what he was doing, he'd stepped forward, planted a soft kiss on my lips, then turned and walked away.

* * *

On the way home, in the warm afterglow of Jason's kiss, I made a decision. I was going to see Catherine. I'd had a few short but sweet replies from her over the last couple of weeks, but I was beginning to worry I'd done something to really upset her – although I was at a loss as to what it might have been. Maybe it was a result of sorting things out with Rob and with Olivia, but suddenly I felt as though, if I wanted things to get better, I needed to take matters into my own hands.

I drove home, showered and changed, then grabbed a bottle of wine and jumped in the car. It was less than a ten-minute drive to Catherine's, and all the way there my hands felt clammy and my stomach was in knots. Why was I so nervous?

When I got to Catherine's street there was another car parked directly outside her house, so I parked a few houses down and climbed out. Catherine's car was on the drive, which was a good start. I hooked my bag onto my shoulder, feeling the weight of the wine bottle against my ribs, and opened her front gate. I knocked on the front door and felt my legs shaking and my pulse thumping in my throat. What if she didn't want to see me? I couldn't bear to lose my friend, I realised.

Before I could form the thought, the door swung open and Catherine was there, Freddie in her arms.

'Oh, Beth. Hi,' she said.

'Hi, Catherine.' I felt suddenly shy. 'I, um...' I stuck my hand in my bag and pulled the wine out. 'I brought this...'

She gave a quick smile, and glanced over her shoulder. I saw a movement behind her.

'Oh, you've got someone here,' I said.

'It's not a great time,' she said at the same time.

We both gave a nervous laugh, like air being let out of a balloon, and Catherine's shoulders dropped as if she'd deflated.

'Listen, you'd better come in. I think I've got some explaining to do.' She reached over and grabbed the bottle from me and turned, indicating that I should follow her. This wasn't the reaction I'd been expecting at all, and I followed her, my mind racing. Who on earth did she have here that she didn't want me to know about? And then my heart almost jumped out of my chest. Was it *Charlie*?

No. Surely not.

We reached her small kitchen and she stood aside, and the person at the fridge turned and smiled at me and said, 'Hello, Beth.'

'Andrea, what are you doing here?' She was the last person I'd expected to see, and the high pitch of my voice must have indicated that. She glanced at Catherine then closed the fridge door. She was clutching a bag of lettuce and some cheese.

'Catherine and I have been spending some time together,' she said.

'Oh,' I replied. 'Oh! That's wonderful.'

'Yes, it has been,' Catherine said. Her voice sounded tight, strange, as if she was trying to force words out through her teeth.

'Is – is everything all right?' I said, glancing from Catherine to Andrea and back again. Catherine looked at Andrea again and gave an infinitesimal nod.

'Let's sit down for a minute, shall we?' Catherine said, pulling out a chair. I did as I was told, and Andrea sat the other side of Catherine.

'What's going on?' I said, looking from one to the other. Had something terrible happened? Had they discovered another secret? Somehow I didn't think it was that. I waited, holding my breath.

'I'm sorry I've been so quiet recently,' Catherine started. 'I—' She stopped. 'There have been some things going on.' She glanced at Andrea again then took a deep breath. 'I've been spending quite a lot of time with Andrea and we...' She looked down at her hands, a coy, shy girl, and all of a sudden it dawned on me what was happening here.

'You two are—' I pointed from Catherine to Andrea and back again. They looked at each other and it was so obvious I couldn't believe I hadn't spotted it immediately.

'We've been getting to know each other,' Catherine said. 'And we've – well, we've sort of fallen in love.'

As if saying the words had released something in them, they let their hands touch on the table and I let out a laugh.

'Oh my God, that's amazing – and such a relief!' I said.

Catherine turned to look at me. 'A relief?'

'I thought I'd done something to upset you – but you were just busy falling in love!' I said.

'You're not mad?' Catherine said.

I frowned. 'Mad? Why on earth would I be mad?'

'I don't know. I – I thought you'd feel betrayed or something. Like I was choosing Andrea over you.'

'But that doesn't make any sense,' I said, puzzled. 'Unless – you didn't think I'd disapprove, did you?'

Catherine shrugged. It was the first time I'd seen her looking so unsure of herself.

'I told you,' Andrea said, nudging Catherine in the side. She looked at me. 'I told Catherine you'd be thrilled for us. But she wanted to wait, make sure we were certain, before she told you.'

I shook my head. 'I can't believe you didn't think more of me than that,' I said. 'Honestly, I'm so thrilled for you. But how long—?'

'I felt something for Catherine from the moment you two came to visit me all those weeks ago,' Andrea said, rubbing her hand along Catherine's forearm. 'But I had no idea whether she felt the same way. Whether she'd ever even considered having feelings for a woman...'

'But when Andrea asked if she could come and see me the next day, I realised I was looking forward to seeing her, and when she got here – ' Catherine said, taking over, the words tumbling out as though they'd been trapped for so long and couldn't wait to escape. 'It took me a good few days to admit it to myself, but it slowly dawned on me that these feelings were not the feelings you usually have for a friend. It felt—' She stopped, looked down at the table.

'It just felt right, didn't it?' Andrea said, and I could see the love in her eyes.

Catherine nodded. 'It did.'

We sat in silence for a moment while I let the news sink in. I had so many questions I didn't know where to start.

'So have you – did you—?' I stopped, unsure how to ask it.

'Do you mean have I ever been in love with a woman before?' Catherine asked.

'Yes.'

She shook her head. 'I haven't, but now I look back it could explain why my marriages to men never worked.'

'And I've known I was gay for a long, long time,' Andrea said. 'I guess growing up with two mothers made it easier for me to understand the feelings, even back then.'

'I can't believe it,' I said. I could feel the smile growing on my face. 'Honestly, I'm thrilled for you both. Truly.'

Andrea grinned. 'See, I told you.'

'I know.' Catherine looked at me. 'I'm sorry I've stayed away. I should have told you. I should have known you'd be happy for me. For us.'

'It's fine. Honestly. I get it. You needed to work out for yourself what was going on before you shared it with anyone else.' I stood abruptly and moved between the two women, then wrapped my arms around them both. We stayed like that for several seconds before I pulled away. 'Now, shall we celebrate?'

'That sounds like the best idea you've had all day,' Andrea said, standing and finding the glasses.

* * *

After Andrea and Catherine had filled me in on the last few weeks and how they had slowly begun to realise that they both wanted more than just friendship, there was a lull in the conversation and I became acutely aware of the fact that I hadn't spoken to Catherine about any of the problems I'd been having. I didn't want to put a dampener on things, but when she asked me how I was, I couldn't lie.

I told her about Olivia not wanting to come home, and how we'd finally got to the bottom of that.

'She'll be coming home tomorrow at last,' I said, tears filling my eyes. 'I can't wait.'

'That's brilliant,' Catherine said. 'I'm so sorry I wasn't there when things were tough. I should have been.'

I shook my head. 'It's fine.'

'It really isn't. I was being selfish.' She gave a sad smile. 'So, tell me what else is happening. How are things with the delicious Charlie?'

She must have seen the look on my face because immediately she gasped. 'Oh God, I've said the wrong thing, haven't I?'

'I—' I stopped, as I remembered that Catherine didn't even know that anything had happened between me and Charlie, let alone that I'd since started seeing Jason. We had so much to catch up on. I felt my face redden, the blush rising from my toes and blooming across my face. 'Charlie and I had a... a thing,' I said.

Catherine's eyes widened. 'I knew it!' she said, smacking the palm of her hand on the table. 'Didn't I tell you they liked each other?' she said, turning to Andrea, and I felt myself blush even more. 'So come on, tell me more,' she said. 'Are you two together at last?'

I shook my head, the words lodged in my throat. 'No, we—' I stopped, swallowed. 'It was just one night and I – I haven't seen him since.'

Catherine stared at me, her mouth open. *'What?'*

Beside her, Andrea put her hand on her arm gently. 'I'm not sure Beth wants to talk about this, darling,' she said.

Catherine shook her head. 'God, I am sorry. I'm like a bloody bull in a china shop sometimes.'

'It's okay. I just—' I what? I'd moved on? I didn't care? Neither of those things were true, and yet I wasn't sure what the truth was. 'After that night we—' I coughed. 'We didn't see each other. He didn't return my calls and then – well, the next thing I knew, he rang to tell me he'd gone back to Helen. Well, not back to her really as they'd never officially split up, but that they'd decided to give it another go...' I trailed off miserably.

'The bastard,' Catherine said.

'But that's just it, he's not, is he?' I looked at her. 'He came to me for advice about how to sort things out with her in the first place. And now that's what he's done.'

'Well, maybe, but he made sure he got what he wanted from you in the meantime, didn't he?'

'Catherine, I don't think that's helping,' Andrea said softly.

Catherine looked down and shook her head. 'You're right. It's not. I'm not being a very supportive friend, am I? I just feel so angry that he's done this to you.'

'Don't be angry. I'm okay.'

'Are you?'

I shrugged. 'I wasn't. I realised I really liked him after we came to see you,' I said, directing my words to Andrea. 'And even though he'd never given any indication that he liked me in that way too—'

'He bloody had!' Catherine interjected, and Andrea shushed her before I carried on.

'Well, anyway, it hadn't been clear to me. But that night, it felt... amazing. Right.' I shrugged. 'But what could I do? Beg him to choose me?' To my horror I felt a tear slip down my cheek and before I knew it Catherine had thrown her arms round me and was holding me and I was sobbing into her shoulder. Finally, she pulled away and I wiped my nose with my sleeve. I felt exhausted, but also, I realised, lighter than I had done in ages. 'Sorry,' I mumbled.

'Don't be daft.'

'You know what, afterwards, after me and Charlie – well, you know.' I smiled. 'When he ignored my messages, and didn't reply for ages, I kept trying to think about what I would have advised someone to do in the same situation as me. And when I couldn't do that I tried to imagine what Lois might have said, or what you would have told me to do.' I hung my head. 'But even though I know you would have said not to take no for an answer, to demand that he spoke to me, I couldn't do it. I couldn't face being humiliated when he told me it had all been a mistake.'

'I would have gone round there and given him a piece of my mind myself,' Catherine said.

'I know. Which is probably why it was just as well I didn't tell you,' I said, giving her a grin. 'But the point is, what sort of agony aunt am I if I can't even take my own advice, or work out what the advice should be?'

'You're a great agony aunt,' Catherine said. She turned to Andrea. 'You've seen some of the replies she's given over the last months, haven't you?'

Andrea nodded. 'I have. You're really good, Beth.'

I shook my head. 'Most of it was thanks to Lois. I used her advice and just made it more relevant to now.'

'You're doing yourself a disserve there, Beth,' Catherine said. 'You stopped using Mum's advice a long time ago. You've got an instinct for it. You're – caring. Empathetic. Kind. And I know you only set the website up to stop yourself from feeling so lonely, but you've helped so many people since it started.' She laid her hand on mine and her skin felt warm. Comforting. 'You mustn't give up on it. Or on Charlie.'

I didn't reply, and the sound of the clock ticking above the door filled the silence. I took a long, shuddery breath in and forced a smile. 'It's fine now. Anyway, I'm kind of seeing someone else.'

'Are you? Who?' Catherine and Andrea both leaned forward and I laughed. 'Look at you two, so desperate for gossip.'

They both grinned at me. 'You bet we are!'

I laughed again and told them about the handful of dates Jason and I had been on. I even told them about the night he'd planned to stay over that had been so rudely interrupted.

'You dark horse,' Catherine said, folding her arms across her chest.

'I don't know about that. I need to move on at some point.'

Andrea nodded. 'And you like him, do you?'

A few days ago I would have been unable to answer that question, unsure about my feelings for someone else so soon after Charlie. But now I felt more confident in my growing feelings for Jason and I nodded, a smile spreading across my face. 'I do. He's really lovely.'

'Ahh, look at you, all loved up and swooning,' Catherine teased.

'Well, it's about time I found someone uncomplicated, eh?'

She grinned. 'True.' She leaned towards me, chin in her hand. 'So, tell me all about him.'

'There's not much to tell,' I said. 'Not yet. We've only been seeing each other a little while. But he's a teacher at school, and he's a few years younger than me, and he's – well, he's really handsome.' I grinned back at her, but she didn't reciprocate. Instead she was studying me with a serious look on her face.

'What?' I said.

'And you're completely sure about this, are you?'

'Catherine!' Andrea chided. She looked at her, eyebrows raised.

'What? I'm only asking.'

'Beth's said she likes him, what more do you want?'

Catherine leaned back. 'I want lightning bolts and rainbows and heart flutters,' she said, smiling. 'Beth, I know how you felt about Charlie, and I just want to be sure you're happy. That's all.'

I smiled. 'I am happy. For now, at least. I have no idea what future this thing with Jason might have but it's fun finding out.'

'And it's taking your mind off Charlie too.'

I wanted to deny it, pretend any thoughts of Charlie were far from my mind. But Catherine would see right through me, so I simply nodded and said, 'Exactly.'

* * *

Later, after we'd polished off a couple of bottles of wine, Andrea suggested I stay over.

'You can't drive home and there's no point in paying for a taxi.'

'But it's the last day of school tomorrow.'

'So go first thing.' She looked at Catherine. 'We'd like her to stay, wouldn't we, Cate?'

Cate. I'd never heard her being called that before and it struck me how close these two had become in the weeks since they'd found each other. I was so happy for them but my treacherous heart still couldn't help a little clench of jealousy that they'd found love so easily.

Except it hadn't been easy, had it? It had taken Catherine most of her adult life to understand who she truly was. How could I begrudge her that?

'No, I need to get home for Buster anyway.'

'Course you do. You should have brought him with you – Freddie's been missing him terribly.'

'I would have done if I'd known you'd be here and answering the door.'

They both had the grace to look sheepish.

'Stay a bit longer, then,' Catherine insisted. 'And we'll pay for your taxi home, won't we, Andrea?'

'Yes, consider it done,' she said. 'We'll even run your car home for you first thing in the morning before you leave for work.'

I sighed. 'You two are going to be a terrible influence on me, I can tell.' I grinned at them. 'Go on, then. But another hour, and no more. It might be the last day of term tomorrow but I'm still a teacher – until midday at least.'

'As if we'd make you drink any more,' Catherine said, giving me a cheeky grin.

'As if.'

A silence fell and I watched the pair of them, holding hands like love-struck teenagers. I would never have guessed what was going to happen that day when we went to find Andrea. At best we'd hoped we might find out some more about Lois – but Catherine had come away having found love. It was all thanks to the *Dear Evelyn Wright* column. All of it was, when you really thought about it. Me finding Catherine, Charlie coming into my life and then leaving again, setting up the *Dear Evelyn* website, working things out with Rob – and now, Catherine and Andrea finding each other.

When it came down to it, things didn't change as much over the decades as we might think. Love – with friends, family or lovers – had always been the glue that held everything together. It was merely the details that changed.

'Beth?'

Catherine's voice interrupted my thoughts and when I looked up it was clear they'd been speaking to me.

'Sorry, I was miles away,' I said.

'Andrea was just asking how *Dear Evelyn* is going,' Catherine said.

'Oh, you know. Okay.'

Catherine peered at me from beneath beetled brows. 'Beth? What are you not telling me?'

I shrugged. 'Nothing. I've just – I haven't really been doing much with it recently.'

'What? You're not giving it up are you?'

'No, but...' I sighed. 'I feel like such a fraud, telling other people what to do when I've made such a mess of things myself. But it's more than that. It's just so overwhelming.' I threaded my fingers together and looked down at them in front of me on the table. 'There are so many new letters every week, so many people demanding things of me, and I'm just one person. With the kids and my job it just all feels a bit much.'

'Can I see it?' Andrea said.

'If you like,' I said.

Catherine stood and fetched her laptop from the worktop. I logged on and showed Andrea the pages and pages of emails that were still marked as unread.

She gave a low whistle. 'I see what you mean,' she said, scrolling down.

Catherine leaned over to peer over her shoulder.

'What's this?' she said, pointing to something. I peered round the screen to see what she was looking at. It was one of the emails asking about sponsorship.

'Oh, nothing,' I said.

Catherine's forehead concertinaed, and she took the mouse and clicked it. A few moments later she looked over the screen at me.

'Have you replied to this?' she said.

I shook my head.

'Beth, you must! This is a brilliant opportunity – these people want to give you money!'

'There are quite a few of them but I haven't replied to any of them.'

'Show me.'

I did as I was told, feeling under scrutiny as I opened one email, then another, and another. Catherine and Andrea read them all.

'Will you let me help you with the advertising requests?' Andrea said.

'I... I mean...'

She clasped my hands. 'Please let me. I'm not busy during the day when I'm here, I sort of float around killing time. I might as well be doing something useful. Besides, from what Cate's told me, I've got a lot to thank you and this agony aunt website for.' She glanced at Catherine lovingly.

'Well, when you put it like that...' I grinned. 'Are you sure though?'

'Of course I am.'

'But there is something we need to get on with as well,' Catherine said.

'What?'

'We need to get some of these questions answered.' She looked at Andrea. 'Are you up for it?'

'Hell yes!'

Over the next two hours we worked our way through dozens of unanswered questions, and for the first time since I'd started this project, I answered them without wondering what Evelyn might have said, or what I thought was the 'right' thing to say. I answered them from my gut, with real heart.

By the time we'd finished it was dark outside and a glance at the clock told me it was almost eleven o'clock.

'I really have to get going,' I said.

'I'll call you a taxi,' Andrea said.

As the taxi took off into the night, I felt more content than I had done in ages. I had my friend back, a project to keep me busy over the summer holidays, a new man in my life, and my daughter was coming home tomorrow. Life was looking up at last.

26

THE WRONG MAN

My friends think I am with the wrong man. We have been together for a few months and he has begun to talk about marriage, but when I told my friends they said they thought I was making a huge mistake. The problem is that they know I am still hung up on my old love and, although he is unavailable, they don't believe I should settle for second best.

I'm afraid I rather agree with your friends in this instance, although only you can know for certain whether you want to marry this man. If, after a long hard think, you decide he isn't the man for you then I think you should call it off sooner rather than later before you get tangled up in making all sorts of promises you may live to regret.

I didn't wait for the doorbell to ring – I was at the front door and throwing it open the minute Rob's car pulled up outside the house. Seconds later, Olivia came flying up the path and launched herself into my arms, and we almost tumbled into the hallway together, a bundle of arms and legs and tears.

As we pulled apart, Jacob came towards me, his little green rucksack in his hand, and I put one arm around him and pulled them both in tightly.

'Oh, it's so good to have you both home again,' I said, my voice thick with tears.

'Why are you crying, Mummy?' Olivia said.

'They're happy tears, love,' I reassured her, and she wiped them away with her finger.

'I missed you,' she said, and the tears started afresh, running down my face and soaking them both. I didn't care.

'Here's their stuff.' I looked up to see Rob by the front door. Just behind him I saw Natalie, hovering awkwardly. She looked blooming, and I was astounded to find that I no longer cared.

'Do you want to come in for a bit?' I said. Rob hadn't seen the house where his children spent more than half of their lives, but today I felt I could bear to invite him in. It felt like my space now, somewhere he was the visitor, rather than me feeling like a visitor in my own home.

'I...' He hesitated.

'Please, Daddy,' Jacob said. 'I want to show you our bedroom.'

Rob glanced back at Natalie. 'I can wait in the car,' she said.

'Don't be daft. You're welcome to come in too,' I said.

She smiled. 'Thank you, Beth.'

We all made our way inside, and while the children showed Rob their bedroom, Natalie and I went into the kitchen.

'Tea?'

'Have you got any herbal?'

'I might have some peppermint?'

'Perfect, thank you.'

I busied myself making tea. 'Please sit down,' I threw over my shoulder. After everything that had happened, it felt surprisingly comfortable having Natalie in my home. I placed a steaming mug of tea in front of her and sat down.

'I wanted to thank you properly,' I said.

She looked up at me, her hands wrapped round the mug. 'What for?'

'Helping me with Olivia.' I held my hand up before she could interrupt. 'I know it was thanks to you that we sorted it out. Rob's not known for his skills at negotiating with the kids.' That was an understatement.

She smiled. 'It's fine. I didn't do much.'

'Well, whatever it was, I'm grateful.'

'I should be thanking you, really,' she said.

'Should you?'

She nodded. Her hand was resting on the small swell of her belly but I didn't think she even knew she was doing it. She looked me right in the eye. 'I don't deserve anything from you. I never blamed you for hating me, for what Rob and I did...' She trailed off, her face flaming.

'I never hated you,' I said. 'Well, maybe at first.' I gave her a wonky smile. 'But you know what, Rob and I had been having problems for ages. I've no doubt we would have split up anyway.' I shrugged.

She shook her head. 'Well, I'm not sure I could have been so forgiving.'

'It took a while, believe me.' I tapped my fingers against the table. 'I'm happy here now though. Truly.'

'Good. I'm glad.'

Before we could say anything more, Rob and the kids burst into the room. 'It's a lovely house,' Rob said.

'Thank you. It's taken a lot of work and there's still a lot more to do, but I love it now.'

He nodded, and for a minute I thought he was going to say something else. But then he changed his mind.

'Well, we'd better get going.'

Natalie stood and as I watched them walk away towards the car to drive home, I felt glad it was me staying here and Natalie going with Rob.

Did this mean I was... happy?

* * *

'I'll warn you now, you're in for a grilling,' I said as Jason tied an apron round his waist and stepped up to the barbecue.

'I'm ready for battle,' he said, snapping the tongs together.

It was a few days later and I'd decided to have a barbecue. The weather had held and it felt like the perfect opportunity to introduce Jason to the children and to Catherine and Andrea. Now the time had come, though, my stomach was doing somersaults.

'Mummy, can I have three sausages?' Olivia said, marching into the garden in a tiny pair of shorts and a crop top that I would never have bought her. I bit my tongue. Halfway across the lawn, she stopped dead. 'Oh. Who are you?'

'Olivia, this is Mummy's friend Jason,' I said, pushing him forward slightly. 'Jason, this is my *very* grown-up daughter, Olivia.'

Jason stuck his hand out and Olivia took it tentatively. 'It's lovely to meet you,' Jason said. 'I've heard lots about you.'

'Have you?' Olivia said, her forehead creasing down the middle. 'I've never heard of you.'

Jason laughed and turned to me. 'Well, your mum and I haven't known each other very long, but we work together, don't we, Beth?'

'Yes, Jason is a teacher at the school,' I said.

She studied him for another few seconds then, in the way that children did, she turned to me, subject forgotten, and put her hands on her hips. 'So, can I have three sausages?'

'You can have as many sausages as you like, love,' I said.

'Good.' Then she turned and stomped back into the house.

'Well, that went okay, I think,' Jason said.

'You did well. Normally she'd pump you for information until you felt as if you'd been under interrogation by the Spanish police.' I laughed. 'Maybe she's saving that for later.'

'I can't wait.' He picked up a packet of sausages from the small wooden table. 'I'd better make sure I cook her enough sausages or she'll never let me come round again.'

I smiled but didn't answer. As I watched him stoking up the coals on the barbecue, I felt a rush of tenderness for him. He was such a lovely man, and I knew many of the women – teachers and sixth formers – at school would kill to be in my position right now. So why had memories of Charlie started flashing into my mind every time I looked at him today? Perhaps it was simply because we were in the garden that Charlie had spent so much time helping me get into shape.

I didn't have time to worry about it any more anyway because the garden gate swung open and Catherine and Andrea arrived.

'Cooee!' Catherine called as she strode across the lawn.

'Brace yourself,' I muttered under my breath to Jason, and he flexed his biceps. My stomach flipped.

'Hello, you two, I'm so glad you could come,' I said, hugging them both one by one.

'I wouldn't miss it for the world,' Catherine said, bending down to scoop Buster into her arms, and smothering him in kisses. She peered over her sunglasses ostentatiously to look at Jason, then slid her gaze over to me and raised her eyebrows. 'Not bad,' she said, grinning as I smacked her on the arm.

'Behave,' I said as she descended on Jason.

'Always,' she called over her shoulder.

'Poor man doesn't stand a chance,' Andrea said, fanning herself with her hat.

'He'll cope,' I said. 'Anyway, how are you? Are you staying for a while before you head back to Lincolnshire?'

'Ah, well,' she said, and her face flushed crimson.

I gasped. 'You're moving in with Catherine, aren't you?'

She nodded. 'I rather thought I might, yes,' she said, and her eyes shone.

'Oh, I'm so thrilled for you,' I said, throwing my arms around her. She hugged me back.

'Hey, hey, hey, what's going on over here?' Catherine said, sauntering back over and draping her arms round us both.

'I've just told Beth about me moving in,' Andrea said.

'Oh, you've stolen my thunder,' Catherine said. 'So, what do you think about that?'

'I think it's bloody brilliant news,' I said. 'I'm so thrilled for you.'

'Thank you, darling, that really does mean the world,' she said. She leaned closer so I could feel her breath on my ear. 'Jason seems very nice. Hot, too.'

I looked at her. 'He is.'

'And yet...?'

I studied her face, trying to work out what she wanted me to say. 'And yet nothing.'

She held my gaze a moment longer, then pulled away without saying anything else. 'Well, I hope he makes you happy,' she said, pointedly.

'He does.'

'Good. Then I won't say any more.'

I gave a small nod, then moved towards Jason. I felt protective of him, as though he was on display, being judged.

'Who wants a drink?' I said.

'I'll come and help you,' Catherine said, and before I could argue she hooked her arm through mine and led me indoors to the kitchen, leaving Andrea and Jason to chat. When we got there, whatever Catherine had been intending to say to me had to be put on hold as Jacob and Olivia were both there yelling at each other.

'Mummy, Olivia says I can't have an apple juice, but she's had two already,' Jacob said. He was almost in tears.

'I haven't had two, Mummy, and he spilt most of his last one so he's not allowed to waste another one.'

'Come on, you two, stop bickering. I'll make us all something to drink and bring it out. Why don't you go and play for a bit? The Swingball is out.'

Olivia gave a dramatic sigh and stomped out, and seconds later Jacob trailed after her. I ruffled his head as he passed.

To my surprise, Catherine didn't quiz me about Jason. Instead, we made drinks and took them outside. 'Here you go, kids,' I said, handing them a cold plastic cup of juice each.

'How are the sausages?' Catherine said as Jason wandered over to get a drink. He slung his arm around my shoulders and pressed his lips into my hair. 'They'll be a while,' he said, grinning and accepting a cold beer from me. 'Cheers.'

'Here's to new friends,' Catherine said.

We sipped our drinks in comfortable silence, just the occasional shout from the kids as they tried and failed to hit the tennis ball round the pole.

'Your garden is lovely,' Jason said. 'What are those called, over there?' He pointed to a large round plant halfway down the right-hand flower bed.

'Er, I have no idea,' I said.

'That's a rhododendron,' Andrea said.

'Is it? I'm not very good with plants.'

'I love them. I'm always happy to help out with the garden if you need it. Although it's looking pretty good.'

'Charlie did it,' Olivia said, popping up beside me, and I felt my whole body flush.

'Oh, who's Charlie?' Jason said, sipping his beer.

'No one,' I said, at the same time as Olivia answered.

'He was Mummy's boyfriend but then he stopped coming round.'

A silence fell and my brain flailed around, trying to think of something say, but without making Olivia feel as though she'd said anything wrong. Jason was looking at me with raised eyebrows.

'He wasn't my boyfriend, Olivia,' I said, then turned to Jason. 'He was just a friend – she gets mixed up.' The words felt stilted, and I tried to sound natural.

'And he's not a friend any more?' Jason tipped the can up and swallowed.

'What?'

'You said he *was* a friend.' His calmness felt studied, and I hoped he didn't think I was lying to him.

'Oh, right. No, he just – I haven't seen him for a while.' *Stop gabbling, Beth.*

I looked down at my feet. The polish on my big toes was chipped, and I curled them over. I wanted the ground to open up and swallow me.

'Ah well, never mind,' he said, eventually, shrugging. 'You've got me here now, right?'

I smiled at him gratefully, and avoided Catherine's gaze because I knew I'd see something in her look that I didn't want to acknowledge.

* * *

In the end the day went as well as I could have hoped. Jason seemed to be a hit with the kids as well as with Catherine and Andrea, and there was no more mention of Charlie. I felt as though I'd passed a test.

Finally, it was time for everyone to say goodbye. Just as Catherine and Andrea were getting ready to leave, Catherine called me from the kitchen, saying she couldn't find her phone.

'Excuse me a sec,' I said to the others, and hurried over. But when I walked inside Catherine was standing at the table, her phone very clearly in her hand. I frowned.

'You found it, then?'

She shoved it in her bag. 'Yes. No. It's not about the phone.' She stepped forward and clamped my arms tightly. Her face was inches away. 'Are you sure you're doing the right thing?'

'What about?'

She sighed, exasperated. 'Jason is very nice, and I can see why you like him. But you don't love him, do you?'

'It's early days!'

She held my gaze. 'Maybe. But I think he hopes you might, in time.'

'And I might.' She released my arms and tilted my chin up gently with her finger until I was forced to look her in the eye.

'If you're still in love with Charlie, I don't think you should give up on him.'

'I'm not in love with Charlie.'

'Aren't you?'

I shook my head but I couldn't say the words. The truth was every time I thought about Charlie, my whole body tingled. But then, Jason made me feel that way too, when he touched me. And Jason was here, and Charlie never would be. So what was the point in even thinking about it?

'I don't know,' I admitted. The words surprised even me. 'But it doesn't matter whether I love Charlie or not because he's back with his wife.' I flicked my eyes up at her. 'So it's all too late.'

'It's never too late to be with the person you love, Beth.'

I held my breath, then let it out in one go and shook my head. 'Jason is a good man. I enjoy spending time with him. I need to look forward now, not back.'

She watched me for a minute, then hitched her bag onto her shoulder. 'Then you have to do what you think is right.' She leaned in and gave me a peck on the cheek. 'I just want you to be happy. You deserve it.'

* * *

Catherine and Andrea had gone and Jason was helping me clear the plates away. Catherine's words were repeating themselves over and over in my mind, and I was looking forward to some time on my own later to try and clear my thoughts.

'Beth?'

I looked over to find Jason watching me from by the barbecue, a frown etched onto his forehead. Clearly, he'd been talking to me.

'Sorry, I was miles away,' I said, smiling at him. 'What did you say?'

'I wondered if...' He trailed off and looked suddenly shy. 'Could I stay tonight?'

My stomach dropped. I'd been longing for this moment since we'd been interrupted the week before, but right now, after my conversation with Catherine, my feelings were all over the place, and all I could think about was having time to myself tonight to clear my head. Besides, since that night we hadn't done anything more than kiss. This felt like a big step, especially with the kids here.

'Sorry, Jason,' I made myself say, stepping towards him. 'Would you mind if we waited until the children are with Rob? I – I don't want to confuse them any more.'

I couldn't ignore the drop of his shoulders and I felt a pang of guilt.

'Yes of course. I should have thought.'

'It's fine,' I said. 'Anyway, it gives us something to look forward to.' Then I stepped forward and planted a kiss on his lips and tried to pretend I hadn't seen how disappointed he looked.

27

NEVER GIVE UP

I know you often have letters from women desperate to find love and wondering whether they should settle for second best. Usually you tell them not to, and I am just letting you know that I agree entirely! I almost married the first man who asked me, but in the end I turned down his offer of marriage and now I am deliriously happy with the man of my dreams. Never settle for second best, I say.

Thank you for your letter and I am so glad you agree with my advice. Of course it's not always the case that one should refuse the offer of marriage to a good man, but if your heart is not in it, as most clearly was the case for you, then it can sometimes be best to consider turning them down. I'm glad it turned out well for you.

Guilt-tripped into seeing my parents, I agreed to take the children to Lowestoft before they disappeared to Greece for three weeks.

I'd been trying not to think about being without them for so long, but it was hovering above me like a cartoon dark cloud and getting away from it all seemed like the perfect distraction.

'You can bring someone if you like,' Mum said, when she rang a few days beforehand to check for the third time what the kids liked to eat.

'I'm bringing the children,' I said, deliberately ignoring her meaning.

'Oh, Beth, you know perfectly well what I mean. Haven't you got a new young man in your life yet? It's been more than a year and you don't want to be left on the shelf forever.'

I took a deep breath, all ready to tell her to mind her own bloody business. But instead I said, 'Actually I have.'

I heard her intake of breath and couldn't resist a satisfied smile. I quickly regretted it though.

'Oh, who is he? What's his name? Tell me you're bringing him with you. You must – your dad and I would love to meet him.'

'He's called Jason, he's a teacher at the school and I haven't asked him,' I said, already regretting being so rash. I felt as if I were being pelted with questions.

In the end I agreed to invite him along, if only to shut my mother up. To my surprise, he said yes.

'I'll warn you, they're intense,' I said. 'And they'll probably assume we're getting married or something. They don't understand why I'd ever choose to be on my own.'

'It's fine, I can handle it,' Jason said.

'I wouldn't be so sure,' I replied.

In the end, it went better than I'd imagined. Mum and Dad pumped Jason for information, but they mostly behaved themselves. Olivia and Jacob were thrilled to see their grandparents again, which filled me with guilt for keeping them away for so long, and the long days on the beach building sandcastles and braving the freezing North Sea were, it turned out, exactly what I needed to take my mind off everything else.

'What if I sneak into your room tonight?' Jason said, nuzzling my neck as we watched the kids build sandcastles on the third and last day, Buster knocking them down as quickly as they could build them. Mum and Dad had put me and the kids in my old bedroom, and Jason was on a pull-out bed in the spare room, surrounded by piles of clean laundry and stacks of books. They might have been keen for me to find someone else, but they wouldn't tolerate sex before marriage under their roof. Their old-fashioned attitude made me think about all the people who'd written to Evelyn, and how difficult it must have been back then when almost everyone felt the same way.

'I'm with the children!' I said.

'I won't wake them up,' he said, sliding his hand down my thigh. I batted him away. 'Stop it, the kids will see.'

He pulled away. 'Would it be so bad if they knew I was your boyfriend?' he said.

I looked at him. I was windswept and unkempt in the wild Suffolk wind, but if anything the beach just made Jason look even more handsome. I felt a shiver of desire as I leaned over and kissed him gently. 'No, it wouldn't. But you're still not coming into the bedroom with us.'

'Spoilsport.'

By the time we left Lowestoft to head back home, I felt happier and more relaxed than I'd felt in a long time. But as the day of the kids' departure loomed closer, I felt the clouds begin to gather again.

'They will be fine, you know,' Catherine said, when I admitted how worried I was.

'I know. I've just never been away from them for so long.'

'Just spend lots of time with me and Andrea, and Jason, and keep smiling. It'll be over before you know it.'

Olivia and Jacob had been beside themselves with excitement at the thought of going to Greece, and as they pulled away from the house with Rob and Natalie, I kept my smile pasted on until they'd rounded the corner. I'd planned to spend the day letting myself cry and miss them, and was just heading to the kitchen to make myself a cup of tea to take back to bed when the doorbell went. I almost didn't answer it, but when it pealed again I thought I should get rid of whoever it was.

'Surprise!' Catherine, Andrea and Jason were on my doorstep, arms piled high with shopping bags, grinning like a bunch of loons.

'What on earth?' I stepped back as they bundled in and headed straight into the kitchen. I followed.

'We knew you'd be feeling down so we've come to entertain you for the day,' Catherine announced, handing me a boules set, a parasol and a packet of sausages.

'Interesting selection of items.'

She grinned. 'We're going to eat food, play games and, of course,' she said, tugging a bottle from a cool bag, 'drink lots of fizz. And if that doesn't take your mind off missing Olivia and Jacob then I don't know what will.'

I felt tears gather in the corners of my eyes. 'I can't believe you've done this,' I said.

'We all love you, you silly sausage,' Catherine said, and I felt my gaze flicking to Jason. He'd already hinted he was falling in love with me – although hadn't *quite* said it – but something was still holding me back from committing to anything. I looked away and back at Catherine. 'I love you all too,' I said, hoping it was enough.

* * *

As Catherine had promised, the time the children were away flew past quicker than I could ever have imagined. Days were filled with tiling the kitchen and replacing the worktops as well as getting the garden finished with Jason's help. Evenings were spent drinking, eating and laughing with my friends, and answering as many *Dear Evelyn* questions as we could. Andrea had begun to reply to some of the companies interested in advertising on the site, and it was beginning to feel as though it was properly taking off.

And, of course, in the end, Jason stayed over. It was as amazing as I'd hoped it would be, and for a while I felt as though I might finally be starting to forget about Charlie for good.

Then the kids were back, full of stories of the amazing time they'd had with their dad, and August began to slide into September and we were gearing up to go back to work. And as the day approached, I felt a knot of anxiety growing in my belly.

At first I couldn't work out what was playing on my mind. I'd been through the first week of term a dozen times before. I was used to starting afresh with a brand-new class, to dealing with troublesome children, planning a whole new year of work. So what *was* bothering me?

In the end it was something Catherine had said that made me realise what the problem was – something I couldn't seem to shake from my mind.

'It's never too late to be with the person you love, Beth.'

And I realised she was right.

Despite the lovely times I'd had with Jason over the summer, and despite hoping I might fall in love with him, given time, the truth was that now, faced with the prospect of going back to our normal routine, and having to tell our colleagues what was going on between us, I was having doubts.

They'd been there all along, hidden beneath the excitement and the headrush of meeting someone new. But now that had faded, reality was beginning to sink in and I realised that, despite what I'd told Catherine, and what I'd told myself, Jason hadn't helped me get over Charlie. He'd simply masked the pain of losing him.

I felt my heart breaking for Jason. I so wanted to love him the way he should be loved. But it felt cruel to continue to lead him on, knowing that, until I'd got over Charlie, I couldn't give him everything he deserved.

And so, three nights before term began, I took myself to his flat with a heavy heart to tell him it was over.

'I wasn't expecting you tonight,' he said as he opened the door, and the delight on his face at my unexpected visit was like a dagger to my heart.

'Can I come in?' My voice was low, and he must have realised there was something wrong.

'Sure,' he said, stepping aside to let me past. I slipped by, careful not to touch him, for fear it would make me back out. I had to do this, for his sake, if not for my own.

I walked into his kitchen and when I turned to face him I almost changed my mind. A shaft of light slipped through the window and his face glowed. My stomach flipped over.

Instead I took a deep breath and said, 'We need to talk.'

'Do we?' His voice cracked.

I pulled myself onto the stool at the breakfast bar. But before I could speak he said, 'You're breaking up with me, aren't you?'

I looked up at him, surprised. 'I—' I started.

He sat on the stool beside me and his knee grazed mine. I tried not to pull away.

'I had a feeling this might be coming,' he said.

'Did you?'

He nodded sadly and the hurt in his eyes made my heart clench. He took a deep breath and said, 'Has this got anything to do with that other guy? Charlie?'

'What? No!' We hadn't spoken about Charlie since the barbecue when Olivia had mentioned him. I hadn't known Jason had even remembered his name but clearly he had. 'No, there's no one else,' I assured him.

'So it's just me, then?' He laughed mirthlessly.

I shook my head. 'No, I swear. You're wonderful. I just don't want to hurt you, Jay. And I know I will.'

'Would it matter if I said I was willing to risk it?'

It would have been so easy to go along with it. To have fallen into his arms and let myself fall in love with him. He was such a lovely man, I felt sure that I would, in time. But I also knew that I would end up hurting him eventually. Because no matter what I told him, or myself, a piece of my heart had been left behind with Charlie, and until it healed, it would be unfair to let anyone else in.

'I'm sorry. This is the right thing to do. I know it is.'

He looked down at his lap and shook his head. 'I don't agree, but I'll respect your wishes.'

I felt a tear trickle down my cheek. 'Thank you.'

He stood and moved away, leaving me looking at him from the other side of the kitchen worktop. 'Promise me you won't be weird with me at school,' he said.

'Of course I won't.'

He hesitated, then gave a small nod and walked to the front door. And as I gave him a peck on the cheek as I left, my heart felt a little bit heavier and I couldn't help wondering whether I'd made a terrible mistake.

* * *

There were only a couple of days until the start of the new term and I had a lot to prepare. As I made my way along past the newsagent's and pub, my mind was miles away, planning lessons and thinking about all the things I needed to get ready for Tuesday morning. So when I almost bumped into someone coming out of the corner shop I wasn't paying any attention to where I was going or who it was.

Then I looked up, and all the air left me.

'Hello, Beth,' Charlie said.

'Hi,' I croaked. The sun was behind him and a halo of sunlight lit up his hair, throwing the rest of him into shadow. I tried to calm my breathing.

He shuffled his feet. 'How are you?'

'I—' I stopped, tried to arrange the words into some sort of coherent sentence. I hadn't seen Charlie since the morning he'd left my house after we'd slept together, and I'd thought I'd be okay with it by now. But his presence still made my insides turn slippery, like liquid, and my skin feel as if it were sunburned. I felt a bead of sweat drip down my temple and I brushed it away absent-mindedly. 'I'm fine, Charlie. I'm good.' I nodded as if to prove the point. I couldn't quite meet his eye and for a moment we stood and listened to the sound of a passing tractor, a welcome relief from having to find something else to say.

The sound faded away, and the silence hummed, expanding until I felt as though it were going to make my head explode.

'How's Helen?' I said, and instantly regretted it. Apart from the fact it was none of my business, I didn't want him to think I'd been thinking about them, together. I wanted to at least give the illusion that I'd moved on. I wished, fleetingly, that Jason were with me, and then pushed that thought away too. He wasn't just a prop to make me feel better. He was worth more than that.

Charlie took a while to reply, his mouth moving silently as though chewing over the words. His eyes flitted over my shoulder, onto the floor, and finally onto me. 'She's fine, as far as I'm aware,' he said, his words landing carefully.

I let them settle for a minute, turning them over in the light, trying to work out what they might mean. Was it just a straightforward answer to my question, or was there another meaning to it? Was he trying to tell me something?

'That's good,' I said, not wanting to jump to any conclusions.

'I haven't seen her for a few weeks.'

And there it was. Like a sucker-punch to the gut, his words hit me right in the solar plexus, and made my head spin.

'Oh!' I said, foolishly. 'I mean, I'm sorry.'

He shook his head. 'It's fine. It's just—' He swallowed, his eyes locked on me. I couldn't bear to look right at him in case I saw something there I didn't want to see. 'It didn't work out, in the end.' His voice was so soft I wasn't sure I'd heard him right, but when I finally looked up, I could see I hadn't misheard at all.

'Oh.' This time the word wasn't an exclamation, but a realisation, a small, rounded sound, that left my mouth like a puff of air.

He nodded. 'I was going to... I mean, I wanted...' He trailed off, and rubbed his hand across the back of his neck.

'It's okay. You don't need to say anything,' I said.

'No, I do.' His words seemed urgent all of a sudden, as though he needed to get them out quickly. He stepped towards me so that I could see his long lashes fanned out across his cheeks, and make out the fine lines around his mouth, the swell of his lips. I wanted to reach out and run my finger across them and it took everything I had to resist the urge. I held my breath as he spoke. 'I wanted to apologise to you. I *should* have apologised to you. I behaved terribly and you deserved better.' He sighed. 'I – Helen and I, we – we couldn't make it work, in the end.'

'I'm sorry,' I said, and I meant it.

He dipped his head in acknowledgement. 'I made a mistake, giving things another go I should have known it was over between us after—' He stopped, his eyes flicking side to side as though he were watching a game of tennis. He didn't finish the sentence and my mind started filling in the blanks. After she cheated? After she told you she didn't love you any more?

After I met you?

Stop it, Beth.

'I am sorry it didn't work out, Charlie. Truly.'

He smiled and his eyes glittered. 'So how have you been?'

'Good. I've been... things have been good.'

He studied me for a moment, his eyes roaming over my face as though trying to commit it to memory. I wished I could reach inside his mind and see what was going through it.

'And are you... have you been seeing anyone?'

I felt a heat rise up my face and swallowed down the lump in my throat. 'I was. I'm not any more.'

He gave a tiny nod. Charlie was closer to me than he had been a moment ago and the air between us was thick. It was hard to breathe, and as we stood there, arms hanging loose by our sides, the rest of the world dropped away. Cars stilled, leaves stopped rustling in the trees, and my heart stopped beating, for a few long, torturous seconds.

And then a car horn blared and we jumped apart, fresh air rushing into the gap between us.

Charlie pulled his hand through his hair in the way I'd become so familiar with, leaving his hair wilder than ever. I wanted to reach out and smooth it down. The urge to touch him was overwhelming and I took another step away from him.

'It was lovely to see you,' I said.

'You too,' he said. I turned and began walking away. I knew he was watching me, and I felt as though each step was going to trip me up, as though my feet had forgotten how to move as I tried to focus on putting one in front of the other. My shoulders were hunched and it was taking all of my concentration not to turn around and walk back to him. I wanted to ask him how he'd been, what had happened between him and Helen, whether he regretted the night we spent together, whether I could see him again. But the corner was approaching and any second now I'd be round it and out of sight. The last shop was on my left now and my heart thump-thumped in my head as I took the final step to turn the corner.

Then he was gone, and I let out a whoosh of air, and leaned over, with my head hanging down and my hands on my knees. Good God, what was wrong with me? I hadn't seen this man for two months, and I'd thought I'd put him out of my mind. But now here he was, filling every single inch of space of it until there was no room for anything else, any rational thought. I slowly stood up and leaned my back against the wall and took a couple of deep breaths. I thought about what Catherine had said, about Charlie making it clear how much he liked me, and I wondered why I'd been trying to deny it to myself for so long.

To protect myself, perhaps?

I wanted to peek round the corner and see if Charlie was still there, staring at the space where I'd been. What if he was though? What would I do? Run towards him and declare my undying love?

Love.

The word stopped me in my tracks. *Was* it love? It certainly felt like the early stirrings of something. But love? That was a big word with even bigger connotations. There was no denying that seeing him again had stirred something in me though, and I wasn't sure how I was going to dampen it down again.

Or even if I wanted to.

I straightened up and turned to walk the rest of the way home when a sound stopped me in my tracks. It was a sound so familiar it took me a second to tune in, but when I did, my heart stopped beating. It was someone calling my name.

There were footsteps, fast ones, and then before I could put the two things together, Charlie had barrelled round the corner and almost bundled into me, skidding to a halt just in time as if he were in a cartoon chase scene.

'You're still here.' His cheeks were red and his eyes were wild.

'I am.' My heart pulsed so fast in my veins it made me dizzy and I pressed my hand against the wall to steady myself.

'Are you okay?' he said, stepping towards me and as his hand touched my arm I felt the air leave my body.

'I'm fine,' I said. He was staring at me so intently I felt his gaze burn into my skin, and it felt as though he was trying to see inside me, to search for something. He was just inches from me, but in the shadow of the building I couldn't make out his features. A breeze slipped between us as I shivered.

'I've missed you.' The words were so quiet I couldn't be sure I'd heard them right.

'Me too,' I said, my voice raspy.

He was closer now, his face a blur, and then his lips grazed mine and fireworks sparked through me and I rested my forehead against his.

'It was Evelyn,' he whispered, and I pulled back slightly.

'What was Evelyn?'

He tucked a stray strand of hair behind my ear and leaned in. 'It was thanks to Evelyn that I knew it couldn't work with Helen.' His breath tickled my cheek.

'What do you mean?'

He smiled. 'Do you remember the letter I answered where someone was looking for advice about whether to stay with their husband, or leave and follow their heart with someone else, and I told them to listen to their heart?'

I nodded without speaking.

'Well, I took my own advice,' he said, his eyes blazing. 'And it was you that was in my heart. Not Helen. And I knew I couldn't pretend any more.'

The world stopped and I tried to steady my breathing. The air fizzed and popped between us, and it felt as though there were no one else in the universe.

'But you didn't come and find me?'

He shook his head. 'I didn't think you'd want me to.'

'Then you were wrong.'

For one agonising minute I thought he was going to kiss me right there and then. But then, simultaneously, we both seemed to remember where we were, in the middle of the street in the village where people knew us, and we sprang apart as though we'd had an electric shock. But our eyes stayed locked.

'Shall we go back to mine?' I said, and he nodded.

We didn't touch on the five-minute walk back to my house, but I couldn't stop thinking about how much finding the *Dear Evelyn Wright* column had changed my life, and how much I had to thank her for.

Sometimes, life could be tough. But at others, such as now, you realised that sometimes the stars could and did align – and a change in fortunes could often be traced back to one small thing. In my and Charlie's case it was the discovery of Evelyn Wright's letters that had set a whole train of events in place that had led us to being here, right now, together.

But Evelyn's letters had changed lives for so many other

people too – including herself, as they'd helped her to find true happiness with the person she loved. I felt grateful she had given me the chance to do the same.

And as the door of my ramshackle cottage closed behind Charlie and me, I knew that another door was about to open wide to a whole new world of possibilities.

And this time, it was a world that included Charlie.

ACKNOWLEDGEMENTS

As always, I need to thank lots of people with their help and support while I wrote this book. The idea for it came to me out of the blue. Maybe it's thanks to a career working in women's magazines, but I had an overwhelming urge to write a story about an agony aunt from the 1950s. Before I even knew what I wanted that story to be, I took a trip to the British Library and spent a happy day going through huge piles of magazines from the early 1950s. I loved travelling back to that time and seeing how much the world – and its attitudes towards women, as well as love, has changed since then. So thank you first of all to the British Library staff who helped me find and wheel those enormous trolleys-full of magazines around! Tanith Carey's fascinating book *Never Kiss A Man In A Canoe* gave me some real inspiration too.

My editor Sarah is amazing. When I told her what I wanted to write, I described a very different book to the one I ended up writing. Halfway through, when I realised my original idea wasn't really working, I said I had a better idea and did she wanted to hear it, and she said 'no, I trust you.' And that is music to an author's ears. Being trusted to tell the story in your own way is absolutely priceless. So thank you, Sarah, for always believing in me – and then guiding me to make the story every better once I'd written it.

Sometimes ideas grind to a halt, and something you thought was going to work, doesn't. On those occasions it can be useful to speak to other authors in order to throw some ideas around. In this instance, I happened to be chatting to the lovely Christie Barlow when I came up against an obstacle with The Lost Letters of Evelyn Wright – and she gave me the seed of an idea that helped me get over those obstacles and make Evelyn and Beth's story work. So thank you Christie, your crazy, brimming-over-with-ideas mind was very useful!

My brilliant friend Serena is probably my biggest champion (joint with my mum, but she has to be!) and always reads everything I write in its early stages. She's great for feedback, but even more importantly is such a massive support to me. When things aren't going well or I worry I can't write a book any more, she always builds me back up again, and tells me how brilliant I am. And I don't even pay her. Love you, Serena.

I've dedicated this book to my boys. Not because I think they'll read it, because they won't – teenage boys don't really read much at all unless it's the football scores, and my husband doesn't read anything except newspaper supplements and websites about mountain biking – but because they're my world, and I can't imagine my life without them in it. Jack, Harry and Tom, you're amazing, even when you drive me crazy, so thank you.

And finally, thank you to my wonderful readers. It really is incredible to think of so many people out there reading the words I've written, the story that's come from my head and, many months later, has landed on your kindle or in your hand in the form of a paperback – or even in your ears as an audiobook! However you read/listened to it, I really hope you enjoyed The Lost Letters of Evelyn Wright, and thank you for your support.

ABOUT THE AUTHOR

Clare Swatman is the author of numerous women's fiction novels, which have been translated into more than twenty languages. A former journalist, she spent the previous twenty years writing for *Bella* and *Woman & Home*, amongst many other magazines. Clare lives in Hertfordshire with her husband and two teenage sons.

Sign up to Clare Swatman's mailing list here for news, competitions and updates on future books.

Visit Clare's website: https://clareswatmanauthor.com

Follow Clare on social media:

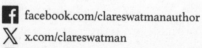

facebook.com/clareswatmanauthor
x.com/clareswatman
instagram.com/clareswatmanauthor